Review

Autumn Leaves is a priceless work of art. It promises to take you deep into places of the human soul, especially our heartfelt desires and fears. As a reader of this story, I can say I was there, because Stefan Vučak presented it so well that it became a part of my existence. Though he already has his main character, I felt like I was the main character because his experiences revealed our universal vulnerability as we seek to live in perfect bliss.

Linda Diane Wattley

Books by Stefan Vučak

General Fiction:
Cry of Eagles
All the Evils
Towers of Darkness
Strike for Honor
Proportional Response
Legitimate Power
Autumn Leaves
F/X-26
28th Amendment
Night Sirens
Broken Rose

Science Fiction:
Fulfillment
Lifeliners
All My Sunsets

Shadow Gods Saga:
In the Shadow of Death
Against the Gods of Shadow
A Whisper from Shadow
Shadow Masters
Immortal in Shadow
With Shadow and Thunder
Through the Valley of Shadow
Guardians of Shadow

Non-Fiction:
Writing Tips for Authors

Contact at:
www.stefanvucak.com

AUTUMN LEAVES

By

Stefan Vučak

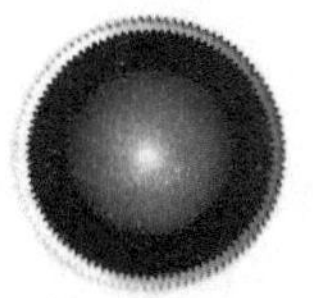

Dedication

To Claudia...when the leaves begin to fall

Acknowledgments

To Charlotte Raby for additional proofreading and insightful suggestions.
https://charlotteraby.wordpress.com/

Cover art by Laura Shinn.
http://laurashinn.yolasite.com

Chapter One

With only a mild jolt, the Boeing 737 touched down, and the pilot immediately engaged reverse thrust, which pushed Dural against the seat. On some flights, the pilots came in with wings rocking and landed with a jarring crunch. Hardly the most pleasant way to end a journey. After two days attending the Australian Clinical Psychology Association symposium in Sydney, he was glad to be home. Two papers on meditative treatment of stress-related neurosis by prominent guests from Harvard's Medical School generated robust discussion between the traditional conservative attendees and the more progressive camp. Dural liked the underlying theories advocated by the papers, although not entirely original, but lack of clinical evidence on their effectiveness provided free ammunition for detractors. He would discuss the papers with his two partners on the efficacy of applying the techniques to their own patients.

He glanced at the black Rado on his right wrist: 18:47. By the time he got home, it would be close to eight. He could have stayed in Sydney overnight networking with fellow psychologists dissecting the presented articles, shared a drink or two, and took a morning flight to Melbourne. It would have meant losing half a day by the time he got back. Anyway, he had two patients scheduled for tomorrow morning.

A more compelling reason to be home was getting Lenora's welcoming embrace and Daniela swarming all over him, demanding he tell her *everything*. His precocious seven-year-old would not give him a moment's peace until he did. She would not be interested in the conference proceedings, considering it dull grownup stuff, insisting instead he tell her about Darling Harbor, the

Opera House, and Sydney's other attractions, hinting darkly it was high time he took her there. With all that waiting for him, drinks with colleagues didn't stand a chance.

When he received the conference invitation, he considered submitting an article that explained aspects of irrational aggression and road rage exhibited by drivers in high-density environments, which he published in the latest edition of the *Australian Medical Journal*, but thought it too radical for the stuffy traditionalists who still thought Freud, B.F. Skinner, and William James had discovered and defined everything to do with psychology. On reflection, he should have presented it and watched the sparks fly. That would definitely have been a reason to stay behind and chew the cud with his colleagues.

The 737 pulled into the QANTAS domestic terminal, and coach passengers behind him scrambled to retrieve bags from overhead lockers, jostling for positions in the narrow aisle. Dural could never figure out the reason for the rush, as no one could exit for at least five minutes. He toyed with the idea of writing a paper on compulsive behavior in aircraft, trains, and buses that buried individual personality traits in a group environment. The coming Australian Society for Psychological Medicine symposium should receive it favorably, but that was not until August.

When the air bridge finally connected and the flight attendant opened the door, Dural slowly stood and retrieved his carry-on and garment bag. Seated in the business class part of the cabin, he avoided the impatient crush of economy passengers. Flights would cost him and his partners a little less if they flew coach, but the extra comfort and convenience were worth the expense. Anyway, it was all tax deductible. With only a carry-on, he was spared the mind-numbing wait at the luggage carousel, potentially half as long as the flight itself, especially after an international haul.

Outside, a fresh breeze stirred his hair and Dural frowned at its keen bite. Melbourne in May did have an occasional pleasant break, and they've had a long, warm summer, but the days now were unmistakably shorter and cooler. Leaves were turning various shades of yellow, brown, and red, littering the sidewalks and nature strips. Except for the eucalyptus. They remained green year-round; dumping leaves and bark over the summer months, but were now settled in for the approaching winter.

He wrinkled his nose at the pervasive stink of petrol coming from buses and cabs streaming past the terminals, and tugged his right earlobe in irritation. Across the busy thoroughfare, the Parkroyal hotel blazed with light against the imposing parking lot complex that serviced short-term visitors. A city shuttle bus rumbled past him as he made his way toward the taxicab rank. An attendant waved his arm, steering cabs into a queue for waiting passengers eager to be out of there. The noise of cars, blaring horns, an occasional thunder of a departing aircraft, the lingering whiff of avgas, were familiar sights and sounds for Dural. Sydney may be more touristy, and it pained him to admit it, its climate milder, but he was Melbourne born and settled into his lifestyle. He had a devoted wife he loved, a doting daughter, a successful practice, and a promising career. What else could he want?

Get rid of your mortgage, dummy!

Another five years or so, he told himself.

A cab pulled to the curb and the attendant pointed at him toward it. Dural dumped his carry-on and garment bag onto the back seat and settled himself in.

"Where to?" the cabby demanded.

"Nine Trinion Street, Prahran," Dural told him as he buckled in.

"That's off High Street, right?"

"Right."

The cabby grunted and pulled the car into the traffic.

Once they hit Tullamarine Freeway, the drive toward the city's glowing spires became smooth. A stream of oncoming headlights made Dural squint. Although past seven and the afternoon rush over, there were still a lot of cars on the road. The Victorian state government said the planned widening of the airport end of the freeway would start in October this year, which would ease the morning and evening crush, but it meant three years of annoying inconvenience by the time all the work was completed in late 2018. If done by then. He and most Melbournians could never figure out why the government hadn't put in three lanes both ways when they originally built the freeway. Didn't they have planners to project population growth and the corresponding need for infrastructure to cope with that growth? Judging by after the effect construction going on everywhere, apparently not. Another inexplicable phenomena, he mused.

Embedded in a river of cars making their way downtown, he allowed himself a small smile, anticipating his arrival home. Daniela would still be up, refusing to go to bed until she saw Daddy, and Lenora could do nothing about it. His daughter a force of nature and nothing could change her, not that he wanted to. He and Lenora wanted another child, but two miscarriages before she had Daniela made that a forlorn prospect. According to the doctors, Lenora was lucky to have had Dan. As it was, their daughter was born three weeks premature. Two subsequent miscarriages convinced her she was unlikely to have other children. Hard to take at first for both of them, but as Daniela blossomed into a lively girl full of energy and bubbling spirits, Lenora told him she did not want to risk another failed pregnancy and the emotional trauma that went with it. He understood and reconciled himself to the inevitable, enjoying what they had. His training as a psychologist helped both of them cope with the disappointment, but he knew Lenora secretly fretted at not being able to have more children, fearing she had somehow failed him. The underlying neurosis exhibited itself in random fits of temper. He tried to make it up to her by loving her unreservedly, content to share Daniela with her.

The cab took the off-ramp to Kings Way, the city towers

glowing jewels on his left, and entered the tree-lined Queens Road. A left at High Street, a few blocks later another left into Trinion Street, and he was there. Tall light poles lit mature trees on both sides of the road with a yellow glow. A relatively old part of town with lots of small plots and narrow, double-story brick and weatherboard houses, with a sprinkling of trendy dwellings put up by well-to-do investors and owners.

Dural and Lenora had only been married two years, and Daniela due in three months, they needed to upgrade from a small cottage they were renting in South Melbourne. Even though Lenora held a good job, the consultancy with his two partners getting established, they were not awash with cash. Perhaps in two years or so, he and Lenora agreed.

His parents were visiting one Saturday, and a chance Internet scan of real estate opportunities in the inner city ended with his father urging Lenora and Dural into making a bid to the agent the owners could not refuse. Although reluctant to load himself with a substantial debt, Dural recognized that such opportunities, when they came, needed to be snapped up. It was 2009 at the height of the Global Financial Crisis. A loan from his old man clinched the deal. The previous owners acquired the old house as an investment, figuring the real estate bubble would keep growing, and splurged to turn it into something modern. The sudden credit squeeze and an overvalued mortgage left them exposed, forcing them to sell at a substantial loss.

It cost another eighteen thousand to finish the renovations, but the outlay had been worth it. An upcoming clinical psychologist and Lenora a junior systems analyst at ANZ, the bank did not hesitate to extend them a bridging loan. They wanted a fixed rate, but his old man told him to hold out for a variable rate. Interest rates were going down and he could lock in a fixed rate once the economic indicators started to turn. Although on a stable financial footing, Dural did not want to overextend himself.

Nevertheless, he insisted he would service the loan, Lenora's income acting as a buffer. In 2010 when the rates showed signs of climbing, He renegotiated his loan to a fixed rate, which the bank undoubtedly regretted now.

He paid the driver and watched the cab's red taillights dwindle down the street. The wind sighed among the branches, making them whisper like rushing surf. Dead leaves swirled around his feet as he opened the small side gate and made his way toward the front entrance guarded by two heavy solid wood door panels. He walked up the three terracotta-tiled steps of the small portico and blinked when the motion-sensor overhead light snapped on. Before he could insert the key into the lock, the door flew open and a small bundle of irrepressible energy dressed in thick pink flannel pajamas slammed against him. He grunted from the impact, dropped his carry-on and garment bag, and embraced the little girl.

"Daddy! Daddy! You're home!" Daniela cried out with a beaming smile, clutching him fiercely. After a moment, she glanced behind her. "Mommy! Daddy's here."

Lenora, tall, strikingly handsome and composed, appeared from the brightly lit lounge. Wearing tight-fitting blue trousers, black sweater rolled up against a long throat, her glistening black hair cascading over her left breast, she gave her daughter an amused smile.

"I sure hope it's Daddy, sugar buns. I would hate to see you hugging a stranger like that," she remarked in a husky contralto.

Daniela laughed merrily and winked at Dural. "Mommy is only kidding. I knew it was you right away." She lifted her arms, which meant he had to pick her up.

"Uh, you're getting too heavy for this," he complained as he lifted her.

"Aw, you're just saying that."

"No strangers in the house while I was away?" he asked teasingly as he cradled her against him.

"No one else came, Daddy," Daniela assured him, then looked suddenly serious. "Unless you count Mrs. Parker across the street. She came about a half hour ago."

"Demanding sugar again?"

Dan shook her head, which set her two ponytails dancing. "She brought us some walnut cookies. They were very good. Weren't they, Mommy?"

"They sure were, darling."

An elderly lady, Mrs. Parker who lived alone these days, her husband having passed away last year. She was one of those golden creatures who became loving and caring as she became old, and the entire street adored her. Forever going around borrowing flour, sugar, and stuff from everybody, returning the favor with gifts of cakes and cookies. Dural had done odd jobs for her, fixing things around the house, as did some of his other neighbors. A prolific gossip, she loved to regale everyone's secrets and goings-on. Old and wrinkled, she was nevertheless full of energy and always about somewhere.

He planted a kiss on Daniela's rosy cheek and squeezed his daughter until she squealed and beat her tiny fists against his chest.

"Stop it, Daddy! You know how I hate it."

He winced and eased off. "Sorry, I forgot. It's just that I've missed you so much."

"Next time, not too hard."

"Deal."

They exchanged a high-five to seal the bargain.

Lenora walked toward him, wrapped her arms around both of them, and her eyes shone as she looked at him.

"Welcome home, stranger," she said and gave him a brief kiss. When she leaned back, he stroked her smooth face and pushed away a lock of wayward hair. She always threatened to cut it short, and Dural would not have minded, but she knew he liked it long and never went through with it. However, she often told him he would quickly reconsider if he had to wash and care for it.

"Glad to *be* home," he murmured.

"Carry me inside, Daddy," Daniela demanded. "You guys can smooch later."

Lenora ruffled her daughter's bangs and laughed as Dural walked into the house.

"Did you bring me anything? A cat? I've been wanting one for *ages*!"

Dural chuckled. The two women in his life both wanted a fluffy, purring creature padding around the house, provided the other did all the caring and cleaning up.

"I'll get you one if you're prepared to take care of it, *and* it stays outside."

"How can I have a cat if I cannot cuddle it?"

"You'll like cuddling it while it's still a little ball of mischief, but that will quickly wear off once it grows up. Like you, cats don't like to be squeezed."

She thought about it and shrugged. An argument she knew she could not win.

"How was Sydney, Daddy? Did you get to do some sightseeing? When are we going there? You *promised*! Tell it all."

He sat on the soft couch and cradled Daniela on his lap. The muted 60" LED TV showed news on the ABC channel. Under the TV stand lay tucked a DVD player and surround system box. On either side, magazines, professional periodicals—his and Lenora's—and all sorts of books that covered a range of their tastes filled ceiling-high bookcases. She liked Harry Potter and that kind of stuff, which he detested, disliking all forms of fantasy and magic. His idea of fun books were science fiction, contemporary political thrillers, naval warfare, among others, but nothing on terrorism. Too morbid and gruesome. Apart from fiction, he collected old texts on psychiatry, ethics, and philosophy. Among the volumes, a hardback on clinical psychology that bore his name.

He also dabbled at writing short science fiction stories, self-published on Amazon. The slim anthology sold well and had some good reviews. If his professional work went belly up, he figured he could always turn his hand to writing novels for a living. His inner self snorted at the absurd idea. On his left, a formal dining table, liquor cabinet, and wine cooler filled the rest of the lounge that opened into the kitchen space. Against the wall, polished stairs led to bedrooms and a bathroom for Daniela's exclusive use. Dural and Lenora shared an en-suite.

Lenora walked to the cabinet and poured two fingers of bourbon, no ice. She handed him the tumbler and placed her hands on her hips.

"You'll see Daddy at breakfast, Dan. Right now, it's time for bed, young lady."

Daniela pouted and looked at Dural. "She always makes me go to bed early, like I'm a kid. My friend Penny is allowed to stay up until nine!"

"Bed," Lenora declared. "And Penny is a year older than you."

"I want a story first," Daniela pleaded. "You've just *got* to, Daddy."

Dural smiled and slid a hand down her hair. If he had to, he had to. She would eventually outgrow this phase when she started to read seriously on her own. She already had a nice collection of books in her room and liked to read paperbacks and e-books, but a story from her daddy still the tops.

"A short one, little grub, if it's okay with your Mom," he told her.

"I wouldn't mind a story either," Lenora said with a grin.

"Fine, then." He took a sip of smooth whiskey and placed the tumbler on the coffee table.

Daniela beamed at him and nestled her head against his chest, her small arms wound firmly around him, her eyes glowing with anticipation as she looked at him. Lenora smiled indulgently and sat beside him.

"Once upon a time there was a beautiful princess. She lived in a grand castle and had servants to fulfill her every wish. She had everything, but she felt lonely. She could not understand why she could not have friends like other girls. She had a gorgeous garden full of bright flowers to walk in, but she was lonely."

"What happened then, Daddy?"

"One day, her father declared that she must marry. The idea did not appeal to her, but she had no choice. The young men who came to court her up to now were all stuck up and acted important. She did not like any of them. She told her father she would marry, but he must allow any young man to seek her hand. Even a commoner. The king looked properly scandalized, but the queen approved. In the end, they posted a proclamation on the main gate, and messengers were sent throughout the kingdom inviting suitors for her hand."

"What then, Daddy? What then?"

Dural glanced at Lenora. She gave him a fleeting nod filled with approval. She occasionally read Daniela stories, but the little imp preferred a story from her daddy.

"Well, after one month, the princess had seen all the noble sons across the kingdom, and she didn't like any of them. This outraged most of the young bloods, but the princess would not be swayed. One day, a tall youth walked through the main gate garbed in ragged, torn clothing. At first, the guards would not let him in, and he pointed at the declaration that said anyone is free to seek the hand of the princess. They laughed at him and allowed him through. When he walked into the reception hall, the attending lords and ladies tittered at his bedraggled appearance. As the handsome youth strode confidently toward the throne, something about him stirred the princess to look at him more closely. When he demanded her hand, the king asked what he could offer his daughter, apart from toiling in the field, hardship and hunger, a life she had little taste for. The youth turned and gazed at the princess. Then he said, I offer her love, respect, and joy in her life, simple as it might be."

Daniela blinked at him. "Wow. What did the king say?"

"Before he could say anything, the princess stood up and slowly walked toward the youth. She stopped before him and looked deeply into his eyes. Can you be my prince, she asked him in a soft voice. He said, close your eyes, kiss me, and wish me to be your prince. If you wish strongly enough, I'll be your prince. The princess looked at him, then slowly closed her eyes and kissed him. When she opened them, she gasped in surprise. She did not see a poor boy, but a splendid prince in fine garments adorned with gold and jewels. From that moment, she knew she would never be alone again and they lived happily ever after."

Daniela sighed softly, her eyes large and dreamy. "A lovely story, Daddy. One day, I'll also have a prince asking for my hand."

"I am sure you will."

Dural kissed the top of her head. "Off to bed now. Want me to take you?"

"I want Mommy to do it. She tucks me in just right."

As Lenora carried her upstairs, Daniela peered over her mother's shoulder and fluttered her fingers at him. He waved back, smiled, and sat down. He picked up the tumbler and took a sip. A pleasant warmth spread through his belly and he gave a contented exhale.

He glanced at the TV, picked up the remote and switched it off. Lenora came down, sat beside him and rested her head on his shoulder. Her hair smelled faintly of lilacs and he longed to run his fingers through it.

"That *was* a nice story," she mused. "If I close my eyes and kiss you, will you turn into a prince?"

"Only one way to find out," he said with a grin.

She closed her eyes and he brought his mouth over her rosy lips. Their tongues danced around each other in delicious abandon as he gathered her into his arms, not wanting the moment to stop. Regrettably, it had to, but only as an interlude to a promise of more.

Lenora looked at him and smiled. "My prince…"

He cupped her face between his hands. "And you will always be my princess."

She laughed and straightened her sweater. "You're a hopeless romantic, Dural Sinclair, and I love you for it. How was the conference?"

"If it weren't tax deductible, I wouldn't have gone," he admitted and took a sip. "Not a total loss, though. Two Americans presented interesting papers on neurosis treatment I found stimulating. I'll have to discuss them with Leonard and Gerard tomorrow. There is stuff in them we might be able to use. It could also be a useful topic at the Research Center. Apart from that, not much excitement."

"No romping around Kings Cross?"

He snorted at the idea of carousing through Sydney's premier drug and red light district. "The only romping I want to do is with you. What about your work?"

He kept himself fit through a regimen of running, workouts and an occasional game at the Albert Park Golf Club, alone or with Leonard. Gerard wasn't much into the game, although he did have a bash at it—which it actually was—for exercise. Dural's work demanded a lot of chair polishing and he hated the idea of turning into a stomach-sagging slob. If Lenora could make the effort, so could he. They shared a run around the Kings Domain Park and the Albert Park Lake—when mutual work commitments permitted. All of them regularly went for leisurely weekend walks through the Botanic Gardens. It gave Daniela an opportunity to run free, climb trees, roll in the grass, and feed ducks beside the Ornamental Lake. Modern suburbia didn't do kids any favors. Sometimes they strolled along St. Kilda Beach where Dan enjoyed chasing gulls, to their squawking annoyance.

At thirty-five, Lenora maintained her trim shape. The years

may have matured and softened some of the curves, but she did not allow herself to spread. She laughed easily and her dark complexion—heritage from her Maori father—had fascinated him from their first encounter in November 2005 at Melbourne Airport. Her classical looks came from her English-born mother. The memory of that chance meeting still vivid as though it happened yesterday.

He recalled as she loaded her handbag and small travel bag into a gray security tray, she dropped her purse. He had not even noticed her until then. Long black hair cascading down her back, merely another woman in a queue. He picked up the purse and touched her elbow.

"Excuse me…" His words failed him when she turned. Her deep violet eyes regarded him with detached curiosity, then widened when she saw the purse in his hand. Her generous mouth opened in a warm smile that highlighted perfectly white teeth. Apart from lipstick and eyeshadow, she did not appear to wear makeup, but hard to tell what women put on their faces these days. Not strikingly beautiful, high cheekbones, he could not look away from her clean features.

He cleared his throat and held out the purse. "You dropped this," he said with a grin.

"Thank you. I would have been lost without it," she replied in a husky voice.

When she cleared the security portal, travel bag rolling behind her, she walked quickly down the long corridor toward her boarding gate, leaving Dural staring after her, totally bemused. He felt an unaccountable connection with her, someone he wanted to know better, but it looked like it was not meant to be. When the speaker announced his boarding call, he was surprised to see her hand her pass to an attendant and enter the air bridge for the same flight he took. His next surprise far more pleasant when he found his seat and saw her in the center seat next to him.

Perhaps it was meant to be after all.

"Good morning…again," he ventured.

She returned an amused smile. "Small world."

"Since we're going to be sharing it for the next hour or so, I'm Dural Sinclair."

Her eyebrows arched. "*Doctor* Sinclair?"

He chuckled. "I did not realize my notoriety had preceded me."

"I saw your book displayed at the Collins Street Dymocks store. I'm sorry to disappoint you, but I am not in need of your services."

HarperCollins released his *Psychology in the Modern World* two weeks ago, and it already generated a stir among his colleagues, not altogether favorably received by the older and stuffier members of the learned community. As Clark Gable told Scarlet at end of *Gone with the Wind*, he didn't give a damn. His research solid, the book dealt with modern issues unfettered by prevailing dogma. Being controversial would also boost sales, as such works were not considered a mainstream attraction.

"In that case, I would rather only talk. If you don't mind, that is."

The aircraft pushed back and the dreary safety presentation droned in the background. Dural tightened his safety belt. He wanted to cross his legs, impossible in the narrow space between seats. Only a short flight, he told himself.

Lenora gave him a surreptitious glance, which showed at least mild interest. "I don't mind, and I don't have anything else to do. Who knows? A psychologist might come in handy after all. By the way, I'm Lenora."

At 179cm, without carrying any love handles, pale brown hair combed straight back, eyes dark gray, Dural knew he looked good. He took in her casual wear, which suggested she was not on a business trip.

"Visiting in Sydney?"

"My brother. We're both from Wellington, New Zealand, and came here to further our careers. His as an electrical engineer, and mine in IT."

"Programmer…analyst?"

"Programmer at ANZ, but I expect that to change in January to senior programmer." Her violet eyes sparkled. "I don't have to ask what you do."

"Nothing as exciting as being a computer programmer."

"Block," she retorted with a chuckle, and he grinned, enchanted by her easy manner and lack of awkwardness.

"Any other relatives in Sydney?"

She shook her head. "My parents are still in Wellington, as is my sister and her husband. She's threatening to move to Auckland. Better job prospects there, and she's right. Wellington may be the capital, but it's really a very small city. She'll never do it, though, what with parents and friends in Wellington. And you?"

He shrugged. "I run a practice with two partners near The Alfred Hospital. All of us also consult at the Monash Alfred Psychiatry Research Center, which is next door to the hospital. I have a small apartment in South Yarra. My old man runs an accountancy firm and my mom is his bookkeeper."

Lenora smiled. "Funny you should say that. My mom does the same thing for Dad. He's a mechanical engineer and owns an auto repair shop with two partners."

Dural glanced at her hands, no ring. She fascinated him. Charming, clearly sophisticated, unpretentious, he found her easy to talk with. At twenty-eight, with university studies and a new practice establishing itself keeping him very busy, he hadn't had many opportunities to form a stable relationship. His two affairs never actually developed. His fault mostly. He simply could not devote the attention a relationship required, and casual romps did not interest him.

"And why are you going to Sydney?" she asked.

"I'm attending the Australian Society for Psychological Medicine conference."

"Sounds dull."

"Might not be. Before you ask, my book will be a topic of discussion. Vigorous discussion, I might add," he said dryly, and she laughed. "It promises to be a lively two days."

"Your partners, also psychologists?"

He nodded. "In various branches of psychology. We all studied at Monash University. Leonard is the oldest and got his PhD first. His parents are quite well off, and he picked up a lot of knowledge from them about running a business. He urged Gerard and me to open our own practice, something I wasn't initially too keen on. I had enough on my hands settling in as a junior researcher at the Psychiatry Center. Leonard told us our professional careers would get a boost if people saw a business logo on our correspondence. Besides, we would make more money that way. I couldn't fault him there. Working at a public hospital not exactly a large six-figure job. His father loaned us an accountant and a secretary to get us going, and took out a lease for us in a building on St. Kilda Road not far from The Alfred complex. Rosalyn, our secretary, is still with us."

She pursed her lips and nodded. "You and your partners did well in such a short time."

"That still remains to be seen. We've only been in business for a year."

When the flight attendants rolled the drinks carts along the aisle, Dural and Lenora declined coffee or tea and kept talking. Before he realized it, the copilot announced they were landing. He had never enjoyed a better flight. What now? She would return to Melbourne and resume her life, and he would resume his. Did he want to leave it at that?

The Airbus A330 squatted down at Mascot and began rolling toward the QANTAS domestic terminal. He turned to Lenora and searched her eyes.

"I would like to resume our conversation when we're both back in Melbourne," he said softly and waited, unaccountably anxious. He knew he was experiencing a normal physiological response to an attractive woman, but his training did not help him cope with the emotional reaction.

She smiled faintly, dug out her purse, and offered him a business card. "Call me."

Five months after they met, Lenora and Dural married in March 2006.

Memories still chasing each other, he took her hand in his and squeezed.

"I got a surprise yesterday, Du," Lenora gushed, her eyes bright. "Woodrow Grant himself called me to his office. I don't usually chat with the Senior Manager for Treasury Projects, and I thought he wanted an update on my work to upgrade the short-term bills settlement system. It's about three weeks behind schedule, but that's not my fault," she pointed out with a raised index finger and arched eyebrows.

"It's always the project leader's fault," Dural pointed out gently.

"You can be such a block sometimes, you know," she mused and fisted him lightly on the shoulder.

"About Woody…"

"I thought he would dress me down, but he never mentioned the project or the schedule slippage. In fact, he congratulated me and my team for our work. What he said next floored me. The Program Manager would give me the official letter, he said, but Woody wanted to offer his personal endorsement on my promotion as project manager. I could have kissed him! I waited three years for this and I finally got it."

Dural stroked her arm and pecked her cheek. "I'm thrilled for you, Len. ANZ merely slow to recognize talent."

"Better believe it, buster," she purred contentedly. "There is another upside to this; an immediate raise in salary to $115K."

"Say, that's great. I'm proud of you."

"Thanks. Despite all those talks by Human Resources about equal opportunity, it's only talk. Women today have to struggle for recognition as hard as ever, even when everybody sees we're better than some men."

Dural tossed back the last of his whiskey. "Fifteen years into the twenty-first century, but many things still have a long way to go." He heaved himself up. "I need a shower."

"Will you tell *me* a story before going to bed?" she murmured, eyes sparkling.

"Any lullaby you want, hon," he told her softly.

"You're good with kids, Du, and Dan worships you. Leonard says the same thing. You know that his little Chris is sweet on her?"

"Len! They're only kids, for heaven's sake."

"Kids grow up to be young people, you know."

"She's seven. By the time she gets interested in such things, Chris will probably be married already."

She laughed. "You *are* a block, Du. Anyway, the staff at Wesley College also told me how kids there like you."

He brushed off Lenora's remarks as frivolous, but he admitted he clicked with kids. A high level of empathy, he told himself. Something that also made him good at his job as a psychologist.

"How about a nightcap before we turn in?" he remarked as he led Lenora toward the stairs.

"You don't want anything to eat?"

"Not hungry. Not for food anyway." He grinned at her.

"Randy old goat."

"We could open that bottle of ice wine we have stashed in the cooler. Ice wine and champagne…a great combination. What do you say?"

"We were saving it for my dad's birthday," she protested.

"I'll get him another one."

"You haven't forgotten to book the flights?" she demanded

sternly.

"All done," he assured her. His secretary cool, charming, and very efficient.

She gave him a speculative glance. "I sometimes wonder about you and Rosalyn. All those late hours at the office…I've seen how she looks at you sometimes."

"I like it when you show your horns, doll," he said, vastly amused, and patted her shoulder. "It tells me I'm not over the hill."

"Yet. Seriously, Du. I don't want to disappoint Dad because you stuffed up our flight to Wellington."

"I told you. It's all done."

"You know, we could visit my parents more often if we lived in Brisbane. Lots of opportunities for psychologists among all those neurotic geriatric retirees on the Gold Coast and Surfers Paradise."

"But not many opportunities for a newly minted project manager," he pointed out reasonably. "All major corporations are either in Sydney or here in Melbourne, and that's where the good jobs are. Something you know very well, and the reason you came here."

She gave a characteristic sniff of disapproval. "Let's move to Sydney, then. I'll be able to see Edmond more often."

Dural sighed. He and Len had walked this ground before and the rocks were showing. New Zealand was picturesque and touristy, but high-paying jobs were not lying around for the picking. He knew she missed her parents, her sister Judith, and old friends, but her desire to be closer to them a nostalgic fantasy. She understood all that, but it did not stop her dreaming about it. Should he treat her fixation as she were one of his patients? The job should not be too difficult. She was organized and very methodical in everything she did, and logical. She had to be to succeed as a project manager. On reflection, a person can be logical and still unreasonable. However, that did not diminish the validity of her emotional desire.

"Len, Daniela is at an important stage of her development and getting comfortable with the idea of spending every day at school. And she's developing friends. Do you want to relocate and start somewhere as an analyst again just when you got your big break at ANZ? I could set up a new practice somewhere else, that's true, but the plain fact is that I don't want to. We're doing great here, hon, both of us. Anyway, we jet off to Wellington every few months to see your parents and sister. Melbourne or Sydney, there isn't much difference in distance," he said and tugged at his ear. There might not be much difference in distance, but this was not about distance.

Lenora paused on the steps and lifted her hands in surrender. "You're right, and I'm being silly."

"You're not being silly, and I'm not insensitive. We have to look at this from all angles. Talk about it later?"

"You still want to take that trip to the Kimberleys in December?" she asked, sidestepping the issue. "I'll have to confirm my leave application."

She knew he loved to travel and see more of Australia, so did she, but not overseas, unless it was to New Zealand. So far, she had not shown any interest in Europe or America. The unpalatable truth he could not avoid, touring around Australia often more expensive than taking an overseas trip. What stopped them adventuring was getting time off work. Daniela not a problem, not in second grade.

"Definitely. I have never been in that part of the country, and what I've seen on TV has me intrigued. We'll be able to visit Broome along the way and Dan will go nuts feeding the dolphins. Now, how about that ice wine?"

She frowned and bit her lower lip, then grinned. "I'll get the glasses."

He hooted with delight and hurried to the cooler.

In bed after a very quick shower, bottles safely in an ice bucket on the side cabinet, Dural lifted his champagne flute in a salute.

"To us."

"To us," Lenora agreed solemnly and clicked her glass against his, the crystal ringing with lingering purity.

After a third glass, the bubbly started to affect both of them.

"You're right. Pink champagne and ice wine is a very nice combination," she declared and took a hefty swallow.

"Last night in Sydney as I strolled along Darling Harbor," he mused absently, "the city bright all around me, you know what I wanted most? I wanted you beside me, Len. I wanted your hand in mine. I wanted to feel you against me. Most of all, I wanted to hear your enchanting voice." He turned his head and looked deep into her eyes. "Did I tell you that you have a most magical voice and it has me bewitched?"

"You did, my prince, but I don't mind hearing it again," she murmured.

Something changed in her eyes and she reached for his glass. She placed it next to hers on the side cabinet and faced him. Without saying anything, she grasped the flimsy nightie and pulled it over her head. Her full breasts swelled as she arched her back. He placed his hands over them and massaged the nipples. She groaned, leaned over him and crushed her mouth against his.

* * *

With electronic certainty, the alarm went off at 6:45. Dural grunted, fumbled for the cutoff switch, and rolled onto his back. Light from the street oozed between the drapes, dispelling the darker shadows. He particularly disliked Wednesdays. The last weekend faded in the memory tube, and the coming weekend still two full days away—three if he wanted to include today.

Getting out of a warm, cozy bed, he found hard. Downstairs would be nice and toasty, the automatic heating system making things comfortable for the frail human occupants.

Not bothering to open his eyes, he listened to the soft patter of rain against the window pane. A rumble of thunder rolled ponderously somewhere in the east and faded into a muted grumble. Lightning momentarily set the shadows dancing, followed by a sharp, crashing protest. The east side of Melbourne always got the worst of the prevailing westerly weather flows. Being a natural heat sink, warm air from kilometers of concrete, brick, and road disrupted the normal airflow. The western suburbs would see heavy clouds overhead with a promise of rain, only to have them roll by and dump in the east. The eastern suburbs got more rain, but they also suffered from flash flooding and high winds. Despite these negatives, people still flocked east, considering inhabitants in the western part of the city blue-collar migrant trash. Not true, of course, but old English snobbery still held sway with many multi-generational families.

Lenora shifted beside him and mumbled something. He leaned over her and nibbled her ear. She sniffed and shifted her head.

"Wasn't last night enough?" she muttered, her voice muffled by the pillow.

Dural allowed himself a broad smile. They never got around to finishing the champagne, having started something more interesting, and definitely more satisfying. A combination of things that made the evening memorable. Mere coupling released sexual tension, but never touched the soul. Their tender, slow lovemaking last night definitely touched both their souls. That's what being a man and wife was all about, the touching and merging of souls.

"Just reminding you, hon, it's time to get up," he told her softly.

"I don't want to get up. I have a meeting with the Treasury team at ten, and they'll blame me for the schedule slippage and the cost overrun, forgetting it's their own fault for insisting on that extra functionality. I *told* them it would delay the rollout, and

I got emails to prove it, not that it'll do any good."

"Deal with it, Ms. Project Manager. That's why you're getting the big bucks now."

"You're a lot of help," she growled and turned over.

An intense flash lit the bedroom, followed almost immediately by a hideous crash.

"That was close," Dural observed.

He heard a patter of small footfalls and knew what would happen. The bedroom door slowly opened and Daniela stood there, a battered Cabbage Patch doll pressed against her chest.

"What's the matter, little grub?" he asked, knowing very well what bothered her. He'd been through these impromptu bedroom incursions before.

"I was frightened by the thunder," she said, looking dejected, eyes downcast.

"It's only clouds talking to each other. They can't hurt you."

"I know, but still…"

"Come here," he said and waved her in.

She broke into a sunny smile that made her glow, and she ran toward the bed. Arms stretched out, she flung herself onto the thick doona and scrambled toward him. He made room for her in the middle and she crawled in, clutching the doona to her chin. She tucked the doll next to her and rearranged its raggedy curls.

"Much better, isn't it, Madam Bisque?" she said and looked up. "It's cold in my room, Daddy. Do I have to go to school today? I would rather stay at home."

Dural knew how she felt. He would rather stay at home too.

"School, I'm afraid. And your mother and I have to go to work."

Lenora sat up and brushed down Daniela's disheveled hair. "You'll be with your friends, sugar buns. Much better than being all alone here."

Daniela crunched her nose. "I suppose. Whose turn to take me to school today?"

Lenora hooked a thumb at Dural. "Your father will take you. I did it for the last two days."

Fair was fair, he admitted. The early and middle grade Wesley College private school a couple of blocks down St. Kilda Road from his practice, and next to The Alfred Hospital complex. The College also provided daycare facilities, as parents did not always find it convenient to pick up their children by 4 pm when classes ended. That sometimes made for a long day for the kids, but Daniela had adjusted well, having attended preschool there when she turned four.

Lenora had a year off work when Daniela was born, and ANZ HR did not bat an eyelid. The government paid for the first eighteen weeks, and she took an additional six weeks as long service leave. The last six months were unpaid. Dural then took six months to look after their daughter, neither of them relishing the idea of having a full-time babysitter during this critical period, or putting her into a toddler center. He did some part-time work for the practice, but he focused on Dan. After a year-and-a-half when able to walk and started to talk, they enrolled her in the Alfred Childcare Center. As a consultant at the Monash Alfred Psychiatry Research Center, the admission formalities were largely waived.

Taking Daniela to school not a big chore. They would ride a tram down High Street to St. Kilda Road and walk a block to the College. He and Lenora never took a car to work. Apart from the expense to park it somewhere, both preferred to avoid the morning and afternoon traffic crush and retain their sanity. Trams were crowded enough. Weather permitting, Dural sometimes walked to his practice or the Center for extra exercise. Getting the Prahran house had turned out to be one of their better investments.

He also had a rental property in the seaside Nelson Bay, some sixty kilometers north of Newcastle in NSW. A deal his old man talked him into. At first, Dural protested. He did not wish to burden himself with a second mortgage, but his father took pains to explain the raw facts of real estate business to him. By 2012, the Australian economy had largely shrugged off the effects of the Global Financial Crisis and business everywhere picked up, including the real estate market.

In partnership with two university buddies, his father operated a management accounting firm that specialized in strategic consulting and bailing out troubled enterprises. Farah, Dural's mom, also an accountant, ran the office, kept the books, and paid the bills. Fairway Consulting did very well, allowing his father to build up a nice share portfolio and acquire a newly built residence in Nelson Bay. After a holiday visit, his old man pushing sixty, the Sinclairs fell in love with the charming place and snapped up the property even before the house was finished.

When the economic upturn became noticeable, his father took him by the arm to his lounge when Dural and Lenora visited once, and convinced him to invest in Nelson Bay. An undiscovered resort destination bound to expand quickly. When it did become trendy, prices would soar, his dad said. Get in now when such properties were still relatively cheap. Dural would never lose on the deal, and holding property always a winner. When your old man turns sixty-five in 2017, his father declared, he would sell his share in Fairway Consulting, pull up stumps, and relocate to Nelson Bay.

Dural bought a house near the beach. Growing rental income and negative gearing helped offset the drain on his liquidity. His father looked after the place and made sure the tenants did not cause trouble. So far, Dural never had any problems, only taking older couples who preferred a long-term tenancy. The way the economy developed, he figured he would be debt free by 2020. In the meantime, his personal shares portfolio with Ord Minnett looked healthier every day.

Dural liked his mother, and had a live-and-let-live relationship with his old man. His father always had a practical approach to life, a byproduct of having to deal with hard businessmen and sometimes creative accountants. He never understood why Dural took his PhD in something wooly like psychology, instead of practicing real medicine as a surgeon. Trying to explain to his dad that being a surgeon wasn't a good profile fit just didn't get through. After seeing how much money there was to be made in psychology, Colton Sinclair reluctantly capitulated. No matter how much parents think they're not molding their children, they never stop doing it.

Colton was not obtuse, holding a degree in accountancy. Dural and his old man were simply on different life tracks, based on divergent experiences and education. Raised in different eras, the generation gap was sometimes difficult to bridge. Farah proved more understanding, acting as a mediator when father and son clashed. Probably a byproduct of her Polish heritage. They lived in North Melbourne and Dural visited about once a month. Christmas and Easter lunches were mostly at their place, something of a tradition. However, he and Lenora had flown to Wellington on three occasions to celebrate with her family. Dural not particularly religious, and neither was Colton, but as a Catholic, his mother was devout. Not a regular churchgoer, holding the Vatican hierarchy morally corrupt. Dural did not argue with her there.

"Daddy, are we still going to Healesville on Saturday?" Daniela demanded absently, fondling her doll.

"If it's a nice day," Dural temporized. "No use going if it's cold or rainy. All the animals will be inside where it's nice and warm."

"Aw, Daddy, you're teasing. Everybody knows that koalas and kangaroos don't have houses. They all live outside. There are birds and things there too, and they're all outside. Besides, last night, the weatherman said Saturday would be fine with a top of nineteen."

Lenora cocked an eye at him, telling him he walked into that one.

He tended to forget sometimes how incredibly smart Dan turned out to be. Only seven and starting second grade, she had more brains than some fourth graders. Put her in an advanced school? He and Len discussed it, deciding to wait until end of the school year. They would ask Wesley College to give Dan tests to see if she could go straight to grade four. Daniela may be intellectually advanced, but Dural did not want to stress her emotional development by thrusting her among older students too quickly, not that he considered nine-year-olds a significant psychological threat.

He rubbed his daughter's hair. "Healesville it is, then."

"Wowsy!"

Dural cocked his head and listened. No rain, and the thunder had stopped, the weather front drifting farther east toward the mountains. He gritted his teeth and pulled back the doona.

"You can go back to bed for another half hour. Your mother and I have to get ready for work. We'll call you at seven-thirty in time for breakfast."

"Aw, can't I stay here?"

"Bed," Lenora said kindly and pointed at the open doorway.

Reconciled to the inevitable, Daniela sighed and looked at her doll. "See what I have to put up with, Madam Bisque? Kids got no rights in this house."

She stood, padded across the bed, and jumped onto the floorboards. With an absent wave, she walked out, the doll hanging at her side.

Dural glanced at his wife. "Does this mean we also have to get up?"

"'Fraid so," she said and stifled a yawn. "You want to use the bathroom first?"

"You get a few more winks while I have a quick shower and shave, and get breakfast started. You ladies seem to have so much more to do in the bathroom."

She threw a pillow at him.

For once—well, it happened more than once—Daniela had washed, tidied her room by 7:30, and helped Lenora make French toast. Her job was to keenly watch the frypan and turn over the browned bread when she figured the bottom side was done. Lenora happy for her daughter to get the eggs ready and soak the toast, but not during the week. Removing runny egg out of a school uniform and getting Dan changed into a new one caused too much unnecessary excitement for everybody. Turning over toast considered relatively safe. Dural and Lenora did not allow commercial cereals in the house, being mostly sugar and of dubious nutritional value, something both agreed on completely. Fruit chunks and natural yogurt provided a far better side dish.

Breakfasts at the Sinclair residence were always rowdy affairs. Dural's job was to work the percolator and set the dishes, and Lenora made sure Daniela's small purple backpack with a koala motif had everything. After all that, she had to get ready herself to face another day at work. It presented a challenge, as everybody kept glancing at the wall clock, the microwave clock, the oven clock, and wristwatches. Dan considered all this rushing about very amusing. All the while, in the lounge TV, wearing his signature blue jacket, Michael Rowland and the effervescent Virginia Trioli pumped out the latest domestic and international news on the ABC channel, to which Dural paid only passing attention, unless something of significance happened to be going on.

Lenora had to take a tram downtown to the ANZ tower in Collins Street, and always hurried her breakfast to be off by 8:00. Missing a tram on High Street no big deal this time of morning, as they ran every few minutes. She gulped down the last of her coffee, snatched her slim leather briefcase, and gave Daniela a quick hug and kiss on the cheek. Some time ago, Dural told Lenora one morning that she would not have to hurry if she only started the breakfast rush ten minutes earlier. She agreed, but she always pushed the departure time.

"Be good. I'll see you tonight."

Daniela squirmed, not liking being pawed, having to put up with a ritual her parents considered important. She wasn't a baby, she told her mom.

Dural pushed back his chair and got up. Lenora slid into his arms and he gave her a fleeting kiss on the mouth.

"Knock 'em dead at that meeting."

"Ready to eat them," she purred, eyes glowing. "You'll be okay picking up Dan this afternoon?"

He nodded. "I'll be fine."

With a flutter of fingers, she headed for the door.

"Bye, Mommy!" Daniela shouted after her.

"Bye, sugar buns."

With breakfast done and the dishwasher fed, last minute bathroom chores completed, Dural led his daughter toward High Street. The weather front had moved off and the sky had a deep, clear blue look that left the air fresh and invigorating. Still a little crisp, both warmed quickly as they walked toward the tram stop.

Cars whispered by and he waved to a couple of neighbors. Daniela held his hand firmly and skipped on the sidewalk, an irrepressible package of energy. When they reached the intersection, a tram clanked its bell and pulled out. A five-minute wait for the next one...

"Can we walk to school, Daddy? It's only two blocks. Can we?"

A little farther than two blocks, but the difference wasn't worth making a federal case out of. Dural did not mind and nodded. The legs could use the exercise.

"Sure thing, little grub. Let's do it."

"Wowsy!"

Chapter Two

Leonard wiggled his butt, made two practice swings, gazed intently down the fairway, then looked down at the ball. He pulled back the driver and brought it down cleanly, striking the ball with a sweet click. Dural watched it fade slightly left around the dogleg thirteenth fairway, avoiding trees waiting to trap a wayward shot, a certain way to make a bogey.

"Not bad, buddy," he acknowledged.

"A good shot if I say so myself," Leonard agreed with a satisfied grin. "Let's see you top it."

Dural chuckled and planted his ball on the tee. A fresh breeze made the branches sway as it sighed down the fairway. Dark clouds lay stacked overhead in a promise of rain. He hoped it would hold off until they finished their game, only six holes to go. Up three shots on Leonard, he had no intention allowing his partner to beat him, rain or no rain.

Relatively short, only 160cm, Leonard surprisingly strong, able to produce some amazing drives. He chipped like a pro, and his bunker shots left Dural gaping. He compensated for that advantage with a superior short game, reading the greens better. Generally, they were about even.

Not today, though. In this round, Dural determined to cream his partner.

He glanced down the fairway, addressed the ball, and swung back the driver. The clean hit sent the ball soaring over the tree barrier, effectively cutting the corner. Watching it disappear, he figured a nine iron would see him on the putting green.

Lightning flickered somewhere over the Bay, followed by a deep rumble.

Dural glanced up and frowned. Despite being Saturday, they had the course pretty much to themselves. Given the inclement weather, he was not surprised. Half an hour ago, it was all different, with sunny breaks as bunched clouds pushed in from the west. Then the wind came, cold and biting his windbreaker could not quite stop. As long as it did not pick up, they would finish their game, even if it meant getting soaked a little.

Lenora and Daniela had gone to the city for some shopping and a visit to the Victoria Market. The place had everything, from clothing, footwear, kitchenware, auto tools and accessories, and of course, a range of souvenirs. It housed extensive fruit and vegetable stalls, and a good fish and meat section, the selections far more comprehensive than what the supermarkets offered. Prahran Market an excellent venue in South Yarra where he and Lenora often shopped, but it could not compare to the trendy and touristy Vic Market.

With two hours or so to themselves, Dural and Leonard agreed to have a game and get the blood circulating. They invited Gerard to tag along, but their partner declined, claiming he had work to do at the Psychiatry Research Center. Dural maintained it was a lame excuse to avoid fresh air. Have a life, man.

Gerard, a little plump, not into vigorous outdoor activities, a bachelor despite Dural and Leonard's efforts to get him married—lots of eligible residents at The Alfred, they chided him— a serious researcher with a PhD in Clinical Neuropsychology specializing in aspects of therapeutic brain stimulation techniques and imaging. He often used his patients as test subjects to correlate their brain activity with the control group normals. Normal, of course, still to be defined.

Leonard, on the other hand, worked in translational research in areas of human factors, education, organizational behavior, decision-making, and social influence. He also researched brain structure to determine if anomalous anatomical differences led to psychotic behavior, or whether psychosis induced physical changes in the brain. Happily married to his wife Helen, a PhD candidate in chemistry at Melbourne University, a nine-year-old son, life was good for him.

Dural handled bipolar disorder, Asperger's syndrome cases—a fascinating area of work—and non-drug-related addictions. He also handled cases on women's psychological and psychiatric trauma across a broad spectrum of causal factors, from family violence, postnatal depression, or inability to cope with life's many problems in a society growing socially and technologically more complex. The three of them often consulted each other on their respective patients, the collaboration helping to define a course of treatment, which over time led to improvement and even a cure.

It kept them busy, and an opportunity to unwind a little with a game of golf not to be frowned upon.

Dural placed the head cover over the driver, shoved the club into the bag, and followed Leonard down the fairway. They rounded the dogleg and hunted for their balls. Leonard spotted his on the right side of the fairway, some twenty meters behind Dural's.

"Lucky bastard," Leonard muttered and headed for his ball.

Dural laughed and waited for his partner to make a shot for the green. Leonard made it, but landed up a gentle slope from the flag, which would make for a tricky put to make a birdie. Dural frowned as he judged distance to the flag, then pulled out his nine iron. Forty meters at most, an easy lofted shot. He set up his feet behind the ball and made a couple of practice swings. With a last glance at the flag, he rested the club head behind the ball.

Out of the corner of his left eye, he saw the searing white bolt strike the elm. The crack made the ground tremble and Dural winced at the sharp stab of pain in his ears. A tingle raced up his arms and bright points of yellow light flared in his head. His nerveless fingers opened and the club fell. He could not feel his legs or body. Ears ringing, he slowly toppled. He hit the turf with his right shoulder, insensitive to the fall. He stared at the green, wondering if he could make par. It did not seem important, just mild curiosity.

Leonard leaned over him and turned him on his back.

"Du! Talk to me."

Dural studied his friend's concerned face and managed a small smile. He tried to tell him that he felt fine, but the words would not come. Gradually, feeling returned to his limbs, a torture of pins and needles that raced through his body, then faded. He swallowed and cleared his throat.

"I...I'm okay," he managed to croak.

"Like hell you are. You're in shock. The current must have traveled through the ground and up your club, but I cannot see an exit mark." Leonard extended his forefinger. "Follow the finger for me."

Dural focused and shifted his eyes as Leonard moved his finger from side to side.

"Looks okay and your pupils aren't dilated. Any loss of feeling?"

"Initial mild paralysis, but it seems to have worn off," Dural said more easily and propped himself up. The ground swayed under him, then steadied.

Leonard placed a firm hand on his shoulder. "Sit there like a good boy and don't move. I'll get help." He stood, dug out his cellphone, and started talking.

Dural attempted to listen, but it was too much effort. In the end, he sat there, not thinking about anything in particular, random images. Cold raindrops touched his face and he looked up at the solid wall of dark gray above him. All very soothing and relaxing. He allowed himself to lay back and felt better. An occasional burst of yellow sparks jumped somewhere at the back of his eyes, but they disappeared when he blinked.

The clouds seemed to descend as he watched them, then finally enveloped him. After a while, he closed his eyes and cold drops caressed his face.

$$* * *$$

Dural felt warm and cozy, not anxious to do anything vigorous. The pillow softly cradled his head and the blanket over him smelled of antiseptic. The very air around him smelled of antiseptic. He took a deep breath, held it, and exhaled slowly. Not a bad way to spend a Saturday, he thought.

Memories came flooding back and he opened his eyes.

He experienced a lightning strike! He remembered the elm, shattered branch, sparks, and flying splinters, and a tingle running through his body.

"He's coming around," a grave voice announced beside him.

Dural turned his head and smiled. "Hi, little grub."

"Daddy! Daddy!" Daniela cried out and leaned against the bed, her small arms trying to embrace him.

He stroked her hair and planted a kiss on top of her head. "Were you worried about me?"

"I sure was. Mommy too. Weren't you?"

Lenora nodded and gave him a light kiss on the mouth. "We all were for a while. Welcome back, stranger."

Dural sat up and looked around the small plain room with a single round table and four chairs. He glanced at Leonard and raised an eyebrow.

"What's all the fuss? I just got a tingle."

"You've been out for the last three hours, my boy," Leonard said sternly. "Lucky for you, it was only a weak lightning stroke, or you would be handling a harp right now, or major physical trauma."

"We ran an MRI on you, Du," Gerard added in his characteristic baritone. "Everything seems normal, but I want to do a full workup on you tomorrow. Neuropsychological effects don't manifest themselves immediately. It can take several days or weeks for symptoms to appear. I'm referring to victims directly struck by lightning. There isn't much literature on near-miss cases such as yourself. How's your hearing?"

"Fine," Dural reflected, and it did seem fine without any background buzzing.

"Mmm. We'll have to test that." Gerard glanced at Leonard. "You too," he said and turned to Dural. "In the meantime, we're keeping you here for observation."

"Where is 'here'?"

"The Alfred Trauma Center," Leonard put in.

Dural made a face. "You mean I'll have to survive on hospital food?"

Lenora chuckled and patted his shoulder. "Good reflection therapy, Dr. Sinclair. You'll have a better appreciation of what your patients went through when you put them here."

Leonard cleared his throat. "We'll check up on you later, partner," he said and gathered Gerard with his eyes.

When the door closed after them, Dural reached for Daniela's arms and helped her clamber up the bed. She smiled and cuddled close. Lenora pulled up a chair and sat down.

"All your shopping done?" he asked.

"You're a block, Du," she declared. "Like shopping is important."

"We did get everything done, Daddy," Dan said brightly. "We even had some American donuts, didn't we, Mommy?"

"We did, sugar buns. That's why I couldn't get you to eat any lunch."

"Aw, it was just crumbed veal anyway. Besides, I did eat all the salad and fruit."

"You did…lucky for you."

Daniela looked at Dural. "Mommy isn't much fun sometimes."

Dural laughed. "Were the donuts any good?" He knew they were good. The van where they made them always popular, sometimes with a lengthy queue, especially on weekends.

"Wowsy, Daddy. And we didn't have to wait long, hardly. A band on the corner played South American music. They were great and helped pass the time. Mommy bought their CD."

Dural flickered a glance at Lenora. She smiled and shrugged.

"Your daughter got her donuts, and I got my CD."

"Seems fair," Dural said. "What do you think, little grub?"

Dan scrunched her nose. "I suppose. Uncle Gerard said you'll be staying here for a while. How long is that?"

"I don't know, but I expect to be home tomorrow. Somebody has to take you to school on Monday."

"You don't look hurt."

"The lightning strike sent a surge of electricity through me, Dan, and Gerard wants to make sure there wasn't any nerve damage. Understand?"

"I guess."

"You should not have been playing golf," Lenora said with brilliant hindsight. "Not on a day like this."

"One of those random things, doll. I played on cloudy days before."

"Can I get you anything?"

"My laptop. I might as well do some work while I'm stuck here."

She smiled. "We'll bring it around later…and some crumbed veal, if our little imp doesn't finish them all first."

Daniela gave Dural a conspiratorial grin. "I tried one. It was quite good. I helped with the batter and the breadcrumbs, and I cleaned up afterward. Didn't I, Mommy?"

"You did, darling. How about we give your dad some rest now, eh?"

"Well…" Dan kissed him on the cheek and he reached for her. Knowing what was coming, she squealed and threw herself back. "You were going to squeeze me. I know it."

"Only a little squeeze," he told her. "Didn't we make a deal?"

"Okay, then."

He embraced her and stroked her hair. "Be good."

"Come home soon, Daddy."

Lenora gave him a kiss and wiped his brow. "I would have died if something had happened to you," she whispered.

"It all worked out fine, hon. I'll see you guys later."

When they left and silence returned, Dural locked his fingers behind his head and sighed. His weekend had not turned out as planned, but it could have been much worse. Messing with lightning did not leave much wiggle room for the victim. He glanced at the Rado on his wrist, only to see a black face. He touched the surface, but the watch remained dark. Probably fried when the voltage surge exited through it. The only metal thing on him, apart from the house key in his trouser pocket. He wondered if he could claim the loss against his insurance.

A knock on the door and it opened. The well-rounded nurse walked in and beamed at him, her short raven hair reminding him of Demi Moore in *Ghost*.

"How are you feeling, Dr. Sinclair?"

"Great. I want to get out of here."

She chuckled. "I have that same feeling every day." She checked the monitor on the side cabinet and nodded. "Buzz if you need anything."

He glanced at the jug of water beside him. "Can I have some orange juice?"

"Of course. Won't be a moment."

As a rich patient in a private room, The Alfred could afford to give him a jug of orange juice. Or his insurance could.

The electronic alarm clock next to the jug and glass showed 4:30 pm. He glanced at the large LED TV mounted on the wall and thought fleetingly about watching something, then decided against it, preferring silence cradled in a warm bed.

Around five, Lenora breezed into the room with his laptop case.

"You're a lifesaver," he hooted. "But where is our problem child?"

"At home with Penny. You know how preoccupied those two get when they're together. I'll bring her around tomorrow," she said and placed the case on the side cabinet.

"Pull up a chair, Len."

"Cannot stay long. I've got to feed my charges."

"No crumbed veal for me?"

She chuckled and dragged a chair close to the bed. "You wouldn't like them cold. Did you have your dinner?"

He shook his head. "Not yet, and I have no idea when they serve meals."

She patted his arm. "I'm sure they won't let you starve." The light went out of her eyes, replaced with concern. "Seriously, Du. Will you be all right? Gerard must be worried to schedule all those tests for you."

Dural waved a hand in dismissal. "He is a worrywart. I guess he wants to make sure my brain cells haven't been scrambled."

"I want to make sure too, you block. Having a few million volts run through your body must have caused some damage."

"That would be true if I were struck by the lightning stroke, but I only got a secondary surge tingle."

"Enough to flatten you."

"I feel fine, Len. Honest." He glanced at the laptop case. "Thanks for bringing that. I'll bone up on lightning strike victims to make sure Gerard doesn't turn me into one of his experiments."

"You're not feeling any aftereffects? Fatigue, loss of energy, headache?"

He raised an eyebrow. "You've been reading up?"

She smiled. "I *am* an interested party, you know, Dr. Sinclair."

"For your interest, then, I really do feel fine, hon. Don't worry." Tempted to mention having occasional flashes of light pop in his head, he did not want to worry her unnecessarily. He would research the subject a little before becoming alarmed. He had seen several documentaries on lightning. The physiological effects on the body were generally well understood, as were the psychological symptoms on people who were struck. None of those programs, though, discussed effects on near-miss victims.

Lenora stood and patted down her trousers. "Just get back to me, okay?" She leaned over him and gave him a peck on the mouth.

"I'm ready right now," he growled, his hormones sizzling.

She laughed and slapped him playfully on the shoulder. "You goat. I'll see you tomorrow."

When she left, Dural filled his glass with orange juice and sipped. He opened the laptop and powered it up. When the Google search screen appeared, his fingers hovered over the keyboard. What exactly should he be searching for? No, a wrong question. He knew what he wanted to find out, but he could not jump directly into deep neurological studies without first understanding the fundamentals of lightning strikes. Define the parameters, examine the evidence, evaluate. Standard freshman methodology. Except for one thing. He had no hypothesis to guide his research.

There were probably academic websites that dealt with the subject, but this was outside his area of expertise. Well, he would have to do this the hard way then. He typed, 'Effects of lightning strikes on the body', and pressed Enter.

Most articles were written for popular consumption and thin on hard scientific data. Nevertheless, it gave him a working framework for more detailed searches. He skipped articles on terminal strike victims and related physiological effects. He wanted data on survivors and what being struck by a lightning bolt did to them in immediate, short and long-term timeframes. Unfortunately, apart from general physical trauma, such as neurological degradation affecting movement, speech, memory, and ocular disorders, little in-depth research was available on hypoxic encephalopathy, cerebral infarction, synaesthesia, and transverse myelopathy. However, the material that did touch on these symptoms only partially addressed his area of interest—victims who experienced an indirect lightning strike. All the papers he read did not explain cases of delayed psychiatric, cognitive, and neurological damage that manifest themselves after weeks or months in various forms of personality disorders.

What was interesting is that all victims showed increased levels of cortisol, which augments hyperstimulation of glutamate receptors. Normally, this induces release of destructive free radicals due to oxidative stress, which in turn gives rise to neuropsychological symptoms. Another teasing piece of information he came across was the possibility that the electrical potential traveling through the body from a near strike could alter cell DNA structure, potentially changing some body functions. He could not find papers that researched this in any meaningful depth.

What was clear, every near lightning strike victim suffered various degrees of physiological and neurological symptoms. The evidence irrefutable. Having several million volts surge through the body is bound to disrupt the brain's electrical pathways. To what extent he was affected, an imponderable. Apart from occasional flashes of light in his head, he felt fine. Would he be one of those delayed effects cases? No use worrying about it, as only time would answer that.

A knock and the door opened, and his plump nurse wheeled in a cart.

"Your dinner, Doctor," she announced brightly. "Is everything okay?"

"Fine, thanks."

The inviting smell of food made him realize he was ravenous and his saliva glands went into overdrive.

She glanced at his laptop and gave a faint smile. "Cannot live without it, eh? Strictly speaking, patients are not allowed to have them here."

Dural raised an eyebrow. "And leave me to die of boredom?"

She glanced at the wall TV. "That thing has dozens of channels, you know, but never mind. I won't tell if you don't." She placed the tray onto his lap, glanced at the monitor, nodded, and breezed out.

Dinner adequate if not exciting, and left him wanting more. Finished, he went to the bathroom down the corridor, brushed his teeth, took care of plumbing needs, and settled back in bed with his laptop, a cup of coffee at his side.

Tired at staring at the screen, he rubbed his eyes. A cascade of colored lights burst in his head. He blinked hard and they faded. Nothing he read mentioned such phenomena in any victim. As far as he could tell, the effect did not impair his memory, cognitive ability, or physiological functions. It had only been a day, though, he told himself, perhaps too early to recognize any change. The possibility of developing some dysfunction weighed on his mind, more concerned what that might do to Lenora and Daniela. Would his wife have to deal with a vegetative husband, someone with wild mood swings and personality disorders, a stranger living in her house, sleeping in her bed? What if he changed and found himself unable to perform professionally?

And his precious Daniela? How would she feel seeing her father change into someone she no longer recognized or even loved? What if he did not want to tell her stories anymore, or refused to take her on day trips? She would end up emotionally scarred, not understanding what was going on, realizing after a while that her father might no longer know her.

He did not want to go there at all.

A rational scientist and not religious in the traditional sense of observing Catholic rituals or going to church. Nevertheless, like most of his colleagues and circle of friends, he recognized the therapeutic effect of having an acceptance, if not necessarily a firm belief, in the possibility of some overriding spiritual power that hovered benignly over all creation. Increasingly, better educated people who questioned, reasoned, sought evidence, had walked away from organized religions, turning to philosophical disciplines for spiritual fulfillment. Regrettably, even these disciplines were now blanketed by ritual observances, enforced by ruling priestly hierarchies.

If a god existed out there, he fervently prayed that his family be spared the ensuing suffering if he changed.

Around 9:30, feeling somewhat fatigued, he put away the laptop. He switched off the main light and the reading lamp, snuggled down in bed, and locked his fingers behind his head, his mind churning over the day's events. He was not being negatively destructive. More a process of objective evaluation and reflection, a normal thing everyone goes through after an unsettling physical or emotional event, and he'd had both.

After some undefined time, he closed his eyes.

* * *

"Most of the tests have come back negative," Gerard announced in his doctor/patient voice.

"You didn't have to wake me at seven o'clock for those damned tests," Dural growled petulantly.

"That's when I had access to the MRI," Gerard said without any sympathy and pushed back his rimless glasses. "There is no evidence of tissue disruption due to heating by electrostatic effects, and you show no basal ganglia damage. However, some tests indicate heightened synaptic activity in every region, the strongest in the frontal lobes, compared to baseline tests you had two years ago. The prolonged period of unconsciousness you experienced is typical of an electrical shock victim. The bottom line, Du? We could not find anything physiologically wrong with you. As for possible psychological disorders manifesting themselves in the future, that remains to be seen. Being crazier than you already are will not stop you from practicing psychology."

Dural snorted. "Crap me dead. You don't know how much I appreciate hearing that, old buddy."

Gerard shook his head. "Sarcasm doesn't become you. Since there is no longer a legitimate reason to keep you here, you might as well go home and be sarcastic to your gorgeous wife and kid."

"And a lot more fun," Dural added with a grin.

"Seriously, Du. Have you noticed *anything* abnormal? You simply don't fit the curve of a near miss lightning strike victim."

Dural was torn. Should he reveal to his friend and skilled professional the episodes of light flashes? Were they merely a side effect of heightened synaptic activity Gerard alluded to, whatever that meant? If the indirect strike *had* affected his brain in some subtle way, too soon to tell. Increased synaptic activity could also imply that his nervous system was simply settling down after a major shock. The bottom line, he appeared to have survived without a scratch, literally.

Nevertheless, as an objective scientist, he should not withhold information that might later be germane to a successful diagnosis of a surfaced symptom. His treatment, if it came to that, could hinge on a seemingly innocent fact.

"I *have* had what I consider to be a post-event symptom," Dural said slowly, and Gerard raised an eyebrow.

"Well?"

"I experienced several episodes of yellow and white light bursts I felt were coming from inside my brain. I had two this morning. They were not phenomena I can attribute to a retinal discharge."

Gerard chewed his bottom lip and frowned. After a moment, he shrugged. "Could be anything. I haven't heard or read of something similar in the literature, but that does not imply absence of an article or articles on this. It hasn't affected your vision, balance, or depth perception?"

"Nothing."

"Mmm. An interesting observation. I'll look into it." Gerard thrust his hands into his white lab coat pockets and exhaled. "Go home, Du, and don't bother coming to work tomorrow. Leonard and I will cover for your patients. I'll check with Rosalyn on what you have in the hopper."

"Thanks for looking after me."

"That's what partners do," Gerard said and raised a warning finger. "If you *do* notice anything physiological, neurological, or psychological—"

"You'll be the first to know."

"Good. I'll tell the front desk that you're checking out." Gerard waved and strode out.

Dural leaned back against the pillow and sighed. Outside, the sky looked exceptionally blue, and bright sunshine colored his immediate world. He glanced at the breakfast tray and shook his head. Hospital food not exactly Vue de Monde, and he would not want to live on it for too long, but hunger pains gnawed at his stomach. He wondered if he could have seconds.

He pursed his mouth and pulled the tray toward him.

* * *

The cab pulled up at the curb and the driver pressed the fare meter button.

"That'll be twelve-fifty," he said without a trace of emotion.

Dural paid him off, stepped out, and the cab immediately surged down the street. As he walked through the small side gate, the front door flew open and Daniela squealed with glee as she ran toward him.

"Daddy! Daddy!"

He swept her into his arms and swung her around him before pressing the little squirming bundle against him, remembering not to squeeze too hard.

"My little grub. Causing trouble for Mom, have you?"

"No way," she declared solemnly, hands wrapped around his neck. "I've been really good."

"Glad to hear it. So, what have you been up to yesterday?"

"Penny came over and we played video games in my room. That was lots of fun. When Mommy came back from the hospital, I helped her make dinner."

"Without leaving any mess?"

She beamed with a conspiratorial grin. "Well, I spilled a little flour on the floor, but it was nothing, and I cleaned it all up right away."

Dural slowly walked toward the entrance, Dan's head resting against his chest.

"We made potato dumplings with a minced meat sauce. It was yummy."

"Did you leave anything for me?"

"Still lots left for lunch," she assured him, then searched his eyes. "Since you're home, does that mean you're well?"

"Seeing you, I could jump tall buildings."

"I don't know why you keep saying stuff like that, Daddy. Superman is so *dated*!"

He chuckled and ruffled her bangs. "How about Spiderman?"

"Well…he is okay, I suppose." A smile lit her face. "I have a video game with him in it. It looks like lots of fun squirting that gooey web stuff from his wrist and watching him swing from one building to another chasing bad men."

"I know about that video. You and your friend Penny spend too much time playing it."

"Aw, Daddy. Not all that much time. It's not like I'm neglecting my reading and all that school stuff."

"In that case, it's okay," he assured her and planted a kiss on top of her head.

Lenora appeared in the doorway and hit him with a grin. "Welcome home, stranger," she said warmly.

"You don't know how good it is to be home, doll."

He stopped in front of her and gathered her to him with his free arm. She melted against him and her soft lips slid against his. After a very satisfying moment, he pulled back.

"Mmm. Worth coming home for," he murmured into her eyes.

"Lots more where that came from," she declared playfully, then her face turned serious. "I'm happy to have you back, Du…and unhurt. You aren't hurt, are you?"

"I'm fine, Len. Gerard gave me a battery of tests and everything is working. Everything."

She chuckled. "We'll find out later."

"There is only one way to prove that I'm not lying."

Daniela tugged at his arm. "You guys done? You're carrying on like teenagers," she remarked with unmistakable disapproval.

Dural ruffled her hair and she squealed in protest.

"Let me down!"

He lowered her and she scampered into the house. He wrapped his arm around Lenora's waist and they slowly followed their precocious daughter.

"Are you truly all right, Du?" she demanded softly, her penetrating violet eyes searching.

"Doing good, hon."

When they entered the house, Dan appeared busy at the dining table setting out cups, spoons, and sundries.

"Daddy, you can sit down and I'll get your coffee. Tea for you, Mommy?"

"Thanks, darling," Lenora said, absently brushed Daniela's hair, and looked at Dural. "I got your car in the garage," she added as she pulled back a chair. "Leonard came over after the accident and took me to the golf club."

"Great. Sorry for all the worry."

"For a while there, I was concerned," she admitted. "Bad things happen when people get in the way of lightning."

"Well, nothing bad happened to me."

Daniela carried the glass carafe of freshly brewed coffee to the table and placed it on a cork ring.

"All done," she declared and walked to Dural. He grunted as he picked her up and placed her on his lap.

"Can we go for a walk this afternoon, Daddy? We don't have to go far. Fawkner Park would be good. Or we can go to the Botanic Gardens instead. We haven't been there in a while. Can we?"

He glanced at Lenora, and she nodded. "Sure thing, Dan."

"Wowsy!" She snuggled close, then her eyes filled with concern. "I was so worried that something awful had happened to you. Weren't we, Mommy?"

"We sure were, sugar buns."

"Next to Mommy, you're my favorite person in the whole world, Daddy."

Dural laughed and wrapped his arms around her.

"Don't squeeze!" she shrieked.

"Only a little, my grub," he said and squeezed gently.

"Why don't you have your coffee, Daddy?"

"Since you insist…"

Lenora picked up the carafe and poured for both of them. Daniela added cream and sugar for him, and stirred.

He took a sip and nodded. "Perfect."

She hit him with a sunny smile and wiggled in his lap. "I got to go and tell Penny you're back. You don't mind?"

"Go!" he said and gave her a playful slap on her behind.

"Be sure you're back for lunch!" Lenora shouted after the little whirlwind, the front door banging after her.

Dural took another sip of coffee.

Lenora held her cup between her hands and looked at him. "Those tests, Du. What did Gerard say?"

"He didn't find anything," he reassured her, deciding not to mention the light flashes. He blinked and almost gaped. For a second, he thought he saw the faintest pale brown glow around her, then it faded.

She stared at him. "What's the matter? You look like you've seen a ghost."

Dural waved a dismissive hand. "Nothing. Gerard worries too much. You know how he treats his patients. Clucks around them like they're machines, and gets all fussy when he cannot account for a missing piece."

She chuckled. "No missing pieces in you?"

"It's all there, doll. Last night, lying in bed, I must admit being a little concerned. The stuff I read on the Internet not very reassuring."

"I thought Gerard planned to run his tests later today."

"He woke me up early to do them. Bastard."

Lenora laughed.

He shrugged. "They didn't take long, although it seemed like that at the time, and he had help from a resident neurologist."

"Any long-term worries?"

"No way to tell, Len."

She took a sip of coffee. "I cannot believe this happened only yesterday."

"It does seem somewhat surreal," he admitted.

"When did he say you can go back to work? I can take some time off to look after you."

"Thanks, I mean it, but the way I feel, I might pop into the office tomorrow. Gerard said he and Leonard will handle my patients, but they won't know all the details to treat them by simply reading my case notes."

"You can always ask Rosalyn to reschedule them."

"We'll see how I feel tomorrow."

Her eyes became soft and dreamy. "Did I tell you how much you mean to me? How much I love you?"

"Not lately, but I don't mind hearing it again." He stroked her hand. "I'd be lost without you, you know that."

"My romantic prince…"

They stared at each other, coffee forgotten. After a timeless moment where everything was perfect and the rest of the world did not matter, Lenora disengaged herself and stood.

"That lunch won't get done by itself, Dr. Sinclair."

"What're you making?" he asked and leaned back against the chair.

"Nothing fancy. Vegetable soup, fried drumsticks, baked potatoes, and an assorted salad."

"No dessert?" He cocked an eyebrow at her, his meaning plain.

She smiled. "We'll have our dessert later." Some light went out of her and she suddenly looked apprehensive. He sat up, alarmed that something might have happened.

"What's the matter?"

She blushed, which surprised him, as she did not display raw emotion openly. "This is so silly, Du. Remember when you came back from Sydney?"

"What about it?"

"Well, I did something I promised myself I would never do again. I allowed myself to hope. After what happened last time…but I had to find out! Can you forgive me?"

His eyes involuntarily strayed to her belly. "You're not—"

"I'm afraid I am."

"Oh, Len."

"You don't want to? It's not too late for me to abort."

He stood. His arms went around her and he kissed her hard. "You know we both wanted another child. I don't want you to go through all that pain again if it doesn't work out."

"If I miscarry, I'll have a hysterectomy," she declared firmly.

"No way. I'll have a vasectomy," he told her. "I don't want you to carry another emotional burden." He stared deeply into her eyes. "We could host."

She shook her head. "We discussed that option already, Du. I don't want a stranger to carry our child."

He frowned. "It's been two weeks. Too early to tell how things are going. We'll know in another month. That's been your pattern. But, Len, are you sure you want to do this?"

She firmed her mouth and nodded. "I'm sure. It's been six years since I last miscarried. If it happens again, I'm in a better position to handle it."

He kissed her again, a gentle, sensuous exchange.

"If this is what you want, Len, we'll handle it, no matter what."

She sighed and melted against him. "I was so afraid you might not want another child."

"What I don't want is seeing you hurt again," he said gruffly. He cleared his throat and stepped back, her hands in his. "Right…About lunch. Want me to make the salad?"

"That would be good. Talk about the tests as you chop. No blood in the salad if you can avoid it," she added impishly.

Dural smiled. His last experience with a sharp knife and a head of lettuce had not turned out as planned…for him. The stinging cut on the side of his thumb healed cleanly, not anxious to repeat the performance.

He strode to the fridge and got out the lettuce, one red capsicum, two Lebanese cucumbers, and two gourmet tomatoes. He carried the plunder to the sink and began washing the stuff.

Lenora pregnant?

Crap me dead.

He understood all too clearly the psychological and emotional implication of her pregnancy, but her desire to have a child could also lead to emotional disaster if she miscarried. She was correct when she said should something happen, she would be in a better state of mind to handle it. That, however, was logic talking. If she lost this baby, logic would be the first thing tossed out with the trash.

And the effect on him? Pretty much in the same rowboat. He

liked the idea of having a son or another daughter, and subconsciously, he already felt himself accepting and looking forward to it. If Lenora aborted, it would hit him hard, as it hit him hard twice before after Daniela was born. Perhaps harder, because it would prove the doctors right without any course of appeal. As a man, he was supposed to react more stoically, not showing open emotion. This macho projection a powerful social force—men facing off against other men. Lenora did not accept this stereotyping, expecting Dural to be tough, a protector who would not flinch in a moment of adversity, accepting an expression of emotional anguish from him.

Anyway, it was done, and both of them would see what happens.

His hands on automatic, the ceramic knife came too close to his thumb as it removed a thin slice of cucumber, accompanied by the first two layers of dermis on the side of the exposed digit. Dural winced and stared at the savaged member.

Lenora looked up. "Cut yourself again?"

"A little nick. It's not bleeding. The skin will add protein to the salad."

The corner of her mouth lifted in a flat smile. "The tests," she prompted.

"Gerard started me off with a whole body CT scan to see if I had any bone or hard tissue damage from the near miss. Then came the MRI tests while solving visual, auditory, and cognitive problems. That took about ten minutes, but it felt like an hour. A muscular male orderly wheeled me back to my room and I counted cracks in the ceiling waiting for the results, chewing figurative fingernails. The tests came back negative and Gerard let me go. I feel great, Len…about everything," he added softly.

She searched his eyes for a moment, then nodded. No need for words. They had lived together long enough to develop an almost telepathic understanding.

Around 11:45, Daniela breezed in like a miniature tornado,

insisting her help was essential if they were to have any possibility of lunch. She hovered before the oven admiring the frying drumsticks—one of her favorite foods—and assorted vegetables. After nodding approval, she got busy setting up the dining table, all the while chattering about what she and Penney were doing, and how glad she was that her dad was okay.

Tea followed the simple and excellent meal, coffee for the grownups, and a small bowl of fruit gelato for Dan. Autumn or not, ice cream always tasted grand, she declared solemnly.

The three of them sprawled on the couch with Daniela cuddling up to Lenora at one moment, then turning her attention to Dural. Both of them tickled and teased her until she cried out for them to stop between fits of irrepressible, carefree laughter.

"A story, Daddy! Tell me a story. Pretty please?"

"Just one, okay?" He ruffled her hair, sat back, and cleared his throat.

"Once upon a time—"

"Why do stories always start with 'Once upon a time'?" she demanded.

Dural glanced at Lenora, who raised both hands in surrender. This one was his problem.

"Well, because these stories are about magic, dragons, and brave knights who always rescue the beautiful princess. So, it's got to start with 'Once upon a time'."

Daniela frowned, digesting this revelation, then tugged at his arm, which meant he should resume the tale.

"Like I said, once upon a time, there was a lovely mermaid. She had fun in the ocean playing with dolphins, whales, and all kinds of fish. She never ventured too close to shore, afraid that bad people would take her and do terrible things to her. That's what her parents told her the land people do. Anyway, she had a happy, carefree life, and the ocean gave her and all the other mermaids and mermen everything they needed to live."

"Sounds wowsy, Daddy," Daniela mused.

"They had a good life," Dural agreed. "One day, the lovely mermaid—"

"What was her name?"

"Uh, Crystalina. Because she wore a tiara of pearls and mysterious blue crystals. She frolicked with a pod of tuna, when suddenly, she found herself enclosed inside an enormous net. She and the tuna were trapped. The net began to close, pressing her and the tuna ever closer. The net broke the surface and a large fishing trawler hauled it on board. The land people were astonished to see her as she struggled to get out. They ran around the net, pointing at her, debating what to do."

"What happened then, Daddy?"

"Well, the land people opened the net and all the tuna tumbled into the hold. The mermaid landed on the slippery deck and she immediately tried to heave herself overboard back into the sea, her broad tail flapping in agitation. The land people stood around her, talking loudly, but she did not understand their language. She was very afraid what they might do to her. They did not look like nice people."

"What then? What then?"

"If you stop interrupting, I'll tell you."

"Aw, Daddy."

He smiled and brushed her head. "One tall young man stepped away from the group, looked into her enchanting green eyes, and picked her up. An old man wearing a beard and a black cap pointed at a door where he wanted the young man to take Crystalina."

Daniela frowned. "Why didn't she die breathing air?"

He glanced at Lenora. She pointed a finger at him, her meaning clear. 'This is *your* child'.

"She could breathe water and live in open air at the same time," he said.

"Sounds okay. What then?"

"Instead of taking her inside the ship, the young man hurried to the side rail, his eyes on the beautiful mermaid. As he was about to throw her into the ocean, she kissed him, and he immediately turned into a lovely merman. The land people started to shout in amazement, but they could not stop the mermaid and her beloved from throwing themselves into the sea where they lived happily ever after."

"Wowsy, Daddy. That was lovely." Daniela sighed and rested her head against his shoulder. "Will you tell me another story tonight?"

"We'll see, if your Mom doesn't mind."

She scrambled off the couch and looked at her parents.

"Can we go for a walk now? Can we? It's quite nice outside, although I'll have to take my jacket," Daniela confided seriously. "It's a little fresh out there."

"Before we can go anywhere, we have to tidy up first and feed the dishwasher," Lenora declared in her 'must obey' voice. "The dishwasher also gets hungry."

"Aw, Mommy. You're teasing. The dishwasher is a just machine. It doesn't get hungry."

Lenora chuckled. "That might be, sugar buns, but we still have to fill it."

Daniela turned to Dural. "We won't be a minute, Daddy."

He smiled. "No need to rush, grub."

Chapter Three

Lenora's eyelids fluttered and her eyes focused. "Morning," she mumbled, her voice furry from sleep.

Dural felt wonderfully rested and at peace. During the previous week, he could feel himself changing in subtle little ways. His memory, for one thing, retained event details that bordered on the eidetic. He always had strong empathy, which helped him enormously with his work, but over the last few days, it is as though he could peer into a patient's soul and distil disjointed narrative into the underlying cause of an alleged or genuine disorder. The episodes of light flashes were gone, replaced by a strengthening ability to observe a person's aura. As with most things, mysticism and quackery shrouded the phenomena, but the body of evidence remained irrefutable. Some people genuinely possessed the ability to see the human bioelectromagnetic field in its various color manifestations that underpinned the person's basic personality matrix. It was interesting to observe shifts in aura colors triggered by mood swings. He found that especially valuable, as he could detect the person's genuine state regardless of what that person might say. Basically, he could not be deceived by a lie or deliberate distortion of an event, keeping in mind that 'fact' was a perceived condition, recorded by the brain subject to many underlying environmental influences that contributed to a person's development.

He sensed small changes taking place inside his brain, but the nature of these changes eluded him. Occasionally, he felt moments of clarity where previously complicated issues suddenly became mundane, then the insight faded. Clearly, the surge of voltage induced by the near miss he experienced had affected his nervous system in some way. Perception of human auras provided direct evidence of that change. He had not observed any negative psychological symptoms in himself, though. Either they had not manifested themselves yet, there weren't any, or they would surface in some future point in time. An imponderable, and spending energy on worst-case scenarios could induce the very changes he feared.

Didn't Luke 4:23 say, 'Doctor, heal thyself', or some such thing?

All that was very well, expect for one minor flaw in that quote. Not sick, but would he know if he were?

He studied Lenora's face and followed the curves of her eyes, nose, mouth, and throat, wanting to reach out and run his finger against her magical soft skin. How she managed to keep it glowing like that, he could not say. Well, he could, judging by the assortment of jars and lotions in the bathroom. Whatever she did, he did not want her to stop.

Content—more than merely content, he realized—happy, he could not wish for more. His life might turn dark if she miscarried again, so would hers for a time, but they would deal with it. They had been through this before. Still, it would be a boon to welcome another child into his family. Daniela for one would be thrilled to play with a real live doll instead of her treasured, slightly tattered, Cabbage Patch creation. She understood the doll was merely a conduit point for her vivid imagination, although she would not express it in those exact terms. In a year or so, she would outgrow the need for the doll as she formed solid friendships. Dural did not want that process interrupted just as she evolved her personality by relocating to Sydney or Brisbane, something he felt Lenora did not fully appreciate.

That's the psychologist talking, Doctor.

Perhaps, but that did not diminish the importance for Daniela to develop more maturity and self-confidence. Wrenching her into a totally new environment and new faces at school would undoubtedly induce an unknown degree of trauma. On the other hand, children were amazingly resilient, and relocation might in fact be a stimulating and, potentially beneficial, event.

Was *he* afraid to relocate in order to fulfill Lenora's desire to reconnect with her family? Picking apart the pieces, he decided not. He would certainly lose most of his personal and professional connections by moving, but that would be a transitory inconvenience, not an emotional psychosis. Gerard and Leonard were colleagues and good friends, and he would always maintain a relationship with them, but the bond they shared did not bind them physically. Even brothers moved apart and continued to live satisfactory, productive lives. No, it was not the prospect of breaking personal ties that held him back from acceding to Lenora's wish, but a simple question of what he perceived to be unnecessary inconvenience to uproot and plant himself somewhere else, having to establish a wholly new professional practice. Did he want to go through that hassle? Was he being selfish? Perhaps, but so was Lenora. Everyone was selfish, wanting to satisfy their wants and desires, sometimes at the expense of those closest to them.

He would have a serious talk with Lenora and attempt to hash out an acceptable compromise for both of them—once the issue of her pregnancy resolved itself. Then again, perhaps he should have that talk sooner rather than later. A positive outcome for her would remove an emotional thorn, stimulating her outlook on life and development of her baby. As for the hassle involved with moving, simply a hassle, not a shattering life event. What he wanted above anything else was make Lenora happy, and if that involved relocating, then that is what they would do.

A small load lifted off his shoulders and the day became brighter.

"It is now, my princess," Dural murmured, admiring the soft silver glow around her.

"That sounds nice. You should say it more often."

"I *have* been saying it often."

"More."

"Okay, more," he promised.

She placed a hand over her mouth and yawned. "Another Monday. I hate Mondays. They should do away with them and jump straight to Tuesday."

"Then Tuesdays would become Mondays and you would not have changed a thing," he pointed out reasonably.

"That kind of logic will not help get your breakfast, Doctor," she declared darkly.

He chuckled and kissed the tip of her nose. "I'll write a petition to the Prime Minister demanding that he abolish Mondays. How about that?"

"Deal."

"How are you feeling, Len?"

No need to elaborate. They both knew what he talked about.

"A touch of morning sickness, but so far so good. I feel happy about it, like I'm glowing."

"I can see that," Dural told her whimsically, unexpectedly finding himself facing a cusp. "Len, I know how much you want to be closer to your parents and brother. Tell you what I'll do. Pick Sydney or Brisbane and we'll move. No ifs or buts. How does that sound?"

Her eyes grew large as she stared at him. "You really mean that, Du?"

"Unreservedly."

"You would do that for me?"

"Len, you're everything I value in this world, except Daniela, and I'll do anything to see you happy and glowing."

"What about your practice and position at the Research Center?"

"As you said before, patients are everywhere, and I'll not be deserting Gerard or Leonard. We simply won't be together every day as working partners, and we can always visit."

She sniffed and her eyes glistened. Her arm went around his neck and she pulled his head against her.

"Oh, Du, you block. If I didn't have to get up, I would make fierce love to you right now."

"You don't *have* to get up, you know," he told her with a smile.

"We need to get Dan ready for school."

He sighed. "If we have to, we have to. Rain check?"

"Tonight, something special, Doctor. You bring the champagne and I'll do everything else."

"Done!" Seeing the golden glow around her was worth all the hassles in the world. "Whose turn to take Daniela to school and pick her up?"

"Mine, but I have a problem. I'll take her to school, but would you mind picking her up? I have a meeting with the Treasury team at four, which I'm certain will run far longer than the scheduled half hour."

"Not a problem," Dural said. "I was glad to hear that your project is back on schedule."

"So am I, but I had to discipline one of my analysts. He turned out to be a bottleneck on a vital set of program specs."

"Way to go, Ms. Project Manager. Kick butt."

"Someone will be kicking *mine* if I don't get up."

"Right!" He threw back the doona and jumped out of the bed. "World, the Sinclairs are coming."

Lenora laughed and exited in a more dignified ladylike fashion.

Over breakfast, Daniela a little out of sorts, moody and irritable, her aura shifted between brown and black.

"Do I have to go to school today, Mommy? It's cold and wet and Phil will pull my ponytails. I hate him."

"Pull his," Dural suggested, and she snorted.

"Boys don't have ponytails, Daddy." She pushed her toast to one side of the plate. "This one is burnt. Look at it."

"Then take another," Lenora told her. "If you don't want another one, excuse yourself and go brush your teeth."

Daniela scowled, then slowly began to spread homemade jam Lenora got at the Victoria Market on the supposedly burnt piece of toast, which actually wasn't. She took a bite, then sipped her smoothy, eyes firmly on her plate.

Dural gave Len a faint smile and shrugged. Kids…

Breakfast chores done, little purple backpack on her shoulder, Daniela waited patiently for her mother to get ready. Lenora emerged out of the bedroom and skipped down the stairs. She gave Dural a quick peck on the cheek and headed for the door.

"Let's go, Dan."

Daniela rushed to Dural and embraced his waist. "Bye, Daddy."

He bent, squeezed her lightly, and kissed the top of her head. "Be good, and I'll see you this afternoon."

She disengaged herself and ran after Lenora, waving at him. He smiled and waved back. The little whirlwind slammed the front door and he winced, wondering how long the thing would bear up to this robust treatment.

Silence descended on the kitchen and he cleaned up the breakfast remains. The electronic weather wall beside the fridge said it was eleven degrees Centigrade outside. Definitely heavy jacket time, he decided as he glanced out the window, seeing the sky obscured by a heavy cloud layer.

In a reflective mood, he lifted his arm and stared at the warm orange glow that enveloped it, bordered by a green tinge, which slowly turned purple as he watched. Each color represented a different personality trait, present mood, and emotional state. His orange glow indicated a kindhearted nature and honesty. It also told him he had a high level of empathy and attuned to emotions, something he already knew, but it was surreal having it confirmed like this. It did not show a hot temper or impulsiveness as some articles he read suggested. Like four horoscopes for the same day, he would get four different answers. Broadly, however, the spectrum of colors and their personality associations were generally accurate. The green tinge definitely accurate, indicating physical creativity, love of stimulating beautiful things, loyalty, an orderly mind, and impatience with fools and the absurd. Purple affirmed his philosophical, intuitive, and inquiring mind that enjoyed exploring everything.

When he thought of Lenora, his aura changed to a subtle shade of silver/white of intense love and satisfaction. This morning, he had made her radiantly happy, and he could sense her surge of unreserved love for him. Her reasons for wanting to relocate may be confusing, driven by subconscious desires, but they were nonetheless potently real. As he knew intimately well, the subconscious can be a harsh taskmaster, sometimes demanding unreasonable action from the conscious self, and would keep nagging until the person satisfied the demand or sank into a psychotic state and eventual emotional bankruptcy. Dural had dealt with such patients and knew how difficult it was sometimes to achieve a workable compromise with the basic primitive that lived in all of them.

With Lenora, the subconscious conflict resolved, she can now devote all her attention to her pregnancy, Dan, and work, knowing that one day, her dream to relocate would become a reality.

Her obvious happiness gave Dural an intense feeling of virtuous satisfaction.

The tram full—it always was this time of morning—but not packed. He held onto the steel stanchion as the tram surged toward St. Kilda Road. Surrounded by a flood of colors emanating from people around him, the sensation almost painful. He blinked hard, wishing for the assault on his senses to stop, and the colors faded a little. It looked like he could exert limited control over the effect, which came as a relief. Over time, perhaps even total control? He would practice and observe the results.

He got off, winced at the wind's cold bite, and headed up the broad boulevard toward the building housing his practice. This afternoon, he had an interesting schizophrenic case with three alternate personalities. Not exactly alternate personalities. More like three versions of himself arguing with each other. This morning, he only had two patients to deal with. An easy day.

When he reached 613 St. Kilda Road, he walked up the wide driveway toward the double glass-paneled entrance. Inside the warm foyer, his footsteps echoed on the tiled floor as he made his way toward the two elevators. Half the fourth floor housed Gap Psychology Consulting. He walked toward the glass panel with their logo carved into the frosted surface, and it slid out of his way. He strode in and Rosalyn looked up from her computer screen.

"Good morning, Dr. Sinclair. I trust you're fully recovered from your unfortunate accident?"

Her bright silver aura offset her short blond hair, pert nose, full lips, and a rosy round face. Her concern genuine rather than a mere polite query, but she had always been warm and considerate toward everyone, something more than one patient had commented on. Fortunate, as Dural and his partners sometimes failed to appreciate her sterling qualities.

"I feel great, Rosalyn, although I'm not anxious to repeat the experience."

"I am sure of that. Mr. Peterson called to reschedule his eleven o'clock appointment. I called Mrs. Fullham and she was happy to come in instead."

"Thanks. Anything else I should know?"

"Central City Security is sending an engineer to update firmware on our CCTV system."

Shortly after starting Gap Consulting, everyone agreed that fitting sound/movement-activated cameras in the reception area and every consulting room served not only the obvious security function, but provided invaluable supporting evidence in case a patient decided to mount an action against the practice. This foresight had bailed them out twice from a potential lawsuit.

Dural nodded. "Anything else?"

"A letter came from Mrs. Clare Unwin, Assistant Police Commissioner, Crime Command. They want us to profile a suspect they believe is involved with one of the Hong Kong Triads. I left a copy on your desk. Doctors Stockton and Morton also have a copy."

He frowned. A year ago, the Victoria Police used him to profile an underworld suspect arrested for the murder of two Maritime Union dockyard workers who were part of a smuggling racket on Melbourne waterfronts. He could break down the suspect's seemingly unshakeable alibi, which led to a conviction. It surprised him to have the police call for outside help. After all, they had their own psychologists. Since then, they requested his services on two subsequent occasions, which he resolved successfully, although not successful from the suspect's point of view.

"I'll discuss the request at our nine o'clock partner's meeting. Are they here?"

"Dr. Stockton is in and asked that you see him when convenient."

"Any special items on the meeting agenda?"

Rosalyn gave him a conspiratorial grin. "You, Doctor."

"Hah! Thanks for the heads-up," Dural growled and ambled toward Gerard's office. He knocked once and entered.

"Ah, Du. Glad to see you. Pull up a rock."

Dural took off his heavy jacket, pushed back a chair, and eased himself into its comforting softness. Gerard adjusted his rimless glasses and stared at him with a slightly absentminded gaze, his bright red aura bordered by a solid orange fringe. Like all professionals, Gerard a complex personality with many complementary traits, and some that did not fit the general pattern. One moment, he could be analytical and logical, and the next, his mood would swing into pensive introspection, philosophy, charismatic conversation, to bursts of frustration and impatience. Seeing the shifts in his friend's aura, Dural began to appreciate the potential insight his gift provided.

"Any lingering aftereffects? Still experiencing those light flashes?" Gerard queried, direct as always, his aura shifting to a diffused purple hue.

Dural shook his head. "Nothing," he said honestly. He expected to be quizzed, but during the week, he decided to keep his newfound ability secret. Revealing it could invariably cause him personal and professional harm, and harm the practice, not counting the negative effects on his family if this were publicized. He would become an object of popular curiosity, and something for Gerard to dissect.

"No physiological symptoms?"

"I feel fine. As a matter of fact, I feel energized," Dural added truthfully. "I have not experienced any unexpected emotional mood swings, and I'm not worried what might happen tomorrow. That's a self-defeating cycle."

Gerard's aura shifted to soft green. "Agreed, and I'm glad you're doing well, buddy. By the way, you'll be a discussion item at this morning's meeting."

"I know. Rosalyn told me. When you say discussion, I trust you'll keep it objective?"

"Du, in case it slipped your mind, Leonard hauled your ass to the hospital. He's not only a friend concerned for your wellbeing, just as I am, but as professionals, you represent a unique opportunity to study effects of a near lightning strike over a controlled period of time. As you undoubtedly researched for yourself, there is very little published material on such victims."

"I did not mean to be inconsiderate, Gerard, and I appreciate your concern, I don't want to be turned into one of your experiments."

Gerard gave a feral grin. "An MRI once a month and a fireside chat?"

Dural laughed. "Deal, you grave robber."

"I've been watching you over the past week, Du. Although you appear your normal self, I still think you should take a few days off. You suffered major physiological trauma and minor neurological damage, evidenced by episodes of light flashes you reported. There might be other damage whose effects are yet to emerge."

"I won't forget what you and Leonard did for me," Dural said, "and I'll let you know, both of you, if I experience any anomalous side effects."

Gerard stared at him over the rim of his glasses. "You're holding something back, Du. I can smell it."

Dural chuckled to hide his dismay. Gerard was not only a close friend, but also an extremely well-credentialed psychologist. Trying to run a deception past him would eventually backfire as accumulation of little inconsistencies became unmanageable and exposed the crumbling façade.

Deception through truth?

"I *am* holding something back, Ger. The thing is, I cannot tell if it's a permanent after-event symptom, or merely a transitory phenomena. I want the effect to mature before drawing any definite conclusion from which quantifiable data can be obtained."

"When you get pedantic, Dr. Sinclair, I know you're giving me a sales con pitch. Spill it."

Dural grinned. "When I said I feel energized, I meant it. Sounds are sharper, colors are clearer, and I'm bathed in a glow of general health and strength. I admit this might very well be an unconscious psychosomatic reaction to having survived an indirect strike. I also experienced moments of insight—"

"Insight?"

"When a nagging problem suddenly resolves itself, but before I can grasp the solution, it fades."

"Mmm." Gerard stared at him for a long moment, then

sighed. "An MRI on Friday. I'll make an appointment for 10 am. We'll see if your feeling of wellbeing has any neurological basis."

"Suits me," Dural said and stood.

Gerard raised a finger. "I want you talking to me if you experience anything else. Clear?"

"I'm your patient, Dr. Stockton."

"And don't you forget it. Go away now," Gerard said with a wave of his hand.

Dural grinned and walked out. He fueled up with coffee from the kitchenette and strode to his consulting room. Although the whole floor was air-conditioned, a lingering freshness from a weekend of disuse made the room feel slightly uncomfortable. He walked to the wall thermostat and reset the display to 23C. After logging into his computer, he pulled up Mrs. Fullham's file.

The only thing wrong with the woman, he mused, was over-indulgence in the finer things in life and lack of exercise. She claimed to have an overbearing, demanding husband, but Dural had determined from the onset that her problem stemmed from clinging to a daughter who had now developed independence. Mrs. Fullham compensated for that loss with food and intoxication.

At nine, they all gathered in the meeting room.

As the company secretary, Rosalyn chaired the partner's meeting. She read the minutes and action points from the last meeting, and presented the company's income and cashflow positions. Dural observed the ebb and flow of emotions between everybody, reflected in changes of their aura, marveling at the steadfast glow from Rosalyn, the comforting blue from Leonard, and Gerard's analytical yellow/purple hue. He glanced at his arm and the shifting colors of his changing thoughts and mood around the solid silver/white that appeared to represent his base personality.

He concentrated, wanting the effect to fade, His aura quivered, dimmed, and settled to a softer shade. He looked up to find

Rosalyn staring at him.

"What?"

Her eyes flickered to Leonard, then focused on him again. "I asked, Doctor, if you wanted to add anything to what I said." A momentary halo of light green merged with her yellow aura. Frustration?

Leonard snorted. "It's obvious to all of us that you're existing on a different astral plane, Du."

Gerard reached across the table, patted Dural's arm, and smiled indulgently. "If you need a session of mind bending, my door is next to yours."

Dural pointed a finger at him. "You're the one who needs a mind bending session."

Rosalyn raised her hand. "Doctors, please stick to the agenda." She turned to Dural. "I asked—"

Dural's memory went into overdrive and her words marched bright in his mind.

"For comment on our financial position. For the month of May, Gap Psychology Consulting had total earnings of $51,600. Partner drawings and employee salary amounted to $30,167. Fixed and variable expenses totaled $16,550, which generated a net profit of $4,883. This represents a decline in earnings of $8,400 from the April position due to partners' involvement with the Monash Psychiatry Research Center, a position that will be carried into June unless the partners put in additional billable hours. The Research Center still to forward payment of $4,800 outstanding for April, and $5,200 for May. A detailed breakdown is available on PAX."

Rosalyn gaped at him and her aura flared bright yellow. Leonard looked equally shocked. Gerard pushed up his glasses and tapped his chin, his unwavering stare contemplating Dural as though he were a petri dish specimen.

She consulted her shorthand notes. "My words exactly," she whispered.

Somewhat in shock himself at this display of total recall, Dural firmed his mouth. "In answer to your question, my billable hours next month will increase, if I remember the list of patients in my schedule. Forty-seven, wasn't it?"

Rosalyn again consulted her notes. "That is correct, Doctor."

Dural turned to Gerard. "It appears you're the one dragging down our profitability. How about it?"

Gerard shrugged. "My work at the Center should taper off next month, which all of you know."

Leonard leaned forward. "How did you do that, Du? You never exhibited partial eidetic memory before."

"I cannot explain it," Dural answered honestly. "Her words simply popped into my mind."

"Popped, eh?" Leonard's eyes strayed at Gerard. "The three of us need to talk."

"Make an appointment with Rosalyn," Dural said irritably, tired of being poked and scanned.

Rosalyn cleared her throat. "About the Clare Unwin letter…"

"Give it to Leonard," Gerard declared promptly.

Leonard shook a finger at him. "Oh no you don't. Let Dural handle it. He's done work for them before and they know him."

Rosalyn looked at Dural. "Doctor?"

Dural scratched his right ear. He did not particularly want the case, but admitted it would allow him to gather additional evidence on the relationship between a person's physical and verbal responses in relation to shifts in aura colors.

"Okay, I'll take it. Call Commissioner Unwin and ask her to send me the suspect's file. I want interview transcripts, including all available videos. Please arrange a time with her when I can interview the suspect, consistent with my availability." Dural glanced at his partners. "Do we do this as a pro bono, same as the others?"

Leonard scowled. "I don't like giving them freebies, Du. We're providing a professional service, and I for one prefer that we charge them accordingly. Four hundred dollars an hour, plus expenses. This is higher than our standard rate, but we need to recoup time away from the practice."

Gerard nodded. "I agree. I want some of my taxes back."

"Fine with me," Dural said and glanced at Rosalyn. "Set it up."

"We'll do. If there is nothing else on the agenda…"

"There is," Dural said with a grin. He glanced at his partners, and looked fondly at Rosalyn, feeling a warm glow of magnanimity. "We have decided to make you an associate partner, with an immediate rise in monthly drawings to 11,667 dollars."

She went pale, then blushed furiously. Her aura changed from light yellow to shifting green and blue.

"Dr. Sinclair, I'm grateful, but I don't deserve this."

"Nonsense!" Leonard declared and his aura changed to bright red. "You're not only a superbly efficient receptionist; you're also an invaluable secretary and office manager. Our consultancy would not work without your dedication."

"Len is right, Rosalyn," Gerard added emphatically. "Don't ever question that you don't deserve this. Du?"

"Agreed. You're a key member of the team, and this is our way of showing appreciation for all the work you have done since we set up the practice."

Rosalyn's blush deepened. "Thank you. I'll try not to disappoint you."

"You never have," Dural said and gathered the others with his eyes. "If we're done…"

"We are," Leonard declared. "Let's get out of here." He heaved himself up and walked briskly toward the door.

Dural strode out of the meeting room and found Leonard waiting for him with a concerned look. They waited for Rosalyn and Gerard to walk out, Gerard giving them a questioning glance.

"What happened in there, Du? Ger's workup on you has not revealed any neurological side effects from the lightning strike.

However, your display of eidetic memory suggests otherwise."

"I honestly don't know, Len," Dural said. "Like I said, Rosalyn's words popped into my head."

Leonard prodded his chest. "We need to explore this."

Dural raised his palms. "All right. We'll talk. Happy?"

"Don't patronize me, Du. This could be serious."

"Look, Len. This might be a side effect, but I want to get more observational data before I allow Gerard to start dissecting me. Fair enough?"

Leonard grinned. "He *can* be somewhat intense sometimes, but he has your welfare at heart. Just as I do."

Dural patted his friend on the shoulder. "I know, and I appreciate it. I'll see you later, okay?"

Going over Mrs. Fullham's notes, Dural decided to end the sessions with some hard truths. There wasn't anything psychologically wrong with her to warrant ongoing treatment and expense that went with it. Milking clients not only unethical, but such practice also exposed the consultancy to damaging litigation.

At eleven precisely, his intercom buzzed.

"Yes, Rosalyn?"

"Mrs. Fullham is here, Doctor."

"Please show her in."

Rosalyn opened the door and stepped aside to allow a richly dressed overweight woman to walk in. She wore a conservative blue jacket and tight black pants that showed far too much of her ample bulk. Her black hair came out of a bottle. No woman in her late fifties had such luxurious looking hair. Dark olive eyes peered at him beneath prominent eyebrow ridges that dominated a thin nose and a pursed mouth that seemed set in a permanent scowl. What surprised him was her brown aura that indicated confusion, lack of confidence, and a tendency to blame others for her faults, which described Mrs. Fullham accurately. He also saw a tinge of black around the brown aura, suggesting hatred, negativity, and depression. Also a characteristic of her personality.

Dural stood and motioned at a visitor chair. "Please sit down, Mrs. Fullham. And how are you today?"

She settled her bulk into the chair and sighed. "Not very good, Doctor. I seem to be having a relapse, and your sessions are not helping me as much as I thought they would."

Dural sat down and pulled at his right ear. "Can I offer you anything? Coffee, tea?"

"No, thank you. About my ongoing depression—"

"Mrs. Fullham. We both know the source of your problem. We discussed it at length during our last session. You'll not see any improvement in your condition until you accept the unavoidable fact that your daughter is now a young woman trying to establish her independence."

"I know all that, Doctor, but I cannot let her go."

"You'll lose her if you continue to smother her with unwelcome attention."

Mrs. Fullham flushed with anger and her aura turned deep black. "How dare you! I never heard the like. And you call yourself a doctor."

"Madam, until you accept the reality that your daughter is a grown woman, your condition will not improve."

"It's all his fault anyway."

"Your husband?"

"He is…you know…trying to force himself—"

"He isn't. We talked about that already. Blaming your strong-willed husband—"

"He doesn't let me breathe! My daughter is the only thing I have left that makes life bearable."

"Are you sure about that?" Dural asked softly and glanced at her bulging waistline.

Mrs. Fullham stood and glared at Dural. "I don't have to take this from you! You'll be hearing from my lawyers. Good day to you."

She stormed out, black aura and all, and slammed the door after her.

Dural sighed and shook his head. Not his most professional session, but he hoped a cold dose of reality would shake the woman out of her self-imposed state of denial, although he did not expect that to happen. She was far too comfortable satisfying her subconscious, which further psychiatric sessions would not resolve.

He would not miss her.

He tapped the intercom. "Rosalyn?"

"Yes, Doctor?"

"If Mrs. Fullham tries to make another appointment, give her a polite brushoff. I don't want to see her anymore."

"Certainly."

Good girl, Rosalyn, he thought comfortably as he sat back against his leather chair.

After woolgathering for a few moments, he turned to the computer screen. Only 11:15, and far too early for lunch. He brought up Mr. Phil Moore's schizophrenic case file. Going over the notes, he admitted that this one had been giving him a hard time. Four distinct personalities, and all his research so far had failed to identify the dominant one. Once he had that, the three shadow personalities could be quietly buried, leading to eventual stabilization of the dominant one. When he saw Moore's aura, he would know. Or would he? This aura business still new to him and he hated to place too much reliance on it at the expense of his professional judgment and training.

After a quick lunch and coffee, he was ready to see Moore. The young man, only twenty-eight, strode into the room, smiled amiably, and waited. A master's graduate in electrical engineering from RMIT, his intense blue aura indicated a good communicator, a charismatic personality, intelligence, and sensitivity. Blue supposedly demonstrated a strong, stable psychological condition. In Moore, that condition was tainted by interwoven bands of red, pink, and purple of his three alter egos. Perhaps not alternate fragments at all, but exaggerated manifestations of a condition that allowed Moore to escape reality for a time. Escape from what? Dural had an angle to confirm his hypothesis.

"Glad to see you again, Phil. Have a seat."

"Thank you, Doctor. The drug you gave me after our last session helped me a lot, but there are still gaps in my memory, which means I was not always myself."

"I would not be too concerned," Dural said. "Your alternate personalities are basically a reflection of your true ego, and you would not have done anything, or harmed anyone, that would conflict with your underlying behavioral values. We've been over that before, but I am glad to hear the drug has helped."

"What do you want to try this time, Doctor? I've had four sessions with you already, and I'm not seeing substantial progress. I don't know if my health insurance will continue to fund this."

"They will. If they throw up a legal wall, call me and I'll straighten them out."

Moore's aura changed to bright pink. "No kidding, Doc? I may be covered, but I doubt BHP will tolerate more absences from work. I *do* have a job, you know."

The aura shifted to red. "A job? You call fixing blown fuses a job? You'd make more money wiring houses."

"I would be doing that if I had listened to you," the purple aura responded.

Dural observed the exchange with interest. "How are your parents, Phil?" he asked quietly and watched the four auras tremble and coalesce into a rainbow.

Two of Moore's alternate personalities denied that his parents were killed a year ago in a car accident. A case of hit-and-run. Dural had tried hypnosis, but it was impossible to hypnotize all four personalities simultaneously to affect an integrated case argument. He had always known that Moore needed to accept the death of his parents in a positive, forward-looking perspective, abandoning what had obviously been a close relationship. Perhaps too close. A subject Moore appeared reluctant to talk about in any depth. Definitely a vulnerability for Dural to explore.

"Leave them out of this, Doctor," the purple aura declared.

"They were buried a year ago, moron!" the red aura interjected. "You need to let them go."

"I *have* accepted that they're dead, Doctor," Moore said softly. "I just cannot get them out of my mind. They're like ghosts, following me everywhere, and my old man telling me I'm not good enough, never prepared to listen to him. Stubborn like my mother. That's how he saw me. If only he had given me an occasional word of encouragement..." Moore's voice faded and he hung his head.

"Phil. Look at me," Dural commanded.

The young man slowly raised his head.

"Did you love your parents?"

"I have always respected them."

"I never loved them!" the red aura snarled.

"My father was a bully who thought he knew everything," the pink aura declared vehemently.

Dural waited for Moore to settle the war raging inside him, and for the red and pink auras to fade.

"Phil, did you love your parents?"

Moore firmed his mouth and his eyes blazed. "I respected them, but I never loved them. I hated their smothering, overbearing domination. Does that make me weak?"

He laughed as his aura changed to purple. "It makes you a sentimental slob! I *told* you to move into your own place as soon as you got your bachelor's, but you wouldn't listen. Mommy's little darling."

"Dad's whipping boy!" the red aura sneered.

Moore's face cleared and his blue aura flared. "I'm glad they're dead, Doctor."

"That's my boy!" the red aura cheered.

"Phil, I need you to do something for me," Dural said. "Something that will also help you."

"What's that? More drugs?"

"No drugs, but something equally helpful. Create a spreadsheet with two columns. In one, list why you clung to your parents, and in the other, why you continued to stay with them when you knew they did not love you."

"They did love me!"

"Did they?"

"They did! They paid for my degrees!"

"Was that love, or merely something your father imposed on you because he never achieved that level of education himself?"

Moore looked torn as emotions chased each other, as did his alternate auras.

"We're told all our life that we must love our parents, when often, they cause us the most hurt," Dural offered gently. "Your spreadsheet will help you resolve your dilemma. Once you have your answer, you'll be free of them, able to be finally yourself. Provided you're prepared to be totally honest." Dural stood and offered his hand. "Ask Rosalyn to make another appointment. Hopefully a very brief one."

Moore lifted himself out of the chair, looking somewhat dazed.

"I'll try to do ask you ask, Doctor. It's just..."

"Phil, do you want to be chained to your past?"

Moore stood there, bathed in shifting auras. After a moment, they merged into soft green, a very positive development.

"I want a future," he declared.

Dural escorted him to the door. "Good luck, Phil."

He closed the door and strode briskly to his chair. He dug out Commissioner Unwin's letter and went over the request in detail, finding that he remembered every word from his first reading. Nothing more he could do until he received the suspect's file.

A quick scan of his current and pending cases embedded all the information into his memory. A feat he still found incredible, although something clearly very useful.

He glanced at the framed picture of Lenora on the corner of his desk. He closed his eyes and tried to recall the image. It was there, but in grainy monochrome. It looked like he could also remember images, and he hoped the ability would develop fully.

At 4:30, he powered down the computer, dragged on his heavy overcoat, and strode out. Rosalyn looked up as he closed the door.

"Picking up Daniela, Doctor?"

"My wife will give me hell if I don't," he said and stopped at her desk. "Now that we're partners, you can call me Dural or Du, and that goes for the others."

She smiled faintly and nodded. "I'll see you tomorrow…Doctor."

He shook his head and walked toward the exit.

A grim sky greeted him outside, and he winced at the cold southerly sighing between bare branches of golden elms that lined the nature strips dividing St. Kilda Road's two inner lanes from the main car and tram boulevard. The crisp air smelled of rain as he made his way briskly toward Wesley College, hands deep in his overcoat pockets. It took only minutes to reach the private school, the main entrance clogged with cars belonging to parents picking up their children. A lollipop lady glared at cars when the walk sign turned green and she shepherded kids across the zebra crossing toward the tram stop. The press of aura colors actually became uncomfortable, and Dural concentrated until they faded to a dull glow.

He waited as a crush of children raced past him and walked toward the day center. Inside, he welcomed the warm blast of air that greeted him. The receptionist at the main desk smiled and spoke rapidly into a microphone attached to her left ear.

"Good afternoon, Dr. Sinclair. I paged for Daniela. She won't be a moment."

"Thank you, Moana," he said. "Cold day outside."

"They're predicting a downpour this evening. If it happens, the traffic will become unbearable. Lucky, I have a tram to take me home."

"Me too," Dural said.

The glass door that led to the daycare center slid away. Daniela broke away from her minder with a happy shout of delight and rushed him, her clean white aura outlining an angel.

"Daddy! Daddy!"

She swarmed all over him and he picked up the wriggling bundle. He gave her a light squeeze and kissed the tip of her nose.

"Have you been behaving yourself, little grub?"

Her arms tight around his neck, she flashed him a sunny smile. "You know I have, Daddy, but you always ask."

"She's been adorable. Most of the time," Mrs. Dangler added with a grin.

Daniela pouted. "That's not fair, as I *have* behaved."

Mrs. Dangler laughed. "You have, little cutie. I'll see you tomorrow." She glanced at Dural. "Good night, Doctor."

"Good night."

Daniela waved at her minder. "Good night, Mrs. Dangler."

Dural nodded to Moana. "I hope you're wrong about that rain."

The young woman shrugged. "I guess it's got to rain sometime."

He lowered Dan to the ground, and hand in hand, led her toward the entrance.

"Wowsy, it's cold," Dan declared when they walked out.

"So, what have you been up to today?" he asked.

"In the morning, we had an English class. Then social studies where we talked about South America. Afterward, we played some sports in the hall. After lunch, arithmetic. You know, Daddy, I actually like it, and Mr. Barnes explained everything so clearly."

"I'm pleased to hear that," Dural said. "Arithmetic is very important. What else?"

"We also had a painting session using watercolors. That was fun. Some of the kids got paint all over them," Daniela declared, and gave a merry, tinkling laugh. "I'll show you mine when we get home. It's in my pack. It's you in your study working. You look funny when you stare at the computer."

He patted her woolen cap. "I look forward to seeing it."

Holding his hand, she skipped as she walked, the flow of words about her day and what she did, a rushing river of events. Listening to her, he shared her bubbling happiness. The world through her eyes simple and complete, and with her, his world also became simple and complete. He squeezed her hand, happy that he and Lenora had the fortune to be part of this little girl's life. He wondered absently what the web of life would weave when Dan entered her rebellious teen years, then buried the intruding thought. He had her now, and basked in her warm glow.

In the crush of children and parents, the combined rainbow of auras faded as Dural approached the main gate. An occasional car horn expressed the driver's displeasure at someone's infringement. At the tram stop on the other side of the boulevard, the driver clanged his bell and thirty tonnes of sudden green death, as Melbournians fondly called their trams, clattered toward the city.

At the pedestrian crossing separating the inner lane and the dividing nature strip, the lollipop lady in her yellow plastic safety jacket lifted her stop sign when the walk light turned green. Her shrill whistle brought cars and bicycles to a stop. A gaggle of kids made their way across and stood patiently under the covered glass waiting area for the next tram going uptown toward the St. Kilda Road Junction.

Daniela tugged at Dural's hand when she saw a tram coming. "Hurry up, Daddy, or we'll miss it," she urged.

"It's not ours. That one is going down Dandenong Road."

"But the one behind it is ours."

So it was. The traffic light blinked yellow, then red. The lollipop lady retreated to the sidewalk and cars surged through the crossing.

"Aw, Daddy. We're going to miss it," Daniela declared and pouted as their tram pulled up behind the Dandenong one. Its doors opened and kids swarmed in, the passengers inside forced to give way before the onslaught.

"Not to worry, Dan. It'll wait," he reassured her. "Anyway, there is always the next one."

The Dandenong tram clattered off and the one going up High Street pulled in. When the traffic light began to blink yellow, the lollipop lady lifted her stop sign. Daniela broke free from Dural's grasp and ran across the crossing, her golden aura bright with excitement.

Time slowed to a crawl as Dural watched his precious daughter sprint past the startled lollipop lady. A blue hatchback skidded on the slick road surface as the driver attempting to beat the yellow traffic light slammed on the brakes. The light turned red and the car, broadside on, clipped the lollipop lady, sending her spinning toward the sidewalk, her stop sign cartwheeling into the air. Dural heard her frantic cry as she landed in a heap, but this was merely a distraction as he stood helplessly watching the hatch slide toward Daniela.

"Dan!"

His cry of agony reached her and she turned her head toward him, eyes growing large when she saw the looming car heading for her. Dural knew it would hit her, and his despair turned to rage at the idiotic driver trying to save a few seconds by beating the traffic light. He forced his feet into a run, but it was all too late.

The car's rear swiped Daniela and she landed hard on the road, arms flailing. Suddenly, everything stopped. The sounds of traffic stopped. The gaping parents and kids on the sidewalk stood frozen trying to absorb what happened. Soft rain began to fall, and Dural felt its icy caress on his face. His chest contracted and sharp thorns of pain made breathing an agony.

He had read how a person's life flashed before him at a poignant moment or event. He actually discussed this with several of his patients, finding their experience a fascinating psychological phenomena. That an accumulation of all life's experiences could be retrieved and seen in exquisite detail between two beats of a heart seemed an impossibility.

With time seemingly frozen, Dural experienced the phenomena himself as Daniela's brief life streamed before him in fast forward. All the little dramas, joys, teary moments, laughter, they all coalesced into the image of his little girl lying still on the wet road, one of her arms outstretched, seemingly for him.

Then it ended and reality crashed into him.

He heard the tram's bell as it moved off. The sounds of cars along the boulevard sharp, the stink of their exhausts nauseating. He heard cries of horror from kids on the sidewalk and rushing feet. He glanced at the blue hatch hard against the curb, its bright white headlights pointing at him in accusation, the car having spun around.

Dural stopped and stared at Daniela's crumpled form. He knelt beside her and grasped one cold hand, her aura now pale yellow surrounded by a pulsing green fringe. Bright blood oozed from a deep cut on her forehead and he wiped it away. He could not tell how badly she was injured, but she had to have suffered several broken bones, even possible spinal damage. He wanted to gather her into his arms and squeeze her against his chest, but he forced himself to simply watch her, blinking at the raw sting in his eyes. Moving her could very well exacerbate her injuries. The cutting pain in his chest made him grimace, and he gasped as something gave way deep inside and flowed hot through him.

He slowly lifted his head and stared at the leaden sky, dark and cold as the life he now faced. Not religious, having thrown off the shackles of a Catholic upbringing, but with rain staining his face, tears leaking, he sought some understanding and reason for what happened, knowing he would not find any. A random moment, a careless driver, an eager young child running toward the tram…none of it made any sense. He wiped his eyes with a bloody hand and swallowed, the lump in his throat going down jagged and hard.

Let it be me, he pleaded silently in a forlorn wish.

When he looked down, he was startled to see people and children around him standing in silence. A vigil of sympathy and compassion. He gave a shuddering sigh, took off his overcoat, covered Daniela, and clamped his mouth.

"I've called triple zero," a gruff voice came from somewhere.

Already? Had that much time passed? It did not seem possible. His little girl struck only a second ago.

He sniffed, brushed his nose, and nodded. An unknown hand tried to help him up, but he shrugged it off, not wanting to let go of Daniela, the connection with her overwhelmingly important. If he let go, he knew he would lose her. If that happened, he would also lose himself. An irrational thought, but he could not let go of her hand.

The hatchback driver got out of his car, looking dazed and bewildered as he took in the tragedy around him. Dural locked eyes with him, the image of the young man dressed in a blue pin-stripe suit, white shirt, and red tie, burned indelibly into his brain. He wanted to hate him, to punish him physically, but the look he saw on that face made him realize that this single instant of inattention would haunt the youngster forever. Perhaps an even harsher punishment than whatever the court decided to give him.

Dural turned his head and absently watched the cluster of people around the lollipop lady's twisted body, wondering at the extent of her injuries. He did not care. Nothing mattered. He felt numb, anesthetized against the dull throb of pain coursing through him. Clinically, he realized he was going into shock, but it was a detached observation of no significance.

He looked down at Daniela's peaceful face and stroked her hand.

Things seemed to happen in a rush then. He heard the familiar wail of an ambulance, and the sharper piercing cry of a police siren. Doors banged and a paramedic leaned over him.

"We've got her now, sir," the voce said gently. "You can let go."

Let go? He would never let go. How could he?

"Sir, you have to let us treat her," the voice insisted more urgently.

Dural glanced at the concerned medic and slowly nodded. He managed to get to his feet and watched the paramedics remove his overcoat, then slide a flexible white plastic plate under Daniela, and fix on a neck brace. They heaved her onto a gurney and pushed it into the ambulance. A medic helped him in and the doors slammed shut. He swayed as the ambulance jerked and pulled away, the siren a distracting background noise.

One medic quickly went over Daniela's vitals, then spread a silver insulation sheet over her. He wiped the oozing blood off her forehead and fixed on a wide pressure bandage over the wound. He then shone a light into her eyes using a pencil torch, gave her a shot of something, and placed an oxygen mask over her face. He then spoke rapidly into a mike attached to his right ear. Dural watched it all with detachment, his mind refusing to connect, refusing to accept reality, the crash replaying before him in shattering clarity, over and over.

He looked up as the second medic reached for his hand and took the pulse. The medic saw Dural's vacant stare and rummaged through a tray of small bottles. He extracted two gray pills and held them out.

"You better take these if you don't want to pass out."

Dural looked at the pills and reached for them. He hesitated a moment, then popped them into his mouth. They caught in his throat and he swallowed, feeling them going down.

"My girl…" he choked, but could not manage to utter the words waiting to be said, ready to burst through. How could he tell a stranger all the tender things he wanted Daniela to hear? How could he tell him the regrets for things they never managed to do, and now might never do? A simple 'I love you, my little grub' now impossible.

The medic glanced at his partner. "Hard to say until we get a CT scan and an MRI."

Did the medic try to shield him from an awful truth? Probably. Dural decided not to push it. He would know soon enough.

"Where are you taking her?"

"The Alfred Trauma Center. We're just about there."

Dural nodded, the hospital practically around the corner from Wesley College.

The medic glanced at Dural's bloody hands and smeared face, and handed him several wet tissues.

Whatever the medic gave him kicked in. His mind cleared and he began to think rationally. Daniela's aura burned dull yellow, brighter around her head. As long as she lived, he would live. He reached into his jacket pocket and pulled out his cellphone. He scrolled down the contact list and pressed Lenora's icon.

"Du, is that you?" she answered after two rings.

It always amused him when she responded with that question. He knew his picture was visible on her phone when he called. One of life's imponderable mysteries.

He gripped the phone and slowly exhaled.

"Len, it's Dan. A car hit her outside the school and we're on our way to The Alfred. You better come over right away."

He heard her startled gasp and sob. "How…how bad?"

"I don't know," Dural said, sparing her additional shock,

knowing what must be going through her mind.

"I'll be there as soon as I can," she managed to say in a strangled voice, and hung up.

The ambulance pulled in under the broad emergency portico and one medic wheeled Daniela inside. The other took Dural to the Admissions desk. The process went quickly once he identified himself. The thing done, they told him to take a seat among a gaggle of other concerned, dejected sufferers, and wait. He found an empty corner seat and sat down, suppressing the shifting auras of those around him. An elderly lady glanced at his wet trousers, crumpled overcoat, then turned to stare vacantly at nothing. He wanted to shut out the sounds of voices and feet on a hard floor, and have some silence. What he could not silence were the surging images and sounds in his own mind.

Lenora…

Daniela had always been his little girl, but Len never showed resentment over that, because Dan loved her mother unreservedly and showed it in many small, intimate ways. The two were close and shared girl things impossible for Dural to understand.

The image of the car swiping Dan, hurling her through the air, kept replaying in his mind. Not healthy, his intellectual part told him sternly, but he could not shut it off…or the feeling of guilt that consumed him. He should not feel guilty for what happened. One of those things, but if he had held onto her hand harder, she would not be now on a cold examination table.

Why couldn't it have been him?

A tall skeletal man in a green operating theater garb walked quickly toward the waiting group, paused, and strode toward Dural.

"Dr. Sinclair?"

Dural stood and draped the overcoat over his left arm. "That's right."

"I'm Dr. Pollack, senior attending trauma surgeon. Please come with me."

Without waiting, the surgeon turned and made his way toward the elevators.

"About Dan…" Dural began, but Pollack ignored him.

On the fourth floor, the surgeon led him down a quiet corridor, stopped at a white door and opened it.

"Please…"

Dural stepped into the compact office, considerably smaller than his own, the smell of antiseptic pervasive.

"Take a seat, Doctor," Pollack offered as he sat down behind his desk. He waited for Dural to sit down, then leaned back.

"Dr. Sinclair, I wish I could break this gently, but I can't. Your little girl has multiple fractures. We can fix those, but there are too many internal organ injuries. She also has a severe concussion and a major subdural hematoma on the right side of her brain. We cannot operate until she's more stable. The thing is, we might not be able to operate at all as she is unlikely to stabilize."

Dural stared at him, then swallowed. "Are you…are you telling me she's terminal?"

"She's resting comfortably under sedation, and we treated her head contusion. Her body is out of shock and her vitals are strong…for now. There isn't much more we can do for her."

"How much time does she have?"

Pollack shrugged. "Hard to say. A few hours. Her body is barely keeping her alive."

"Is she conscious?"

"Not at the moment, but we can bring her out of it at any time."

"I want to see her," Dural declared firmly.

The surgeon nodded and stood.

On the seventh floor, the children's intensive care ward looked deserted. A nurse walked out one of the rooms, glanced at Dural, and strode briskly down the corridor, her footsteps loud on the hard gray linoleum floor.

Dural found himself in a small ward filled with life-support equipment and blank monitors. Beside the window, Daniela lay beneath a white blanket, her purple backpack beside the bed. A saline drip bag hung from the support stand. The monitor traced wiggly lines on a green screen.

His breath caught as he stared at the little bundle, a white bandage around her head. He turned to Pollack.

"My wife is on her way over. Please have someone bring her up."

"Of course." Pollack raised his hand to touch Dural in a gesture of sympathy, changed his mind, and walked out.

Dural pulled a chair closer to the bed and sat down. He reached for Daniela's hand and held it tenderly, his thoughts a random jumble of images, past and present, and things of what might have been.

Outside, dusk had settled and the street bright with lights. Light rain fell, blurring outlines, softening the harsh impact of reality.

Reality…

The monitor beside the bed traced wiggly lines.

He stared at the contours of his daughter's face, going over every line, curve, indentation, the glow of her aura bright around her head…an angel's halo. In a cauldron of seething, turbulent emotions, he found it difficult to concentrate, to think clearly, to review the accident objectively. He gave up the struggle and simply watched his precious girl. What about his own sands of time when she was gone? He did not want to venture there just yet.

He watched and waited, and the invisible rain continued to fall.

A knock on the door jerked him out of his pensive mood and he turned his head. Pollack walked in and stepped aside. Lenora stood there, face ashen, her eyes fixed on him, reflecting the turbulence and horror of her emotions. She walked slowly toward the bed and gazed down at Daniela. Dural stood and embraced her. She gave a strangled cry, wrapped her arms around his neck, and sobbed.

Pollack stuck a needle into the drip input slot, then turned. "She'll come around in a few seconds. I'll be on standby in case her condition worsens."

Dural nodded. "Thank you, Doctor. For everything."

The surgeon opened his mouth to say something, then clamped it shut and hurried out, shutting the door after him. What was there to say?

Lenora pulled away and dabbed at her eyes. "Oh, Du. I cannot believe this is happening."

"I know, Len. I know."

"How bad?"

Her aura rippled through a cascade of shifting colors, reflecting her confusion, uncertainty, and pain of her emotions. Dural grasped her hand and kissed it.

How could he tell her something he wanted to deny wasn't real? How could he shield her from what was going to happen? If he could somehow take on her pain, he would do it without hesitation, but that was not possible. He would have to help her adjust, to cope, to accept...somehow. As he would have to adjust and cope.

"We're going to lose her," he whispered brokenly, the words torn from somewhere deep inside him that left a searing, gaping wound.

He saw shock and consternation in her eyes as she struggled to comprehend the impact of his words. Her mouth opened and she gaped at him. Then her eyes filled and a fat tear rolled down her left cheek.

"No," she managed in a barely audible voice. "No. This is not possible."

He gathered her in his arms and held her tight, his own feelings threatening to spill in a torrent of uncontrolled rage and helplessness at the unfairness of it all.

"Daddy?"

Dural let go and turned to Daniela watching them with her big eyes. He leaned over her and kissed her cheek.

"Hi there, little grub."

"Why are you crying, Mommy?"

Lenora took her daughter's small hands and pressed them against her chest, forcing herself to smile.

"I'm simply happy to see you, sugar buns."

"I don't feel too well, Mommy. Will I be able to go to school tomorrow?"

Lenora's gaze flickered at Dural. "Perhaps not tomorrow, but soon."

"I can't feel my legs, Daddy."

"You've been in an accident," Dural said, fighting to keep his voice even. "Do you remember anything?"

Daniela crunched her nose. "I remember you calling me, and I saw the car coming at me, but I couldn't move. I don't remember anything else."

"You're in a hospital—"

"I can tell by the smell."

"—and the doctors put your legs to sleep to help you get better more quickly."

Daniela digested that for a moment, then let out a slow sigh.

"Tell me a story, Daddy. Please?"

Dural swallowed a lump that felt like a ball of thorns and cleared his throat.

"Okay. Here goes. Once upon a time, a beautiful princess lived in a magical castle of glass and crystal. She had servants to fulfill her every wish, gorgeous clothes, and horses to ride. She should have been happy. Instead, she was mean and cruel. After a time, her father the king got tired of his daughter's meanness and decided to give her to the first beggar to come to the castle. The princess was horrified, but her father would not be moved.

"One day, a handsome youth dressed in ragged, torn clothing

came to the castle begging for food and shelter. The guards informed the king and he led his daughter to the gate. The youth was startled when the king gave her to him, telling him to tame her.

"The youth lived in a humble cottage, and there were no servants to wait on the princess. Instead, she had to work in the field tilling and gathering hay, and cook. She missed her servants and cried, hating the hard life she had to live, and was nasty and spiteful to the youth, who was always kind to her."

Daniela snorted. "She wasn't very nice, was she?"

"No, she wasn't."

"What happened then?"

"Well, it took a while, but the princess began to change. She started being nice to the young beggar, and actually smiled a little and laughed sometimes."

Daniela sighed. "I'm a little tired, Daddy. I would like to rest for just a moment, but finish the story, please. I want to know how it turns out."

She closed her eyes and her breathing slowed. The monitor beside her gave a beep and the heartbeat wiggle flattened. Lenora gasped and clutched Dural's arm. One by one, the other indicators slowly flattened, and the aura around Dan's head flickered and faded.

For a moment that had no time, Dural gazed at his daughter's peaceful face as his chest constricted and he found it difficult to breathe. A searing bolt of heat raced through his body and he shuddered. He gulped and exhaled loudly.

"One day," he began faintly, "the princess looked at the beggar and saw for the first time how tall and handsome he was. Without saying anything, she walked up to him and kissed him. In that instant, his cottage turned into a soaring castle and the beggar transformed into a prince. He gathered the princess into his arms and said he loved her. A magnificent carriage emerged from the front gate and stopped beside them. The prince helped her get in and the carriage took them into the castle where they lived happily ever after."

Dural exhaled slowly, then gently caressed Dan's cheek.

"Sleep, my princess."

He turned and smiled wanly at Lenora's tear-streaked face. He spread his arms and she walked into his embrace.

"Oh, Du." She clung to him and sobbed brokenly, crying against his chest.

The door opened and Pollack walked in. He quickly checked the monitor, took Daniela's pulse, flashed a pencil torch into her eyes, and straightened.

"I'm sorry for your loss, Mrs. Sinclair…Doctor. There wasn't anything more we could have done."

"Thank you," Dural said gravely. "Can you give us a few minutes?"

Pollack nodded and softly padded out.

Dural held out his hand to Lenora and her fingers clamped him hard. They turned and gazed at their sleeping girl.

Chapter Four

Dural stood on a rolling grassy meadow that stretched down into a steep valley bordered by snowcapped mountains. Warm sunshine bathed his face and he breathed deeply as a crisp breeze stirred his hair. Vivid blue, the sky clear of clouds.

A dark shadow suddenly obscured the sun and Daniela tugged at his arm.

"Look, Daddy! It's going to hit us."

He lifted his head and saw the looming fiery world draw closer. He looked at her and smiled.

"It won't."

"But it's so close!"

He reached out with his hand and saw the approaching planet shrink until it rested in the palm of his hand. Bright sunshine once again spilled across the swaying grass.

"See…" But Daniela was gone.

A wave of dread swept through him and he shivered. The dread came from the world in his hand. He concentrated and focused. He saw a schooner anchored in a lagoon, palms nodding over a smooth beach, small waves lapping against white sands. A figure on the boat waved at him, then darkness shrouded the image. He frowned and hurled the miniature world at the boat.

He watched the boat grow larger and the surrounding darkness faded. He gasped when he recognized the smiling figure waving at him.

"Daniela!"

Bright light struck the boat and the image disintegrated.

"No!"

Dural jerked awake in a dark room, struggling to breathe, the image of his daughter vivid in his mind. Lenora moaned beside him and turned over. This was the third time he had this particular dream, and it always ended in the same way with him destroying the boat…destroying his daughter. He did not subscribe to the suggestion that dreams were messages from the subconscious, although he had read the literature, but the fact that he had this particular one again disturbed him.

He rolled to his side and waited for the oblivion of sleep.

* * *

Rosalyn walked up to Dural and stopped. Her mouth quivered and her eyes glistened.

"I'm so sorry, Dr. Sinclair," she managed to choke out, her emotions ready to spill into tears.

Dural embraced her tightly. "Thank you," he said and kissed her cheek.

Rosalyn sniffed and glanced at Lenora. "Mrs. Sinclair…"

Lenora made a brave attempt to smile, gave up, and nodded. "I know."

Rosalyn swallowed and quickly walked toward the front door, trailing other guests leaving the reception. Dural saw her dab at her eyes, his own emotions clamped down hard.

Gerard extended his hand and Dural grasped it warmly.

"Great funeral, Du. I was impressed."

It had been a great funeral, Dural reflected. The St. Kilda Cemetery took care of everything with unobtrusive efficiency. A simple civil ceremony, the cremation, and planting of the urn in the Family Tree plot, all done with sensitivity. He was surprised and pleased to see a number of kids from Daniela's class, and with Len, went out of his way to thank the parents.

"I'll be back on deck in a couple of days," he said.

Gerard waved his hand. "Take all the time you want, Du. We'll handle your case load." He glanced at Leonard. "Right?"

"Absolutely." Leonard swallowed; unable to find the words to heal a raw, gaping wound. There weren't any. He patted Dural on the shoulder and followed Gerard out.

Dural stood there and watched his two friends disappear out the front door. Disappear into another life, another time. A wave of loneliness washed over him. He turned to Lenora and swept her into his arms. She sagged against him and held him tight. He stroked her head, his hand traveling down her back. He felt her pain, anguish, loss, because they were his. Except he had no tears to sweep it away. The only tears were those inside him, burning, searing where they flowed, consuming him with fire, anger, and deep-seated resentment that fates chose to be so cruel.

After a while, she pulled back and her mouth twitched. "I better say goodbye to my parents."

Yesterday morning, the entire Tipene brood—minus the grandkids—descended on Melbourne and parked themselves at a hotel on Southbank beside the Yarra. Dural arranged a dinner at the trendy Eureka 89 restaurant on top of Eureka Tower that gave them a stunning view of the city at night. He also invited his own parents who came down from Nelson Bay for the occasion, but they declined, wanting Lenora to have quality time with her own family. After a teary reunion, everybody valiantly tried to forget the reason that brought them together.

Now, it all seemed like a fading dream.

Dural led Lenora toward the entrance and the waiting taxis. She walked through the side gate and stood before her father.

"Come soon," he said gruffly and patted her arm.

"I will, Dad."

Her mother hugged her and the two exchanged a few more tears. Her brother and sister waited stoically for their turn. Dural shook hands all around and watched the two cabs speed off, trailing white vapor from the tailpipes. Mouth tight, he took Lenora's hand and they walked back into the house.

Around him, the caterers were quietly cleaning up, silent

ghosts in a silent house devoid of laughter and sunshine. Would he ever see laughter and sunshine here again? He knew that in time, the pain of grieving would fade, heralding a new beginning, but it would be a beginning without Daniela in it.

It will fade, he told himself, perhaps the only comfort he could look forward to.

After what must have been an eternity of random thoughts, memory flashbacks, regrets, lost dreams, the chief caterer cleared his throat.

"Dr. Sinclair, we're done here, sir."

Dural gave him a wan smile and shook the proffered hand. "Thank you for everything, Mr. Rogers."

Rogers glanced at his two assistants and they walked out, softly closing the door after them, the click of the lock unnaturally loud and final. Closing of a chapter.

Dural let out a heavy sigh and glanced at Lenora. At any moment, he expected to hear Daniela slam the door to her room and come rushing down into the dining area. Only silence echoed in the corridors of his mind.

"I don't know about you," he said, "but I could use a stiff drink."

She pursed her mouth and shrugged. "Why not?"

He made the drinks and they settled on the couch.

"Nice of your parents to come," she said after taking a sip.

"Dinner at their place tomorrow night." Dural searched her face. "I can call it off if you don't feel like going."

She shrugged. "I don't mind. I still cannot believe any of this, Du," she said softly, the tumbler held tight between her hands.

"I know, hon. I know."

"Remember when you closed the door on her fingers and she lost a fingernail?"

Dural's mouth twitched. "And she insisted I tell her a story to make it all better. She was in a lot of pain, but never complained."

"No more stories, I guess," Lenora murmured, then gave him

a sidewise gaze. "What I still cannot figure out is how you came up with all those outlandish tales."

"I don't know. They just came. The writer in me?"

"Whatever…Du…"

"I miss her too."

"I'm taking a week off work."

He looked at her in alarm. "You don't want to do that, Len. You'll be alone brooding, and that's the last thing you need right now."

"You should take a week off yourself. We could do things together."

"And do what? Sit here and rake over old memories? We need to put this behind us and move on."

She searched his eyes. "Move on? This is your professional advice, Doctor?"

He blanched, stung by the venom in her words. "Len, listen to me. You think I'm not hurting? I would give anything to have her back, but it can't be done. It will take time, a lot of time, but we'll have to get over this. She will always be with us and we will never forget her or stop loving her, but we must accept that she is—"

She lifted a hand. "Don't say it. Intellectually, I know you're right, but it seems all so unreal, like a bad dream. Taking time off will help me adjust and clear my head. The thought of going back to my project right now turns my stomach." Her eyes bored into him, her expression cold. "I'm surprised that you're so callous about this. You can be such a block sometimes, you know."

"What do you want me to do, Len? Throw myself into your arms and sob myself to sleep?"

"You could say you're sorry," she snapped, and her face turned white in contrition. "Oh, Du, that was so stupid of me. I didn't mean it."

Didn't mean it? Perhaps not consciously, but deep down, she did mean it. She blamed him for Daniela's death. Could she be right? The image of the accident replayed in his mind. An irrational guilt, but knowing he could not have done anything to stop it did not seem to help.

He sighed and patted her hand. "Forget it."

She leaned toward him and rested her head on his shoulder. "It's only—"

"Yeah. The 'if only' scenarios will haunt me forever," he said gruffly and took a sip, the whiskey a trail of fire inside him.

She pulled back. "I still want to take some time off, Du."

He exhaled and nodded. "I don't think it's a good idea, Len, and that *is* the doctor part of me talking, but if that's what you want…"

She smiled. "Don't worry. I won't fall apart on you."

"If you want a break, take up your father's offer and visit. Better than being alone here."

"Not right now, but I'll think about it."

"I'll stay home with you if you want. Maybe taking a break is not such a bad idea."

"No, got to work. I'll handle this."

Painfully conscious of Lenora's seething emotions, Dural hoped the prospect of a new baby would settle her down. Did he do the right thing deciding a return to work?

All your training and case experience not much help now, eh, Doctor?

Life sucks, he decided.

It certainly looked like it right then.

After a moody evening with nothing much said, Dural's attempts at conversation met hollow silence—Lenora setting a dinner plate for Daniela before she realized what she was doing—she went to bed early, refusing his attempts to console her, not appreciating that consoling her, he would also get some emotional closure. He watched her climb the stairs, then pursed his lips and walked to the bar cabinet. He poured himself a snifter of Otard cognac and sprawled onto the couch.

Outside, a keening wind whispered among the branches, reflecting the turbulence of his thoughts.

Looking around, everything appeared the same, yet hollow somehow. What used to make it normal had been ripped out of the house, leaving behind a silent shell of memories. At any moment, Daniela would softly pad down the stairs as she had done so many times before, her raggedy doll at her side, eyes downcast, expression uncertain. She would lift her head and quietly ask if she could stay with him for a while. Her room dark and cold, and she did not like how the wind sounded. He did not mind these interruptions, glad to see she wanted his company. He would reach for a blanket he kept beside the couch for such occasions and hold it up. Her face would light up with joy as she flung herself at him. He then wrapped her squirming body and she snuggled against him demanding a story.

He glanced at the empty stairs.

"Come down and I'll tell you a story," he whispered.

After a while, he took a sip and listened to the wind.

Lenora was already asleep when he opened the bedroom door. Face relaxed, hair spilled across the pillow, she looked angelic and his heart went out to her. Bathroom chores done, he undressed, gave an involuntary shiver, and crawled into bed beside her. He turned off the side light and stared into the ceiling's impenetrable blackness. Sleep eluded him and he stared into darkness. Long after he should have fallen asleep, Lenora stirred, turned, and buried her head into the crook of his arm. He kissed her forehead and waited for the dreams to come.

* * *

"You should go back to work, Len," Dural said, eyeing her over the rim of his coffee mug.

Dressed in her favorite purple kimono with the red dragon motif, Lenora appeared not to hear him, the scrambled eggs he made for her untouched.

"It's been a week, and you're still moping around, spending a lot of time in Dan's room. That's not good. And you started drinking."

She kept gazing into nothingness.

He sighed and placed his mug on the table. "You wanted time to sort yourself out. Fine, but what you're doing now is retreating from reality. You cannot go on like this. *We* cannot go on like this."

She sat there, cup between her hands, and her eyes found him. "You don't seem to miss her at all."

Her savage words ripped something in him and he clenched his fists.

"That was unfair, Len. Just because I choose to have some normality in my life does not mean I have forgotten her. I will never forget her, but brooding in her room will not bring her back. Don't you see what you're doing to yourself?"

"What am I doing, Du? I'm keeping house. I make your bed, and I cook for you. What else do you want from me?"

"I want my wife back. Don't shut me out."

She snorted and her eyebrows rose. "Shut you out? How can I shut you out when you're not here? You don't care what is happening to me. You don't care what happened to her. Ever since your accident, you changed, Du. Changed into someone I don't know. You have become cold and detached, like people around you don't matter anymore."

Her aura flared deep black, and Dural sat back in shock at the hate emanating from her.

She *did* have a point of sorts, surprised at her perceptiveness. He could feel the slow changes happening to him, his eidetic memory, his ability to see past irrelevancies and resolve problems with clinical impartiality. Even Gerard and Leonard remarked on it, but Dural dismissed their observations as proof of his recovery. Those things had not made him cold. He could feel, love, and yes, hate, like everybody else. Anyway, he had always been organized and methodical in everything he did, even remote at times.

So, why did Lenora think he no longer cared? Guilt transfer?

He felt his face drain.

"Len, have you miscarried?"

Her lips quivered and her eyes became bright, ready to spill the glistening tears.

"Three days ago," she whispered brokenly and clutched the cup to her chest.

He got up and took a step toward her. She immediately pushed out her arm.

"Don't."

Not knowing how to comfort her, he stood there, his emotions raw. He now understood what happened. Having lost Daniela, she had now lost the only chance she saw to turn her life into something bright again. And he was a convenient object against which she could focus her anger and disappointment. It was all his fault. That is how she rationalized it, and he could say nothing to change that perception. Was it his fault in a way?

"Oh, Len. I am so sorry."

The tears spilled and ran down her cheeks. "I cannot forget that you let her die, Du. Now, I have nothing."

"I don't count?"

She dabbed at her eyes with a napkin and sniffed. "I don't want to talk about it." She rose and headed for the stairs. He grabbed her arm and swung her to face him.

"You don't want to talk about it? It's not all about you, you know. I didn't let her die. A stupid accident, and I'm not responsible for your miscarriage."

She glared at him. "So, it's my fault, is it?"

"It's no one's fault. Some things simply happen. You knew the risk when you allowed yourself to become pregnant. I wanted that baby as much as you did."

"Did you? I wonder."

"Venting your loss at me will not bring either of them back."

"Let go of me," she hissed and shook off his hand. "I'm leaving."

He looked at her in confusion. "Leaving?"

"I'm going to Wellington for a couple of weeks." Her eyes softened and she sighed. "I'm sorry, Du. I did not mean to be so waspish. It's just…"

He took her hand and squeezed it. "I need you with me, Len."

"I thought you said visiting my parents would help me cope."

"I did, but that was before you decided to take a week off work. I'm not sure it's a good idea for you to leave right now."

"I have to do this. We'll make a fresh start when I get back."

"Want me to come with you?"

"I want to do this by myself."

"When are you going?"

"I have a flight this afternoon."

"You arranged this without even telling me?"

"What's to tell?"

His shoulders sagged. "I'll take you to the airport," he said in resignation.

She shook her head. "Don't bother. I'll get a cab."

He searched her eyes. "You think I mind?"

Her aura flickered from black to brown and a veil fell across her face. All her words about being sorry, wanting a fresh start, were lies. Did she hate him because Daniela was gone and she miscarried?

"Go to your patients, Du," she snapped and hurried up the stairs.

Left without any appetite to finish breakfast, he washed everything and went up. Lenora kept stuffing clothing into a hard case, ignoring his presence. He brushed his teeth and picked up his heavy overcoat. At the door, he paused and turned.

"Don't go, Len."

She kept jamming clothing into her case.

There were lots of things he wanted to say right then. Instead, he closed the door and made his way down the stairs. He thought he heard a muffled sob, but it could have been his imagination.

Bright sunshine greeted him as he stepped out, and the wind had faded. Fresh, the air felt invigorating and Dural breathed deeply. A tram clattered as it headed up High Street. Feeling the sun's warmth on his face, he decided to walk. He wanted to think, although he had been doing nothing else since...

Lenora miscarried...

She could be impulsive, but never anything like this. Admittedly, the situation they both found themselves in now different. They usually discussed everything before making a major decision, and her announcement to spend time with her parents disturbed him. It was not the trip *per se* that concerned him, but the underlying psychological state that led to her decision. He could not shake off the image of blackness surrounding her, a wall she had thrown up between them. One she did not want him to cross.

Clinically, he understood her desire to make a clean break, separate herself from the place of her grief. That grief, though, had turned into anger...anger directed at him. If it were only that simple. Such things rarely were, he admitted ruefully. He should have taken up Leonard's offer of a counseling session. It might have helped Lenora cope better, but she would not hear of it. Not with someone she knew, she maintained.

Two weeks, she said. And afterward? He would know what to do once she returned and he saw her reaction when they met again.

Was he losing her?

He did not believe it. He did not want believe it. Understandably distraught, she took it out on him. Her old man would straighten her out. Quietly wise, Nikau Tipene projected love and warmth to all. The older man had surprised him more than once with views Dural found unsettling. Views on multiculturalism, religious extremism, and growing nationalism across most developed countries. The new century, Nikau declared, a stubby of NZ ale in hand, would be a time of serious reappraisal as geopolitical forces readjusted from short-term profitability to environmental issues on an increasingly crowded globe.

Dural hoped the old Maori would give him his wife back. If he could not? He did not want to go there. Not right now. Len was going through a bad emotional period, and he did not know how to reach her, how to help her.

Rosalyn greeted him with her usual warm smile and effervescent spirit.

"Nice to have some sunshine for a change," she remarked brightly and leaned back from her computer screen. "This cold weather is strictly for the penguins."

"It *has* been rather chilly," Dural agreed absently, thinking about his patient list for the day. "Tomorrow is Saturday and you can rug up at home."

She pouted. "Not much chance of that, Doctor. Saturdays are my usual washing up, cleaning, and shopping days." She smiled and her eyes sparkled. "It won't be a total loss, though. I've got a date tomorrow night."

He broke into a broad grin. "That'll generate some heat, all right."

"We shall see," she replied mysteriously. "And you? Anything special lined up?"

"A quiet weekend, I'm afraid."

"You should take Mrs. Sinclair out. How is she, by the way?"

"She's flying off to New Zealand this afternoon to spend some time with her parents."

Rosalyn's eyebrows climbed. "Is everything all right, Doctor?" Her intelligent eyes regarded him with concern. She did not pry or gossip, maintaining a strictly professional attitude at work. After hours, though, over a drink, she loosened up somewhat, but never descended into personalities about her three partners.

However, she was very good at reading between the lines.

Should he tell her? Dural wanted to shrug it off, but whom was he fooling? It would all come out sooner or later, and Rosalyn was a friend entitled to some personal confidences.

"She miscarried and is down a bit."

"Ah, that sucks…Du. After everything that's happened…"

"I know."

"Before I forget, Dr. Stockton made a 4:30 pm appointment for you at the Research Center for an MRI."

He nodded and sighed. With everything that's been going on, he missed the last appointment and Gerard had been on his case about it, reminding Dural that he was also a patient. Like he cared about a damned MRI right now.

"Thanks."

He disposed of four patients before lunch, and three in the afternoon, which should improve his billable hours position. All were women with postnatal and related stress disorders. Ironic when he thought of Lenora. They left buoyed and cheerful, relieved not having to take medication.

If he could only treat Lenora's condition as easily. Did he do the right thing, though? He coped with his grief by burying himself in work, keeping a normal routine. She had withdrawn, taken to drinking, seeking a place where she could escape from the memories. No, not escape, but somewhere where she could consolidate and recover, and she did not allow him there. Was she right when she said he cared more for his patients than he cared for her?

During coffee breaks, he chatted with Leonard and Gerard, only half listening to their list of litanies and patient problems. Seeing him moody and distracted, they left him alone without pressing him to open up, something he appreciated.

He did get one surprise, not altogether sure whether to be pleased or annoyed. The file from Commissioner Unwin no longer in his case directory. When he queried Rosalyn, she said

Dr. Morton took care of it. Dural did not have to ask why he had been sidelined. During the week, he had not been operating at full capacity. He reminded himself to ask Leonard how it turned out.

At 4:15, he wished Rosalyn a pleasant weekend and walked to the Research Center for his MRI. The chore done, he took a cab home, something he rarely did. A chill southerly made it unpleasant to walk, and the sight of packed trams made him wince with distaste. The last thing he wanted was to be jammed in a crush among anonymous bodies wearing vacant, bored faces, enduring stoically the time to wherever they were going.

Dural strode through the side gate and paused at the front door out of habit, expecting Daniela to swarm all over him. He unlocked and stepped in, surprised to find the heating system still on. Lenora had not bothered to switch it off when she left. He turned to the alarm pad and frowned. She had not bothered to reset it either, which was highly unusual, as both of them were very conscious about security. Not that the neighborhood had break-ins, but one could never tell. That she had not set it showed something of her state of mind.

He changed into jeans and a light alpaca sweater, and padded into the kitchen. The cooktop empty, and nothing prepared in the fridge. Although hungry, not in the mood to cook, he satisfied himself with a grilled Hungarian salami and cheese sandwich, washed down with neat bourbon. Not the most nutritious meal, but right then, he did not give a damn about nutrition. It filled the emptiness in his belly, if not the emptiness in his heart. Lately, he had been craving fatty foods, driven by some inner need, ignoring Lenora's pointed comments about his waistline, which had not grown, he countered.

As he ate, dabbing grease off his chin with a napkin, he became aware of deep silence permeating the house. He listened, hoping to hear something, anything, but the only thing he heard was his breathing. It unsettled him more than he cared to admit.

He had lived alone before and did not mind it. That, though, had been many years ago during his bachelor days. Nine years ago, to be exact, he reminded himself. Since then, his life always had noise. Now, this cloying, indifferent silence pressed on him.

Two weeks…only two weeks, he told himself.

Coffee mug in hand, he sprawled onto the couch and switched on the TV in time to catch the six o'clock news. He normally watched ABC without commercial breaks, but he could not be bothered to change channels. The intro music faded and Peter Hitchener's corpulent face smiled from the screen.

"In summary, the All Ordinaries gained thirty-five points following the signing of the China-Australia Free Trade Agreement. There is growing speculation that Malcolm Turnbull will challenge Prime Minister Tony Abbott for the nation's top job. Donald Trump announces his run for the White House. Tension mounts in Europe that Greece will default on its debt. Pressure is growing for Congress to introduce gun control measures following a mass shooting in Charleston. Tomorrow's weather, rain during the day with a top of nine degrees.

"Welcome to Channel Nine's news hour on June 19, 2015. The details."

Dural reached for the remote and switched off, not interested in watching a mind-numbing hour of depressing news. Violence, crime, shootings, car smashes, political shenanigans, it all seemed insignificant and banal. Not exactly insignificant, as his life to an extent was influenced by Canberra intrigues and world events, but he found that he no longer cared. He really didn't.

No matter how much he wanted a measure of sanity to prevail around the world, he realized there would never be any sanity. Merely an indulgence in wishful thinking. A hope that chaos would not rule when he woke tomorrow. He thought himself capable of anything, but he dreaded the idea of social anarchy where the mob and the gun ruled.

He sipped his coffee and eyed the array of DVDs stacked on

the wall shelf. After a moment, he got up and studied the titles. Not interested in action, war, or a western, he pulled out *The Age of Adaline*. Lenora and he saw the film in April when it hit the cinemas, and liked the storyline, supported by good acting. He fixed himself a whiskey, dimmed the lights, and slipped the DVD into the player.

The movie ended and so did his day. He showered and went to bed a bit earlier than his usual time.

'I'm leaving.'

Lenora's words kept replaying in his mind as he longed for oblivion.

Over breakfast the next morning, nursing a second cup of percolated coffee, Dural decided to do something personally painful. Something that in all likelihood would also create a scene with Len. Her tongue lashing would not be pleasant, but like a sweeping fire, it would pass, leaving behind room for new growth. At least he hoped it would.

He cleaned up around the kitchen, gritted his teeth, and walked slowly up the stairs, feet and heart heavy. He paused before Daniela's door, not entirely sure he should be doing this, and opened it. Standing there, he swept his eyes around the room as though seeing it for the first time. In a way, he saw it for the first time. This was Dan's space and she could do pretty much anything here as long as she kept everything neat. If she did not, there was punishment through loss of privileges. Like all kids, Daniela kept testing the boundaries of her freedom, but learned early it was easier to follow the rules, however unreasonable to her, than fight the system.

He glanced at the large poster of Spiderman above her small writing desk, and his mouth twitched. It was one of her favorites. The beaten-up Cabbage Patch doll stood prominently on the bed between two decorative pillows. He was surprised it had survived the treatment Dan dished out to it, a testament to the ruggedness of its manufacture and Len's running repairs. Lenora tried to wean her away from the thing one Christmas by giving her a nice Barbie doll. Daniela merely sighed and looked at her worn doll in the eye.

"Don't worry, Madam Bisque. They can't bribe me with any old Barbie to give you up," she declared, then looked hopefully at her mom. "Can I give it to Penny? She's into this kind of stuff."

Len glanced at Dural for support. He promptly lifted his palm in surrender, not wanting any part of this.

Lenora smiled, knowing when she was beaten. "You can give it to Penny if you like, sugar buns."

"Wowsy!"

The message had been received—Daniela and the Cabbage Patch doll were an inseparable pair.

They observed popular Christian festivals such as Christmas and Easter because it was an accepted social thing. Dan loved the egg hunt through the house and the backyard, although not allowed to scatter the Easter eggs, meant to be secret, something she frowned on darkly. Her favorite time, though, was decorating the Christmas tree. Dural remembered fondly one episode two years ago when Len and Dan finished hanging on little bonbons, candy sticks, and colored globes, covering everything with filmy strands of cotton wool to emulate snow. They hung several sparklers on the lower branches and dimmed the lounge, the effect complete when they turned on the tree lights. Dan insisted they set off one of the sparklers 'just to see how it looks'. Lenora lit one, and Dural admitted the effect was startling, but not as startling as when a spark set off the cotton wool and it all disappeared in a sudden puff. After a shocked gasp, they all looked at each other and burst out laughing.

Dural and Len taught Daniela morals and ethical principles, but never indoctrinated her in any Christian denomination. Raised an Anglican as most Maori were, Lenora did not attend church services. She said they gave her bad vibes. A Catholic, Dural did not attend services either, not seeing any relevancy in an outdated ceremony where attendance was a social habit rather than a genuine spiritual experience. They discussed with Daniela, as much as she could absorb at her age, the turbulent history of all major religions and philosophies, and the effects they had on Western thinking, keeping it objective, allowing her to form her own views. All in all, he thought they had not done a bad job of it.

He and Lenora did make one concession to religion. They had Daniela baptized, otherwise Judith would never have forgiven her daughter. A small thing to keep peace within the family.

Dural walked to the bed and stared at the doll as memories of Daniela dragging the thing wherever she went cascaded through his mind.

The cold, detached part told him to get on with it, but he could not bring himself to do it. He should be sharing this moment with Lenora, allowing her to cleanse herself by finally letting go. He picked up the doll and lovingly placed it on the work desk. The backpack joined the doll. He would make this concession to the past. With a heavy sigh, he stripped the bed and threw the sheets onto a pile in the middle of the room. Hard at first, but he made himself purge everything that threatened to turn the room into a shrine. His mind churning, he opened the wardrobe and ran his hand lovingly over the hung dresses, pants, and shirts, her smell everywhere. After a moment, he clenched his teeth and slowly began removing the clothing, adding them to the pile, surprised at its size. He bagged salvageable items the local Sacred Heart Mission Op Shop might use, and binned the rest. He saved her books, photos, and personal DVDs, wanting to add them to the collection downstairs.

Finished, he washed up and made himself look into Daniela's room one last time. A bare room now with a bed, a bookshelf, and a small writing desk, all traces of its previous owner removed. He quickly walked down the stairs into the lounge and fixed himself a stiff bourbon.

Lenora had to adjust to the bitter truth that their little girl was gone and they needed to move on. He had not liked seeing darkness draped over her and the unsettling way she had left. Despite his patience and silent support, what troubled him was her refusal to let him share her grief, refusing his attempts to comfort her.

Did she blame him for Daniela's death, or was that merely a natural backlash for losing her baby? The psychologist in him could not decide. After two or three sessions with a patient, picking apart the underlying problem, he generally had a recovery plan. With Lenora, he was stymied. He could not help her if she remained buried in the gloom of her thoughts, refusing to talk about it. She not only did not talk, she shunned his attempts to touch, hug, or kiss her. Couldn't she see that he also hurt, that he suffered? Sharing an embrace would help both of them.

His cell went off. He picked up and touched the caller icon.

"Hi, Leonard. How's things?"

"It's a bright morning, Du, and I thought I'd have a game of golf. Care for a bash, old man? I'm sure Lenora can spare you for a couple of hours."

So, Rosalyn had not gossiped.

"She wouldn't if she were around," Dural said. "She flew to New Zealand yesterday to see her parents."

He could almost hear Leonard's thoughts in the ensuing silence. His friend wasn't anybody's dummy and could read the signs.

"Anything I can help with?" Leonard offered.

"I'll let you know when she gets back."

"A game might be the thing for you right now, Du. The fresh air will clear your head."

"If I don't get poleaxed by another lightning strike."

Leonard laughed. "Not a chance. It's a blue sky out there if you haven't noticed. Afterward, we'll have lunch at my place and share a bottle. Helen will be glad to see you. How about it?"

"It's Saturday, Len. The course will be packed."

"Looking for an excuse not to get creamed?"

Dural chuckled. Smashing the little white sucker around the fairways might be the therapy he needed at that.

"Okay, you quack. I'll meet you there. Ten-thirty?"

"Ten-thirty works for me," Leonard said and hung up.

* * *

For the first time in days, Dural felt himself slowly settling down. Daniela still burned bright in his mind, but her loss no longer seared his insides, the pain now only a dull throb always there. He adjusted, although at night, alone in the house, he occasionally descended into melancholy introspection, hoping The Dream would not return. When he became moody, he found solace in music. A nice piece of Brahms or Mozart helped him look at brighter aspects of life, helped him look at tomorrow.

He called Lenora a couple of times, but their conversations were short and cryptic. She refused to open up, maintaining a barrier between them. There were moments when she said she missed him, but the words did not carry genuine feeling. When he asked what she was doing, she said she spent a lot of time in solitary walks, reflecting. He did not like that, suggesting that she socialize with her parents and sister. She did, she said, but she could not party every day.

Dural rang Nikau, and the old Maori told him to be patient. He said that women felt grief far more deeply than men, something Dural knew wasn't true. What he did know, Lenora needed time to reconcile herself with her loss and grasp reality again. Nikau said she did not look depressed or sullen, but she did have several deep discussions with Judith. What they discussed, he could not say, as his wife did not talk about it, and he did not push it.

"Give it time, Du," the old Maori said softly. "The girl is hurting."

"She has shut me out."

"She just went through two major traumas in her life. She's trying to cope and put everything together again. The problem she's facing, the pieces no longer fit. As a psychologist, you should understand that."

"That's the problem, Nikau. I understand all too well," Dural said heavily. Who was there to help *him* cope? "I cannot support her, though, if she keeps me at arm's length."

"She's not one of your patients, Du, but your wife. Simply be there for her, my boy. She'll come around."

Dural replayed the conversation they had last night, going over every word trying to discern their underlying nuance and meaning not overtly said. In the end, he gave up, suspecting he overanalyzed.

He only hoped Lenora's old man was right.

Unusually mild, the sun starting to hug the horizon, the sounds of traffic a background distraction, he turned into Trinion Street. The golden elms were still mostly bare, but new growth already spurted, and leaves were budding. He did not expect to see new growth in late June, but welcomed the sight of fresh greenery among the ever-present gums. Cities were natural heat sinks and generally a couple of degrees warmer than the outer suburbs. For plants, all the difference they needed to grow.

Humming the opening theme to *Chariots of the Gods*, a surprisingly fresh look for its time at many unexplained phenomena around the world, although decried by many, he felt energized, looking forward to preparing himself a special dinner. He and Lenora usually reserved Fridays or the weekend for elaborate cooking over a nice glass of red wine, but he felt in the mood to treat himself, even if only Thursday.

He found it surprisingly difficult being alone, used to having her around, sharing everything, sometimes talking deep into the night, or simply cradling each other with unstated understanding. He missed that intimacy, and the silence at home he came to these days grated on him. Only eight days more, he told himself, and they would be together again, moving on…together.

It amused him that he had become so domesticated that he could not spend a few days by himself.

Still humming, he paused before the side gate to his place, opened it, and walked toward the small portico lit by a central downlight. He frowned when he saw the lounge and kitchen windows lit. Did he forget to turn off the lights this morning? He did some things so automatically—both of them did—not consciously aware of doing them. Like turning off the hotplate or locking the front door. At work, he wondered more than once if he locked the damned thing, the thought nagging at him all day. When he eventually got home, he would sigh with relief when he found the door locked. He and Lenora had a bad one during a trip to New Zealand. Neither remembered locking the front door, although Daniela assured them they did. Dural told Len the security system would alert him on his cell if anyone crossed the intruder trip zone. As it turned out, both had fretted needlessly, much to Dan's amusement.

He unlocked the door and stepped into the warm interior. Nothing unusual about that, as the heating timer always kicked in at four. He walked through the lounge and headed for the stairs, then stopped when he saw used dishes on the kitchen bench.

She was home? A flutter of dread rippled through his body.

"Len!"

He heard footsteps and she stood on top of the stairs, Daniela's doll clutched to her chest. By the tight set of her mouth, he could tell she seethed with fury, and he knew why.

"How could you do it?" she snarled.

He did not pretend not to understand. "It was a catharsis, Len," he said wearily, not relishing an argument when he sought to pull them together.

"A catharsis? There is nothing left of hers in the room!"

"No, there isn't."

"What did you do with the stuff?"

"I gave most of it away and trashed the rest."

She gaped at him. "You threw everything out? That's why you wanted me gone. Not to help me. You wanted to erase her from your own mind. What about me and how I feel? Do you want to erase me as well?" Her eyes blazed. "I hate you. I actually hate you, and I'll never forgive you for this."

"Len, you were spending too much time in there. You were turning the room into a memorial and descending into depression. Grieving over her is one thing, but you were losing yourself in that room. I couldn't let that continue."

"*You* couldn't?" She tilted her head and looked at him with a puzzled expression. "What's happened to you, Du? We used to talk things over before doing something." She swept a hand at Daniela's room. "You killed her! And now you're trying to kill her memory. You're a bastard and I wish you were dead instead of her."

Cloaked in an aura of darkness, she stomped toward their room.

Enraged at the unfairness of it all, he pressed his fists against his temples. "Tell me how and I'll change places with her!" he shouted after her, the image of Daniela lying on the wet road sharp in his mind. "What the hell do you want from me!"

Damn it all.

If someone repeated something often enough, would it become truth? He clung to only one truth. He did not kill Dan. Unreasonable as it was, Lenora came to believe a lie, and he did not know how to shake her out of it. Teeth clenched, he trudged up the stair after her.

When he got to their bedroom, he paused and took two deep breaths. Nothing would be gained by shouting at each other, destroying more between them. He opened the door and stood there. She lay sprawled across the bed sobbing. He wanted to take her in his arms and make the hurt go away, but in her agitated state, she would spurn him. He took off his overcoat and folded it across the dresser chair, then bit his lip and walked to the bed. The edge sagged as he sat down. She flinched when he touched her shoulder.

"Len…"

"Go away, you murderer," she mumbled into the doona. "I don't ever want to see you again."

Dural winced at the malice of her words. Right now, it would be all too easy to storm out and slam the door, letting her stew in her misery. That, however, would not solve anything for either of them.

"You know why I cleaned out her room? I wanted to spare you the pain of doing it yourself. I didn't want to, but I made myself do it. Maybe I was wrong not telling you first, but she isn't gone, Len. She will always be with us in our thoughts, but you cannot keep burying her every day!" he added hotly.

She turned and wiped her cheeks. "You should have told me, Du."

He reached for her hand and held it. "I'm sorry, Len. I really am. I thought it would help both of us."

"Do you have any idea how I felt when I walked into her room, only to find it empty? You drove a knife through my heart then." She glared at him. "You didn't do this to help me. You were purging your own guilt. When you threw out her stuff, you threw her out with it. That's how it looked to me."

He buried his head between his hands and sighed. He swallowed a lump that threatened to choke him and looked at her.

"I won't forget her, Len. Not that I want to, but there are things I wish I *could* forget. Seeing her tear herself from me, the oncoming car, her crumpled on the road…The images, they're with me always. Why couldn't it have been me? I have been asking myself that every day, but it wasn't me." He gazed deep into her eyes. "Just one of those things, Lenora. As long as she remains in our hearts, she'll be alive for us. In our hearts, not with the things in her room."

Tears slid down her cheeks and she sniffed.

"It's just that I miss her so," she moaned. "I expect to see her at the door, that wretched doll in her hand, asking you for a story." She allowed the tears to run. "But she never will again, will she?"

Dural swept her into his arms and held her tight as she broke into heaving, wrenching sobs, her body shaking against him. She wept and he held her, crying inside, wincing as his chest constricted from pain that would not go away.

After a while, he pulled back and wiped her wet cheeks.

"Why did you come back?"

She sniffed and dabbed at her nose. "I had a terrible row with my father. It was partly my fault, I guess. I thought being with my parents would help me settle down and come to terms with what happened. Instead, their fawning, cloying attempts to cheer me up only made things worse. I should have stayed with Audrey. My sister is very much down to earth and wouldn't have smothered me with sympathy."

"Your dad. What happened?"

"He always has to be right…like you. Talking to him was like talking to you, and I wasn't looking for another series of psychiatric sessions. Eventually, it got on my nerves. Both of you treated me as though I was a simple child, and you knew best how to make things better. Losing Daniela shook me to the core, and my miscarriage sent me over the edge. Withdrawing into myself may have been a little extreme, but I didn't lose it. For you, I was a patient. For Dad, a sounding board for his lame get-over-it philosophies. I couldn't take it and I stormed out. My only regret is making Mom very upset, but we talked on the phone as I waited to board my flight and sorted things out." Her eyes puffy and red from crying bored into him. "Men just don't get it. I thought that you of all people would, seeing how women make up most of your patients. When I came home and saw Daniela's room…" She sniffed and dabbed at her nose.

Lenora's words cut deeply into Dural and he struggled to say something in his defense, but he couldn't find the words without sounding condescending, and he supposedly knew everything. After all, he had a PhD to prove it.

What she said made a lot of sense, from her perspective, but her muddy pink aura suggested a level of dishonesty and delusion. As he looked at her, her aura changed to deep green, normally a sign of insecurity and a feeling of being victimized. It revealed something of her true state of mind, but Dural had begun to realize that a person's aura, although a fairly accurate barometer of the base personality, did not always reflect the rational, conscious part. As he knew too well, the conscious and the subconscious always warred with each other. Mostly over small things easily reconciled, but conflict over something major, unless resolved, had the potential to develop into psychosis.

What he should do is run controlled experiments to quantitatively define aura patterns generated by the subconscious and the conscious to derive a reliability index. It would not be too difficult, seeing how the practice provided a pool of readily available test subjects. From a superficial indication of a person's base state he now perceived, unreliable as a diagnosis tool, he would have a definitive methodology to analyze and treat his patients. Too bad he did not have that now.

Were Lenora's auras a reflection of her conscious self and a natural reaction to two major traumas? Did he read too much into an involuntary subconscious reaction? Unless he overcame her belief that he was responsible for Daniela's death, reconciliation might not possible, and they would never be able to move on.

Could she be right, though? Was he responsible?

He had kept that part of himself firmly shut and did not want to venture there, afraid what he would find. Slowly, he opened that door and the truth stared back.

"What are you thinking?" she asked, eyes glistening.

"That I may be a block," he said heavily, then brought her hand to his lips and kissed it. "This is hard for me to accept, let alone say, but I think it must be said. All this time, I kept telling myself it wasn't my fault, that I couldn't have done anything to save her, but I've been in denial. I *could* have stopped her if only I'd held her hand harder. I saw the traffic, and I saw how eagerly she wanted to catch our tram. I should have anticipated that she would want to break away from me." Saying the words seared his soul, but they also wiped away the guilt he had locked away. Not a total cleansing, but it helped him reconcile with his own sub-conscious self.

Lenora bit her lip, not saying anything.

"All this time, I thought you didn't care," she whispered at length. "And her room?"

"A mistake. I see that now. If it had to be done, we should have done it together." He squeezed her hand hard. "It may not help now, but I'm sorry, Len."

"Du…" Her arms went around his neck and she sighed against him. "You *are* a block."

They held each other, and Dural felt a flood of relief wash through him. Everything would be all right now…in time.

She disengaged herself and wiped her eyes.

"These last couple of weeks, it's all been a bit much, and I didn't know what to think. It's irrational, I know, but I still resent that you're alive and she isn't. I resent that you buried your re-sponsibility for her safety, blaming it all on the driver, and I resent that you've been a block when it came to how I felt. I'll get over it, and I'll have to accept that she's gone. If I snap at you, make allowances, okay?"

He leaned forward and kissed her, a light touch, but a wealth of feeling lay behind it. She did not respond, her aura flaring dark brown—rejection. He tried not to read too much into it, but the cold, logical part of him didn't like it.

What the hell was happening to him? To hell with all auras! He would be better off not seeing or using them.

Had the indirect lightning strike changed his personality after all? He *knew* that some symptoms took weeks or months to manifest themselves. Was his growing objectivity and detachment one of those symptoms? Was he losing his humanity, turning into a walking computer? Perhaps he should see Gerard again.

"Just don't hate me," he said softly. "I can take everything else."

"Part of me wants to hate you, Du. The silly, unreasonable part, but I don't hate you. I'm still angry with you, though. Just give me a little time." She exhaled and clambered off the bed. "I better call Dad and patch things up. He was very distraught when I left."

He stood beside her. "That would be a very good idea."

"Talking of good ideas, maybe I should get back to work. Try and make things more normal."

"Whatever you think, Len."

She raised an eyebrow. "No sage advice, Doctor?"

He gave a wry smile. "My sage advice didn't work that well for either of us."

Her mouth twitched as she patted down her pants.

A small beginning.

"How about we go out for dinner?" he said eagerly. "We haven't done that in a while. What do you say?"

Lenora pursed her lips. "I don't know. I've had a pretty harrowing day and I feel like crashing out early. Tomorrow, perhaps?"

"Mmm. How about we order in? Pizza, Chinese, whatever."

"Well…"

* * *

"There is no doubt about it, Du," Gerard declared and pushed back his rimless glasses. "The MRI doesn't lie. Your body has generated approximately two percent more brain mass in mostly even distribution. Two percent might not sound much, but given that the human brain contains upward of 100 billion neurons, that's a lot. Unsurprisingly, this has increased your mental capacity across the board, raising your IQ to around 160. The tasks I had you do during the scans prove it."

Dural stared at him. "One-sixty?"

"We know that electrical stimulation enhances neural stem cell proliferation, neuronal differentiation, and integration into functional neurons. You were subjected to a massive electrical surge, which clearly gave rise to profound neurogenesis. Instead of having your cerebral cortex scorched, your accident has actually proved beneficial." He leaned forward and glared. "You must have noticed some change. Hell, Leonard and I already commented on your clinical impartiality. Out with it, and don't stare at me with those baby gray eyes of yours like you don't know what I'm talking about."

Dural pulled at his right ear, not certain what to say. One thing he could not say was that he had the ability to see people's aura. A straightjacket was the least he could look forward to. However, he could not deny the obvious, and unless he gave Gerard something, his friend would keep digging.

"I guess the MRI only confirms what I already knew," he said simply. "With the exception of enlarged brain mass, that is, which by the way explains my increased appetite earlier on. As for my detachment...It's true that lately, I have been able to analyze and diagnose my patients with greater ease, but I have always been analytical."

Gerard's mouth twitched. "I know. Leonard and I used to kid you about it at the university."

Dural smiled. "That didn't stop either of you from asking my help with an assignment."

"No, it didn't, but this is different. Remember the Davenport case? Of course you do. Your eidetic memory. A borderline psycophrenic, but you determined that his condition was caused by issue avoidance, not a personality disorder. Namely, sticking to a failed marriage and an abusive wife rather than take the obvious step and get a divorce, which I recommended."

Dural remembered the case clearly. "I couldn't see your problem. His unreserved love for his wife made him submissive, which suppressed his masculinity and set up a conflict with his ego. He didn't want a divorce. What he had to do was stand up to his wife, but feared rejection."

"Your solution didn't set me aback, but the speed with which you made it. Less than an hour after I let you read my notes."

"You would have got there, Ger. Your notes were clear enough."

"My point, Du, is how you explained your solution without ever talking to my patient. I also talked to Leonard when you helped him with a similar case. Face it. The accident appears to have enhanced all your cognitive abilities. It also made you cold."

Lenora had said the same thing. Dural felt a flush of anger wash through him. "Cold? I would like to know what exactly you meant by that."

Gerard leaned forward. "Why are you agitated? Did I flick a raw nerve?"

Dural studied his friend, then shook his head and gave a rueful smile.

"You son of a bitch. You had to dig for that one, didn't you? I'm not talking to my friend, but a clinical psychologist, and I am his patient."

"Yes, you are, and I'm trying to make you face up to whatever is happening to you."

"Okay. That near miss has clearly changed me, I admit it, but underneath it all, I'm still the same old me. In some ways better perhaps, but just because you cannot explain it, Doctor, is not an excuse to undermine the effects as pathological."

"I'm not." Gerard pushed up his glasses. "Is everything all right at home?"

The abrupt tack made Dural frown. "More Psychology 101?"

"Idiot! Forget the accident. You walked away from it with something positive, and I'm glad not to have lost you. However, you represent a unique case and I am understandably curious. My question, though, was personal. You're coming out of a major trauma, and as your friend, I am concerned and want to help you."

Dural sagged in the chair and exhaled. "Sorry, Ger. I didn't mean to snap at you. The thing is, everything is not well at the Sinclair residence. Lenora has miscarried."

"Oh shit."

"Yeah."

"And she blames you for it?"

"She blames me for letting Daniela die."

"Christ, Du! It was an accident."

"I know, but I cannot help feeling that I could have stopped her."

"Put on your professional hat, Doctor. Could you have stopped her?"

Dural replayed the incident in his mind, going over every detail.

"In hindsight—"

"In hindsight? You're playing 'if only' games with yourself and you know it. Stop carrying guilt over something you could not have done anything about."

"I'm trying not to, but Lenora doesn't see it that way, and maybe she's right."

"I'll talk to her if you want."

Dural shook his head. "I already suggested that, but she won't have any part of it."

"Because we're friends? I can recommend a colleague."

"She isn't interested. A week ago, she went to Wellington to see her parents. I thought the trip would help her, but it created a problem with her family. When she came home, we had a pretty heated argument, and I thought we patched things up." Dural leaned forward and gazed at his friend. "She looked for closure, Ger, and I gave it to her. In a way, it was also closure for me."

Gerard bit his lip. "You told Lenora that you were responsible?"

"I can make excuses, but I *was* responsible. The admission has settled her down, and in a way, settled me down. She went back to work and looked more reconciled."

"Purging yourself like that showed you're fallible like everybody else," Gerard mused. "On the other hand, it might reinforce her perception of your guilt and engender further negative episodes."

"I'm afraid you might be right. Over the last few days, she has become increasingly withdrawn and is drinking too much. Frankly, I don't know what to do."

"Talk to her and be there for her. Be patient."

"She hates it when I talk like a doctor, and she won't talk to me as a husband."

"Have you thought of taking her on a trip? You like traveling, and Europe is warm this time of year," Gerard added with a smile.

Dural shrugged. "I wouldn't mind, but she isn't into travel much, unless it's to New Zealand to see her folks. We did make plans to see the Kimberleys in December, and she appeared keen to go."

"There you are. Fresh scenery, different people, it might snap her out of it."

That trip, though, included Daniela. "I'll think about it."

"You okay with another MRI next week?"

"As long as you don't pontificate over the results."

"Peace! I want to see if your brain has outgrown your skull."

Dural laughed. "Bastard. You mentioned accelerated neuro-genesis. Is there a possibility of a negative response?"

"Like a tumor, you mean? It's always a possibility where there is rapid cell differentiation, but the literature is thin on this. You'll have to put up being monitored for the next few years." Gerard glanced at his watch. "I guess we better make our way to the partner's meeting before Rosalyn comes after us. Mondays…they should ban them."

Dural bit his lip. That's what Lenora used to say.

He sorted out serious psychological problems for his patients and saw them resume productive lives, but he found himself floundering helplessly when it came to helping his own wife. Frustration hardly came close to describing his turbulent feelings. He understood the problem, of course. His patients came to *him* seeking resolution, whereas Lenora didn't, allowing herself to slide down a slope of moodiness and depression.

Just be there for her as Gerard advised?

Be there as a constant and underlying reminder of everything she loathed. Admitting that he could have somehow prevented Daniela's death served to temporarily ease her churning emotions, but did nothing to bring closure and a return to a semblance of normality. He could see it in the way she looked at him, in her words, and refusal to engage in any intimacy, not even a hug or a peck on the cheek.

She needed time, she said.

Fine, he would give her time, but there were limits. This was not only about her. He wanted closure himself and open a door to a brighter tomorrow. They couldn't go on like this. If that door remained closed? Dural clamped his mouth with resolve. He would open the damned thing himself and walk through it—alone if necessary. He would not allow her to drown in introspection. The life they had before now gone, but they could rebuild and move forward. It would be a life without children, though.

Hell of a thing to say when what seemed like yesterday, he

looked forward to extending his family. Crap can come from anywhere at any time.

Fates had certainly crapped on him.

After six when he finished with his last patient; a young commercial airline pilot laid off by Jetstar because of macular degeneration. A former Air Force F/A-18 Super Horner driver, he saw a bright future and financial security for himself. Now, he would never be able to fly any type of aircraft ever again. No career, an uncertain future, and a floundering marriage.

Dural was not the only one fates had crapped on.

He shut down the computer, gathered his overcoat, and walked briskly through the empty reception area. Rosalyn was gone. Another hot date, she confided earlier. A date on a Monday night? Love knew no time, he reminded himself, recalling wild outings with Lenora. Despite urging her to go out over the last few days, she always had an excuse not to.

Although windy and dark, the sounds of evening traffic loud, he decided to walk home. The sky clear, but he smelled rain in the air. Winter in Melbourne was the peak of shits, and he understood why his parents preferred to spend time at Nelson Bay. It wasn't much warmer there either this time of year, four or five degrees only. Right now, that sounded like tropical paradise.

When he turned onto Trinion Street, it felt like stepping into another world. Tall trees along the nature strip on both sides of the road glowed soft green under street lamps, and the silence palpable. Nothing stirred. Windows in surrounding houses glowed dull yellow behind drawn drapes. He reached his front yard, paused, and strode toward the entrance. The driveway gate open, but he didn't think anything of it. Len could have been out shopping.

A wave of warmth swept over him as he walked in, and he sighed with relief. He hung his overcoat on a wall rack, took off his shoes and slid his feet into leather slippers.

"Len?"

The TV was off and the kitchen empty.

He walked up the stairs and opened the bedroom door. Lenora lay propped against the bedrest, a photo album on her lap, a crystal tumbler in hand. On the bedside cabinet beside her stood half a bottle of Canadian Crown Royal. She did not usually drink whiskey, but Dural shrugged it off. She was free to drink whatever she wanted. He just did not like her drinking so much. The album was something else. Was it simply something to pass the time while she waited for him to come home, recapturing memories, or something deeper? Don't read too much into everything, he chided himself.

She looked up without expression.

"How was your day?" he asked as he made his way to the walk-in wardrobe to change.

"Do you really care?"

Her cold answer made him frown. He tore off his tie and looked at her.

"Yes, I care. Why wouldn't I?"

"Well, if you must know, the bank took my project from me. How do you like that?"

"Took your project? Why?"

She waved the tumbler. "None other than Woody Grant himself, Senior Manager for Treasury Projects no less, called me into his office this morning and gave me the cheery news. He dressed it up with sympathy for my loss and was very understanding. However, my project schedule had slipped seriously and he had no choice but to relieve me. Take more time off, he offered, and that's what I'm doing. I'm taking two weeks off. He said I can take over again once I'm back. Don't you think that was nice of him?" Her eyes bright from too much whiskey, she downed what remained in the tumbler.

"You're tipsy," he told her sternly.

She pursed her mouth, glanced at the tumbler, and nodded. "You're right." She reached for the bottle, topped up, and raised the tumbler. "To Woody," she declared and took a deep sip. "And my project."

Dural placed both hands on his hips and glared at her.

"What the hell's the matter with you, Len? You've been walking around like a zombie these last few days. Get a grip on yourself."

"That's exactly what I'm doing, Dr. Sinclair. Getting a grip on myself."

"It won't happen out of a bottle."

"And how would you know?" She spread her arms. "Go ahead. Let's have it out. I'm ready for one of your counseling sessions. Maybe it'll take two. Whatever." Her eyes bored into him. "Well? What are you waiting for? Don't worry, my insurance will cover it."

He walked to her and plucked the tumbler out of her hand.

"Have a shower and sober up," he snapped.

"That's your advice? Wow. So profound." She giggled and swung out her legs.

Emotions ready to explode, he stood over her. "You want to have it out? Okay. Let's do it. Dan is dead and nothing will bring her back. Could I have done something to stop her? Perhaps, but it was an accident, and you cannot hate me for that. You miscarried, and I'm sorry as hell, but you knew what might happen. If you're blaming yourself for that, then stop it! I'm certainly not. We have to accept what has happened and move on. You cannot live in the past."

"The past is all I have," she moaned and her eyes filled.

He grabbed her shoulders and shook her. "The past and that bottle?"

She glanced at the photo album and the tears ran. "And these."

He knelt and held her head between his hands. "You have me."

"Do I? You walked away from me just as you walked away

from Dan."

"Christ almighty! How did I walk away from you?"

"You could have come to Wellington with me, but no. Your practice was more important."

"I offered to go with you!"

"You were being polite. I could tell."

"You wanted time alone and I gave it to you. Against my better judgment."

"And I screwed things up with my dad."

Dural glanced at the floor and sighed. "What do you want from me, Len? Tell me, and I'll do it, but I can't do anything if you don't talk to me. You want to go to Wellington? Fine. We can do it tomorrow. You want to go to the Kimberleys like we planned? You want me to stay at home with you? Tell me what you want!"

She sniffed and wiped her eyes. "What I want is to have her back, but that's one thing you cannot give me, can you?"

"I would give anything to have her back. I would take her place if I could." He squeezed her shoulders until she winced. "She is gone! Accept it!"

She shook him off and stood. "I'll never accept it, and I will never forgive you for taking her from me." She picked up the tumbler and splashed whiskey into his face. "This counseling session is over, Doctor," she hissed and threw the tumbler to the floor. With a sharp crack, the crystal shattered. She turned and stomped out.

"Len! Wait!"

He slowly stood and wiped his face, badly shaken by her vehemence. He heard the garage door roll up and rushed down the stairs. She should not be driving, not in her distraught condition and half drunk. He jerked open the door leading to the garage and saw her accelerate down the driveway. The car skidded as she went into a tight right turn. Recovering, she sped toward High Street.

Dural stood in the doorway and stared at the empty garage. A thin wind made him shiver. Time passed as memories shouted at each other. He reached for a button on a panel of switches next to the door and the roller door slowly rumbled down.

Should he call the police? They wouldn't do anything unless there was an accident. An accident he did nothing to stop. Like with Daniela…The thought made him shake his head, seeing Lenora hurt, seeing others hurt. Cars mangled, sirens wailing, lives destroyed. So what? His life was already destroyed.

Silence echoed loud as he slowly walked up the stairs. He paused beside the bed, then cleaned up the broken glass. Looking at the whiskey bottle, he took it downstairs, got a tumbler, and poured himself two fingers. He tossed it back in one swallow. It burned as it went down.

Crap me dead.

He refilled and took a long swallow. The liquor made his head buzz, but he didn't care. Why shouldn't he get drunk? To hell with everything!

Feeling he had a bit too much, he walked into the bathroom and splashed water on his face. Looking at himself in the mirror, he saw ashes. Some psychologist he turned out to be. His mind in neutral, he changed into slacks and a thin sweater, and made his way down to the kitchen. Nothing on the hotplate. Two used dishes and a fork lay in the sink. Thinking she had cooked something and did not want it to spoil, he opened the fridge. He gazed at the clutter, but there wasn't a pot or frypan there.

He walked to the CD library and dug out Beethoven's sixth symphony. With the haunting strands of the first movement on medium volume, he strode back into the kitchen. Chewing his lip, he pulled out a slab of speck from the fridge, two eggs, and a block of cheddar cheese. With everything on the bench, he rummaged in the pantry for a large onion. He finely diced the onion and a thick slice of speck and tossed them into a frying pan, and added olive oil. As the stuff sizzled, he poured himself another drink. With the onions browned, he broke two eggs over the mixture and grated in the cheese. Done, he scraped the mess onto a plate and carried it to the dining table. He ate mechanically, preferring not to think, but it didn't work.

The heater fan kicked in and he could hear the whisper of warm air coming up from the vents.

Finished just as the second movement wound down, he washed up, pulled out the CD, and sprawled on the couch. The seven o'clock news on the ABC wrapped up with tomorrow's weather report—sixteen with breaks of sunshine—and Leigh Sales introduced the *7.30 Report*. Not in the mood to sit through half an hour of current affairs, he pressed the program button on the remote to show channel selections. *Kelly's Heroes* at 8:30 the best of the pick. He had seen the movie already and liked it, Clint Eastwood with a great cast, but Dural did not feel like waiting that long. He glanced at his collection of DVDs and frowned. *Why not?* He got up, walked to the wall unit and scanned the rows of movies. He pulled out *Kelly's Heroes* and stuck it into the player. The opening song and the stirring melody washed over him as he settled back on the couch. It helped to shut out the silence…and other things.

As Eastwood raced his jeep through the bombed-out town to escape the Germans, Dural wondered if he would ever watch the movie again, his eidetic memory giving him the ability to replay it in his mind whenever he wanted. A memory was not the same thing as direct visual stimulation, he reminded himself.

When the movie finished around ten, he went upstairs, completed his bathroom chores, and crawled into bed. It took a while for the silence and the darkness to cradle him in their embrace. Hands behind his head, he gazed into blackness trying to find the ceiling. Tired of hashing over the evening's events, having analyzed and reanalyzed everything to death, he turned over and waited for sleep.

He blinked when he heard the sound of the garage door coming up, and glanced at the bedside electronic clock: 11:43. She came up and padded toward the spare bedroom. The door closed behind her and silence returned. He strained to hear something, anything, but there was nothing. The walls were too well insulated.

It took a long time before darkness took him.

Chapter Five

Dural got up, had a shower, dressed, and went downstairs to make breakfast. He flicked on the lights and TV for the ABC news to have some background noise. He did not listen to what was going on. The Yemen civil war heating up; Greece looked like it might strike a deal with the EU for its loans; Deepwater Horizon spill still spewing oil; ISIS on the march; more insane car crashes. All too depressing. When the coffee finished percolating, he walked up the stairs and knocked on the spare bedroom door.

"Coffee's up, Len. Do you want any breakfast?"

Not hearing anything, he went back down and poured himself a mug. Plain scrambled eggs with toast satisfied his hunger and he washed up. Finishing his bathroom chores, tempted to check up on Lenora, he refrained. If she did not want to talk to him, he did not want to push her. When he got home, she might be more settled, he told himself. Downstairs, he put on his overcoat, snagged the umbrella, and walked out.

Although overcast, patches of blue sky and sunshine made the crisp morning inviting. A deep breath and a long exhale cleared out the cylinders, and he strode briskly toward High Street. A tram clattered past the stop as he turned toward St. Kilda Road, another anonymous figure among other pedestrians. Exercise, that's what people should do more regularly. Instead of taking a car, a walk to the corner shop would add years of life. Regrettably, walking these days seemed to be frowned upon. A necessity when nothing else was available. When he smelled the exhaust-laced air, he wondered about those extra years.

As usual, Rosalyn was bright and chipper. She positively

glowed, and he did not have to see her aura to tell. Both parties had obviously enjoyed last night's outing. Tempted to check her aura, he clamped down on the impulse. Until he understood the effect far better, he had to resist being swayed by a possibly misleading phenomena. Undeniably useful, but also potentially dangerous if it caused him to make an incorrect diagnosis.

What he did find invaluable was his eidetic memory. He still took notes during a consulting session, but as supporting evidence, and a requirement in case of legal action. They were now not his primary source of information that formed a basis for determining treatment. Notes simply could not capture every body movement, facial expression, word, and mannerism. Not unless they were so detailed, he would be spending all his time writing them. On the other hand, he had to be careful not to have them too cryptic. They had to be informative enough for Leonard or Gerard to follow should he want their input.

Sandra, his first patient, a young woman in her early twenties. A pro bono case, he and his partners handled from time to time. He chose the talk therapy method, which he preferred over medication treatment. Drugs were valuable and helped many patients overcome their problems, but he did not like using them except in severe trauma cases.

According to her GP's notes, Sandra grew up in a turbulent family, an alcoholic mother, and a sexually abusive father. After one such horrific episode, she had herself sterilized at a backyard clinic. Shortly afterward, her parents died in a car smash, and at nineteen, she found herself alone for the first time in her life.

She had a sister, but three years earlier, she was killed in a skiing accident, and the shattering experience caused the family to slowly disintegrate. Gradually, Sandra's life settled into a routine. She resumed her studies at Melbourne University and graduated as a graphics designer. Despite her resolve never to get involved with a man, she fell in love with a work colleague, which led to her present problem. She wanted the relationship to work, and so did he, but he wanted more—children.

Dural leaned back against the chair and pursed his lips. "Sandra, can you tell me why you're here?"

She pulled up the sleeves of her sweater and tossed back her curls. Her long honey hair glistened under the lighting. She opened her small mouth to say something, but it took several seconds for her to find the words.

"What do you mean, Doctor? I was referred to you—"

He leaned toward her. "You want your relationship with Harold to grow, but you're afraid he'll leave you if he learns you had yourself sterilized. How does that make you feel?"

"According to my doctor, not talking to him has made me neurotic. He said if I don't do something about it, I'll become addicted to the cocktail of prescription drugs I'm now using to paper over my dilemma. His words. If that happens, I'll not only lose Harold, I'll also lose myself."

"What else did your doctor say?"

"That I have to tell Harold everything," she said quietly.

"And you're unable to do that."

Her features twisted as she fought for control. "I can't! He wants children…and so do I," she murmured and shuddered. "But it's too late."

"From your file, you only had contraceptive sterilization, which can be reversed."

She snorted. "Yeah. Wait ten years on a public hospital list, and my private insurance doesn't cover this procedure. I could do it tomorrow, but I don't happen to have six thousand dollars on me right now."

Dural leaned forward. "Sandra, look at me."

She dabbed at her eyes.

"Are you being honest with yourself?"

"Honest? Of course I'm being honest. That's why I'm here."

"What do you want for yourself? You're not suffering from any psychological disorder that warrants treatment. You are merely caught in a moral dilemma, one I am happy to help you resolve, but you must be honest about what you want. Forget your abusive father. You appear to have overcome your hatred of men, or have you? Are you looking for an excuse to break off with Harold?"

"I…I do love him." She blinked rapidly and the tears ran. "I think I love him. Oh, God," she moaned and buried her face between her hands. "I don't know what to do."

Dural allowed her a few minutes to collect herself.

"I'm asking you again, Sandra. What do you *want* to do?"

She wiped her cheeks and sniffed. When she looked up, her eyes were hard with resolve.

"Harold wants to marry me."

"Is this what *you* want?"

"Yes," she whispered.

"Then you know what to do."

"Tell him everything."

"That's right. If he is any kind of man, he'll understand and support you."

"What if he doesn't and walks away?"

"That's part of your dilemma, Sandra, and the reason you're taking all those drugs. If you want a future with him, you must talk to him."

"What about children?"

"This clinic will fund your treatment at The Alfred. I know a good surgeon who could do it. If you want, I'll arrange for you to see her."

She gaped. "You would do that?"

Dural gave a brief smile. "But…"

Her face clouded. "I know. I must talk to Harold. I should have done it already, but I'm afraid he would walk away."

"If he does, then he's not the man you thought he was. Whether you lose him or not, reversing your condition will give you a healthy psychological boost, and you'll be in a far better position to face your next relationship."

"I don't know, Doctor. I'm so afraid—"

"And that fear has stopped you from resolving your problem." Dural gave her a hard look. "Time to make up your mind, Sandra."

She bit her lip and sniffed. "If I don't do this, I'll lose it all, won't I?"

"You risk sliding into deep depression and eventual psychosis."

Sandra took a deep breath and exhaled. "I'll talk to that surgeon…and Harold."

"Rosalyn will call you with an appointment."

She stood and gave a weak smile. "Thank you, Doctor. This is not going to be easy for me, but I feel better about it. I also want to thank you for your generosity."

Dural rose and escorted her to the door. "Take care, and don't hesitate to call if Harold becomes difficult."

She beamed and kissed him on the cheek. He closed the door after her, a wry smile on his face. His phone rang and he picked up.

"Yes, Rosalyn?"

"A letter arrived from Parker and Associates. They want to discuss a damages claim filed by Mrs. Fullham."

The waspish woman with a supposedly domineering husband. He did not believe that any law firm would actually take on her case.

"Send me a copy, and include one for Gerard and Leonard."

"A copy for Arnold, Becker and Strong as well?"

"Definitely. Call Paul Becker and arrange an appointment with Parker *et al*, excluding Mrs. Fullham."

Dural could picture Rosalyn's smile. "Very well, Doctor."

"When is my next appointment?"

"At 10:50."

He sat down, frowned, and dialed to make an appointment

for Sandra. A simple case her GP should have resolved without resorting to prescribing psychotropic drugs. The prevalent use of pills as a ready cure-all was a growing problem worldwide. Instead of spending time in quality consultation to dig out the real issue, patients—and doctors, for that matter—resorted to pills for an answer. Add pushy pharmaceutical reps interested only in bonuses to the equation—he had seen several such drug pushers and did not like any of them—and harried GPs who often did not understand or bothered to research what was being sold to them, medicine had turned into a ten-minute turnstile business, leaving broken bodies and shattered minds in its wake.

It should not be like this.

Now he was getting gloomy.

He strode to the kitchenette and fixed himself some coffee. At the computer, he quickly went over the case notes of his next patient. Another pro bono referral. He and his partners did not mind doing an occasional one, provided they did not turn the practice into a charity clinic.

The notes were brief, but telling. Another young woman, pregnant, her ex refusing to pay support, stuck with a substantial loan she could not service, the case sounded more like something for A, B & S.

As a professional, he should be objective and impartial, not get emotionally involved with patients. A catch-all phrase for not caring. Except it did not work. A surgeon can be detached cutting a draped body, but Dural could not. His patients bared their soul and expected him to solve whatever bothered them. He had to care. Right now, though, facing problems of his own, he did not want to shoulder his patient's problems as well. Not now. Should he take some time off until the situation with Lenora is settled? Being there for her might help at that.

He glanced at his wristwatch; still forty minutes before his next appointment. He reached for the phone and dialed.

"Arnold, Becker and Strong. Steffi speaking. How may I help

you?"

"Hi, Steffi. This is Dr. Sinclair. Can I talk to Paul Becker if he's available?"

"Good morning, Doctor. I'll check. Please hold."

A few seconds later, a click and Paul's throaty voice made Dural smile.

"How are you going, you old quack? Haven't heard from you in a while."

"Sorry, Paul. Things have been piling up lately. Let's have lunch somewhere and I'll fill you in."

"Sounds good. I'll arrange it with Rosalyn. What can I do for you?"

Dural quickly filled him in. "Can you see her? She has emotional problems, caused mainly by legal issues. If you clear them up, or at least get something positive done for her, it would go a long way toward reducing her other difficulties."

"The case too tough to handle, eh?" Paul laughed. "I always knew that behind your polished professional veneer lay nothing but smoke and mirrors."

Dural chuckled. Paul was a friend who did not mince words. He was also a formidable trial lawyer. Gap Psychology Consulting had done business with A, B & S and they bailed them out of several tricky litigation cases.

"What's the deal here? Is this a pro bono?" Paul asked.

"Given her financial situation, it probably will be. Centerlink is in a position to help, but by the time Social Services wheels turn, she might be on the street."

"Hah! The wonders of our bureaucratic machinery. Okay, send her over. I have a slot tomorrow at 1:40."

"Thanks, Paul. I appreciate this." Smiling, Dural replaced the phone, paused, and walked out. "Rosalyn, please call Mrs. Evans and cancel our appointment. Tell her to see Paul Becker tomorrow at 1:40. Give her the address. Also, can you ask Gerard and Leonard to take my patients this afternoon? If not, have them rescheduled with my apologies."

"Fine. Is everything all right, Doctor?"

"I'm going home."

She nodded without showing any reaction. "I hope things work out…Du."

"So do I," he said and walked back to his desk. He shut down the computer, took his overcoat and umbrella from the small cabinet, and strode out.

He caught a passing cab and slid onto the front seat. Now that he made his decision, he wanted to get home quickly and discuss everything with Lenora. Somehow, he had to sort out the situation between them. Sleeping in separate bedrooms would only serve to deepen the rift, as would silence.

The cab pulled up outside his house and Dural paid it off. He watched it make a U-turn and head toward High Street. Pleasant warmth enveloped him as he walked in.

Lying on the couch, Lenora turned away from the TV, looked at him for a second without expression, and continued to watch the movie. A bottle of white wine and a half-full glass sat on the coffee table. Dural hung up his overcoat next to her heavy jacket, noticed her suitcase, and his heart beat faster. He walked slowly toward the couch and looked down at her.

"We need to talk," he said evenly, not liking to see her drinking.

"About what?" she replied without looking at him.

"About us."

She took a sip of wine and stood, wearing black slacks and a heavy navy sweater. "Okay, let's talk about us, if that's what you want."

He inclined his head at the suitcase. "What's that?"

"I'm going to Wellington. I planned to be gone before you got home."

"You're going back to your parents?"

"Actually, I'll be staying with Audrey."

"How long do you plan to be away?"

She shrugged. "A couple of weeks. I'm not quite sure. Until the divorce papers are done."

Dural felt himself go pale as though someone had punched him in the gut.

"Divorce? What the hell are you talking about?"

"It's not a complicated thing to understand, Du. I file, you get served, we settle, and that's it."

"Just like that, eh? Mind telling me why?"

She leaned toward him and glared. "Because I don't have anything left here to make me stay, and seeing your face every day only makes me more determined to leave. You took everything. Everything I loved, and I cannot forget that—ever."

He reached for her, but she stepped back.

"Len, think what you're doing. You're understandably upset, but we can handle this."

"Think? I've been doing nothing else since Dan died and my miscarriage. I lost my baby because of you. If I had not been so stressed, I would still have it, and you're responsible. You're responsible for everything."

"How..." he began, but she was not listening.

A car horn sounded. Lenora turned and walked toward the entrance. She put on her coat, slung a small leather bag across her shoulder, and opened the door. Without looking back, she picked up her suitcase and strode out.

Dural heard the trunk slam, and a moment later the cab sped away. Numb, he stood there as cold air washed over him. He closed the door and locked it, walked to the coffee table, picked up the remote and shut off the TV. The DVD player kept going. He stared at it for a while, then lowered himself onto the couch.

Divorce? She *couldn't* mean what she said.

He placed both fists against his forehead and stared at his shoes, thinking that he should put on slippers. Lenora did not like people walking around the house in shoes. The absurdity made him snort and shake his head.

Everything they talked about the other night meant nothing. After her Wellington trip, he thought they had reconciliation and acceptance. Perhaps they did, but it clearly did not last. She needed counseling, but he could not force her. His wife blamed him for everything, and that was that.

End of a life. End of everything.

This couldn't be happening. He'll wake up and she would be there, warm in his embrace.

He reached for the bottle, then stopped. That would not solve anything.

It would kill the pain, Doctor.

For how long? Then another bottle…and another…

He dragged out his cellphone and pressed an icon in the contacts list. It took three rings before a gruff voice answered.

"Nikau Tipene."

"Hi, Nikau. It's Du."

"Du! Great to hear from you. What's up?"

"It's Lenora."

"What happened?"

"She's gone, Nikau. She's flying to Wellington to see Audrey."

"When did that happen?"

"Ten minutes ago."

Silence ate into time as Dural waited.

"Talk to me, Du," the old Maori said gently.

"She wants a divorce. I thought we had things settled…"

"Shit."

"Yeah, that's what I thought."

"Impulsive girl. I'll try and sort her out."

"From what she said, your last encounter with her didn't end that well."

"No, it didn't. Mostly my fault. Judith and I talked about it and she straightened me out. Women have a different slant on these things."

"You got that right. Anyway, I didn't call to cry on your shoulder," Dural said and chuckled, but without humor. "Then again, maybe I did. I just wanted to tell you."

"I'll talk to Audrey. Du, this is not the end of the world."

"It might as well be for me."

"Don't you go blaming yourself for everything. Hear me?"

"You should be in my profession, Nikau. Talk to you later," Dural said and hung up.

He stared at the cell, then placed it on the coffee table. He did not know how long he sat there, thinking about nothing and everything. For the first time in his life, he realized that silence could actually hurt, and he hurt everywhere.

* * *

Following his own advice, Dural went to work the next day. Staying at home brooding would only drive him into gloomy moodiness, and he had never indulged in melancholy introspection. Although if he were to start, he could not pick a better time for it. On top of everything, it was Wednesday, and he never liked Wednesdays, which did not help his disposition.

For once, he beat Rosalyn to the office. A small moral victory, as this did not happen often. He started the coffeemaker and logged into his computer, hating what he was about to do, but his calculating self told him he was merely being prudent.

Lenora had access to his ANZ working account and Saver reserve funds account that earned a meager 2.5% interest, but better than nothing. She had her own accounts, and he never pried, although he did have access. Not sure of his liquidity position, he logged into the ANZ Online Banking portal. His Access account served as a common pool into which he and Lenora deposited $2,000 each to meet ongoing monthly expenses. The rest of her salary was her own. At end of every month, excess funds were transferred to his Saver account. Right now, the Access account had a little over $4,000, and the Saver under $9,000.

Tempted to transfer a portion out of the Saver account, he logged off instead. Regardless of what went on between them, he trusted Lenora not to clean him out. However, people under emotional stress were prone to take irrational actions they would otherwise never contemplate. Even if she did withdraw everything, it would not break him financially, but if he barred her access, it would send a definite signal it was all over between them, and he did not want to precipitate anything as long as there was the slimmest chance of getting back together. Every day she stayed away reduced the likelihood of reconciliation. His only hope lay with Nikau and Judith. Last night, he contemplated going after her, and rejected the idea immediately. Seeing him, she would only flee somewhere else. She might not do that at all and he was being unfair to her. Still, a no-win scenario no matter what he did.

Prepared to peek into her accounts, he refrained. How she managed her finances was her own business. With his encouragement, she held a nice shares portfolio managed by Ord Minnett, and a stake in two managed funds. Out of his partner drawings, he regularly deposited $3,000 into her Saver account. Financially, she did very well from their informal arrangement.

A knock on the door and Leonard peered in.

"Hi, Len. Come on in. What can I do for you?"

Leonard shut the door after him and sprawled his ungainly length into a visitor chair.

"Oh, nothing in particular. Just checking up on my partner."

Dural cocked an eyebrow. He could see concern in Len's look. "Just checking up, eh? Have you been talking to Gerard?"

"He is a professional clam, Du. You should know that by now."

"A nice evade. So?"

Leonard shrugged. "You've been dragging your ass around like the weight of the world has landed on you, and I'm naturally concerned. A post-lightning strike development?"

Dural sighed. "In a manner of speaking. Lenora is divorcing me."

"What? You can't be serious. You two are walking examples of a perfect marriage. An envy of everyone who knows you. When did all this happen?"

"Yesterday. She took off for NZ to see her sister, which as they say, yanked the rug from under my feet. Whatever she's thinking, I can't talk her out of it."

"Because of Daniela and the miscarriage?"

"She's blaming me for everything."

"Ah shit. I'm sorry, Du."

"So am I."

"Well, that explains your long face. What are you going to do?"

"Nothing much I can do until she serves the papers—if she's serious."

"Mmm. You thought of going after her?"

"I'm undecided."

Leonard bit his lip. "Yeah, it could work either way. You've got yourself in a crack for sure."

"A very helpful diagnosis, Doctor."

"That's what you get for a freebie. Seriously, Du. I'm sorry as hell. Anything I can do?"

"Not right now, thanks."

Leonard snorted. "Women! Did you suggest counseling?"

"She doesn't want to hear of it, and she refuses to talk to me."

"Three psychologists at her disposal and we can't do a damn thing."

"Hence my long face."

Leonard frowned. "You're not blaming yourself for any of this, are you?"

"Gerard asked me the same thing. I'm blaming myself...a little. Coming back to work after Daniela's death may have been a mistake. Looking back, perhaps I should have stayed with her, but she wanted time alone. Perhaps I should have been more sensitive and supportive." Dural tugged at his right ear. "I thought I did the right thing at the time."

"Some things simply happen. Easy to be smart in hindsight."

"Yeah. Anyway, you don't have to worry that I'll sink into some depressive manic state."

"It can happen to the best of us, partner."

"If you see me sliding down, kick my ass," Dural said with a smile.

"It will be a pleasure."

"Bastard."

Leonard heaved himself up and paused. "My door is always open, Du."

"I appreciate that, Len. I mean it."

When he left, Dural sat back feeling buoyed. Life may have landed him in the rough, but he had friends who genuinely cared for him. Just knowing that gave him a lift. Still, if Lenora went through with the divorce, he might find himself with an unplayable shot.

Call Audrey? Tempted, then decided against it. She and Lenora were very close, and she would likely take Len's side. No, his initial impulse was right. He would wait and see what her parents could do. At the back of his mind, he still toyed with the idea of flying there and talking it out with her. Surrounded by her family, she might be calmer and amenable to reason, but emotion cannot be treated with reason.

Fondling his coffee mug, Dural did not have too many options to play with.

Divorce…he grappled with the daunting possibility that Lenora would actually leave him. After nine years of love, friendship, companionship, she appeared prepared to throw it all away, but the suddenness of her decision to leave him shocked him most of all. How many ways can he say he was sorry?

If she did leave him, what then? Memories would echo in an empty, silent house with no one to hear them. He wondered what he would wake to every morning. Immerse himself in routine: wake, work, home, sleep, wake…

There had to be more to life than that.

He gave a wry smile and shook his head. If nothing else, his current predicament had given him valuable insight into what some of his patients must have gone through. He sat up and frowned. Now, why the hell did that thought pop into his head? He felt and hurt like everybody else, but he could not deny a level of detachment within him that made him look at himself with unsympathetic coldness. Feelings and emotions did not seem to matter. Facts, evidence, that's what life was about. Everything else was a distraction, an illusion.

He rubbed his forehead, fearful of his growing duality. Afraid of what he might be turning into. To retain his sanity, he had to confront his new self and integrate it with what he knew was his real personality. He had been aware of this creeping psychological change, or was it physiological, for some time, but refused to accept its effects rationally. Was this change a manifestation of the near miss lightning strike he feared would one day appear?

Had he started to lose himself?

He lost Daniela, their baby gone, and it looked like he would lose Lenora as well. If he lost his humanity, what would be the point of living?

Wait, his inner self told him. Sound advice. He should not work himself into a state over something that had not yet happened. Going down that path could result in a self-fulfilling event.

Dural gulped down the rest of his tepid coffee and turned to the computer. He had a patient in fifteen minutes, and that patient would not care for his problems. He scrolled down the screen, the words reflected in his memory.

A referral from A, B & S, a thirty-four-year-old partner in a law firm set up by the ACTU—Australian Council of Trade Unions—to represent workers with an employee grievance, sued her doctor for getting her hooked on opioids. Dural did not care about the law action. He had been digging through her mind to establish why she started using opioids to begin with. During their last session, he thought he had it, and his notes tended to confirm his hypothesis.

Ms. Russel hated being a lawyer, knew it, but could not bring herself to walk away from a six-figure salary that supported her comfortable lifestyle and social position. She wanted to be a journalist and a writer, but her father, a prominent barrister in his own right, threatened to disown her if she left law. To paper over her inner conflict, her GP prescribed an opioid, and now, she had two problems: addiction and a career she hated, one feeding the other.

His advice? Leave law before it destroyed her life. In time, if he had any smarts, her father would come around, and she should not worry about inheritance or social position. Those were merely gauzy trappings without substance. He did not try to dilute the difficulties she would invariably face during her transition, but with a positive frame of mind, she should overcome them. Young, smart, highly educated, she should not have too many obstacles securing a job as a legal consultant with a major newspaper chain or television network.

"Edith, decide what you want and act on it," he told her more forcefully than he intended. In a more conciliatory tone, he added, "Denial has led you to addiction and is the reason you're here now. Seek treatment at one of the clinics that specialize in opioid addiction. I'm not in a position to help you further."

When she left, Dural fixed himself a fresh cup of coffee. Sipping the fragrant brew, he wondered where Rosalyn got the beans. In all the years they've been working together, he never bothered to find out, taking it for granted like the weather.

Decide what you want…the words kept nagging at him. Disgusted, he sighed and strode out.

"Rosalyn, I need you to do something for me."

"Of course, Du."

"Please book a flight to Wellington for tomorrow morning, with a return on Saturday."

She raised an eyebrow. "I'll get it done right away. It's Mrs. Sinclair, isn't it?"

"She wants to divorce me."

Rosalyn's eyes grew huge. "I never…This is horrible."

"I want to talk her out of it before it's too late. Reschedule my patients if Leonard or Gerard can't take them. I'll fill them in over lunch."

"I hope it works out for you, Du."

He smiled weakly. "So do I."

A weight rolled off deep inside him and he strode to his office with a lighter step. He should not have allowed Lenora to walk out, but in her mood, short of restraining her forcibly, there was not all that much he could have done to stop her. Wallowing in his self-pity, did he want to stop her? Sipping his coffee, Dural decided he should have.

* * *

The Air New Zealand Airbus A320 plunged through heavy clouds and sagged into a steep starboard turn, which generated several startled gasps from the passengers. Wings rocking, the narrow-body jet leveled out and steadied as it lined up for its final approach to Wellington's Rongotai Airport.

Strapped into his aisle seat, Dural only saw glimpses of the city as the aircraft came in. He did not miss out on anything, having been here a number of times with Lenora and Daniela. Dan, of course, had to have a window seat, her face pressed against the plastic divider watching the proceedings intently despite having a camera view from the plane's entertainment system. Not the same thing, she argued. Dural admitted she had a point. They should do away with windows altogether, he mused. It would certainly simplify construction. Some of the concept designs he saw from Boeing and Airbus had cabin-long electronic panorama screens. Dan would have loved it.

He always had an aisle seat when flying, considering a window seat a superfluous indulgence and a pain if he wanted to visit the restroom or simply stretch his legs. Not a problem on a short haul, but he considered three-and-a-half hours to NZ a longer flight. The thing was, Lenora liked an aisle seat for the same reason. Solving the conundrum was simple—swap seats every two hours or so, unless both happened to have the same urge.

The aircraft dropped out of the cloud layer into patchy sunshine and Dural glanced at his new Rado watch. Tempted more than once to stop wearing the thing, as the smartphone in his pocket was able to give him a time check, but he wore it out of habit. Once it broke down, he told himself. Unfortunately, or perhaps not, good electronic watches lasted almost forever. Getting close to 2:45 pm, the flight pretty much on schedule. Still, by the time they landed and the aircraft taxied to the terminal, then having to wait for the air bridge to mate, then finally disembark, the entire trip would be around four hours. Longer if he added the time to get to Melbourne Airport, clear passport control, and then hang around to board. All that waiting and staring at duty-free stalls was enough to drive a man to drink. Not surprising then to see most airports well-endowed with bars.

One thing he did not do was use his aura trick, and he found he did not miss it. With the initial novelty worn off, he found the kaleidoscope of clashing colors emanating from a crush of people actually painful. He *did* allow himself a brief peek at an attractive passenger as they boarded, a transitory moment that did not mean anything. Everybody's libido continued to work regardless of other personal considerations.

The A320 landed with a soft crunch and Dural nodded in appreciation. Some pilots brought their aircraft down with the intention of driving the gear through the wings. Pressed against the seat when the reverse thrust kicked in, he pursed his mouth and sighed, wondering if coming had been such a good idea after all. Too late. He spent most of the flight going over various scenarios when he met Lenora, which merely reinforced his anxiety. Could they patch things up? He hoped so, but his cold part did not believe it. Well, his other self can screw himself. Life was more than logic and facts. The psychologist in him sneered. It certainly was, and lately, he'd had a bucketful of it.

No matter. Get her alone and take it from there.

Nikau Tipene met him once he cleared Customs. With only a carry-on bag, he spared himself the mind-numbing wait at a luggage carousel. The old Maori—Dural wondered why he considered him old, being only fifty-eight—embraced him, and grabbed the bag.

"Good to see you, Du. How was the flight?"

Dural shrugged. "No problems, but I wish the butterflies fluttering in my stomach would land," he said dryly, and Nikau laughed.

"What you need is a stiff shot of bourbon, and I've got just the stuff—Canadian Crown Royal, your favorite poison."

"That'll be useful. Have you seen Len?"

The older man shook his head. "She's been spending time with Audrey, but don't worry. I spoke to her briefly and it's all arranged. I invited both of them for dinner tonight. That's your chance to sort things out between you."

"Yeah. She doesn't know I'm here?"

"Not from me."

"Nikau, getting Lenora over for dinner under a false pretext might backfire on me, you know."

"We're not conspiring against her."

"You're trying to help, I know, but she might not see it that way."

"Well, you can blame me if things don't work out."

Dural suppressed a snort. That would really solve everything. He wanted a chance to talk things out with Lenora, but she might not be ready, and would naturally resented being pressured by her family.

"By the way, how long are you staying?" Nikau asked.

"I'm flying back on Saturday. I wish it were longer, Nikau, but I'm a working man and I've been neglecting my patients lately."

"Sorry as hell about all this, Du. When I spoke to Lenora, I tried to draw her out, but she wouldn't talk, and Audrey refuses to let me in on what they've been doing. I can sympathize with Lenora's point of view, and I understand where you're coming from. For what it's worth, both of you need to calm down and think seriously about the consequences of what you're doing. What's more, you need to help her get over whatever resentment she holds against you."

Dural gave a mirthless grin. "You should be in my profession."

"Talk is cheap, my boy. It's how you act that counts."

"I'll keep that in mind. By the way, thanks for meeting me," Dural said as they walked toward the parking lot. "I could have taken a cab, you know."

"Not to worry." Nikau waved a hand in dismissal. "My repair shop won't fold if I'm not around for a couple of days."

"How is Judith taking it?"

"Upset, as you can imagine. I think she spoke to Len, but she wouldn't say. I still cannot believe how Lenora flew off the handle like this. It's not like her."

No, it wasn't, Dural agreed morosely.

Despite being New Zealand's capital, Wellington was a relatively small city compared to a metropolis like Melbourne. Once Nikau steered the Corolla onto Cobhan Drive running along the coast, with the ocean on their right, the drive to Hataitai only took some ten minutes. A right turn onto Maxham Avenue, and another right up hilly Raupo Street, Nikau pulled into his drive-way. An old part of Wellington, all the plots were narrow with small, mostly weatherboard cottages. The Tipene residence must have been somewhat crowded with three growing kids, but with everyone settled elsewhere, the cozy house these days more than adequate for Nikau and Judith.

When Dural walked into the house, she was all over him with a hug and an affectionate kiss on the cheek. All smiles, wiping her face, she led him into a small lounge next to the kitchen.

"I'll put the bag into your room," Nikau declared and disappeared down the corridor.

Holding Dural at arm's length, Judith beamed. "You haven't changed a bit. A handsome rogue as always."

"And you're radiant as ever. Nikau's partner still after you?"

She giggled. "Rick is a bad man and he'll come to a gory end." She dragged him to the sofa and turned off the TV. She liked to hear some voices when she worked in the kitchen, she told him once. "You had a good flight?"

"Comfortable enough, but I wish it were under different circumstances," he said, and her face clouded.

"You youngsters don't know how to tough it out. I could have left Nikau a dozen times, but we walked it through. On the other hand, what happened to Lenora—"

"Is tragic," Nikau boomed from the bar cabinet, "and she overreacted."

Judith glared at him. "Brute! Just like a man to say that."

"It's true," Nikau said as he held out a crystal tumbler. "I would cut off my right arm to have it undone, but blaming Du is crazy."

Dural took the tumbler, raised it in a salute, and sipped. Judith patted his knee.

"Don't worry. She'll come around."

"Have you talked to her?"

"We had some words."

"And?"

She bit her lip. "I don't know. I honestly don't. Something important has been ripped out of her life and she's floundering emotionally, looking for an anchor and stability."

He stared at her. "An anchor? There are two of us living in my house, you know."

She gave a forlorn sigh, "She blames herself for losing the baby, and she's taking it out on you."

"I never blamed her for that, and I told her."

"She understands, Du, but she's distraught over Daniela. You just happened to be around as a focus for her anger, rage, and unfairness of it all."

"You never told me anything of this, Judith," Nikau remarked darkly as he lowered himself onto a padded seat.

"Because you're blaming her for everything. Both of you are." She turned to Dural. "All she wanted was a shoulder to cry on, and you weren't around when she needed you."

"Is that what she told you?" he snapped, feeling the accusation in her words cutting through him.

"Whether you realize it or not, you two were looking for excuses to blame the other, when in reality, no one is to blame."

Dural swallowed hard, not wanting an argument. "I offered to come with her, but she wanted to be alone with you. I offered to stay at home with her, but she didn't want that either. I was ready to take time off work anyway, but she stormed off, telling me she's divorcing me."

"Wanted…wanted, but you didn't do any of it, did you?" Her clear blue eyes bored into him in sentence of his guilt. "You should have just done it."

He slammed down his tumbler. "Christ almighty! So, it's all my fault, is it?"

Nikau stood, placed both fists on his hips, and stared at his wife. "You've said enough, Judith. This isn't anybody's fault, and you're being unfair to Du. Lenora has always been headstrong. She's been hurt and is lashing out at everyone close to her. Remember the argument we had when she was here? She called me an insensitive pig and said I didn't love her. She lashed out and didn't mean it. She's now lashing out at Dural, but I fear that this time, she does mean it."

Judith's look softened and she stroked Dural's shoulder. "I'm sorry, Du. I didn't mean to fly off at the handle like that, but you don't understand how women feel about these things." She glanced at Nikau. "You don't either."

Dural took a deep breath and exhaled loudly. "Then tell me what I don't understand."

"You're a successful psychologist, learned and sensitive, but you approach personal problems with logic and reason. All men do when they don't overreact. Women feel more, but often, we don't express it too well, tending to hold it inside. That's not good, because holding it inside sears the heart. When we do let it out, it tends to be verbally violent. Afterward, we're sorry, but the bridges are burnt and we don't know how to get back. Perhaps it's pride," she said wearily and shrugged.

Dural studied the older woman, marveling at the wisdom of her words. She should be the one doing psychology, he mused. All his years of study and patient treatments, he thought he understood it all. Looking back, though, everything he knew came from books and professors who were mostly men, expressing a man's perspective, the woman's real needs a mere footnote. Ironic when he thought about it. Men treating women's problems with a man's psychological template.

Did men really understand women?

He would have to dig up some texts written by women and find out.

Somewhat calmer, he picked up the tumbler, took a sip, and slowly shook his head.

"I don't know what I expected by coming here. Sympathy, a pat on the back, a promise that everything would be okay? I certainly did not expect a dressing down."

"Du—"

He raised a hand. "It's all right, Judith. You didn't say anything wrong. What do I do to make things right?"

She smiled. "Hug her when you see her."

"That's it?"

"That's it."

Dural glanced at Nikau. "Is she always like this?"

The older man grinned broadly. "Every time. If it weren't for her, I'd be another drunken bum on the waterfront. Seriously, Du. The thing with you and Len might take more than a hug."

"Yeah, but it would be a start, no?"

They spent the rest of the afternoon in much pleasanter conversation. Judith finished preparing dinner and started laying out the table, refusing their help. Nikau took Dural to the back porch and offered him a cigar. Not a smoker, he refused, but the old Maori insisted, claiming it would settle him down. Lighting up, Dural was surprised at the pleasant fragrance and the cigar's mildness. Years ago, he tried cigarettes, but it wasn't his thing. Sitting with Nikau, a glass of heavy shiraz in hand, eyes gazing over the modest backyard garden Judith cultivated lovingly, his nerves faded, and he felt more confident about seeing Lenora.

Around six, Judith poked her head from the back door. "They're here."

Crap me dead.

Nikau grinned at his expression and tapped his shoulder. "Tell her you're sorry. Women like that."

Dural felt himself emotionally sagging. Did he feel sorry for himself? Perhaps a little, he acknowledged. Feeling sorry for himself, wallowing in wounded pride, would not get his wife back.

"I'll do it. Whatever it takes."

He followed the older man down the corridor to the lounge.

Judith and her two daughters were finishing a round of hugs. Lenora turned when she heard footsteps and went pale.

"What's he doing here?" she demanded, and Dural was shaken by the intensity of the black aura cloaking her.

He slowly walked toward her and stopped. "I'm sorry, Len...for everything." He made to take her in his arms, but she stepped back and turned to Audrey.

"Take me home," she grated between clenched teeth and strode toward the front door.

"Len!" Dural cried out, his heart ripping. He heard Judith sob, but his eyes were on the only woman he ever loved, seeing her walk away from him, hatred and loathing in her heart.

"Len! Don't do this. Please!"

She opened the door and hurried out. Audrey glanced at Dural and gave a fleeting, pained look.

"I'll talk to her...again," she said, then looked at her mother. "I'm sorry, Mom."

Judith patted her arm. "It's okay, my dear. Go."

Audrey walked into her father's embrace. "Dad..."

Nikau stroked her back. "I know."

Dural heard car doors slam. A moment later, the engine kicked into life and the car pulled away. He glanced at Judith and Nikau, and walked slowly toward the back door. He sat down, picked up his glass, and swallowed the wine in two large gulps. The cigar still smoldered and he puffed it into life until the tip glowed red. Wreathed in smoke, he stared at the surrounding rooftops as dusk settled around him.

Nikau appeared, sat down, and picked up his cigar. They smoked in silence. Dural figured there wasn't much to be said. Numb, in shock, confused, angry, his emotions coursed through him.

He felt totally screwed.

"I'm leaving in the morning, Nikau," he said after what seemed a very long time.

"Why the rush? Spend the weekend. We could talk, walk around town and see the sights."

"I'm a working man, remember?"

"Not until Monday."

Dural's mouth twitched. "True."

They puffed on their cigars.

"I'll drive you to Audrey's place in the morning," Nikau said. "Maybe she'll come around."

With a surge of determination, Dural stood. "Take me there now."

Nikau looked at him for a while, then nodded. Without saying anything, they walked into the house and through the front door.

"Hey! What about dinner?" Judith cried after them.

It did not take long to reach Aro Valley, the drive spent in silence. Nikau pulled up behind Audrey's Mazda and they walked to the entrance. She gaped when she opened the door.

"Where is she?" Dural demanded.

"In the kitchen."

He nodded and pushed past her.

"But—"

Nikau shook his head and held her back.

Dural found her with a glass in her hand, a bottle at her side, her expression stony. When she saw him, her orange aura immediately turned black, bordered by a brown halo of confusion and uncertainty.

"What do you want?" she grated.

Dural did not say anything as he walked toward her. He paused, leaned over her, and gathered her in his arms. God, how he missed her! Missed her warmth, her love, and being with her.

She stiffened and sat there. He pulled back and searched her eyes.

"Tell me what you want and I'll do it."

"I want you to go away. We don't have anything anymore. You took it all."

His eyes misted and he blinked back the sting. "You can't mean it. We have each other. Doesn't that count for something?"

"It used to once, but not now."

"I love you, Len."

"You love yourself."

Her eyes were empty. Something to see with without revealing anything inside. Not even hate. Eyes of a stranger.

"I can't give you up."

She didn't say anything, turned, grasped her glass, and gazed at a white wall.

He straightened and looked at her, not believing this could be the end. Everything they had, everything they shared, dreams and hopes, it all lay in ashes at his feet. Cold like her heart. Her aura told him everything he did not want to know. This blackness was her, not some subconscious manifestation.

He walked out, nodded to Audrey, and slowly made his way to the car.

Darkness had settled and took him in its embrace.

* * *

Four-thirty when the cab dropped him off. Light rain followed him all the way from the airport through the city. If nothing else, he gained three hours in the shuffle with time zones. It did not make up for the loss he left in Wellington. Would he ever get her back? The portents did not look hopeful.

Fuck it all!

Across the street, Mrs. Parker stuck out her head from behind a three-meter holly bush.

"Dr. Sinclair! Away again? I haven't seen Lenora in a while. Sick or something?"

"Visiting her parents in Wellington!" Dural shouted. Saying anything more and the whole suburb would know it. She simply could not help gossiping. He waved at her and unlocked the front door. Inside, he dropped the carry-on and deactivated the alarm, then switched on the heating system to drive away the deep chill that had settled over the house. Even with the heating on, he doubted the chill would go away anytime soon.

Still feeling sorry for yourself, Doctor?

He felt damn sorry for himself and did not mind admitting it. Screw everybody. Screw the world.

Nikau and Judith were supportive and tried to cheer him up; telling him it would all work out, knowing it was a lie. Who were they kidding? He had his talks with Nikau, a walk through Wellington and the seafront, but there wasn't any fun in it. Dural was glad when Saturday arrived and he headed home.

In time, Lenora might come around. He hoped so. If she did not...

Life would go on without her. An empty, shallow life without laughter, music or song, but it would be a life. He would adjust.

He showered, changed into casual clothes, and went downstairs to fix himself a drink. Not feeling like eating, the meal served on the plane adequate, he sprawled onto the couch and sipped his whiskey.

"Hell of a day, Du," he mumbled and gave a heavy sigh.

Without willing it, he replayed all recent conversations with Lenora, picking over her words, gestures, and expressions. He had done this before, and his effort now did not reveal anything new he could have done to keep her. Memories, all he had left. It would have to do.

He caught up on the latest news, then unpacked his carry-on and went to bed with Mary Stewart's *The Hollow Hills*, the second book in her Merlin story. *The Crystal Cave* absolutely enchanting, but *Hills* had a special magic that captivated him. Right now, he could use a little magic in his life. A fresh drink at his side, snuggled under the doona, he began to read.

Bright sunshine splashed the bedroom with color when he

woke. Feeling lazy, he clasped his hands behind his head and luxuriated in the warm bed. He had nowhere he needed to go and nothing to do, except a little washing and housecleaning.

A rough outline for a book had bubbled in the background for a while, but he simply had not the time for necessary research, preparing a detailed outline, and actually writing the thing. He did have a title, though, *Stress Management in the Modern World*—a broad brush that covered a multitude of disciplines, but he thought of a subtitle, *A Woman's Perspective*. He bit his lip and nodded. Yes, that would do nicely. Given recent events with Lenora and what Judith said, he needed to understand that perspective far better. He wanted to write the book not only for personal enlightenment, but to serve as a driver to change the established mindset of practicing colleagues. Dealing with men was easy. He could relate directly with their problems. Women, on the other hand, wanted most of all to be treated as equals, with the same feelings, desires, hopes, dreams, as any man. They process things differently, because their brains are structured differently, but that in no way made them inferior or less capable. On reflection, he feared that on more than one occasion, some of his automatic assumptions might have caused him to adopt an inappropriate approach and treatment of his female patients.

He figured his eidetic memory would come in very handy on this project. First thing, though, he needed to dig up books written by female psychologists—he had two or three already in his library—to formulate a mental framework. Monash University had an extensive collection, and so did Melbourne Uni.

In the meantime, he had ideas for two short stories to add to his anthology—and now time to write them.

Morning chores done, he drove to Prahran Market to pick up fresh fruit and veggies. With Lenora gone, he would have to roll up his sleeves and put in some serious cooking time. He wasn't bad at it, but he could not compare his amateurish efforts with her expertise. Start with simple things and work up, he told himself comfortably.

Monday served him another gorgeous day: clear, sunny, without a breath of wind. He walked to work with a distinct bounce in his step, a hearty bacon omelet, and two cups of ground coffee ensuring a great start. Even Rosalyn noted his cheery mood when he strode in.

"My, something good must have happened to you, Du."

"It's all doom and gloom," he told her, "but I refuse to be beaten."

Her face clouded. "Mrs. Sinclair—"

"Still hates me and wants to divorce me."

"I'm sorry to hear that."

He waved a hand. "One of life's shitty deals. Anything I need to know for the morning meeting?"

"Nothing in particular."

"Good."

"Dr. Stockton handled one of your patients on Thursday, and Dr. Morton did one on Friday, but I had to reschedule three for later this week."

"I'll thank them later."

Dural snagged a mug of coffee from the kitchenette and walked to his consulting room. He took a sip and powered up his computer.

"Bring it on," he murmured as he checked over Leonard and Gerard's notes on his patients. He quickly went over the list of emails and sent several replies.

At nine, everyone settled in the meeting room, Rosalyn opened the proceedings by reading the previous minutes.

"Our revenue is a little down—"

"My fault, and I apologize," Dural said and tugged his right ear. "As of today, I am back on deck full-time." He looked at each of them in turn. "You all know what has been going on in my personal life lately. Last week, I went to Wellington hoping to sort it out with Lenora. Unfortunately, the trip did not end well, and she's determined to divorce me."

Leonard and Gerard exchanged glances.

"I want to thank each one of you for your support. I may not have said it already, but it was appreciated…and will continue to be appreciated." He looked at Rosalyn and nodded.

She cleared her throat. "I speak for all of us, Du, and I want to say we're all devastated by this news. Let us know if there is anything we can do to help."

Gerard pushed up his glasses and nodded. "Absolutely."

"With you all the way, Du," Leonard added.

"Thanks guys. I mean it."

Rosalyn straightened her pile of papers. "As you know, the practice faces potential legal action from Mrs. Fullham, represented by Parker and Associates. Dr. Sinclair has an initial meeting with them tomorrow at eleven."

"Any potential problems?" Leonard asked, and Dural shook his head.

"Paul Becker will be at the meeting. I understand he already discussed the case with Parker *et al*, and I expect tomorrow's meeting will be the end of it."

Gerard nodded. "Going over your notes, Du, I tent to concur. Still, these things are a damned nuisance and jack up our liability insurance."

"Can't be helped," Leonard said.

"Any other points?" Rosalyn added.

"I have something," Dural said and looked at Ger and Len. "I'm planning a book that deals with a range of female psychological problems, with a special emphasis on presenting a woman's point of view, which my initial research has shown to be grossly unrepresented. Both of you have extensive experience in the field, although not necessarily with female patients. If either of you want to contribute, I'm happy to make this a collaborative project."

His two partners looked at each other and grinned.

"I'm in," Leonard said. "Give me a chapter breakdown once you have your topics defined and I'll write something. I may add a topic or two myself."

"Same for me," Gerard agreed.

"You'll have it." Dural nodded to Rosalyn. "I'm done."

The rest of the meeting went quickly, mostly dry business things.

Leonard snagged him outside the meeting room.

"I get suspicious when I see you bright and chipper, Du, considering."

Dural chuckled. "Frankly, old buddy, I'm all torn up inside, and I want to punch the next guy I see. Not a good idea, though. I'll just have to muddle through, but thanks for your concern."

Leonard patted his shoulder. "Whatever you need, you know that."

"You're a good friend, Len, and so is Ger. I'll yell before I swallow that bottle of sleeping pills."

"Do that," Len said and made his way to the kitchenette.

In his office, mug at his side, going over notes for his next patient, Dural sighed.

Life can be a real bitch sometimes, he decided.

On his way home, he wondered what Lenora thought right then. Did she walk along the waterfront, watch surf crash against the wet sands? Was she alone in her room staring at nothing? Did she think about him, reconsidering? Was there anything he could do to get her back? Hard to see what with her in NZ.

She wanted him to share his grief with her, without judgement, without being told the one and only way to deal with it was getting on with her life. Jumping back into a normal work routine had not been the best choice for her, and he'd been too thick to see her side. He knew well that people experience and handle grief differently. Anger and denial were part of it. If Lenora had taken Daniela home that day and witnessed the accident, Dural might have experienced anger and resentment against her. A natural reaction. Perhaps, but cold clinical analysis did not help him much here.

If he had his choice, he would prefer having telepathy instead of seeing people's aura. What if he could not turn off the flood of thought from billions around him? On reflection, perhaps seeing someone's aura was not such a bad thing after all. It was a *kind* of telepathy.

"The girl needs time," Nikau told him gently as they sipped wine at the airport.

That really helped, Dural thought moodily.

Yesterdays happen with no regard for tomorrow.

Pedestrians hurried on both sides of High Street, and the line of cars streaming out of town had slowed to a crawl. What were all those people thinking? Did they even think, or did they simply run on automatic, anxious to get home or to wherever they were going? Too much thinking, that was the problem, and the cause of most neuroses. Better not to think. Just work, come home, work, snatch a moment of happiness here and there, and hope fates don't smear him beneath their feet.

He turned into Trinion Street and home. An empty, silent home.

The meeting with Anthony Parker of Parker and Associates the next morning did not take long. Paul Becker handed Parker a slim folder containing transcripts of Dural's notes and DVD recordings of Mrs. Fullham's consultations, and sat back.

"You can take Dr. Sinclair and Gap Psychology Consulting to court, Mr. Parker, but you'll be wasting your time and your client's money. I understand you work on a contingency fee, with a $2,000 retainer and forty percent of any settlement."

Parker cleared his throat and pulled down his coat lapels, his initial bravado somewhat deflated. Clearly aware of Paul's reputation and standing with Arnold, Becker and Strong, he appeared to be reconsidering the whole matter.

"An outright settlement, Mr. Becker. Forty thousand dollars."

Paul grinned. "You don't have a case, Mr. Parker. If you think otherwise, serve us with a writ and I'll see you in court."

"Humph! If that's your position…" Parker slipped the folder into a slim briefcase, rose, and made his way out without looking at Dural.

Paul leaned back and shook his head with wry amusement. "I doubt we'll be hearing from Parker and Associates anytime soon."

"You know him?" Dural ventured.

"I know of him. We were both at the Victorian Law Association function once and one of my colleagues pointed him out. Small-time suburban lawyer who competently stops at handling domestic issue cases, car bender claims, and minor industrial accidents. With you, he doesn't have a case and knows it. He tried to shake you down."

"What if he brings in a heavy hitter like Maurice Blackburn Lawyers?"

"They would throw him out the door. Trust me. We're done here."

Dural escorted his friend to the elevator. "Thanks for handling this, Paul."

"That's what you pay me for."

Thankfully, the rest of the day far less exciting.

That evening, feeling inspirational, he decided to start writing one of his short stories. Pen in hand, a Mozart symphony playing in the background, he stared at the blank A4 pad. He always wrote the initial manuscript longhand, and then transcribed it into the computer. He tried composing directly into the computer, but it didn't work for him. The words seemed to flow more easily with a pen in hand.

He met her at Moonport, he wrote, and gave a sardonic grin. A variation of his first encounter with Lenora, but he planned a more satisfying ending for his hero.

Once he started, the words poured out with a satisfying glow of creation. After six pages, he rubbed his eyes and decided to call it a night, happy with the result. Another session or two and he would have it done. After some editing and polishing, he would add the story to his anthology, but would not publish the revised book until he had the second story written. Publishing on Amazon Kindle, Smashwords, and IngramSpark was easy. The ongoing grind of marketing on social media outlets wore him down. That is probably why he did so little of it, but he did not write to make a fortune. He wrote because he was driven by a fire deep inside him. A fire he could not quench. Not that he wanted to.

Despite feeling good about the writing he had done, sleep did not come easily that night.

On the way home on Friday, he stopped at the post office to pick up mail from his private box. Having a box was handy. It stopped the flood of useless advertising he would otherwise have to endure, although Lenora did not agree with him, keen to check out the latest specials. He compromised by installing a metal cylinder on the fence for junk mail, and hawkers took advantage of it. With Lenora gone, he should take the thing down. His eyebrows rose when he saw the sender's address on the slim white envelope: Wellard, Wellard and Starke. He never heard of them, but he could smell lawyer ink when he saw it.

Resisting temptation to open the envelope, dark thoughts followed him home. It looked like Lenora was determined to go through with it. Mouth tight, he walked into the house, threw the mail on the kitchen benchtop, and went upstairs to change.

With a glass of mild Pinot Grigio at his elbow, he tore open the envelope. He quickly scanned the documents, shook his head, pulled out his cell, and pressed an icon in his contacts list.

"Hi, Dural. What's up?"

"Apologies for calling you after hours, Paul, but I need your help again."

"Oh? Another lawsuit?"

"I wish. This is personal. I received a divorce Affidavit of Service from Wellard, Wellard and Starke."

"Wellard, eh? A reputable bunch."

"It's Lenora."

"Shit, sorry to hear that. Have you signed the Acknowledgment of Service?"

"I just finished reading the accompanying letter."

"Don't do anything. I'll send a courier to pick up the documents. How do you want to handle this?"

"As amicably as possible. She has no claim on my property at Nelson Bay, my partnership with Gap Psychology Consulting, or any other asset I acquired prior to our marriage. If she wants sixty percent of our Prahran house and my shares portfolio, I won't fight it, but I keep the house. That's not negotiable."

"You're being generous. Let me look over the papers, and we'll discuss this in detail. I'll text you a meeting time. Probably sometime on Monday afternoon. Suits?"

"'Twere best done quickly, as someone said," Dural agreed.

"No way this can be patched up?"

"Believe me, Paul, I tried."

Dural heard a heavy exhale, which about summed up his own feelings.

"I have been your business manager ever since you started work at The Alfred, and I know everything you've been up to financially. Do I?"

Dural chuckled. "You do, you shyster."

"Asset disclosure must be total, Du."

"I understand."

"I'll have a talk with Wellard and aim for an informal settlement. Dragging this through the divorce court won't do anyone much good."

"Agreed."

"Take care, Du. I'll see you on Monday."

When the connection broke, he placed the cellphone on the benchtop and took a long swallow of wine. It seemed the appropriate thing to do.

Time drifted aimlessly, as did his thoughts. Lenora was actually leaving him. It hardly seemed real. After nine years being together, sharing everything, loving each other, overcoming the hard times, and enjoying the good times, it had all fallen apart. Glass in hand, he stared at the dark TV, dark like the night outside, seeing in it the unwinding of his life. He topped up his glass and sat there thinking of nothing, everything, shattered tomorrows, lost dreams.

Thick silence followed him as he walked heavily up the lonely stairs into the lonely bedroom…alone.

* * *

Dural closed the door after him and locked it. He shook off his loafers and slid his feet into leather slippers. Looking at them, he tried to remember when he got the things, but the memory did not come. It had been a while, and they seemed to last and last, showing no sign of serious wear apart from some scuff-marks.

After a fresh breeze outside, he relished the warmth inside the house, the heating system having automatically switched on at five to make the place toasty. Winter was slowly loosening its grip and leaves were sprouting in earnest, which added pleasant greenery to barren branches. September could still be nasty, but the bitter southerlies had subsided. He looked forward to spring and a chance to take more frequent walks. Going to the gym not the same thing.

He made his way upstairs and changed into black jeans and a loose navy surplus sweater. His footsteps sounded loud as he walked down. Everything sounded loud these days in the hollow rooms. No voices, laughter, banging of doors, cries of pain, or shrieks of joy…empty house. Empty life. He lived in a shell of yesterdays, and he could not break into tomorrow, and did not want to. The yesterdays still held him fast. For now, he preferred his yesterdays to the silent, empty tomorrows. It would take time for the scabs to dry and fall off. Until then, they were a poignant reminder of the wounds they covered. The surface scabs might fall off, and outwardly at least, he would appear whole again, but the gashes inside him would continue to bleed for some time to come.

That is where the negative side of his eidetic memory showed itself. He could not forget. Others could forget as time softened the pain, leaving behind the laughter and the joy, enabling the body to heal, to move on. For him that path was closed because he could not forget. He kept picking at the scabs and they bled. Eventually, he would compartment the hurt and walk into tomorrow, but he could not do that yet. Not yet.

After the divorce, it took a few weeks before he began to feel somewhat comfortable without Lenora being around. He had a routine, and it helped him compartment memories he could never forget. Not that he wanted to forget, but the memories did not haunt him anymore. Life went on, and it carried him with it.

In the kitchen, he opened the fridge and took out a pot of veal stew he made yesterday. He ladled a helping into a frypan and placed it on the cooktop. Waiting for the thing to simmer, he started the percolator. He poured the hot stew into a bowl and carried it to the dining table. A crusty roll and coffee at his side, he began to eat, not thinking about anything in particular. Finished, he washed up, poured himself a snifter of cognac, and sprawled onto the couch. He switched on the TV and watched news on the ABC.

A kid and three of his mates had stolen a car and wrapped it around a tree. Two of his mates were killed and the other seriously injured. The kid walked away with a broken arm and a lacerated side. Dural sighed and shook his head, wondering what ghosts would haunt the kid for the rest of time. One careless moment, that is all it took to destroy four families.

When a clip of parliament Question Time came on, Prime Minister Malcolm Turnbull and the Opposition leader Bill Shorten verbally slugging at each other, Dural had enough and switched off, not in the mood for more stupidity.

Silence returned and he sat there nursing his cognac.

What now? Watch a DVD, search Netflix for something, or read a book perhaps? He could work on his new book, Gerard and Leonard had already contributed articles, but his heart was not in it. Right then, reading a book sounded like a good idea. He would pick one of his old favorites, top up his snifter, crawl into bed, and go pleasantly to pieces for the night.

He walked to the bookshelf and browsed through the stacked volumes. Larry Niven's *Protector* caught his eye and he pulled out the slim book. Dated by today's standards, it was one of Niven's better early works and eminently readable. Book in one hand and cognac in the other, he started for the stairs.

The doorbell chimed and he turned, a frown creasing his forehead. Somebody wanting to sell him a new gas or electricity plan? Mrs. Parker after a cup of sugar? He placed the snifter and book on the coffee table and walked toward the door.

Lenora stood there in a cream turtleneck sweater and black jeans. Her violet eyes regarded him without expression, mouth set in a tight line, glistening black hair draped across her left breast. Shades of red and orange smeared her aura, clinging tight around her like a protective shield. She licked her lips and shifted her feet.

He stood there, his hungry eyes taking her in, wanting desperately to embrace her.

"Can I talk to you for a minute, Du?" Her husky contralto set off a cascade of pleasant memories.

Wondering what brought her, never expecting to see her again, he stepped aside and extended a hand. "Come in."

She hesitated, walked into the lounge, and swept her eyes around the familiar layout. "You haven't changed anything."

"Did you expect me to throw it all away?"

She winced and Dural kicked himself for being an idiot.

"That was thoughtless. I'm sorry. Care to sit down? Coffee or some wine perhaps? I have a bottle of chardonnay in the fridge."

"Nothing, thank you." She made her way slowly to the couch and gingerly sat on its edge, hands clasped tight in her lap. He took the soft seat opposite the table, picked up his snifter and sipped.

Looking at her enchanting features, the soft lips, the deep pools of her lavender eyes, he felt a tug of desire. He could not help it. She had captured his heart long ago and he could not shut her out. Not yet. Maybe he never would. One of those things that tomorrow might reveal.

Muddy blue hues clouded her aura. Clearly nervous, she kept shifting her gaze.

"How have you been?" he asked at length before the silence became too awkward.

She gave a small smile. "Not too good. The last couple of months…"

"I know."

"And you?"

"Day by day." He searched her face. "I missed you."

"And I missed you," she whispered, her eyes misting.

Her answer surprised him. When they met for the last time at Wellard lawyers, she barely looked at him, sitting rigid and cold, cloaked in hate.

"Are you back at work?"

She nodded. "The project goes on…and life goes on."

"It does, despite everything," he agreed. "Still at ANZ?"

"Still."

"You have your own place now?"

"I'm renting a rundown terrace in Richmond. It's only temporary until I find something I can buy. Being staff, ANZ will give me a good rate on a loan."

"I'm glad you're settled now."

She cleared her throat. "Can I have that chardonnay, please? This is more difficult than I thought it would be."

"What is it? If you have come to pick up some things, you've already taken everything."

"It's not that."

Dural stood and strode into the kitchen. He poured a glass of icy wine and walked back into the lounge. She took the glass, gulped down half the wine, and gave a sheepish smile.

"I needed that."

"I can see." Dural crossed his arm. "Why did you come, Lenora?"

Her aura flared in shades of brown agitation.

"Because I missed you, Du," she whispered, clutching the glass to her belly. "After Daniela…I went crazy for a while and I took it out on you. I hated you with a sick hate, and I hated myself, but I couldn't change what was happening. I wanted to hurt you, and divorcing you was my revenge. And I did hurt you. I could see it in your eyes during the divorce proceedings, and I was glad you suffered." She took another gulp of wine. "You had taken everything I valued in life, and I took from you what you valued most…me. I thought my revenge complete and I would move on. For a while, my work kept me busy, kept me from thinking, from remembering, but then the lonely nights came. After a while, the taste of revenge became bitter and I realized I had nothing but silence. By walking away from you, I threw away the last thing that also mattered to me. I had my settlement, but I had nothing."

"I had those silent nights myself," Dural said softly, "and they're still with me."

She glanced at the book on the table. "Niven?"

A ghost of a smile tugged the corner of his mouth. "Some light reading before I turn in. I didn't feel like watching TV or a movie."

She fiddled with the stem of her glass. "Do you miss her?"

The wound inside him ripped and bled, and he clenched his fists. She saw that and winced.

"I shouldn't—"

"I miss her, Len. I miss her desperately. If I could, I would do anything to give her back to you. I would give my life."

"I know that…now."

"You don't know how sorry I was when you miscarried. I tried to tell you, but you pushed me away."

"It was my last chance to have something—"

"And I took that from you as well. In my own way, I also pushed you away." He snorted with painful regret. "And I thought I knew it all."

She reached across the table and touched his hand, and he felt the old tingle race up his arm. "You didn't. I did that to myself."

"Thank you for saying that," he whispered, but the pain inside him still burned.

"If only we could turn back time," she moaned and her eyes filled. She sniffed and blinked rapidly.

He sighed and nodded. "If only, but we can't." He took another sip. "Why did you come, Len?"

"To turn back time," she said firmly, her aura flaring bright yellow.

Her words churned his emotions. It would be like before, he told himself. She would be his again, and they would…

They would what? Things could never be the same again. Daniela gone, the baby gone, and Lenora gone as well, at least the one he knew and loved. The Lenora who sat here no longer the woman he loved. A shell from his yesterdays.

"Too many burnt bridges, Len," he said after an endless time.

"We can rebuild them, Du," she insisted, eyes boring into him.

Eyes he could never resist.

"You had time to think things through before we finalized the divorce. You didn't have to rush it. I wanted to give you all the time you needed to sort yourself out, but you didn't want to wait. It's too late now. The fire has died."

"Has it, Du? You're saying the fire has died, but your eyes are telling me something else. You still want me. I can tell."

"I would be lying if I said I didn't want you, but the wife I want is gone. I want a memory, but I cannot have what you can no longer give me."

She grasped his hand with fierce determination. "I can, Du! I'm still the same."

"You're not. Neither of us is anymore. Too many burnt bridges."

"We can start over! I admit it might take some time, but we can work things out. I cannot let you go, Du. I still love you."

"With Daniela's ghost and the ghost of your baby in the same room with us?"

Her features broke and fat tears slid down her cheeks. "They'll always be with us," she choked, "but that doesn't mean they have to haunt us."

Dural's cold, calculating self surfaced, and he gazed at Lenora with detachment. After years of comfortable, secure marriage, she found life alone tough and wanted the old security back. Being alone not as satisfying as she had imagined. She has the revenge she wanted and all the bitterness that went with it. He didn't need her. He didn't need her presence to remind him every day what she had taken away. He had his life...and the silence, and the empty rooms.

Her tears touched something he wanted to bury, but couldn't, and he could not be so cruel and insensitive to rip her apart with cold rejection. He reached with his finger and brushed her wet cheek.

"It wouldn't work, Len," he said gently. "It would be a

doomed future. What happened has changed both of us. Pretending otherwise is an exercise in delusion. We cannot turn back time, simple as that."

"And there is nothing I can do or say to make you want to even try?"

He reached for her hand and held it tight. "It's too late. You made it too late when you signed the divorce papers. You didn't have to do that."

"I made a mistake, Du!" she cried out in desperation. "You want to condemn me for that? You want to condemn yourself?"

"You didn't make a mistake. You made a choice."

"And you cannot forgive me, is that it?"

Dural sighed, wanting the pressing weight on his chest to roll off.

"I understand what you did and why, and I wish it were otherwise, but I have nothing to forgive. You did what you thought was right for yourself regardless of consequences. Life is a one-way street, Len, and both of us have crossed the intersection." He slowly shook his head. "I cannot go back."

She arched her eyebrows. "Wounded pride?"

He gave a wan smile. "If it were only that simple. When you left, you tore out something deep within me, and the hole is only now beginning to fill. I wish I could say that you can fill it, but I can't. I cannot love you the way I did before, and I don't know if I could fall in love with who you are now. The old you would always be between us, and I'm not sure I could handle two of you in my life. If you want, you can blame my cursed eidetic memory for that!" he grated harshly. "I'm sorry, Len. More than you know."

She searched his eyes. "That's it, then? You want to doom both of us?"

"I would like to think that I'm giving you a fresh start."

She pursed her lips and exhaled slowly. "A fresh start..." After a time, she placed the glass on the table and stood. "My revenge was not as sweet as I imagined it would be."

"It never is," he said and rose.

A faint smile creased her cheek. "If this is for keeps, can I kiss you one last time?"

He opened his arms and she sobbed as she walked into his embrace. Her soft mouth opened and he crushed her lips with his. Their tongues danced in abandon and flames roared around him. Gods, did he want to walk away from her?

After what seemed like an eternity, he pulled away. He cupped her face between his hands and kissed the tip of her nose.

"If only we *could* turn back time."

She sniffed and nodded. "I thought we could, but I was being selfish. If it means anything, I don't hate you anymore."

"Walk in peace, Len."

"Goodbye, Du."

She turned abruptly and hurried toward the front door. A blast of cold air made him shiver when it closed after her and silence crept into the house.

Lenora!

Not too late, he told himself. He could still run after her, and she would be his again. All he had to do was go after her. To his horror, his feet remained rooted. They could not bring back yesterday, simple as that.

The damn bridges…

Her scent lingering around him, he picked up her glass and took it to the kitchen. He washed it and placed it onto the drying tray. The weight on his chest hung heavy, and he still bled inside after he thought the wounds had scabbed over. What a crock. The gods were laughing at him, but he failed to get the joke.

He refilled his snifter, picked up *Protector*, and slowly walked up the stairs to yesterday's echoes.

Chapter Six

Leonard bit his lower lip as he glared at the 7th green guarded by three bunkers as though it was an enemy to overcome. His ball safely on the fairway some fifteen meters from the flag. He swung the club back and forth a couple of times, then placed the head behind the ball. With a glance at the flag, he slowly swung back and followed through the strike. The ball soared neatly and fell about a meter from the flag, rolled, and stopped a hand's width from the cup. He turned and grinned with evident satisfaction.

"Top that, partner."

Dural sighed and shook his head. "Crap me dead. Good shot, Len."

His own ball was on the putting green some three meters from the hole. He would have to sink it to make par, leaving Leonard with a simple tap in for his.

He pulled out the putter from the bag and ambled toward the green. The Albert Park Lake shimmered in dawn's golden light. Two skiffs were tacking to catch a faint breeze, their white sails bright. A lone canoer stroked briskly to make the far shore. Melbourne's jagged skyline glowed under the sun's glare, which promised another hot day. March weather can be finicky, but 2019 had delivered a long, hot summer, showing no sign of abating. Dural loved hot weather, not caring much for winter's rain and Antarctic winds.

Still early—not even seven—the course practically deserted, but would fill quickly as the morning wore on. By afternoon, players would be queuing at tees waiting to start. Dural preferred playing on Saturday mornings when people still had shopping and other chores to do. He disliked the feeling of being rushed. Sundays were patchy, as a lot of players chose to come early to avoid the crush that inevitably ensued later.

He stepped on the hard green and waited for Leonard to mark his ball. Dural's was above the hole and had a slight right to left drop. He could either tap in gently allowing for the curve, or strike firmly, speed overcoming the tendency to curve. Of course, if he missed, the ball would run past the hole, leaving him with a bogey on his scorecard. He glanced at Leonard leaning on his putter and smiled.

"Watch this."

"I'm watching."

Dural scowled. "Don't enjoy yourself too much."

"And why shouldn't I enjoy myself? It's a gorgeous morning, we have the course virtually to ourselves, and my partner is about to fumble it, which by the way, will make me two up." Leonard took a deep breath and exhaled slowly. "Yes, sir. A great morning if I say so myself."

"Enjoy yourself, then," Dural growled and lined up his putter behind the ball.

He measured the distance to the cup and fixed his eyes on the ball. He swung back and struck it with a sharp tap, keeping his head down. He looked up and watched the ball speed toward the cup, catch the right lip, spin around, and clatter into the hole. Grinning from ear to ear, he tilted his head at Leonard.

"Well, smart boy?"

Leonard winced and shrugged. "A lucky shot. That's all." He tapped his in and they marked their scorecard.

At the short par three 8th tee, Dural pulled out a four iron from his bag and made a couple of practice swings as Leonard prepared to make his drive.

"Gerard on board for tomorrow?" Dural asked as he eyed the dry fairway. The Club watered the course, but persistent northerlies had reduced the lush grass to scrawny brown shoots. A little rain and it would come back.

"All set," Leonard declared. "I cannot wait to see Rosalyn's face, or Suyin's."

"Me too," Dural agreed. "I'm still betting that Rosalyn will refuse."

"Ten bucks on it?"

"You're on, but I won't mind losing. She deserves it."

"Agreed. The practice can afford to move them up."

"Talking about our new partner, have you been watching Gerard?"

"Our love-struck boy? I certainly have. Who would have thought it. The crusty, unshakeable bachelor felled by a Chinese beauty. Do him good, I say." Leonard made two trial swings and gave Dural a quizzical look. "You could do with a change yourself, my friend."

"I had my fling, old buddy. After four years on the singles bench, I am firmly off the market."

"Don't close the door yet. It can strike from the blue."

Dural laughed. "I've already been struck once, remember? And on this very course. I'm not anxious for a repeat demonstration, thank you. I might not be as lucky."

Leonard leaned on his three wood driver. Somewhat short, he did not have the driving range Dural had, but he made up for that slight impediment with a cunning short game.

"I still cannot believe how quickly it all happened. A lecture at Melbourne Uni, boy meets girl, he talks her into taking a job at The Alfred's Therapeutic Brain Stimulation division, and now, she's a partner."

It did happen quickly, Dural admitted. Meng Suyin, thirty-four, divorced, a bright eight-year-old daughter, a PhD in Clinical Psychology, the serenely beautiful woman with a jade face brought Gap Consulting a stream of Chinese and Asian patients. Initially taken on as a part-time associate, her revenue-earning value and professionalism quickly recognized, and six months ago, they made her a half-share partner.

What he did not expect was the change in Gerard. Slightly overweight, not interested in outdoor activities of any sort, considering them a waste of his time, preferring to bury himself in the practice and the Psychiatry Research Center. Since he met Suyin, he became a changed man. He lost weight, started an exercise program, and fluttered around the woman as though attached to her with a rope. What she thought of his advances was hard to say, because during business hours, she was a model of unflappable professionalism. However, the looks they exchanged, and how they talked to each other, she appeared to like the attention.

"Something is brewing between them, all right, and I'm glad," Dural said. "They definitely have more than a casual workplace friendship."

"Suyin will sort him out. The chipper way Gerard walks around these days, he appears to think so himself."

"We'll have to get him a set of clubs," Dural declared, and Leonard chuckled.

The few times Gerard struggled with an uncooperative ball produced much amusement for everybody, but to give him credit, their partner kept at it and started to enjoy himself as his skill improved. Dural pictured him on a fairway with Suyin as his caddie and grinned. They made a fine couple.

Leonard positioned himself, glanced at the green 141 meters away, and swung back. The club made a sweet click with the ball, and Dural watched it arc gracefully to land on the green.

"Good shot," he said.

"It'll do," Leonard said and pocketed the tee. "I'm anxious to see you top it."

"Watch and learn," Dural growled and positioned his ball. His shot clean and crisp, and the ball landed two meters or so from the flag. He glanced at Leonard. "You'll have to make birdie to beat that, partner."

"Watch me," Leonard declared confidently.

Dural bagged his club, not sure he wanted to broach this. However, the situation had been developing for too long and he wanted to lance the problem before it became serious.

"Len, about Suyin…"

"What about her?"

"You may not even know that you're doing it, but ever since she joined the practice, you've been hovering around her in a way that's more than professional courtesy."

Leonard's aura flared dark orange, indicating repressed emotion.

"You're crazy! We had an occasional coffee together, but there is nothing in it. I'm only being friendly."

"If you say so, but you're the one dragging his tongue on the floor."

Leonard thought about that for a moment, his aura muddy green of insecurity. "Perhaps I *have* been somewhat overly attentive around her, but no more than you."

"Gerard doesn't know a thing about women, and he could misunderstand things."

"Christ, Du! Now you've put me off my game." Leonard shook a finger at him. "What's more, I think you did it on purpose, you bastard."

"Don't say I didn't warn you."

Rolling the bag carts behind them, they slowly made their way down the fairway. Dural had planted the seed of warning, and hoped it would sprout. The practice did not need that kind of internal disruption…if there was something to it.

On Sunday, Dural went all out and cooked an elaborate lunch. He did not do it often, but waking that morning, he felt in the mood. On occasion, he liked to invite his partners for a Saturday dinner. After overcoming her initial reluctance, even Rosalyn came sometimes. Married now with an irrepressible thirty-month freckled, pigtailed daughter—Gap Consulting paid for her daycare at the Alfred Childcare Center—Rosalyn the hub around which the other partners revolved. One time, she brought her husband. Evans Pickering was a construction manager for Grollo, and the things he told them about building a high-rise left everybody doubled with laughter. How the two happened to meet, fall in love, and marry, Dural did not know, and Rosalyn never said. Their business, he decided.

Monday morning warm with a blustery northerly likely to make it a lot warmer. Dural had his air-conditioning going through most of the twenty-five-degree night. He walked to work, a light gabardine jacket slung over his shoulder. Patients, everybody agreed, wanted reassurance and clinical professionalism, which a rolled up sleeve and open collar would not engender. Still, the tight business dress code was slowly changing, but not in his profession. Dural did not mind. His patients paid a lot and expected a lot.

He filled his mug with coffee and made his way to the meeting room. After a nod to Gerard and Leonard, he sat at his usual place near the end and sipped. Rosalyn straightened her paperwork and glanced at the wall clock. Suyin rushed in, mumbled an apology, and sat beside Gerard.

Dressed in black pants and business jacket, raven hair glittering as it fell straight to her waist—she normally had it tied in a bun—her clear white complexion had a trace of blush after rushing to make the nine o'clock meeting. Her small mouth framed with restrained red lipstick, a trace of blue eyeshadow, perfectly complemented her large black eyes. She caused heads to turn wherever she walked. Looking at her serene features, Dural was not surprised that she managed to turn Gerard's head.

Rosalyn cleared her throat. "All of you have appointments, so I'll keep this short. You can get the details from PAX." She read last week's minutes, which Leonard seconded, then followed with a financial report for March.

"The billable hours are up by fourteen percent on February. After partner drawings and expenses, we have a net profit of $11,780. As you know, Dr. Sinclair has an appointment with the NSW Police and will not be available tomorrow. However, Victoria Police will provide adequate compensation for his services."

Dural had not been keen to waste his time on a small white-collar scam case, but Inspector Frank Farmer from Finance & Cyber Crime turned out to be very persuasive. The Director of Public Prosecutions wanted to drop what they considered a minor case at best, happy to let the Australian Securities and Investments Commission handle it, but Farmer was convinced that Dural could break the perpetrator. He hated to let a criminal slip through his fingers, small or large. Reluctantly, Dural agreed to interview the suspect. He only had two patients tomorrow, and Rosalyn rescheduled them.

Philip Kresta worked as a senior accountant for Galloway Investments, a small-time firm specializing in securing clients interested in purchasing speculative, high risk stocks. Most of their clients tended to fall into two categories: someone wanting to dabble in the shares market in the hope of raking it in on the cheap, and the more sophisticated gamblers who did not mind losing a bit of money. Kresta had nothing to do with initial stock purchases or trade sales. His scheme was a variation of the recovery room scam, where he sent investors emails warning them of an imminent price fall, and offered to buy back their shares for a fee, usually ten percent of the stock value, to limit their losses. Once the client sent in the fee, he initiated a sales order. So far, everything appeared superficially legitimate. Since most investors expected to lose money on the deal anyway, they were suitably grateful to Galloway Investments for recovering some of their outlay, depending on the stock value at the time of sale.

No ethical violation prevented the firm's two traders from buying speculative shares when a client placed a sales order on Kresta's 'advice'. He did not cheat on the received fees, but used his insider knowledge that a block of reasonably good shares would become available and placed a 'hold' on the stock. He then purchased the shares on his own account, waited for a marginal increase in price, then sold off. This did not generate a huge income for him per transaction, but it all added up over the year he ran the scheme. Overall, a neat little scam.

After reviewing the case material, Dural came to appreciate Farmer's point of view that no crime was too small to ignore.

Rosalyn finished her report and looked around the table. "If there are no further discussion points—"

"I have an item," Gerard said. "I propose that we lift our hourly rate to $290. Our expenses across the board have increased, and I feel the new rate is justified."

"Second the motion," Leonard said immediately.

"Dr. Meng?" Rosalyn queried, and Suyni raised her hand in assent. "Carried. I'll change the necessary documentation and notices, and update PAX."

"I want to add something else," Leonard said and looked at Suyni across the table. "Dr. Meng, the partners want to acknowledge your valuable contribution to Gap Consulting by offering you a full partnership, effective immediately."

Suyin gaped and everyone clapped, Gerard loudest of all, his grin threatening to split his face. She blushed and hung her head. When she looked up, her eyes were bright with emotion.

"Thank you for this undeserved honor," she said quietly, her words like enchanting music. Dural often wondered how the Chinese and Japanese managed to make English sound so lyrical. "I'll try not to disappoint you."

"Keep those patients coming is the best way not to disappoint us," Leonard growled good-naturedly, and everyone laughed.

She smiled and nodded. "I'll try."

Leonard fixed his eyes on Rosalyn. "Equally pleasant, we have also decided to make Mrs. Pickering a full partner."

Dural joined in the cheering and clapping.

Moved, Rosalyn cleared her throat. "Thank you, Leonard, but I cannot accept. I'm happy to remain an associate partner."

"This is not open for negotiation, Rosalyn," Leonard said firmly.

She lifted her chin. "As a partner, I have a say in this, and I vote no."

Leonard grinned. "The rest of us outvote you."

"Well, since you put it that way…" Rosalyn beamed, and the room burst into another round of clapping.

"To celebrate, I'm having lunch brought in," Leonard added when order returned. "However, whatever plans you've made for Friday night, cancel them, because we'll be hitting Crown Casino for an opportunity to lose some money and cry into our wine afterward."

Everybody cheered. Leonard smiled at Rosalyn. "That's it. I'm done."

"In that case," she said, "this meeting is adjourned."

As the others filed out, Dural looked at Suyin. "A moment, Doctor."

She stopped and waited. When the room cleared, he closed the door, not sure he should go through with this. Her aura glowed deep red with a pale orange border.

"Suyin, Gerard is a very close friend of mine, and I would hate to see him hurt in any way."

Her thin eyebrows rose a fraction, breaking her usual calm demeanor. "I'm not sure I understand," she said softly.

"I think you do. He is very much in love with you—"

"And I love him."

"I'm glad to hear it. If Leonard or I have given you an impression that we're more than colleagues, it was unintended, and I want to apologize if you thought otherwise."

Her eyes sparkled with amusement. "That was a very gallant thing to say, Du. Believe me, I would never betray Gerard by flirting, and I'm sure Leonard had no ulterior motive behind his amiable advances."

Dural chuckled. "So he said. How about a coffee?"

She cocked an eyebrow. "Are *you* flirting now, Dr. Sinclair?"

He laughed and opened the door for her.

* * *

Showered and shaved, Dural crawled into a lightweight navy blue gabardine suit, a pale blue silk shirt, and knotted on a dark red wool tie. Satisfied, he left the bedroom open to air during the day and strode briskly to Daniela's room, which he now used as his office. He snagged a slim calf leather briefcase and went downstairs to the kitchen. The wall clock beside the bench said 05:59. Lips pursed, he walked into the lounge and switched on the TV just as the ABC intro music started.

Michael Rawland in his signature light blue suit, smiled into the camera.

Welcome to the show on this Tuesday, the fifth of March. The main points.

The Labor Party is determined to push through cuts to negative gearing and halve the capital gains tax discount should they win election likely to be held on May 18. More Australians are working into their 60s and 70s. Fires continue to burn east of Melbourne with temperatures for today forecast in the high 30s.'

The camera shifted to his co-host. *'Cardinal George Pell is awaiting sentencing for sexually abusing two choirboys in 1996. He continues to claim innocence.'*

Dural snorted with derision. Innocent indeed. With all the evidence around the world, Vatican and Pope Francis were still in denial mode, paying off families to be silent, and relocating pedophile priests where they can continue committing atrocities.

'In the U.S., speculation is rife regarding contents of the Mueller report into Russian involvement in the 2016 presidential election. The Royal Commission into the Banking, Superannuation and Financial Services Industry claims more corporate scalps. I am Virginia Trioli. The details.'

Dural strode into the kitchen, half listening to the news. He fixed himself a bowl of homemade muesli, having bought the ingredients, coffee, and sat at the dining table to watch the news. Finished, he switched it off and washed up. In his office, he powered up the computer. He quickly checked his emails and scanned Facebook, shaking his head with amusement at President Trump hate posts and Democratic Party antics to select a candidate for the 2020 election. Dural did not favor Sanders or Biden, considering them old-era politicians—part of the swamp. What the party needed was a fresh face able to unite America under a vision designed for the twenty-first century. Right now, the Democrats seemed hell bent on handing Trump another term, which in his opinion, would be disaster for America and the world. The President's evident irrationality and instability worried him, as did the escalating U.S./China trade war. He gave a mental shrug. Whatever happened, it was America's problem, although the political whirlpool could snare Australia should the trade war escalate.

The time stamp on the bottom-right of the screen showed 06:55. He powered down and heard a car horn. That would be his cab. Downstairs, he grabbed his briefcase and hurried to the front door. He set the alarm and locked up. Still around 24C after a humid night, Dural glanced at the blue sky. Another scorcher in Melbourne, and Sydney was not likely to be any cooler.

He climbed onto the back seat and the cab immediately pulled away from the curb.

"No relief until Friday," the cabby announced cheerfully with a glance at the rearview mirror.

"So they say," Dural replied as the cab stopped at the High Street intersection.

"What terminal?"

"QANTAS domestic."

The cabby gave him another glance and turned his head to watch the road, Dural not in a talkative mood. Not morose or anything, he just wanted silence. The cab turned into High Street. From St. Kilda Road, it entered Kings Way and caught the West Gate Freeway onramp that led to Tullamarine Freeway and the airport. This early in the morning, all the traffic headed into the city, and he had a clear run out. Watching the stream of cars, trucks, and vans on the inbound carriageway, he wondered how people did it. Day after day the same thing. Some did not have any choice, public transport acutely lagging behind the city's exploding growth. He was immensely glad to have his Prahran house within easy walking distance to work, and regular trams made a trip into the city painless.

He almost did not get the house, Lenora wanting it for herself, understandably enough. She acquiesced when her lawyer convinced her to accept sixty percent of its market value, less the outstanding mortgage. Dural was prepared to give her half outright, provided she also serviced half the mortgage. He intended to sell his Nelson Bay investment property to finalize the divorce settlement, which had not been at all vitriolic as he suspected it might, but a fatherly talk with Paul Becker made him realize the magnitude of his mistake. Real estate everywhere boomed, and Nelson Bay had become a trendy tourist and retirement location. Get a bank loan to cover the settlement, Paul urged. Dural's income would easily service the load. Given his assets and shares portfolio, ANZ happy to make him a loan. He, on the other hand, was not overly keen to add an additional burden on top of his existing outlays. Although rental income comfortably serviced his

Nelson Bay mortgage, the divorce had seriously reduced his shares portfolio and liquidity position. In the end, he accepted Paul's advice and took out a second mortgage, consolidating it into one. Looking back, he was glad he listened to his friend. In another four years, he would be mortgage free. He could do it in three if he sold off his remaining shares, but they served as a handy buffer in case things went south.

Dural called Nikau Tipene occasionally and sent them Christmas cards, but he had not visited since the divorce. Lenora was still at ANZ, now a senior project manager. Some nine months ago, according to Nikau, she became involved with someone she met at the bank, and the relationship serious enough that the Tipene family were hearing wedding bells. He wished her well.

The cab drove past the old Holiday Inn and took the up ramp to the departure level. The modern Parkroyal Hotel and the looming parking complex behind it blocked the bright, sunlit sky. He paid off the cabby and walked directly toward the security gates. With an e-ticket and no luggage to check in, he quickly found himself in the cavernous departure area with its shops and food outlets. His watch said 07:42. He had around fifteen minutes to kill before they announced the boarding call for his 8:15 flight to Sydney. Not enough time to snag a coffee, he wandered around, then slowly made his way along a crowded corridor to his departure gate, the walk interrupted regularly by public speaker flight announcements and calls for lost passengers. A neatly dressed QANTAS attendant called the boarding for QF416 and he joined the economy class queue. On longer flights, he usually went business class, but Sydney was a short one-hour twenty-minute hop and not worth the extra expense, the indulgence coming out of the Gap Consulting bottom line, as Rosalyn reminded everybody. The Victorian government, though, footed this flight, but were too stingy to let him go business class.

In a crush with other passengers, Dural moved down the air bridge toward the waiting B737. The flight attendant in the doorway smiled politely, checked his boarding pass, and directed him to the port side of the aircraft. He walked past the business class section and checked seat numbers beneath the overhead lockers. All row seven seats—almost as good as being in business class—were empty, and he eased himself into the aisle one, not bothering to buckle in, expecting the seats next to him to fill before takeoff.

He was looking out the small window at the open tarmac when he heard someone clear her throat.

"Excuse me, but I think you're in my seat."

Soft, the gently modulated voice made Dural picture rolling autumn fields filled with wild flowers. He turned his head and saw shapely legs enclosed in black trousers. As he raised his eyes, he made out a young woman wearing a black business jacket over a faintly pink T-shirt. Slim, tall, around 170cm or so. Smoky Mediterranean features, think black eyebrows, short jet black hair that fell straight over her ears, small mouth, and pert nose, the effect stunning. She returned his scrutiny with a lingering smile. In mid-thirties, he figured, hazel eyes bright with amusement, she was clearly used to men's scrutiny.

He felt a primordial jolt of desire rush through him. He couldn't help it, the feeling totally spontaneous. After a moment, he pulled himself back into the real world, reached into his jacket pocket, and dragged out the boarding pass.

"Seven C," he told her warmly, enchanted by the shift of expressions on her face. Her aura flowed from purple/blue to red. She appeared like she looked, a confident, complex woman. If he could believe her aura—whose interlocking meanings he now understood completely—she was also highly intelligent and accomplished.

She frowned, checked her e-ticket, and with a lift of her mouth, held it out.

"Seven C," she said brightly.

"Well, what do you know? I tell you what. I'll shift into the center seat—"

"And if somebody comes to claim it?"

"I'll ask the flight attendant to bump me to business class by way of compensation."

She thought about that for a moment. "Why should you get the business seat—if one is available?"

"You want to throw me out of mine," he pointed out reasonably, enjoying the encounter.

"If you insist that this is your seat, I'll talk to the flight attendant about getting bumped into business class."

He glanced at passengers waiting to move down the aisle and shifted to the center seat. "We're causing a minor blockage."

She waited for him to move, sat down, and grinned. "I don't know how this could happen," she told him, eyebrows turned up. Her lightly tanned skin smooth without any blemishes.

"With computers and everything, I expected they would spot something like this when we had our boarding pass checked," he agreed.

She slid a slim brown briefcase under the seat in front of her and leaned back. Dural wanted to draw her out more, but however enchanting the prospect, he would probably not get that chance. Another fleeting encounter.

Some five minutes later, nobody had claimed the window or center seat, and he could not see anyone else boarding, which was unusual. Morning flights were normally packed. His good fortune. Flight attendants were going down the aisle closing overhead lockers and checking that everyone properly buckled in. He tightened his seatbelt and glanced at his companion.

"I guess I won't be getting that business class seat after all."

She looked at him and smiled, which lit her face and made her smoky eyes sparkle with devastating effect. He could gaze at them forever, then chided himself for being a gawking adolescent.

"We could swap if you like," she said.

"I don't mind this, unless you want the window."

She shook her head. "I prefer the aisle. Since we're going to be glued for the flight, I'm Aviana." She held out her hand.

Aviana…meaning like a bird, and he pictured her delicate, willowy form soaring through the sky on gossamer wings. A good fit, he decided.

"Dural," he said and took her slim hand in his. "Your attire suggests Sydney is not a pleasure trip."

"Business, I'm afraid. I'm going up to handle an extradition case, but there's been a holdup."

"You're a lawyer?"

"Yes. I cannot talk about the case, but the NSW Police are bringing in some stuffy old psychologist to block my extradition submission. A Dr. Sinclair. What about you? Also business?"

Vastly amused, Dural grinned. "I'm seeing a hotshot lawyer defending a white-collar scammer. I'm Dr. Sinclair, stuffy old psychologist."

Her mouth opened and an attractive flush colored her cheeks. "This will teach me to be more circumspect when talking to strangers."

Dural chuckled. "I couldn't stop you even if I wanted to, which I didn't."

"Having fun at my expense?"

"Guilty as charged."

She realized the humor in the situation and laughed. Her aura momentarily enveloped her in a silver glow with a thin gold border. Her hazel eyes probed into him, and he allowed the moment to linger without breaking contact.

He met Lenora on a flight, and now…

Don't make something out of nothing, Doctor.

"I understand you have a practice in Prahran with two part-ners," she said.

"Have you been checking up on me?"

"Vic Police gave me your resume when I took the case."

"And?"

The aircraft pushed back.

"Ah, moving at last." She sighed and tightened her belt. "I expected to read about a dry university professor full of himself, but instead, I was startled. Two books behind you, and according to the CV, a remarkable record for breaking down suspect testi-monies. I must admit being surprised at the depth and range of material your latest book covered. Unusual to read something like that written by a man. I was intrigued to meet you in person."

"That resume, clearly no picture or personal details."

"Only bare facts, I'm afraid. I should have checked your books on Amazon…"

"And now that you have seen me?"

She smiled, showing even white teeth, and raised a finger. "Not old or dry. However, I cannot wait to see you operate."

"So, you're a partner at Wellard, Wellard and Starke. I've also been checking up. Bare facts only."

"You know them?"

"Only from the brief I got for this case, but I know of them. Four years ago, they handled my ex-wife's divorce."

"Your profile said you're divorced, but I didn't know that my firm was involved." She studied him for a moment. "Your fault or hers?"

The aircraft jolted along the taxiway as it made its way toward the runway.

Dural shrugged. "No one's really. Simply one of those things. We lost a seven-year-old daughter in a car accident, and shortly after, my wife miscarried. She took it badly."

"I'm sorry to hear that," she said softly, and he could tell she meant it.

"It's over and I moved on." He had moved on, but Lenora was still there inside him, and always would be. Not something he could erase, or wanted to. Even though she was gone, she had enriched him, made life worth living. What was life now? A day-to-day proposition without purpose?

"And you?"

"I never married," she said. "After getting my honors degree from Melbourne Uni, I was with the Victorian Corrections Department for four years handling all types of prisoner cases, then five years with the Office of Public Prosecutions where I worked courtroom cases. Then with Wellard for the last seven. Two years ago, they made me a junior partner."

Dural raised his eyebrows. "Impressive. I'll have to watch myself today," he said seriously, then they both laughed, and he felt very close to this woman.

The aircraft lined up on the active runway, paused, and the pilot applied full thrust, which pushed him against the seat. He felt the nose come up and they were airborne. The aircraft steadily gained altitude and brilliant sunshine filled the cabin. After a few minutes, the seatbelt sign went off with a soft *ting*, and he heard clicks throughout the cabin as passengers unbuckled, despite being warned to have their seatbelts fastened at all times in case of unexpected turbulence.

Aviana nodded with satisfaction. "That's what I like on my flights. No excitement."

Dural grinned. "Have you ever had any excitement?"

"A couple of wild landings in high wind. You?"

"Same here. Actually, it feels worse than it actually is. They wouldn't land if it weren't safe."

"That's what my father always tells me. He's an aircraft engineer with Virgin. Pushing sixty-three, but has no plans to retire. Loves his job too much. Claims he would be bored to death playing golf every day. What about your parents?"

"Retired. My old man used to be a partner in a small management accounting firm. They have a place in North Melbourne, but spend most of their time in Nelson Bay up from Sydney."

Aviana's captivating eyes brightened. "I've been there once. Nice area."

"I have an investment property there. My parents look after it and collect the rent."

"You go there often?"

"Not much. My work keeps me pretty busy, but I try going up a couple of times a year to check on the place and spend time with them. When I do have a spare week or so, I travel."

"Any place special?"

"Not particularly. I've been to the States, seen a bit of Europe, and I visited China once. Fascinating country, and the pace of development is unbelievable. A totally different world from Mao's repressive era. My next planned trip is to South America: Machu Picchu, Lake Titicaca, the Amazon jungle. I'm looking forward to it."

"When will that happen?"

"Probably around January next year. Depends on how things go."

"I was in Egypt and Israel nine years ago," she said. "Standing before the Great Pyramid made me shiver. I almost cried, though, when I saw flakes peeling off those magnificent red granite blocks caused by pollution. History is very loud there. So was Israel, but I wouldn't go there now."

"I know what you mean," Dural agreed. "Last year, I wanted to visit South Africa and Kenya, but the way things are over there right now, it won't happen for a while, if at all. Not until things settle down."

She nodded and her eyes took on a dreamy look. "I would love to visit Russia and England. My parents were born here, but my grandparents came from Kent before they settled Down Under. English history is simply awesome." She glanced at him. "Ever been there?"

He smiled. "It's on my to-do list."

The flight attendants wheeled in the food and drinks carts, and Dural got himself coffee. Aviana chose tea.

"My English background," she remarked sheepishly. "I do like coffee…decaf," she added quickly. Noting his amused expression, she raised an eyebrow. "What? You have something against decaf?"

He lifted an open palm. "Not at all. I simply prefer the real thing."

"Mmm." She nibbled a fingernail. "What do you do when you're not mind bending?"

"Oh, read. Play golf, mostly with one of my partners. Alone, if I have to. I also write short stories."

"A fiction author as well! My, my. What do you write?"

"Science fiction."

She winced. "Not into that stuff, or fantasy."

"You prefer romance?"

She pointed a finger at him. "A typical male response, assuming that all women are naturally drawn to tear-jerking love throbs and hunky guys."

He laughed. "And you're not?"

She studied him for a second. "Now you're teasing."

"A little. Seriously, though. What books give you a lift?"

"I don't have a preferred genre, which allows me to sample a wide range of material, fiction and non-fiction. I do like reading about early history, and I have several books on archaeology. I'm particularly interested in formative human theories, but I reject the hypothesis that man evolved in Africa and migrated across the planet. I also reject the notion that modern humans are only 200,000 years old. There is too much evidence sitting in museum basements that refutes that theory."

"You follow the regional continuity model?"

She looked surprised. "You know about that?"

"That modern humans evolved more or less simultaneously everywhere? I'm aware of the theory. You then also reject the replacement and assimilation models?"

She waved a hand. "Both are variations of the continuity model, and both accept the existence of early human variants, which through interbreeding led to the emergence of *homo sapiens* as a single species. If the replacement model had any validity, we would not be seeing any racial variations. There would be a single, uniform human."

Dural nodded. "You know, the assimilation model would be valid if you accepted the premise of forerunner civilizations. The remnants interbreeding with the Neanderthals and the new humans."

"My, you do have a roaming mind, Doctor," she mused, "and I think you're right. Worked artifacts millions of years old dug up around the world tend to support the hypothesis of forerunner civilizations. Before you ask, I'll answer your next question."

"Which is?"

"Why we haven't found evidence of those civilizations. Given the geological timescales—"

"Any evidence would be erased," Dural said softly, marveling at Aviana's depth and knowledge.

Without jumping into a shaky conclusion, that depth might also explain why she never married. Most men would find her formidable intellect intimidating. Maturing far earlier than men, it did not surprise him that women found most males their age still juveniles driven by libido. An empirical generalization, he admitted, but women preferred a partner several years older when a man began to emerge out of a boy's shell. He wondered more than once why evolution would create such an anomaly. Being the protector and food provider, male maturity should have been the priority. From an evolutionary point of view, though, perpetuating the species the priority.

Then again, she could simply have made her career a priority.

Aviana gave him a quizzical smile. "Why the thoughtful face?"

"Oh, just thinking that it's been a while since I had such a stimulating conversation with someone."

She beamed. "Are you hitting on me, Dr. Sinclair? And here I was, thinking you were not a wolf."

He laughed, genuinely tickled by the idea. "I wanted to draw you out. Understand my opposition…your client, you know."

Her dark eyes sparkled, and he sank into their magical depths. Hitting on her? He would not mind it at all, but he did not look for another relationship, comfortably settled into his lifestyle. Nevertheless, he did miss the talks he used to have with Lenora, the quiet moments of intimacy, being together without words having to be said, doing things together.

She gazed at him over the rim of her cup, and he wondered what went on in that probing mind. Her shifting auras did not help him pin down her base self, a typical reaction everyone exhibited under conversation and emotional stimulus. He would have to see Aviana in a quiet, relaxed setting to see her underlying personality, but he already knew what that was. He had seen the purple/blue glow surrounding her when they met.

"A nice evade, but I still think you're hitting on me. All men are wolves. They cannot help it. It's only that some hide it better than others."

He looked at her frankly. "I'm simply passing the time until we land."

"Hmm." She nibbled a fingernail, not believing him. "While you're calibrating me, I calibrated you for the same reason."

"I am sure you did," he said dryly. "And have you finished calibrating?"

"Not yet, but we don't meet officially until ten-thirty. That gives me some time to finish the job."

"Be my guest."

A momentary clash of wills as they stared at each other, he broke into a lazy grin.

He got a refill of coffee and listened to the engine hum, very aware of Aviana's presence. After Lenora, he never dated, and had no interest trawling bars and clubs for the hell of it. With Gerard and Suyin busy making something together, it left Dural firmly in the singles ranks.

Looking back over almost four years since his divorce, although he missed Lenora, and still loved her desperately, he learned to shut the door on his past and reconciled himself to the stark reality that it would never open again. At forty-two, he was now beyond that stuff. Hell, he did not have a bad life as a bachelor. Certainly simpler in many respects, although it took a while getting used to doing all the chores, which for only one person not an onerous burden. He had freedom to do whatever he wanted, whenever he wanted. True to an extent, but as a working professional, those freedoms were also somewhat curtailed. He was not an employee able to quit on a whim. As a partner in a thriving practice, he had responsibilities to keep the business viable. And he *liked* what he did.

He sipped his coffee and wondered what brought on this moment of introspection. Was he making excuses to himself for not wanting another relationship? It is not as though a relationship was something entered into a calendar and then acted upon. It simply happened or did not. Did he deliberately avoid a relationship? Did he even want one? His life was stable, organized, and satisfying...most of the time. Why spoil it with sticky sentiment.

What *did* he want?

His thoughts floundered. When he boiled it all down, he was not sure what he wanted. So far, he was happy to coast along on the waves of life.

Like he told his patients, 'Don't get worked up over something that has not happened, and might never happen'.

He found himself surprised by the depth of feeling stirred into life by a chance encounter with a vibrant, exciting woman who had achieved a measure of stability she apparently did not want to disturb either. He could only imagine her horror if he blurted some indication of attraction for her, for there was undeniable attraction. Simply another middle-aged lecher, that's what she would think. Cannot a woman be friendly without being mentally pawed?

Pleasant company, that's all she was, he told himself. Leave it at that.

He glanced at the golden aura enveloping her, sensing her softer, sympathetic, understanding side, the poetry in her soul, and was fascinated. To have so many such fine qualities left him bemused and confused. Then again, why couldn't she be complex, strong, demanding—she had to be in her profession—and accomplished? Were those things only the province of self-absorbed men?

Their eyes locked, and he had an irrational desire to sweep her in his arms, picturing himself on an empty beach, dancing as surf boomed in the background, the air filled with spray, the stars cold and bright in the sky. He recalled a desert scene from a film *The Doctor*, where William Hurt danced with a terminal cancer patient, the accompanying music making Dural tingle. That was the kind of music he wanted to hear when he danced with Aviana.

"How did you happen to get involved in police work?" she asked, her voice warm and inviting, and the vision faded.

Jerked back to reality, he collected his thoughts. "Well, it started with a couple of requests to our practice for an independent psychological evaluation. I don't know how they picked us. They must have liked our work, and we had a new line of business."

"Mostly from you," she added.

Dural smiled. Mostly from him, and he knew why. Leonard and Gerard did not want to be bothered with criminal cases, and his special ability, coupled with an eidetic memory, got results and generated healthy fees.

"My training helps me gain an insight into a person's psychological profile that enables me to peel away attempts at obfuscation and outright deception, and lay bare their base state. Most people find such a confrontation intimidating and break down."

"You make it sound so easy. Does it work every time?"

He grinned. "Not always. I had two failures in four years, if you want to call them that. Both suspects were completely truthful and the police were forced to drop the charges."

"You do this sort of thing often?"

"I try to avoid it if I can. Two or three cases a year at most. I guess in a way my success at breaking down suspects has backfired on me and the Victoria Police are hounding me to accept a semi-permanent consulting position. It's interesting work, but not something I want to do regularly."

"I'm surprised you took on a small-time scammer like Kresta, then."

"Inspector Frank Farmer from Finance & Cyber Crime was very persuasive," Dural said dryly, and Aviana smiled.

"Your profile says you lecture at Monash and Melbourne Uni."

"From time to time, but it's not billable work."

"Neither is writing books," she remarked with a whimsical smile, and he chuckled.

"You got me there, but the two texts I produced were a distillation of experiences and observations in my field, and hopefully disseminated different insights for our profession."

"Somewhat of a crusader, eh?"

He frowned. "An interesting comment, one I would never have thought of, but accurate, to an extent. Despite advances in our field, too many of my colleagues are still wedded to traditional philosophies postulated by Freud, Pavlov, and Carl Yung, to name a few. They have some validity, but their theories were formulated to explain a different age and culture, and no longer fit our modern social matrix."

"That type of thinking has probably earned you derision from some quarters."

"It certainly has, but I'll get over the disappointment." He studied her amused expression. "What about you?"

"What do you mean?"

"Anything on the horizon apart from trial law?"

"I would like to be a magistrate or judge one day. Dispense justice, rather than argue points of law set in a precedent, which too many cases these days are based on. Law has become overly adversarial, where equity is considered a quaint notion. Offenders claim mental irresponsibility and the courts often take their side at the expense of the victim. I seethe when I see someone literally get away with murder by claiming temporary insanity. It sucks."

Dural nodded. "I could not believe a case I saw on the news once where a burglar injured himself in a bungled robbery and sued the owner for damages—and won! The system has gone insane."

"I heard about that one," she said with a shake of her head. "The prosecutor was an idiot. Anyway, the burglar received a stiff sentence on appeal by the Director of Public Prosecutions."

The seatbelt sign came on and the purser announced imminent landing, asking passengers to stow their tray and have the seat fully upright.

"I'm catching a cab to the Metropolitan Remand & Reception Center," Aviana announced with a sidewise glance. "Want to share?"

He beamed at her. "I'd love to."

She snorted. "Like I said, wolf."

He laughed, unable to help himself. "However, a cab won't be necessary. A police car will be waiting for me—for us—outside the terminal."

Her eyebrows climbed. "Wow. You really are getting the VIP treatment."

"It's a fair way to Silverwater, and a police car will get us there more quickly."

The B737 landed with a mild jolt, turned onto a taxiway, and headed for the terminal. Sydney Mascot was a large international airport, and it took the aircraft a while to park itself at the QANTAS domestic terminal.

After more than thirty years of argument, wrangling, and plain procrastination, the federal government had finally started construction of a second airport at Badgerys Creek, including a rail link to the city, due to open late in 2026—more likely in 2036! Everyone recognized the need for another airport—surrounded by the city, Mascot had nowhere to grow—but not on their land! Put it somewhere else, everyone cried in anguish, concerned about noise pollution and disturbing the wildlife. Nothing much around Badgerys Creek except paddocks and cows, but people complained on principle. Of course, they also complained about the inadequacies of Mascot airport.

When the aircraft stopped and mated with the air bridge, a mad scramble ensued as passengers hurriedly opened the overhead lockers to retrieve personal items. Once they had their bags or packages, they stood listlessly in the aisle, or reached for their phones. For youngsters especially, life without their cellphone would be unimaginable. Dural glanced at Aviana and shrugged. Always the same on every flight. It would be at least five minutes before they could disembark, and waiting less stressful sitting down.

Finally on the move, Aviana retrieved her briefcase, stood, and followed others toward the hatch. Inside the noisy, crowded terminal glittering with shopfront lights, Dural spotted a young man dressed in a dark suit holding up a sign with his name on it.

"I'm Dr. Sinclair," he said, "and this is Ms. Aviana Kinsley, representing the defendant."

"Glad to meet you, Doctor…Ms. Kinsley," the youngster said, wearing a large grin. "I'm Detective Sam Dexter. Any luggage?" Dural shook his head. "Excellent. I have a car outside. Depending on traffic, it will take us approximately thirty minutes to Silverwater. Please follow me."

Hot and sticky outside, Dural winced, not looking forward to the day. Well, it *was* summer. Autumn officially, but it felt like summer.

Traffic out was heavy, but moved steadily. Dural glanced at his watch: 9:44. Plenty of time for their appointed meeting. With a long queue at the Parramatta Road entrance, Dexter lit off the siren and sped past weary drivers. Dural spent the rest of the trip in silence.

He had visited the Remand Center before, and absently watched the flow of cars for want of a better thing to do. He wanted to talk more intimately with Aviana, but not with Dexter overhearing every word. In the end, he had to be content exchanging bland chatter. They reached the forbidding complex that housed male and female prisoners, and Dexter led them through reception where they received visitor badges, then took the elevator to a second floor conference room.

"Inspector Cummins will be along shortly, Doctor. Relax while we bring up the prisoner." He pointed at a table tucked into a corner. "Help yourselves to coffee and buns."

"Thanks," Dural said with a nod.

Dexter glanced at Aviana. "Ms. Kinsley…" he acknowledged and walked out.

The air-conditioning made the large room somewhat cooler than Dural liked, and he hoped this would not take long.

At 10:25 according to the wall clock, a tall man in a lightweight gray suit and black tie strode in. Introductions and handshakes were shared all around. Inspector Cummins pulled out a small Sony recorder and placed it on the table.

"Apologies again for dragging you all the way up here, Doctor, but Ms. Kinsley insisted on having this hearing before we initiated the extradition process."

"You have circumstantial evidence at best, Inspector," Aviana said sternly, looking cool and composed, her purple/blue aura tinged with silver.

"It's not my case, Ms. Kinsley," Cummins retorted indifferently. "We're simply holding Mr. Kresta at the request of Victorian Police."

Dexter brought in Philip Kresta, and Dural was intrigued to see a relatively young man, perhaps in his early thirties at best. The police mugshot had him looking older. Neatly dressed in a dark pinstripe suit, thick black hair combed straight back, dark brown eyes shining with intelligence, Kresta looked confident.

Dural noted the man's predominantly red aura, signifying enthusiasm, energy, strong will, and directness, and frowned. The faint blue outline suggested a master communicator, charismatic personality, and intuition. He was not altogether surprised. Young operators full of unshakeable confidence in their ability ran most stockbroking trading desks everywhere.

Inspector Cummins cleared his throat and switched on the Sony recorder.

"Mr. Kresta, Ms. Aviana Kinsley is here to annul our intention to grant extradition to Victoria on the charge of fraud and insider trading. Dr. Sinclair is here to observe the proceedings and ask you some questions."

"What kind of doctor?" Kresta asked in a pleasantly deep voice.

"I'm a psychologist."

"A shrink, eh? This should be interesting." He turned to Aviana. "Thank you for coming up, Ms. Kinsley."

Aviana looked directly at Cummins. "I protest the unlawful detention of my client, Inspector. The charges are without foundation."

"That's not for me to argue, Ms. Kinsley. Take it up with the arresting officer in Melbourne. I'm simply processing an extradition for a pending court case."

"An invalid extradition. As senior accountant for Galloway Investments, Mr. Kresta was entitled to take advantage of stocks coming into his firm to trade on his own account."

True, Dural acknowledged. Trading firms did not buy stocks simply on a client's order, but held in their own right a portfolio of the most commonly traded shares the company's clients wanted. That entailed some risk, but that was why they had floor traders to offload stocks likely to go belly up. The larger firms also issued client advisories to dump suspect stock, without a fee, but those were usually watch-and-act notices.

Cummins nodded. "Granted, but he traded shares not in any danger of losing value after falsely advising the firm's clients to sell. In other words, he manipulated the market, and according to ASIC, Ms. Kinsley, that's fraud and insider trading."

Dural noted the light hue of black that sprung around Kresta, then quietly faded. Dural needed an outright admission of fraudulent behavior, which might be tough to get. He leaned forward.

"Mr. Kresta, you were formerly a trader with Ord Minnett in Melbourne."

"That's right."

"Why did you leave what was a high six-figure position?"

Kresta's aura changed to light gray, which revealed a secret to be kept, then turned dirty brown, indicating momentary insecurity.

"After two years, I wanted to expand my horizons, and Galloway Investments gave me that opportunity."

"To promulgate a recovery room scam? Something you were guilty of at Ord Minnett."

Black aura flared around Kresta. "Unfounded, Doctor," he replied calmly, but Dural sensed increased tension.

Aviana glared at Cummins. "For goodness sake! I resent this speculative line of questioning, Inspector. Victoria Police have no direct evidence to charge my client with anything, and I demand an end to these proceedings."

Dural ignored the outburst. "Mr. Kresta, why did you take it on yourself to send Galloway's clients emails advising them to sell, when in most cases the shares were reasonably solid? A client takes a risk and gambles on making a profit. You seem to have adopted a most unusual protective attitude. One that has netted you a substantial profit when those stocks came online."

Kresta smirked, but not with humor. "I simply provided our clients with advice—"

"For a fee. Ten percent of the stock's market value, I understand."

"They did not have to take my advice. So I made a profit. That's not insider trading. I had no prior knowledge which way the stocks would go."

"It is when you manipulate a client for your own advantage, and something that might influence the market."

"You can't prove shit, Mister!" Kresta growled and crossed his arms.

"You don't have to say anything more, Mr. Kresta," Aviana told him sternly, and gave Dural a speculative stare.

"I'm sure you're aware what insider trading means, Mr. Kresta," Dural said softly. "It's taking advantage of a stock position based on privileged information not available to the marketplace. You manipulated your firm's clients to obtain insider information."

"I did nothing illegal!" Kresta shouted. "The stocks were junk anyway."

Just another little push, Dural figured.

"It comes down to intent. You intentionally misled your firm's clients for a fee, and that's fraud."

"I saved our clients money, and I made some on the side. So what? Most of them were too stupid to realize they were being used." Kresta snorted, then paled as the enormity of his words sank in.

Dural smiled and sat back. Kresta should have kept his mouth shut. The case against him circumstantial as Aviana said, but he had to demonstrate his superiority by bragging about the cleverness of his scheme.

Cummins glanced at Aviana. "Ms. Kinsley?"

She turned to Kresta. "I advise you not so say anything further until a preliminary hearing has been called. Wellard, Wellard and Starke will contest the charges." She looked at Cummins. "Extradition will not be opposed." She stood and picked up her briefcase. "If there is nothing else…"

Cummins nodded. "Thank you for your time. Dr. Sinclair, a car will take both of you to the airport." He turned to Dexter and pointed at Kresta. "Get him out of here."

Outside the conference room, Aviana looked ready to kick the wall. Dural did not have to see her aura to know that.

"The fool only had to keep it zipped!" She glared at him. "How did you do that?"

"Getting what amounts to a confession? Personal insight. You could still win the case, you know. It's a comparatively minor white-collar crime, and Galloway's clients were not hurt."

She snorted. "With Kresta's admission on tape? Damn, it was supposed to be a simple extradition hearing!"

He laughed at her frustration. "You don't like to lose."

"No, I don't like to lose."

"When is your flight back?"

"Two."

"Same here. Maybe we'll get double booked again."

Her eyes glittered with amusement, and he found himself lost in them. "Wolf, and a prong."

"A prong? Is that bad?"

"Work it out, Doctor."

At the airport, Dural faced a deliciously amusing dilemma, which Aviana sensed and clearly enjoyed. Since both had pre-booked e-tickets, they had different seat allocations. He wanted an adjoining seat, but hesitated to ask if okay with her, not wanting to be a genuine wolf. Realizing how ridiculous it all was, he turned to her as they entered the check-in lounge.

"Would you mind if we sat together? I still have a few things I want to find out about you."

She beamed at him. "You had to drag that out, didn't you?"

"You're having fun at my expense," he accused her, but his eyes were bright.

"Just getting some of my own back. And no, I don't mind."

At the check-in counter, he had no problem changing his seat to 8B, as Aviana had 8C. The flight attendant smiled at him.

"Sit where you like. The flight is practically empty."

Early afternoon flights usually were, as Dural knew. Changing a seat or trying to get one on standby almost impossible for anything after three. New boarding pass in hand, Dural accompanied Aviana toward the security portals.

They still had forty-five minutes before the boarding call, and he invited her to have lunch with him. Not exactly restaurant cuisine, but a food court takeaway would have to do. Studying what was available, they decided on Chinese. He picked Singapore noodles, and she had grilled prawns with vegetables. An apple juice for him and orange for her, they found an empty table and made themselves comfortable. The lounge busy, but not overly crowded. Business would pick up in the afternoon crush.

He forked through his noodles, which were quite good for a takeaway, and watched Aviana pick delicately between the prawns, stabbing square pieces of green capsicum with deliberate intent.

"Opponents?" he queried lightly, and she grinned.

"Not exactly. I always go through my veggies first before tackling other stuff."

"Any favorite foods?"

"Not particularly. I can handle just about anything, but I draw the line with pungent cheeses. And you?"

"I'm not fond of strong cheese either. A childhood experience that left an indelible memory. I always give the supermarket cheese section a wide birth."

Her laugh a pleasant tinkle. "I know what you mean. I do like cheese, mind you. I can take cheddar, Edam, and Gouda. Stuff like that."

Time flew, and lunch was an exercise of mutual discovery. Waiting to board, they found themselves talking about books. Aviana did not like fantasy, but admitted that Mary Stewart's Merlin story had a magical attraction for her. Dural's eyes lit up.

"They're some of my favorites," he declared happily, pleased to have another thing in common with her. "I did not like *The Last Enchantment*. The writing had lost the magic prose of her first two books."

"I must admit being disappointed when I read it," she agreed. "Still, when I feel nostalgic and moody, I drag out *The Crystal Cave* or *The Hollow Hills*, and I'm lost in that old English countryside and history." She lifted a finger. "And I'm not saying that because I love England. It's Stewart's writing. Being a woman, her words have a clarity and fascination not found often with male authors."

When they boarded and buckled in, Dural admitted the check-in attendant was right. The cabin had perhaps a dozen passengers. Ten minutes before scheduled departure, with everybody on board, the aircraft received tower clearance for early departure and was pushed back.

Once airborne, Dural loosened his seatbelt a little.

"If you don't mind talking shop, how did the police find out about Mr. Kresta? My brief didn't go into too many details."

"An external audit queried his fee payments," she said. "Although he did not profit from them, some of the amounts were substantial and the irregularity reported to the managing director, who thought Kresta was far too smooth for an accountant."

"Why did Galloway hire him if they thought he was suspect?"

"Because of his trader experience at Ord Minnett. A floor trader and a management accountant rolled into one package is pretty rare, and they snapped him up. The irony is that they wanted Kresta to keep an eye on the company's two floor traders. With the audit report in hand, the managing director fired Kresta on the spot and called the police."

Dural slowly shook his head. "If he hadn't sent those advisory emails, and limited himself to phone calls, he could have gotten away with it forever."

"Too clever for his own good," she agreed.

"You don't mind defending him?"

"He approached Wellard and I'm a lawyer. It's my obligation to defend him to the best of my ability. I could have rejected the case, but there was no moral conflict in taking it. Kresta is a scammer, but he had not actually defrauded or financially damaged his clients." She gave him a scrutinizing stare. "You must find yourself in a similar position sometimes. Taking on patients who don't need genuine psychological counseling, I mean."

"Sometimes," Dural admitted candidly. "All our patients are referrals, and the notes we get from forwarding GPs are not always detailed enough to make an on the spot diagnosis. However, my partners and I never milk a patient if ongoing sessions are not warranted."

"I never thought you did, Dural," she said softly and touched his forearm, which sent a pleasant tingle up his arm.

The first time they touched and he enjoyed the sensation.

She searched his eyes. "If you don't mind talking about it, can I ask you something personal?"

"No guarantee I'll answer."

"You said you lost your daughter in an accident…"

The memories rushed back, as did the awful feelings. She noted his reaction and was immediately contrite.

"I'm sorry. I should not have pried."

"That's all right," he said gruffly. "I was picking her up from school. Our tram had pulled up and she wanted to catch it. Before I knew it, she broke away and ran across the road. A driver running a yellow light clipped her, and she died in hospital that day."

"Oh, God. How dreadful. I really am sorry."

He exhaled and smiled wanly. "In some ways, both of us had trouble moving forward in our marriage. We were divorced a couple of months later."

Distressed, Aviana cleared her throat. "I should not have raked over an old wound. Forgive me?"

"Life moves on," he said, glad to have a break when the attendants wheeled in the food and drinks carts.

Coffee cup in hand, he stared at the crawling brown and green landscape far below.

"What do you do for fun?" Aviana demanded cheerfully after a time.

"Laugh at our politicians," he quipped, and she chuckled, genuinely amused.

"And we have a lot to laugh at," she added. "All the polls are saying that Labor will win. What do you think?"

"They will, and this country needs a change of government, but they have a very ambitious social reform agenda. Perhaps too ambitious, and voters don't like being handed sweeping changes in one large package, regardless how necessary."

"I don't like their policy to cut back negative gearing and halve the capital gains discount," Aviana mused. "That's fiddling with money I earned the hard way, and I think it's a copout policy to appease the factional left of the party. Buy one less F-35 fighter and it would cover any shortfall in the social services program."

"I agree with you there," Dural said, appreciating her incisiveness. "As do a lot of voters, I am sure. The Morrison Coalition doesn't have a social agenda, promising a steady as you go policy, hoping Bill Shorten and Labor will make a fatal gaffe. With capital gains and negative gearing, they may very well have done it. I do hope, though, come election day, party wreckers like Tony Abbott and Eric Abetz are booted out. What about you?"

"I keep my finger on the pulse, domestic and international. However, I'm constantly amazed at what is going on. Once elected, politicians everywhere descend into factional partisan squabbling, forgetting why they were elected."

"I know what you mean. I look at the American fractured Congress and simply shake my head, wondering if it's happening. Same thing with the Brexit debacle. The politicians there really messed things up for England."

Aviana sighed and nodded. "I feel the same way. Sometimes I get so depressed, I don't even bother watching the news."

"*Hollow Hills* to the rescue?" he said with a broad grin, and she snickered.

"With a glass of chardonnay at my side." She sipped her tea. "Apart from laughing at our politicians, what else do you do for fun?"

"I read, play golf, and write short stories."

"So you said. Not very exciting, I must say."

"Just a dull psychologist, I'm afraid," he agreed candidly.

She nibbled a fingernail. "Oh, I don't know. There are possibilities."

"Such as?"

"I think you're the type who would enjoy a concert, theater, and a play."

"Theater and concerts are fine, as long as they don't include opera," Dural declared firmly.

She arched her eyebrows. "An opera hater? I am astonished."

"They don't do anything for me. I must say, though, I love some of the opera orchestral pieces. It's the singing bits that turn me off."

"Dr. Sinclair! You haven't lived until Verdi's *Nabucco* has rolled over you."

"Well, I do like the *Marriage of Figaro*," he admitted with a grin. "And I like Beethoven's ninth symphony."

"Okay, you're not completely hopeless, but we'll have to work on broadening your horizons."

He squinted at her, intrigued at the possibilities her words created. "Meaning that we'll be seeing more of each other?"

"If you'd like."

Despite her cheerful banter, he sensed a reserve, a barrier she had thrown up against something dark in her life, and he wanted to see what lay on the other side.

"I would," he said, the words having a certain finality about them. "I hesitated to ask because you would brand me a wolf." He frowned and tugged his right ear. "Since you did the asking, what does that make you?"

"In charge!" She laughed.

He smiled. "If we're going to be seeing more of each other, it's just Du."

"Du...I like it."

"While we're on names, how did your parents come up with something so non-English as Aviana?"

"Oh, it was Mom. She wanted to name me Estella after her grandmother."

"Not a very English name either," Dural said.

"My family are Catalan, but we've lived in Australia since the Second World War. Anyway, my father wanted to name me Anna. Dad didn't like Estella, and suggested Viola. So they compromised. That's what they told me anyway."

Dural lifted an eyebrow. "And Aviana is a compromise?"

She shrugged. "My mother can be very determined. When my younger sister was born, they chose a solid English name for her, Dinah." She looked at him. "How about you?"

"I'm not sure why they named me Dural, which by the way, means durable."

She grinned. "Durable, eh? Mmm."

"Seriously, it's an Aboriginal word meaning valley. My father is English and my mother Polish, so it's somewhat of a strange choice. I guess they wanted to go native. They ran into each other at a café in London and married after a two-month romance. Life was tough in England then, and Australia offered virtually free boat passage to anyone with an English passport. So, in 1967, they came to Melbourne and found life equally tough, but full of opportunities. Housing was cheap, and there were more jobs than people to fill them."

"Any brothers or sisters?"

"I'm the only one. And you? A big brother lurking somewhere to pound me for hitting on his little sister?"

She laughed, and he laughed with her, finding her…unique and irresistible.

"Only Dinah, so you can relax."

He got a refill of coffee and immersed himself in the background engine hum.

Aviana glanced at a slim black watch on her left wrist. "Another fifteen minutes and we should be down by three. A quick flight."

"Must have caught a tailwind," he said. "What then? Home?"

"Afraid not. I must go back to the office and prepare a tactics paper to defend Mr. Kresta."

"Sounds like Wellard *et al* are hard taskmasters."

"They demand performance, but they also reward it. They're okay to work for. I get involved with some major cases and learned how they were handled. Kresta is simple, but I don't want to fumble it by being careless."

"You expect to get him off?"

"I do. He might get a warning from the Australian Securities & Investments Commission, and possibly a fine, but no criminal record. He may be a moral scumbag, but straightening him out is more in your line of work."

He raised a hand. "Sorry. I'm not in the priest business."

They spent the rest of the flight talking about the raging fires across Victoria and New South Wales, the drought, youth crime, predominantly by Middle Eastern gangs, and inaction by governments the world over to curb carbon emissions, something Aviana was particularly passionate about. Australian energy and climate change policy a mess because the federal government did not have one. For ten years, both parties put it in the forget it basket, scuttled each other's proposals, and within the Liberal Party, sensible initiatives were derailed by far-right agitators and Tony Abbott, sore at being ousted as Prime Minster by Malcolm Turnbull. Without a clear federal policy, energy retailers took advantage of a deregulated market to raise gas and electricity prices to ridiculous levels. People were paying a very heavy cost for government inaction.

"Scott Morrison promised to do something about that," Aviana said.

"If the Coalition wins," Dural added. "I'm not holding my breath either way."

She looked at him. "Where do you stand on climate change?"

"It is happening, but I don't believe that man caused it. Pumping carbon and other gases into the atmosphere doesn't do it much good, but we cannot discount natural cycles and volcanic emissions. Earth is emerging from a prolonged ice age into a historically warmer and more normal period. Then there are sun cycles to consider, and all weather is controlled by the sun."

"I fear global apathy and influence exerted by multinationals over the political process to do nothing," she remarked seriously.

"Many countries *are* tackling climate change," he pointed out, "as are individual corporations. The use of renewable energy is climbing, but there is always the question of cost. Consumers, myself included, will pay only so much for their base load power. In my opinion, it's also unfair to ask the likes of India, Brazil, and China to abandon coal generators and embrace renewables. They're developing economies trying to modernize using coal sold by Australia and others. Simple economics. It took the West over a hundred years of rampant, polluting industrialization to achieve our standard of living. We cannot ask these countries to abandon coal as a cheap source of energy simply because the developed world doesn't like it." Noting her bemused expression, he gave a sheepish shrug. "I'm preaching again. Sorry."

She nodded and pursed her lips. "You and I could have lots of arguments on that topic. Some other time perhaps."

The 737 landed smoothly and they disembarked quickly. Waiting at the taxi rank, Aviana reached into her briefcase and held out a business card.

"Call me."

He gave her his, and smiled. "I'll do that."

She climbed into the cab, glanced at him, and nodded. The cab pulled away and merged with the stream of cars, cabs, and buses exiting the airport.

Dural sighed with satisfaction and glanced at the clear sky. Filled with traffic noises, the air smelled of aviation gasoline. He could feel the heat soak into his jacket, and found it somewhat overpowering after enjoying the terminal's air-conditioned comfort.

He slid onto the back seat and the cab surged from the curb. As it entered Tullamarine Freeway, Dural replayed the day's events in his mind, relishing the promise of days to come.

Chapter Seven

Dural found himself facing an interesting dilemma. Meeting Aviana had set into motion a range of feelings he was not certain he wanted to pursue. At forty-two, life was orderly, comfortable, and uncomplicated. His days had a reassuring routine that provided a backdrop of security and a level of satisfaction. Not exciting perhaps, but he had never sought excitement or taken unnecessary risks. Evaluate, plan, and act. That had been his mantra all his life. More so since the divorce.

Onions beginning to soften, he added two tablespoons of pork mince into the frying pan, and stirred the sizzling mixture. With the mince nicely browned, he added two beaten eggs and waited until they began to congeal. He slid the omelet onto a plate and carried it to the dining table. A touch of pepper and salt, a squirt of ketchup, and breakfast was done. He reached for the coffee mug, took two large swallows, and began to eat. The TV muttered in the background, but he only half-listened, his mind on other things.

Cold and clinical, Lenora said, and he did not deny it…exactly. Alone, the empty house echoing his footsteps, he felt free to be himself without having to watch every word or gesture, having to pretend he was still the same old Dural, when in reality he had turned into someone else. The near miss lightning strike had changed him irrevocably, and in his view, changed him for the better. His eidetic memory and ability to see a person's bioelectromagnetic field were merely the obvious manifestations of that change. The others were more subtle, but in many respects, also more profound.

What he feared most after his accident was emergence of some physiological impairment, typical in lightning strike victims, or a personality-changing psychological event. Thankfully, none of those things happened. To identify and track the less obvious changes, he turned himself into a patient, and like every good psychologist, he kept detailed notes of his observations. Not that he needed them, his memory serving as a perfect filing system, but it was habit, a result of his training. The notes also helped him focus and evaluate his responses.

Apart from a scan last July, he no longer had any MRIs, although Gerard still maintained a watchful eye on him. With a slight increase in brain mass, Dural confirmed through a standard series of cognitive tests that his IQ had actually increased and he was sharper. Did those changes make him feel superior? In a way they did, and reduced his tolerance for the foolish and inane things people did, which might have made him appear colder and clinical to others. He preferred to use the term objective, and to a degree, more calculating. He still had feelings, though. He still felt emotional pain, anguish, sorrow, compassion…and love. If anything, his empathy quotient was stronger, which led him to confront his dilemma.

A chance meeting with a vibrant, intelligent woman had stirred something he thought safely buried at the bottom of his emotional pile, and churned his placid lifestyle into a muddy river of sensations. He could return to his moribund life and wait for the mud to clear by simply writing Aviana off as an interesting, diverting encounter. He would have clarity and certainty again, but he reminded himself that clear waters held little substance. The silt of experiences made the river of life stimulating, lively, and enriching. A placid pond might be pretty to look at, but it was a place to pause and reflect, not live.

Aviana had placed him on an emotional limb and he did not like the breeze. No, she had not done anything to encourage him.

He had placed himself on that limb willingly. Otherwise, he would not be feeling the wind.

What do you want, Doctor?

A very good question, Dural admitted. He knew the answer, of course. He was a psychologist after all, and did not need a PhD to tell him what he wanted. Aviana's clear face crystalized in his mind and he went over her every feature: captivating eyes, full lips, clean honey complexion, laughter, incisive conversation, her intellect. There was no order to the images her face conjured. Fleeting impressions that formed an enchanting mosaic whole. He felt undeniable physical attraction, but not juvenile lust. He wanted more from a relationship. Unless he misread the signals, she also appeared to want more, and left the door open for him to walk through.

What he thought to be a dilemma was merely indecision on his part. The wound of his divorce had healed, although the scars were somewhat tender, and the love he had for Lenora still smoldered, but no longer burned. She had chosen to move on, and he had learned to accept her decision. Wishing otherwise was delusional speculation. Did he drive her away by not being supportive enough, or understanding enough? Perhaps, but she was gone, and mulling over the 'if only' would not change things.

Aviana apparently wanted to see him again, and he wanted to see her. What was there to ponder then?

Step into the muddy river, Doctor, and see where it carries you. She also took a risk, he reminded himself.

Dural scraped the last of the egg and onion off the plate, downed the coffee, and carried the plate into the kitchen. He washed up, switched off the TV, and made his way upstairs. Twenty-eight today, the weather presenter said, with possible rain late in the afternoon, which meant that anything could happen. Satellites and monitoring stations notwithstanding, he found it amusing that weather forecasting was still so inaccurate. One of life's more puzzling phenomena, as was nature. Not that weather occupied his thinking a lot. Like day and night, it simply happened. Nothing to get worked up about. Still…

He set the alarm, locked up, and walked toward the side gate. Across the street, Mrs. Parker looked up from her weeding, smiled, and waved.

"Dr. Sinclair! Off to work, are you?"

"Somebody has to keep the economy going," he replied cheerfully.

"Not if Labor wins the election," she declared firmly. "They'll spend this country into recession."

Mrs. Parker carried her advancing years with enduring dignity, and those years had not dulled her mind in any way. If anything, they made her a sharper gossip, he mused.

"We'll see what happens on May 18," he said and started walking toward High Street. "Enjoy your day."

"You too, Doctor."

A gentle northerly swayed small branches and made the leaves whisper among themselves. Patchy gray clouds hovered above the southern horizon, presumably heralding the promised change. He would not mind seeing some rain. Summer so far had been fairly warm, even quite hot at times, and dry, which inevitably resulted in forest fires. Regrettably, some deliberately lit. He simply could not understand the mentality of someone wanting to generate destruction and derive pleasure out of the misery lost homes and property caused to the people affected. He had read papers on the subject and the underlying psychological analysis behind them, but that still left him perplexed. Some said a firebug's brain was wired differently. Without cutting one up and seeing for himself, what he wanted to do was wire the guy to a post, set him alight, and watch how the brain coped with that.

Rosalyn looked up from her computer screen when he walked in and beamed. Patricia poked her head from behind the reception desk and smiled, the pixie twinkle in her eyes suggesting that she had pulled a fast one on her mother.

"Hello, Uncle Dural," she said brightly, freckles adding charm to her cherubic face.

"Hi there, Pat. Looking after Mom?"

She frowned. "I got to go to daycare."

"The little monster was being uncooperative this morning and I ran late," Rosalyn said and shot a dark look at her daughter.

"It's not true," Pat declared promptly. "The toast got burned."

"It got burned because you were playing with the setting."

Pat gave Dural a conspiratorial grin. "It was only a little burnt. Honest."

The kid was a handful for Rosalyn, who adored her 'little mo'. Incredibly smart for her age, able to form coherent sentences, Dural not surprised that Pat would be a difficult package. Rosalyn took six months maternity leave when Pat was born, and the practice had to take on a temp receptionist. Rosalyn logged into PAX from home and kept doing the books, even though Dural and the others wanted to relieve her of that chore. The work filled her days, she told them. The temp was efficient and professional, but everyone was glad to have Rosalyn's firm hand at the helm again, with Pat amusing herself around the reception desk, entertaining the patients. At first, only for one day a week, which after three months turned to two days. After three more months, that went to three days before Rosalyn agreed to place Pat into a daycare center. Neither liked the arrangement, but Pat adjusted quickly as she made friends.

"How was Sydney?" Rosalyn asked.

"I managed to obtain a confession, and the accused will be extradited to Melbourne."

"Well, congratulations." She gave him a penetrating look. "And?"

"And what?"

"Something else happened. Didn't it?"

"I had an interesting time with the accused's lawyer, if you must know."

She chuckled. "I do want to know. Planning on seeing her again? I'm assuming it's a she."

"Yes, to both questions."

"Good on you, Du. It's about time you crawled out of that crab shell of yours."

Gerard walked in with Suyin at his side. Dural nodded to her and she nodded back.

"Ah, the prodigal returns," Gerard boomed cheerfully.

He spotted Pat and growled. The little girl squealed and disappeared. A moment later, she showed her head again. Gerard growled and she laughed, a tinkling of running water. The two played that game all the time, much to Suyin's indulgent amusement. To everyone's surprise, himself included, he took charge of the girl when Rosalyn was busy and he did not have a patient. Everyone helped, and Pat had taken a shine to all of them, but she liked Gerard best of all.

"Daycare?" Gerard asked, his head tilted at her.

Pat nodded. "Daycare."

Gerard glanced at Dural. "Everything taken care of in Sydney?"

"He found himself a girlfriend," Rosalyn added, ignoring Dural's stern look of disapproval.

"I should post everything on PAX," he declared darkly.

Gerard stroked Suyin's arm, gave her a beaming smile, and turned to Dural.

"Go for it, partner."

"Crap me dead, guys. I just met the woman," Dural protested, which caused everyone to laugh good-naturedly.

Not minding the mild ribbing, he strode into the kitchenette and fixed himself a mug of coffee. In his consulting room, he powered up the computer and checked his email list. The annual Australian & New Zealand Association of Psychiatry, Psychology and Law—ANZAPPL—congress held on the July 6 weekend. He shot off an acceptance and CCd Rosalyn and the other partners. Since the congress was in Melbourne, no need to secure accommodation. Scrolling down the list, he saw that everybody had already sent acceptances.

The Australian Clinical Psychology Association had a one-day conference on June 12, and he put himself down for it after checking his memory drawers to ensure he did not have a patient appointment clash. Trust Rosalyn to be on top of such details. The Australian Society for Psychological Medicine had a get-together in August, Dural not certain he wanted to attend. He would read the attached agenda later and decide, although he did want to present a paper on irrational compulsive behavior on aircraft, trains, trams, and buses that buried individual personality traits in a group environment. Perhaps he should jest send in the paper and see what happens.

Leonard and Gerard displayed a mild dislike having to attend professional conferences, but they served a very useful purpose, bringing together local and international practitioners, and helped disseminate new developments and ideas in the field. Reading medical journals simply not the same thing. Dural did not mind attending most conferences, but he rationed his appearances, including making guest lectures at Melbourne Uni and Monash. Networking was the price they all had to pay for being in the profession and maintaining their accreditation.

Inspector Frank Farmer thanked him profusely for securing Kresta's confession, and The Office of Public Prosecutions now had the case. The interview transcript from Inspector Cummins should make this a no-contest. Wellard, Wellard and Starke had filed a plea bargain motion, and Farmer suspected the matter would be handled in chambers. Dural did not care how Victoria Police handled the case. His part was done.

The other quandary he found himself in, one very silly, was his indecision to call Aviana. He did not want to appear too eager and perhaps scare her off by bothering her. On the other hand, she said she did not mind seeing him again, and if he did not call, she might interpret that as lack of interest on his part. He had not dated in a very long time and was not sure of the playing rules these days.

His inner self sneered at him. *Do you like the woman? Of course, he liked her,* he told himself. *What is the worst thing that could happen if you asked her out?*

Dural allowed himself a faint smile.

She could only say no. A definite do not call me again no, or a rain check. It would hurt if she said not ever, but it would not be a fatal bruise. He would write it off as a fond encounter and move on. If she said yes, he would take it one moment at a time.

Problem resolved, he glanced at his watch: 8:20; ten minutes before his first patient.

Howard Tanner's history perfectly fitted the statistical bell curve generated by modern high-pressure demands exerted on successful professionals. A high-flyer retail banking executive at the Commonwealth Bank, at thirty-six relatively young for the position, a commerce degree and an MBA behind him, a wife in the real estate business, a boy and a girl growing into handfuls, Tanner had dug himself into a hole. He and his wife liked the comfortable lifestyle their incomes provided, but career success had exacted a cruel price. They were not spending enough time with each other and the kids.

Dural did not need a session to root out Tanner's problem. The referral notes from the GP were clear enough, and Tanner himself understood his quandary. He was intelligent enough. What he struggled with was accepting the obvious solution from the two available to him.

After making his patient comfortable, coffee in hand, Dural started the session.

"The notes from your GP tell me you were reluctant to see me. Most people are," he added with a smile, closely observing the shift of auras around the younger man: resolution, uncertainty, confusion, compassion. "Have you ever seen a counselor before?"

Tanner sipped his coffee and shook his head. "First time, Doc. To tell you the truth, I never thought I would need one. Somewhat ironic finding myself here."

"It can work out like that," Dural agreed. "However, you're smart enough to recognize the need to see me, which means you understand the nature of your problem. I would like to hear you describe it in your own words."

"Nothing much to tell. Simple in one way, and very complex in another. I work fifty hours a week, sometimes more. Veronica works all sorts of odd hours, especially on weekends. As a real estate rep, she's on call all the time." Tanner gave a rueful snort. "You can see where this is leading. We're slowly becoming strangers, and we're not giving our kids the attention they need. They have withdrawn into game playing, and I'm having arguments with Veronica."

"How does all this make you feel? Sad, angry, helpless?"

"All of it, Doc. The crummy part is, I know what I should do, but I cannot bring myself to do it."

"How would you resolve your problem?"

"Easy. Work less and spend more time with my wife and kids. If I don't, they'll grow up without knowing a real father, and Veronica and I'll lose what initially brought us together. We'll end up strangers living under the same roof."

"You said the problem would be solved if you worked less. What about Veronica working less?"

Tanner wagged a finger at Dural. "No way. I couldn't ask her to do that. She worked hard to establish recognition, and she likes the people interaction of her job. Become a sit at home housewife with dinner waiting for her husband and kids?" Tanner laughed, but without mirth. "She's not the type, Doc, and I wouldn't want her to be."

"And your solution?" Dural prompted gently, watching the interplay of conflicting auras with interest.

"It's up to me, isn't it?" Tanner said slowly.

"Tell me. Does Veronica spend time with the children?"

The younger man frowned in concentration. "During the week, yes, and she's always there for them after school. It's the weekends where I miss her the most, and I hardly see her at all during the week. By the time I come home, I'm too mentally exhausted to mess with my kids or talk with her. If I worked less, it would fix my domestic problems, but I could kiss my career goodbye."

"Are you working long hours because the bank demands it, or because you like it? A stimulating pressure cooker job can be uplifting. It can also become addictive, and you get hooked before you know it. Can you tell me which category best fits your case?"

"The bank will not collapse if I worked a more normal week, is that it?"

Dural smiled. "I doubt that very much, Mr. Tanner. Your colleagues—"

"What about them?"

"What sort of hours do they put in?"

"Mmm. I can see where you're going with this."

"Do you?"

"I'm a smart guy, Doc. My degrees say so. Smart at my job, but dumb when it comes to my family. The answer to your question, and perhaps answer mine at the same time, my colleagues are people like me. They have ambition, families, and from our casual chats, most of them are content. On reflection, they don't work fifty hours a week. They put in extra time when there is a need for it, but we have subordinates who are supposed to do the hackwork. Perhaps I should delegate more. I do tend to micromanage somewhat."

"Do you see that as the solution to your problem?"

Tanner bit his lip. "If I want to keep my family it is." He shook his head. "A couple of hours extra every day won't be a problem, I told myself. See what that got me? Seeing a shrink."

"You understand what you must do, Mr. Tanner. More importantly, you understand why you must do it. Can I make a suggestion?"

"Shoot."

"Arrange a free weekend for yourself and Veronica. Go to Daylesford, Yarra Valley, Bright. Anywhere where you can be alone. I'm sure your children won't mind having a weekend to themselves either," Dural added dryly, and Tanner laughed.

"I'll send them to my sister. She'll love to have the little fiends."

"Another question. When was the last time you two had a proper vacation together?"

"Shit! Let's see…after Veronica became pregnant with our son."

"Your first child?"

"That's right."

"Perhaps it's time you two took another one, wouldn't you agree?"

"She always wanted to see Darwin and Kakadu," Tanner mused, then frowned. "Nice idea, but that'll be hard to manage, Doc. Between her work and my projects—"

"Will the bank collapse, Mr. Tanner? Will Veronica lose her job?"

Silence stole into the room as Tanner lost himself in thought. After a while, he looked at Dural with new determination.

"That's a no to both questions," he said and exhaled with apparent relief. "Thanks for sorting me out."

"The battle between a career and family is a common one, and there are no easy answers. Implementing your decision might be difficult to begin with, and you may need more counseling. I would recommend another session in two weeks' time, but I'll let you make that decision. You can always contact me if you need help."

Tanner stood and held out his hand. "Thanks, Doc. Having a long talk with Veronica tonight will, I trust, go a long way toward patching things up. A movie outing with the kids perhaps? We shall see."

"Good luck, Mr. Tanner."

Dural escorted his patient out and then wrote a summary into the computer. He hoped he would not see Tanner again, but suspected he would. Withdrawal from any type of addiction is painful, and work addiction can be the worst of all.

He got himself a coffee refill, sat down, and visualized Aviana's business card. Smiling, he punched numbers into his smartphone.

"Aviana Kinsley."

"Hi, there. It's Dural," he said, relieved how calm he felt.

"Du! This is a pleasant surprise."

"Are you free to talk?"

"I have a couple of minutes. What do you have in mind?"

"Lunch at The Deck at Southbank at 12:30."

"I have never been there before."

"It's off the Princes Bridge. You can't miss it."

He heard a merry chuckle. "Every time someone tells me I cannot miss it, means it's very easy to miss."

Dural laughed. "How about this. I'll meet you at the Southbank side of the bridge, and we'll go hunting for this restaurant that cannot be missed. Deal?"

"I did not expect you to call so quickly," Aviana temporized.

"If you cannot make it today, same time tomorrow?"

"I can see that I won't get you out of my hair unless I say yes."

"Then 12:30 today it is."

"Wolf. Okay, see you then."

"I'm looking forward to it, Aviana," Dural said softly. He heard a click and she was gone.

He sat back against the chair, coffee mug in hand, and smiled.

At 11:25, his third patient out of the way, Dural picked up his mug to wash it before attending to a hydraulic problem. He opened the door and stopped. Leonard walked beside Suyin toward the kitchenette and his arm strayed possessively around her waist. Dural saw her flinch and he gritted his teeth in anger.

He took care of his hydraulic problem, walked to Leonard's office and strode in without knocking.

"Du! What's up?"

"You are what's up, you idiot!" Dural hissed.

Leonard blanched, his aura dirty gray of inner guard. "What the hell are you talking about?"

Dural pointed at the CCTV camera. "Turn that off."

Leonard reached into a drawer and held up an electronic fob. "Okay, it's off. Now, mind telling me why you're biting my head off?"

"I warned you, but you didn't listen. Suyin doesn't need your protective arm around her waist to find the kitchen. What if Gerard saw you? Have you lost your mind?"

His friend gaped at him in shock. "I didn't mean anything by it, Du."

"Fool! You're a happily married man, Len. Do you want to ruin that? Do you want to ruin Gerard?"

"Christ, Du! It was nothing. A fleeting touch. I was only being friendly."

"Too friendly, and she didn't like it. In future, keep your hands in your pockets!"

"I'm not chasing, Suyin! No one was happier than me to see Gerard finally find someone to love. I don't want to come between them."

"Then stop acting like a juvenile." Dural studied his friend and pulled at his right ear. "Is everything all right between you and Helen?"

"What? We're fine. I may have been neglecting her a bit lately. Her work as Assistant Prof at Melbourne Uni sometimes makes for long hours, but we're solid. Why do you ask?"

"You've done Psychology 101, Len. Trouble at home means a roving eye at work."

"You're crazy. I love Helen."

"Then stop this barnyard dance around Suyin before this gets out of hand. Do you want a sexual harassment suit on your hands?"

Leonard slumped in his seat, then gave Dural a pleading look. "It was nothing!"

"Keep it that way, because I'll have my eye on you. All of us have invested too much into this practice to have it undone by playing the love triangle. Don't prove me wrong," Dural said earnestly and walked out, hoping his friend had taken the message seriously.

Around twelve, he told Rosalyn he was going out, and she gave him an impish grin.

"Your lawyer friend?"

"Feel free to post it on Facebook, why don't you."

Her laughter followed him to the elevator.

Outside, the sun burned from a clear sky, and the dark clouds hanging over the Bay had not made a move. His next appointment not until two. Provided Aviana did not have to rush, he looked forward to a relaxing lunch. He figured she would have told him if she were short of time.

He crossed St. Kilda Road and joined a small gaggle at the tram stop. Thirty tonnes of sudden green death hissed smoothly toward them and stopped with a squeal of brakes. The double doors snapped open and Dural climbed on board, the tram practically empty. It would fill quickly as it made its way downtown, picking up office workers heading for the city. He tapped on the Myki charge card, took a back seat, and stared vacantly at the plane and golden elms lining the inner roadway. Some time back,

Yarra Trams wanted the trees cut down because in fall, they dumped piles of leaves along the tracks. The resulting outcry quickly squelched that idea, the traveling public demanding that Yarra Trams improve their services instead.

As the doors snapped shut, the driver clanked the bell, and the tram surged forward with a whine of electric motors.

By the time he reached the Arts Center, there was standing room only. He squeezed his way toward the door, tapped off his Myki, and sighed with relief when he stepped into fresh air filled with the scent of blooms coming from the flowerbeds. His watch said 12:25 and he hurried toward the Princes Bridge some forty meters ahead, Melbourne's jagged skyline providing a postcard backdrop.

Aviana looked cool and composed in a crisp white shirt and dark slacks, eyes hidden behind tinted green sunglasses. She saw him, pulled off the shades, and waited for him to walk up.

"I hope I didn't keep you waiting," he told her warmly, basking in her smile.

"Just got here myself."

He extended an arm at the Southbank entrance. "Shall we?"

A long tourist boat drifted slowly upriver, the occupants snapping pictures or filming everything with tablets and camcorders. The promenade teemed with people against a background of cars and clattering trams. Across the boulevard, Kings Domain Park heralded an oasis of calm. Couples sat beneath broad tree canopies enjoying a perfect summer's day.

The Deck restaurant looked calm and inviting, the ceiling-high windows giving an excellent view of the city. An attractive Asian attendant, neat in her blue blouse and green skirt, smiled and steered Dural and Aviana toward a window table. She waited until they were seated and handed them a large black bound menu.

"Today's special is pork loin on the bone, and I would recommend the chocolate cherry semifreddo."

Dural nodded and she drifted off.

Aviana looked quickly around the elegantly appointed room, large square tables arranged in no apparent order, not all of them occupied, the long bar with its arrays of bottles, and lifted an eyebrow.

"This is nice, Du."

"The service is quick, especially at lunch, and the food is good."

"You've been here before?"

"A few times. There are some nice restaurants along High Street my partners and I frequent, but they're a little out of your way for a lunch outing."

"Next time, I'll take you to a place in Collins Street," she said. "The prices are merely ridiculous instead of scandalous."

"Deal," he said with a grin, and opened the menu. He scanned the beverages list and looked up. "Some wine to help things along?"

"A glass of white, please. Something crisp without being too dry," she said, eyes on the menu. "A Sauvignon Blanc perhaps?"

"Done."

Their minder came, an electronic pad in hand. "Are you ready to order?"

"Two glasses of Avera Hills Sauvignon Blanc," Dural told her and glanced at Aviana. She bit her lower lip, then looked up.

"I'll have the roast snapper."

"Any dessert?" the attendant queried.

Aviana stole a glance at Dural and gave a sheepish smile. "The cherry semifreddo…how large is the serve?"

The attendant grinned knowingly. "I can get you half a serve."

"Great. I'll have it."

Dural nodded approval. "And I'll have the char-grilled Angus rump done medium. A half serve of semifreddo for me as well."

"Excellent!" The attendant tapped in the orders into her pad, beamed at them as she gathered the menus, and sauntered off.

Dural tilted his head at Aviana. "Cherries? A weakness?"

"Somewhat," she admitted. "Especially the dark red ones, but they're late-season fruit. Until they become available, I satisfy myself with whatever is out there." She studied him. "And what is your weakness?"

"Kiwi fruit and mangoes with a touch of cognac poured over them."

Her eyebrows rose. "Wow. That's some combination."

"You'll have to try it," he assured her, and a faint smile teased her mouth.

The wine came in tall, fat glasses and Dural raised his in a salute. "To charming company," he said. They touched glasses with a clear melodious *ting*.

She took a sip and nodded. "Nice. Thank you."

Tables began to fill as diners drifted in, and the ambient noise rose a little, but remained subdued. The restaurant's elegance acted as a sound suppressor.

Dural's gaze drifted to Aviana's hazel eyes, highlighted by light eyeshadow. She met his look without pulling away, her purple/blue aura giving way to orange with a pink border, revealing her goodhearted, loving nature. He felt a momentary twinge of guilt spying on her like that, then shook it off. He wanted to know this woman, and seeing the play of colors surrounding her only enhanced his positive perception of her.

He glanced at the city. "We should come here one evening. With the skyscrapers lit, it makes a great view."

She turned her head toward the unbroken muddle of towers.

"Do you go out much?" she asked after a while.

"An occasional lunch or evening with my partners. Otherwise, I'm pretty much a stay at home person."

"Doesn't sound very exciting," she remarked.

"That's me. What about you?"

She shrugged. "Pretty much the same, I'm afraid. My work keeps me busy."

He sighed and shook his head. "Two dull people. We'll have to do something about that before the condition turns psychotic."

"This isn't a counseling session, is it, Doctor?"

He chuckled. "Just an observation."

She took a sip and held the glass stem with delicate fingers. "Seriously, what takes up your time when you're not playing doctor? I know you said you golf and write stories, but there must be more behind that professional façade."

"Well, I read a lot. Fiction and non-fiction. I like listening to music when I'm writing or working around the house. Mostly classical, but I like a lot of the popular '60s and '70s stuff. My parents were into Neil Diamond, The Seekers, Petula Clark, and ABBA. I guess their influence rubbed off on me."

"Ah, ABBA. I love them," Aviana declared. "I cannot stand modern music. Especially rap." She shuddered. "It makes my hair stand on end. Somewhere along the line, singers—if I can call them that—lost the art of writing good lyrics and producing stirring melodies." She grinned at him. "Showing my age, I guess."

"Good taste, I would say."

"What else goes on in that head?"

"Like with most people, a whole lot of irrelevancy. Everyday life is filled with a myriad of small activates we don't remember. In my case, I remember everything, which fills my brain with a lot of useless clutter."

"What do you mean, you remember everything?"

"I have an eidetic memory."

She regarded him for a second, weighing up what he said. "Everything way back from your childhood?"

"Actually, this started about four years ago. I played golf with one of my partners and an indirect lightning strike knocked me out. Fortunately for me, the electrical surge didn't fry my nervous system, and I walked away to talk about it."

"You were lucky."

"I'll say. Most lightning strike survivors develop debilitating physical and psychological problems, either immediately or over time."

"Have *you* developed anything, apart from your memory?"

"So far so good," he said smoothly. This was not the time to reveal everything.

Their attendant walked up carrying two large plates.

"Enjoy," she said cheerfully and weaved her way between tables.

Dural eyed his Angus rump, keen to stick a fork into it. Aviana eyed her fish and squeezed lemon over it. He filled her spare glass with water and poured for himself.

"*Bon appétit*," he said with a smile.

"Mmm. That roast looks good," she murmured, watching his plate.

He carved off a chunk and placed it beside her fish. "Now you have the best of both worlds."

"Care to sample some of mine?" she asked, knife and fork poised over the fish.

"A little piece."

She cut off a slice, smeared some tartare sauce over it, and forked it onto his plate. He cut off a corner and popped it into his mouth. The snapper had a delicate, smooth flavor and he nodded.

"Not bad."

She did the same with his roast and chewed thoughtfully. "Want to swap?" she asked with a tilt of her head, and he immediately pushed his plate toward her. She laughed. "Just kidding, but thanks. I'll have it next time."

They spent several minutes on food, Dural pleased to see Aviana enjoying herself. He took a sip of wine, feeling its glow spread through him. He did not need to look into a mirror to tell he was bathed in silver/golden light. He had an impulse to reach across the table and touch her hand. She noted his scrutiny and raised an eyebrow.

"What?"

"I love the gusto with which you approach life," he told her.

She smiled faintly. "Wolf, and prong."

He laid down his tools and leaned toward her. "Okay, what is this prong thing?"

"It doesn't mean anything in particular. I use it when I feel the situation draws attention to something you said or did."

"My ex-wife used to call me a block when she thought I was being thick," he told her, and she chuckled.

"I like that. Perceptive woman. I might borrow it. This memory thing of yours. It must come in pretty handy at times."

"Think of it as a Google or Wikipedia database in my head."

She stared at him, then laughed, which drew amused glances from patrons around them. After a moment, she dabbed at her eyes.

"Oh, that was good." She suppressed a titter, took a sip of water, and shook her head. "Perfect description."

Main meal finished, Dural spent time in idle conversation, drawing her out, content to bask in her glow. Their attendant removed the plates and returned with the dessert. Eyeing her portion, Aviana took a bite and sighed.

"When I'm in heaven, I'll insist they serve semifreddo every day. With more cherries on top," she added.

He tried a spoonful and nodded. The chocolate base creamy and not too sweet, the cherries adding just the right offsetting tartness.

"I don't indulge like this often, but I must say this is delicious."

"Indulgence is good for the soul," she declared firmly, then glanced at her watch. "Goodness! One forty already, I've got to fly, Du. This has been heavenly."

"Tomorrow?" he asked hopefully.

She bit her lip and shook her head. "Afraid not. Heavy day, but I could make it on Friday. Does twelve suit you?"

He consulted his memory—no patient clash—and nodded. "Twelve is fine."

"Good. We'll meet outside the Louis Vuitton building on Collins. My treat."

"I know where it is. Wellard has their offices there."

A pixie gleam lit her eyes. "I'll have to watch what I say when I'm with you. I'm not sure I like the idea having a permanent recorder around me."

"It's a chance you'll have to take," he told her lightly.

The attendant brought the bill and Dural left her a handsome tip.

Outside, several gray clouds had drifted in, but there was no letup from the heat. He walked Aviana to the tram stop, squinting against the sun's glare. As the tram pulled up, she put on her shades and turned toward him. He gave her a peck on the cheek and nodded.

"Until Friday."

She beamed at him, stepped into the tram, and he watched it glide toward the Flinders Street station stop. Content, he crossed the boulevard to catch a tram going up St. Kilda Road. Despite complaints, the city tram service quite good, and he only had to wait a couple of minutes. He boarded the almost empty carriage, sat down, and watched the lush park on his left as the tram pulled out. He would be a little late for his appointment, and would apologize, hoping Mr. Greenwood would not be too annoyed having to wait.

It stopped almost directly opposite the Gap Psychology Consulting building. Dural jaywalked across the inner St. Kilda Road lane and hurried inside. As he strode into the reception area, he winced when he saw Mr. Greenwood browsing a magazine in the waiting lounge. He hated to keep his patients waiting. His excuse that he enjoyed Aviana's company too much over lunch would not stand up to close scrutiny.

"Give me two minutes and send in Mr. Greenwood," he told Rosalyn as he strode toward his consulting room.

About to open the door, Gerard walked out, spotted him, and raised his hand.

"Du, just the man I want to see."

"Sorry, Ger. I'm running late. I've got fifteen minutes at four, though."

Gerard scowled and shook his head. "No good. I've got a patient then."

"I can make it after work," Dural offered. "Five-thirty or so? Unless it's something urgent."

"No, after work will do," Gerard said, face troubled, and walked toward the kitchen.

Seeing his friend's expression, Dural wanted to stop him, but Gerard would have stayed if it were something serious.

By 5:40, Dural had enough of therapy sessions, Bishop Greenwood's case the toughest. Every patient was important, and he cared for each one of them. Listening to their problems, he sometimes found it difficult not to get emotionally involved. That was the drawback of his enhanced empathy. Treatment became especially challenging with patients who were in denial or blame mode, refusing to accept they were the causal factor, as was the case with Mr. Greenwood.

Married into a successful paper and plastics recycling business, he started drinking too much and blamed his wife for a failing relationship. Mrs. Greenwood and her brother owned the business, and Bishop, a mechanical engineer, looked after the reprocessing plant. His wife complained more than once that his job was to manage the plant, not act as a greasy maintenance technician. He was supposed to attend executive meetings and help set company policy. The problem, which Bishop recognized, he liked getting his hands greasy, and the other engineers were unwilling to complain when the boss interfered with their legiti-mate work. This led to arguments with his wife and brother. He was not merely another hired hand, they told him, but part of the administrative team. If he could not handle the load, perhaps he should look for other opportunities to exercise his skills.

Today was Bishop's third session, and he still refused to rec-ognize that blaming everyone else for his failings would not solve his problem, and deciding what he wanted out of his marriage and career the solution. Dural had slowly broken down Bishop's defensive barrier and achieved measurable progress. During the next session, he figured Mr. Greenwood would be ready to con-front his demons.

He finished typing notes from the last case and shut off the computer, glad to end the day, then rang Gerard to say he was free. His partner showed up right away and sat down without waiting for an invitation.

"I'm in a bind, Du, and I would like your input before I decide what to do."

Dural hoped it was not about Leonard as he pulled out the electronic fob and switched off the surveillance camera.

"Shoot."

"It's no secret that I'm in love with Suyin, and she told me more than once that she loves me."

"I'm glad to hear it, Ger. So, what's the problem?"

"I want to propose to her, but I cannot bring myself to do it. I fear if I don't do it soon, she might lose interest." Gerard twitched his glasses into place and groaned. "Why do men have to propose all the time? Women should be upfront about these things too."

Dural chuckled. "That's a rhetorical question, Ger. It's one of those social things, and for her, it could also be cultural. Tell me. Are you scared she will say no?"

Gerard pursed his mouth. "I'm sure she would say yes, but..."

"You're scared," Dural said gently.

"I'll level with you, Du. I'm terrified. How did you handle this with Lenora?"

"I was afraid at the prospect of committing permanently to someone."

"But you did it anyway."

"I did when I remembered why I wanted to marry her. I wanted to be with her always, not just on dates and outings. I wanted to give her everything I had, and I'm not talking about money or a house. I wanted her to have me, warts and all, and make a life together."

"That's how I feel about Suyin," Gerard said and snorted. "Look at me. Pushing forty-two, balding, not a body hunk, I'm surprised she wants me."

"Looks aren't everything, Ger, and women want more than just a hunk. Although that helps when you're younger, but neither of you are teenagers, and other things become more important. You're honest, successful, smart, and you care. Not only for her, but for people in general, otherwise you would not be a psychologist. You represent stability and reassurance that she and her daughter will have a future with you."

Gerard waved a hand. "I know all that, Du. I have been counseling others on these very things."

"You cannot bring yourself to practice what you preach, is that it?"

"I guess. So, what do I do?"

"Take her to dinner, go for a walk, or simply bring her a cup of tea and tell her how you feel, then gently slip the ring on her finger. That's all it takes."

Gerard looked skeptical. "That's all?"

"That's all."

"What if she says no?"

"Then you get your ring back. Seriously, though. She's probably waiting for you to ask and is frustrated that you're too chicken to do it."

"And she's right." Gerard sighed dejectedly. "There is something else, Du…Leonard. He and Suyin—"

Dural raised his hand. "Before you go on, I want to straighten you out. I have seen how he tends to flutter around Suyin, and I have spoken to him about it. Believe me when I tell you, there is nothing in it."

"It did not look like that to me. We talked about it, and she doesn't appreciate his advances. Is he planning to leave Helen?"

"Of course not. He was shocked when I asked him the same question. Leonard has simply allowed his boyish gallantry to run away from him. "

"Are you sure? I don't go out, and finding someone at my age to love me is remote. When I met Suyin, I knew right away that we had a connection. But if it comes to competing with Leonard, his poise and sophistication, even if he is a short runt, I wouldn't stand a chance."

"Ger, there is nothing between them, I tell you. If you want, I'll ask him to apologize to you."

"You and Len, we've been together since university, and I thought I knew both of you as well as anyone can know someone. However, men change and they do strange things when it comes to women. Our friendship is important to me, Du, and I won't stand in Len's way if—"

"Stop right there!" Dural commanded. "This is not about Len and Suyin. This is about you and your fear of rejection."

Gerard chewed his lower lip, then exhaled loudly. "You're right. I'm making excuses, aren't I?"

"Get off your ass and propose, you fool."

"Do you think Leonard would care to be my best man?" Gerard asked with a whimsical smile, and Dural relaxed.

"I'm certain he'd be honored. If he gives Suyin one more inappropriate look, I'll hold him down while you punch out his battery."

Gerard chuckled and stood. "I wouldn't mind at all. Thanks for the heart-to-heart, Doctor."

"Rosalyn will email you the bill."

Looking happy, Gerard waved and walked out.

Seeing his friend's contented glow, Dural also felt happy. Suyin was just the thing Gerard needed. He was right about one thing. Men were apt to do strange things when it came to women and the drive to procreate.

Dural hoped he was not making a fool of himself with Aviana.

* * *

Rosalyn looked up from her computer screen and raised an eyebrow. "Two lunches in a week. Wow. What's next? An evening out?"

"I might be going out for a walk, you know," Dural told her with a grin.

"Of course," she deadpanned.

He shook a finger at her and strode out.

Sunny, bright, warm, the very air felt alive, shimmering with energy. Feeling buoyed and satisfied with the world, he crossed St. Kilda Road and waited for the downtown tram. Wherever he looked, people's aura glowed bright, relishing a perfect day. Being Friday invariably contributed to the general wellbeing.

The city center teemed with pedestrians, and he suppressed the flood of auras crashing into him. Easy to tell the tourists from the locals rushing to wherever they were going. The tourists, mostly Chinese and Japanese—the Europeans tended to carry a small backpack—gawked at everything, chattering to each other, happily snapping pictures, seemingly oblivious to the stream of cars, buses, and trams that combined to form a blanket of ambient noise.

When the walk sign turned green, a throng of bodies swept Dural going up the street. A throaty motorcycle roared along the tram tracks past crawling cars. Upper Collins Street housed fashion boutiques and trendy stores, expensive doctors and dentists, and lawyers. A Collins Street address on office stationery meant success and money, and a BMW no longer enough. He and his partners considered opening their practice here, but rents were murderous. Anyway, a St. Kilda Road address also meant they were part of the elite.

He crossed Russell Street and stopped at the corner, the gray old Louis Vuitton Building reflecting the sun's heat. The nineteenth century stone façade hid exclusive stores and offices. The three blocks to the State Parliament lay in almost perpetual shadow cast by towering buildings on either side, tall trees protecting the sidewalks.

Aviana emerged from the main entrance, turned to face down the street, and smiled when she spotted him. Neat in a pale blue shirt, sleeves reaching partway down her forearms, dark blue knee-length skirt, high heels but not spikes, she looked elegant.

"Dressed to wow them," Dural remarked and planted a kiss on her cheek.

"Looking cool yourself," she quipped and wrapped her arm around his. "Busy day?"

"The patients keep coming, as do your clients, no doubt," he said with a grin.

"That they do." She noted the green walk light and tugged at his arm. "Let's cross. The place we're going to is just ahead."

On this side of the block, there were only stores and the Regent Theater. He checked that thought.

"We're going to the La Pesce?"

"If you don't like seafood, we can go somewhere else."

"Seafood is fine with me."

They pushed their way through the lunchtime crowd and paused before the trendy restaurant entrance. Dural opened the door and waited for Aviana to walk into the cool, dim interior. The signature black floor, black tables and chairs, walls clad in chest-high black wood paneling, the La Pesce Restaurant popular with patrons. Aviana confirmed her reservation at the reception desk and a young woman wearing a white blouse and black skirt led them past crowded tables toward the back. The interior had a rustic charm and smelled of seafood and fine wine, but not spirits, which would have dulled the palate.

Their minder waited for them to be seated and held out leather-bound menus. Aviana took a finger-thick bread stick from a tall glass and crunched on it as she studied the menu.

"Some wine?" Dural asked. "Something crisp without being too dry, right?"

She cocked an eye at him. "Nothing wrong with your memory. A chardonnay this time?"

He looked at their attendant. "Two glasses of Serafino chardonnay."

"Very good," the woman said, nodded, and strode toward the bar.

"You've been here before?" Aviana asked.

"Once or twice," Dural said. "I like the atmosphere, and the seafood is first-rate, although I don't have it all the time."

"I like it because it's close to the office. Most of us come here quite often. When we get tired of prawns and oysters, we get stuck into something heavier."

"Are you a white or red meat lover?" he asked.

"I can take either one, but with steak, I usually like it medium rare. You?"

"Same here, but I prefer it seared with a bit of crunch."

She grinned. "I'll have to remember that."

The wine came and the attendant looked at them. "Ready to order?"

The service during the evening was usually subdued, and time was meant to be savored, but lunches were somewhat rushed affairs, understandably enough.

Aviana shut the menu with a snap and looked up. "Tiger prawn spring rolls to start, and for the main, I'll have the garlic crayfish. No dessert."

"I'll have the scampi spring rolls," Dural said, "and veal Saltimbocca."

The attendant scribbled into her pad, smiled, and gathered the menus.

Dural picked up his glass and held it up. "To another Friday."

Aviana chuckled and they clicked glasses. She took a sip and nodded. "Nice. Anything lined up for the weekend?"

"Not much," he admitted. "Cleaning up, washing, shopping; Saturday is my chores day. You?"

"Same here. It'll be a hot one, they said. Thirty-four."

"That's a bit warm for me," he mused and gave her a speculative look. "Since tomorrow will be a boring chores day, how about we close it off on a more pleasant note?"

"Wolf. What did you have in mind?"

"I haven't decided yet."

"A mystery dinner. How can I refuse?"

"You can't. If you do, you will never see me again, which will leave me crushed."

Her laugh lit her face with radiance. "We can't have that, can we? Okay, you're on."

"Good. Now, where do I pick you up?"

"I have a little terrace cottage in South Melbourne…94 Cobden Street." She noted his bemused expression. "What?"

"My ex-wife and I used to rent a place on Napier, a street up from you."

"Small world," she said and sipped her wine.

"Have you lived there long?"

"Oh, eight years now. Three years ago, I had it renovated and turned the place inside out. I got rid of those horrid narrow corridors and opened everything up. The place had three small bedrooms, but when I finished with them, I now have two, larger and much more comfortable ones. The wide windows I put in give me lots of light and a sense of spaciousness. I thought of getting an apartment in Southbank, and I would be right in the city. My dad pointed out that purchasing an apartment would cost the earth and I would also be up for hefty body corporate fees. It would be like paying off a double mortgage, so I decided to stay put. The street where I live has trees on both sides, the neighborhood is quiet, and there is lots of shopping nearby."

"I know what you mean," Dural said, recalling the tidy terrace he and Lenora had. "I would not have minded staying where I was, but I rented, and with a child on the way, both of us wanted something permanent. When an opportunity came to buy, I snapped it up."

The entrees came and Aviana observed her spring rolls with relish.

He looked at her. "Share?"

Without saying anything, she placed one on his plate and took one of his. He forked his into the Thai sweet chili sauce and crunched off the end. The roll had a delicate vegetable flavor, which the sauce complemented perfectly. Aviana clearly liked her tiger prawn roll.

"I could eat these all day," she declared, dipping hers into a mushroom sauce. "Almost all day."

"Your parents…I know you said your father is an aircraft engineer with Virgin, but your mom?"

"Retired for years. She used to be an investigative journalist with *The Age* paper. These days, she dabbles with computer graphics and designs book covers for authors." She lifted an eyebrow. "Maybe you can use her."

"For my next book," he promised.

"By the way, when is the next opus coming? Fiction or professional?"

"Science fiction, and I'm about halfway through it, although I have been doing research for another professional work."

"Your book, space opera? Starships blasting each other, and the hero rescues the damsel in distress?"

He chuckled. "Not exactly. It's a little more subtle, and Star Wars films have overdone the space opera genre in my view. People are starting to look for more substance in films."

"I know," she said and sighed. "I haven't been to a movie in…Goodness! I can't remember when."

Dural loved the way she handled herself without making disclaimers before making a point. She told it like she saw it without apology. Something very useful in her line of work.

The attendant came, took away the small plates, and returned with the main course. Dural admitted the crayfish looked inviting. His own thinly sliced veal filled with prosciutto, served with mushroom sauce, potato mash, and seared beans, made his mouth water. He forked two slices onto her plate and added a spoon of sauce over them. She smiled and gave him a chunk of crayfish.

"Your clients won't mind the garlic breath?" he asked playfully.

"A peppermint Tic-Tac and I'll be right." She took a bite and sighed. "This is good."

Time seemed to stop as food preoccupied their thoughts. Aviana dabbed her lips with a napkin and took a sip of wine.

"How did you get into psychology?"

Dural grinned. "If my father had his way, I would be a surgeon. He thought I wasted my time with something wooly like psychology."

"Sounds like a strong-willed man."

"He is, but he came around later when he found out how much the practice earns. Between you and me, I think he gave up trying to change me. I was actually a computer nerd in high school and never considered psychology as a career."

She raised a whimsical eyebrow. "You a nerd? Really?"

"Truly. I liked things methodical and organized, and computers fitted my mindset. One day, I happened to watch a documentary on SBS about mental illness and modern treatments. I could not believe what they did in the old days. They literally took the equivalent of a screwdriver, plunged it through a patient's nose, and scrambled the frontal lobe of the brain."

She gaped. "They didn't."

"I kid you not. After that, I became interested and started reading up. One thing led to another and I took up clinical psychology at Monash Uni. I'm still methodical and organized in everything I do, and I apply that to my work."

"I'm sure you do. You have that look."

"What look?"

"Detached and clinical. I don't mean cold, but when you look at me sometimes, I feel like a specimen under a microscope."

"Probing for hidden neurosis," he told her brightly.

"And I have a few, but I don't think I could afford you."

"The first one would be a freebie." He chewed on his veal and took a sip of wine. "Is there anything particularly dark lurking behind those eyes?"

Her mouth tightened for an instant. "Dark dreams."

He could sense she did not want to go there and dropped it. "What about you? How did you happen to get into law?"

"Well, I was a bit of a bookworm myself in high school," she said and immediately raised a finger in warning. "Don't say it."

Dural lifted both arms in surrender. "I wasn't going to say anything."

"Good, because there would have been consequences."

"I believe you."

"Prong. Anyway, what I found is that almost every politician and industry leader studied law. Not necessarily to practice, but a law degree has clearly opened doors for them normally closed to other professionals, or are harder to open. I was fascinated how law can be used to protect individuals, their rights, property, and uphold justice, which sounds trite, but it's true." She gave a shy smile. "I must admit, I was also influenced by TV series like *LA Law*. They're highly stylized and really corny, but I could see how a law degree would help me make a difference."

"And have you made a difference?"

"Definitely. As with anything, law is a double-edged sword, and some in my profession consider justice a quaint notion."

"I know what you mean. How did your parents react to the idea of having a lawyer in the family?"

"They didn't particularly care one way or another, happy that I pursued a career. Dinah, though, was all for it, liking the idea of having a rich sister."

"Are you close to your sister?"

"We're pretty close. She's a partner in a dentist practice in North Melbourne, not far from the Victoria Market. We share lunch sometimes and get together for dinner now and then. Her twin ten-year-old girls are a handful whenever I visit, but she doesn't seem to have any trouble coping. Things get very boisterous when all of us descend on our parents, but Mom is a great entertainer and loves to fuss over us."

"My mom is the same," Dural said. "I don't get to see them much these days—"

"They're in Nelson Bay a lot?"

"Especially during winter. When they do come down, I get invited to come over to their place in North Melbourne, or I do the entertaining."

She raised an eyebrow. "You cook?"

"I make a mean omelet, you know," he said seriously, and she laughed.

The restaurant full and noisy with conversation. Instead of being distracting, it provided a protective blanket. By one o'clock, the magic ended and both of them had to return to the real world.

Tempted to pay the check, Dural realized that Aviana wanted to be treated as an equal, and wanted him to respect her independence. Outside, the glare and heat hit them and he squinted. They turned right to walk up the street.

He saw a gangly youngster riding a sports bike speed down Collins Street past stationary cars and mount the footpath. Startled pedestrians jumped aside. The bike had thin tires, straight handlebars, and no mudguards. The youngster had Uber Eats splashed in yellow on his T-shirt, and wore a boxy black pack on his back.

An elderly lady stood her ground and the bike swerved, heading straight for Aviana. Dural instinctively pushed her across the sidewalk, and the bike and rider slammed into his right side, sending him sprawling. He hit something hard and sparkling lights burst in his head.

Chapter Eight

Dural drifted through black vastness without end. It pressed on him with smothering warmth, pulling at him, and he struggled to breathe. When he did breathe, it was not air, but cloying, suffocating darkness. He wanted to scream, but his body could not move, frozen in a morass of nothingness.

A circle of gray light expanded before him and he found himself inexorably drifting toward it. A bright green ring formed around the circle and began to pulse. Inside the ring, white radiance cast shafts of light into the surrounding blackness. Life lay on the other side, a compelling voice told him, but there was also something else behind the light, a lurking menace. He struggled to stop his drift toward the ring, but he only seemed to move faster. Come to me, it beckoned, its pull becoming stronger as he drew closer.

The green ring almost within reach, it blanketed the pervasive darkness, and he could feel its malevolence. Summoning all his strength, he flung out his arms and screamed rejection of its pending embrace. The ring pulsed wildly and the whiteness inside it turned blotchy gray. About to plunge through, denying its pull, the ring flared and exploded in shards of light. The gray circle faded and disappeared with a final bright wink. Dural found himself once again immersed in impenetrable darkness. Only this time, it did not feel alien or hostile, and did not press on him. Instead, it cradled and comforted him as he drifted endlessly.

Gradually, he began to feel and hear. He could tell he was prostrate. A regular soft beep came from somewhere on his left. He felt warm, and the perpetual night gradually gave way to soft gray fog. It felt good lying like that, no longer drifting, the night-mare of the circle fading. A sense of deep peace stole through him. The nothingness merged into a cascade of sensations and he could feel the bed under him, feel the crisp sheet covering him, smell the antiseptic in the air, and sounds crystalized into meaning.

"He's coming around," a voice from memory said, and he struggled to match it with a face.

He blinked, squinted at the bright overhead light, and turned his head toward the sound. A face formed and he knew it.

"Dr. Pollack," he managed to croak and cleared his throat.

A tall glass filled with a pale pink liquid and drinking straw appeared before him.

"Drink this," Pollack said gently. "It will help bring you around."

Dural realized he was immensely thirsty and eagerly sucked the slightly tangy liquid. Finished, he sighed and became aware of another much more pleasant face hovering close to the bed.

Aviana bit her lower lip, eyes glistening, then smiled and tenderly touched his cheek.

"Hi there, wolf."

Dural managed a faint grin, not fully himself yet, and pressed her hand against his cheek.

"Hi there."

Whatever Pollack gave him cleared his head rapidly and the room jumped into focus. He tried to pull himself up and winced as his right arm gave a protesting twinge. He looked down to see it encased in a black brace. His head throbbed like a nagging toothache, as did his right side.

The Uber Eats driver!

"No need to tell me what happened," he said dryly. "Did they get him?"

Aviana nodded. "They got him, Du, and he's in a world of trouble: not observing the road rules, riding illegally on a pedestrian path, endangering life, causing willful harm to a person. He has been remanded, but the magistrate will probably grant bail for a court appearance on summons."

"Couriers!" Pollack snorted. "Openly flaunting the law. Those lunatics almost ran me down twice by running a red light and speeding through pedestrian crossings. I cannot understand why the police don't clamp down on them."

"If you decide to file a civil action suit against Uber Eats, Du, I'll get Wellard to take the case," Aviana told him.

Dural did a mental wince. This might be a problem, as Arnold, Becker and Strong did all his legal work.

He glanced at his arm. "And this?"

"Nothing to worry about, Doctor," Pollack said. "An incomplete fracture of the ulna. You'll have the brace for about four weeks and it'll be good as new. You can take it off at night after the first two weeks. Don't lift anything heavier than about half a kilo. If you want to grab a carton of milk out of the fridge, use your left hand."

"Got it."

"Your arm is fine, but your head trauma gave me some cause for concern."

"Oh?"

"When the bike and rider hit you," Aviana said, "you landed on the sidewalk and struck your head."

"Mild concussion and residual subdural hematoma," he added. "Not critical enough to warrant draining, but you'll have headaches for a few days until the body absorbs the bleed. You were fortunate not to have a fractured skull, and you've been out for the last four hours."

Four hours? The bang on the head must have really shaken him up. Another thought exploded in his mind.

"I need a phone. My partners at Gap Consulting—"

"Were notified." Pollack said. "Now that you're awake, you can call them."

Dural turned his head to the bedside cabinet and saw a reading lamp, an electronic radio/clock, his wallet, and smartphone. Everybody must have been worried when he didn't come back after lunch. Probably thought he had eloped with Aviana, he mused wryly.

"There is something else," Pollack went on. "You have two badly bruised ribs on your right side, Doctor. You'll feel like you've been kicked by a horse for a week, but there will be no permanent tissue damage. The ribs are amazingly elastic."

"How long will I be laid up here?" Dural asked.

"I'll keep you under observation overnight and take another MRI tomorrow. If everything checks out, I'll let you go on Sunday," Pollack said and his aura immediately changed to dirty gray. He held something back.

Dural wanted to push this further, but not with Aviana around in case it was something unpleasant. *Later,* he told himself.

"Thanks, Doctor," he said with a nod.

Pollack glanced at Aviana. "Ten minutes," he ordered and walked out.

Dural raised an eyebrow. "Ten minutes? That's not much time to do anything."

She chuckled and her aura melted from gold into soft orange. "That's how long I can stay." She patted his shoulder. "You need your rest."

He noticed that she still wore the same blue shirt and skirt. He also saw a red scrape on her right forearm and a large gray smudge on her sleeve.

"What happened there?"

"When you pushed me, I landed against a wall. It's nothing, and Dr. Pollack told me not to bandage it." She leaned over him and soft lips touched his. Her light fragrance enveloped him and he gazed deeply into her hazel eyes. "That's for saving me," she whispered and pulled away.

"If that's what I get for saving you, I'll have to do it more often," he mused, and her light laugh sent tingles of warmth through his body.

"Wolf."

"Aviana, about Uber Eats…"

Her eyebrows rose. "You don't want to sue? It'll be an open-and-shut."

"I do, but—"

She looked blank, then laughed. "Poor, Du. You thought I would be offended if you used your own firm?"

"Something like that."

"Who are they?"

"Arnold, Becker and Strong."

"Wow. Heavy hitters." She patted his shoulder. "Don't worry about it, and I shouldn't have sprung it on you like that."

Relieved, his eyes roamed across her features. "Have you been here all this time?"

"I wanted to make sure you were all right," she said simply.

He grasped her hand and gently squeezed. He did not have to say anything, the meaning of his touch clear. He turned his head toward the large window. Bright sunshine streamed through gauzy curtains.

"What time is it?"

She glanced at her watch. "Just on six."

"Long lunch. Your partners won't be happy with you."

She smiled. "They won't mind, provided I don't do it too often." She patted down her skirt and gave him a whimsical look. "I guess tomorrow's dinner is off."

Crap me dead. He had forgotten all about that.

"A postponement only," he reassured her. "Next Saturday? I should be up and about by then."

She studied him. "How about we make it at my place? I haven't cooked for a man in a long time and I want to see if I still have it."

Dural lifted his brace. The arm barely gave a twinge. "I don't mind waving this in public. Might come in handy."

"My place," she said.

"A lunch in between?" he asked hopefully, and she grinned.

"We'll talk about it." A shadow fell across her face and she looked serious. "Du…I appreciate what you did for me."

"I would have done far more to protect you from hurt, my soaring bird," he said softly. Not exactly a declaration of love, but she could not mistake the intensity of his words.

Should he declare outright his feelings for her? He did love her, he realized, but did he rush it? After all, they only met a few days ago and had two lunch dates. She appeared to like him, but that did not necessarily mean she loved him. A significant difference, and he did not want to make her uncomfortable or force her into making a decision she might not be ready for or even want. *Let the situation mature,* he told himself.

Her aura flared bright green, eyes glowing with inner fire.

"I'll see you later."

When the door closed after her, he unconsciously wanted to lock his fingers behind his head, but the stab of pain from his right arm made him wince. Staring at the door, Aviana's image bright in his mind, he allowed himself a lazy smile. They'll be seeing each other later, all right.

He sighed with satisfaction, picked up his phone, and went to the contacts list. About to tap an icon, a knock on the door made him look up. His two visitors walked in and he broke into a wide smile.

"Good to see you guys!"

Gerard frowned, glanced at Leonard, and shook his head. "Look at him. Malingering again, letting down the practice."

Leonard nodded. "Sad to see. We'll have to break his other arm, I guess."

"If you two want to swap places, be my guest," Dural told them.

"How are you, partner?" Gerard demanded as he pulled a chair toward the bed.

Dural raised his brace. "Apart from that, I'll be walking out of here on Sunday."

"Lucky for us you have a hard skull," Leonard added as he sat down. "Otherwise you could have been hurt."

"As for letting down the practice, you penny pinchers, I'll be in on Monday, bum arm and all," Dural said amiably.

"What about your ribs?" Gerard asked.

"Just sore for a few days. It won't interfere with my work."

"Are you sure everything is all right up there?" Gerard tapped his head.

"Pollack said I'm all clear." Dural regarded the two men, considering himself fortunate to have friends like that. "But I'll have another MRI tomorrow."

"Rosalyn thought you were still dating when he called," Leonard said with a grin.

"You've got a low mind, Len," Dural told him darkly, and his friend laughed.

"By the way, who's the girl?"

"Someone I met on my Sydney trip."

Gerard pointed a finger over his shoulder. "The woman we saw in the corridor? Blue shirt and skirt?"

"That's her."

"Wow. Are you building something there, Du?"

Dural grinned. "Possibly, you old goat."

"Regards from Rosalyn," Gerard added. "Suyin extends her apologies for not coming. She'll make up for it by dropping by tomorrow."

"Please thank them, but there is no need to fuss. It's only a broken arm."

"So, what happened?" Leonard asked. "Pollack didn't go into details."

"An Uber Eats courier ran me over," Dural said.

"Ran you over? He was riding on the footpath?"

"In a hurry and didn't want to dodge cars."

"Did they get him?" Gerard put in.

"They got him, and I'm considering taking action against Uber Eats."

"You do that," Leonard said emphatically. "Those couriers are a menace, openly ignoring the road rules." He stood and patted Dural on the shoulder. "You take care, Du."

"Thanks for coming," Dural said and meant it.

"We were finishing up at the practice." Gerard glanced at Leonard. "And this clod had some explaining to do."

Gerard did not have to spell it out. Dural looked at them, his face serious.

"I'm glad to hear you guys worked it out."

"One woman in my life is enough!" Leonard declared, turned, and slapped Gerard on the shoulder. "Let's get out of here, partner, or we'll be eating scraps." He noted Dural's puzzled expression and chuckled. "We're all having dinner at my place. Helen and Suyin are doing the cooking. That's why she didn't come. I wanted to invite you, but you were having your extended lunch."

"Enjoy yourselves," Dural told them.

"Glad to see you're okay, buddy," Gerard said and strode toward the door.

Almost as soon as the door closed after them, came another knock. An elderly take-charge nurse walked in with a large tray.

"Dinner, Dr. Sinclair," she declared and placed the tray on the side cabinet. She helped him sit up, then swung the portable table across his lap and placed the tray on it. "Buzz if you need anything."

He nodded and watched her walk out. Eyeing the tray, he did not feel particularly hungry. He drank the orange juice and water, and started on the blueberry yogurt, finishing with an apple. He pushed back the table and leaned against the cushions, wincing when his side protested.

Hell of a day, eh, Doctor?

Aviana…To think that she stayed with him all this time…

Thinking of time, he wondered what he would do with himself, stuck in this room for another day. The prospect of staring at a TV did not hold much appeal. He could work on his new book, he mused. Do some editing, not at all difficult with his memory, or continue writing. Editing was work and he did not feel like working right now. He turned, groped for the buzzer, and pressed the button. A few minutes later, a young nurse walked in and smiled.

"Done with your dinner, Doctor?"

"Yes, thank you. Can you bring me some more orange juice, please?"

"Of course," she said and picked up the tray.

"One more thing. I would like an A4 writing pad and a pen."

She frowned. "A writing pad?"

"That's right."

"Mmm. I'll see what I can do."

"Thank you."

The orange juice and writing pad appeared promptly. Dural rubbed his hands with satisfaction, sat up, and swung the table across his lap. He fingered the pen, the brace not bothering him too much, and opened the pad. The last two pages he wrote scrolled through his mind and he nodded.

Pen in hand, the words began to flow.

* * *

Morning caught Dural energized, eager to get out into the world and stomp on it. He looked around the bare room and felt he could count the hairs on a fly's legs, except there were no flies around to do it. He fancied he could hear an ant scampering about. No ants, but that did not diminish his euphoria.

Lying against the pillows, left hand behind his head, a good breakfast—if somewhat plain—doing its thing in his belly, life was great. He watched some news on the ABC, and switched off when Bill Shorten came on to talk about Labor's social reform program if he won the election, taking the result as inevitable. Perhaps it was, but Dural suspected that Aussies did not like being taken for granted. He could not stand Shorten's bland, expressionless, lecturing voice, or Morrison's condescending smirk as though he was the guardian of truth and everybody should shut the hell up. In Dural's opinion, if anything was going to lose the Coalition the election, it would be that smirk.

His morning was spoiled somewhat, being wakened at 6:45 by an insensitive male orderly and taken down to Radiology. His gauze-like one-piece hospital gown hardly adequate in that refrigerated dungeon. At least the attending nurse had the kindness to drape what could generously be termed a blanket over him before the MRI started whirling around his head.

He turned toward the window: blue sky clear of clouds. He wanted to be out there than in this antiseptic hole. Since he was stuck here, he would buzz a nurse and ask for a book. Happy with what he had written last night, he could not write all day. He needed to reenergize his creative drive. Not a tap he could turn on at will, although it did drip sometimes. There were days when he did not write a word, stuck in a mental pothole. Not a problem with the book's plot, but finding the right words to get him going again. When he got the blues, he did not force it, knowing his mind would sort things out eventually, and the urge to write would push him into action.

A knock and the door opened. Pollack strode in wearing a white lab coat, pulled a chair toward the bed, and sat down. His muddy gray aura did not bode good news.

"How are you feeling this morning, Doctor?" he asked.

Dural grunted and sat up. "I feel great, ready to eat them up. Do I have to spend the day here?"

"I'll see if I can let you go this afternoon." Pollack cleared his throat. "Dr. Sinclair, the MRI yesterday showed an anomaly on the left side of your occipital lobe, and the scan this morning confirmed it."

"What sort of anomaly?"

"You have a four-millimeter meningioma in a sulcus fold of the cortex. I checked your history—"

"You accessed my MRI records without permission?" Dural demanded coldly, not wanting to process the fact that he had a brain tumor. Not the kind of news easily digested, with all sorts of dire consequences racing through his mind.

"Dr. Gerard Stockton gave me permission. I was the attending surgeon when you were admitted after your indirect lightning strike."

"Still, you should have told me yesterday."

"I was not sure yesterday without consulting with a neurologist first. She went over your MRIs this morning and confirmed my initial diagnosis."

"Is it benign?"

"It is. The growth sack is encapsulated within a membrane, and there are no feeder tendrils into the surrounding tissue. Your MRI last July was clear, which means this is a recent growth. Meningiomas are extremely slow growing, but four millimeters is a lot for nine months. Have you experienced any unusual symptoms, such as persistent headaches, vertigo, nausea, visual impairment, muscular weakness or unusual smells?"

Dural shook his head. "Nothing."

"That's encouraging."

"So, what's the prognosis?"

"You'll have another scan in six months. If the nodule has stabilized and remains encapsulated, we'll leave it in there."

"But if it increases in size?"

"The pressure on the surrounding gray matter layer may generate symptoms that would warrant surgery. Fortunately, the tumor is easily accessible should it need removal." Pollack shifted in his chair. "Dr. Stockton also told me the lightning strike resulted in significant neurogenesis."

"Are you saying it triggered development of the tumor?"

"It might have, as meningiomas, and tumors in general, are quite rare and not hereditary."

"You mentioned surgery. Is that the best option?"

"Excising the growth *in situ* is highly recommended to prevent cell metastasizing. Before surgery, I would suggest a biomarker MGMT promoter methylation test to gauge effectiveness of TMZ chemotherapy, should it be required."

"What about immediate treatment, such as genetic transfer therapy or radiation?"

"Gene therapy is certainly an option, but I would hold off for six months until we get your next scan. I don't like radiation treatment, although some of my colleagues will disagree, unless surgery is not possible due to location of the tumor. Radiation causes too much damage to surrounding neuron cells and connecting dendrites, and there is a real possibility of gene mutation that could promote growth of a more virulent tumor."

Dural snorted and shook his head. "You certainly know how to spoil a fun day, Doctor."

Pollack's mouth twitched. "People walk around with brain tumors all their lives without knowing they have one. Your meningioma is such a case, Dr. Sinclair." He stood and patted down his lab coat. "I'll see you this afternoon."

When the door closed, Dural poured himself a glass of orange juice and sipped.

Crap me dead.

His training gave him a lot of knowledge about the brain, tumors, and treatments, but not current on the latest developments. That was more in Gerard's line of work. From what he did know, although potentially serious—no brain tumor can be taken lightly—he had not drawn the short straw on this one. Like Pollack said, he could have a full productive life without experiencing any adverse symptoms.

What now?

Wait six months. There simply was not enough information to form a definitive prognosis, and projecting a worst-case scenario on the information he did have was an exercise in destructive futility.

Should he reveal his condition to others? After some thinking, he decided not to say anything. The one thing he did not need was fawning sympathy if he revealed his condition. Besides, it might be nothing.

Aviana...

Should he tell her or keep his mouth shut? There was an argument to be made for either option. If their budding relationship developed into something permanent and his tumor became aggressive, could he ethically allow her to commit herself, only to have her life wrenched should he die or become incapacitated?

He might have died when that Uber Eats moron ran into him!

He could plan and organize for his future, but fates ran things in their own unpredictable way. What would be unfair was to deny Aviana and himself happiness regardless of the sand left in his hourglass of life. Was he being selfish? Perhaps a little.

Cool things off between them for six months? He rejected that immediately. She would sense it and demand an explanation, and rightly so. If not prepared to commit fully, he should make a clean break now rather than string her along even if she were willing, or restructure their relationship on a purely platonic basis.

No, with someone like Aviana, there was no middle ground. Anything else would be living a lie.

He pictured the little black nodule in the fold of his brain and sent all his hate at it. The sucker won't have it all its own way. He would fight the bastard, benign or not.

Dural climbed out of the bed and stood before the window. He could not see much—drab buildings of The Alfred complex, but it was a doorway into the world outside. What surprised him, he felt no emotional agitation. Pollack could have given him today's weather report for all the impact it had. Why should he be agitated anyway? He was alive, healthy—cosmic jest thrown in for free—with a comfortable lifestyle and a job he loved, his future bright…hopefully. Okay, he had a small gray cloud on the horizon, but it may never reach him. A future he could not influence and not worth worrying about, his objective self told him. Life was a day-to-day proposition at best.

He would give that future six months.

His cellphone went off and he hurried around the bed to the side cabinet. He read the caller ID and grinned.

"Hi, Gerard. Great morning, eh? Perfect day for a golf game, except that bastard Pollack won't let me out of here."

"It could have been far worse, partner. Talking about things being worse, has he given you the update?"

"A few minutes ago. Don't sweat it. I'm handling it."

"About your file—"

"No need to worry, Ger. He had a legitimate need to know."

"A meningioma. Christ!"

"We did talk about this possibility four years ago, but as you said, it could have been worse. Anyway, it might not amount to anything."

"How do you want to handle this?"

"Keep it confidential. Nobody has to know anything. If things deteriorate in six months, I'll take it from there."

"Got it. Are you still scheduled for discharge tomorrow?"

"If I'm a good boy, Pollack might let me go this afternoon."

"Hang in there, partner, and I'll see you on Monday. My door is always open, Du."

"Check. My regards to Suyin."

"Will do."

"By the way, how did last night go?"

"We had a great time. Too bad you couldn't make it."

"Next time, I think us guys should cook."

"Not a bad idea. Talk to you later."

"Later," Dural said and switched off. Grinning, he crawled into bed.

The fates giveth, and the fates taketh away.

* * *

The cab turned into the leafy tree-lined narrow street and Dural fancied himself transported into a quaint European village. Nothing stirred beneath a hard blue sky and long shadows. An occasional sparrow fluttered among drooping branches as the cab disturbed their slumber. Behind mostly neat fences, terrace houses, some of them touching each other, lined both sides of the street. Most had green corrugated tin roofs, but some had slate or moss-covered tiles. Painted drab gray or something dull, the brickwork did not glare at passersby. Parked end to end, cars jammed both sides of the street.

Suddenly, the cab stopped and he was there. A tall acacia shaded the sidewalk, its branches reaching toward the cream terrace façade with its wide windows and fresh dark brown tiles. He paid the driver and watched the cab whisper up the road. Still warm, pleasant scents drifted through bottomless silence. He took a deep breath and exhaled with satisfaction.

A dark red Mazda 3 stood parked beside the sidewalk, its residential permit prominent inside the windscreen. Parking on these narrow streets impossible without a permit, the residents having the right to tow away the trespassing car. The houses being so narrow, unless built with a garage in mind, residents had to park outside. It was no different where he lived, except his place had a garage, a deciding factor when he bought it.

He opened the small gate in the neat black picket fence and strode toward the front entrance. He pressed the doorbell button and waited. Hurried footsteps came from inside and the lock clicked. Aviana opened the door and smiled broadly, her purple/blue aura a radiant halo around her. Dressed in an olive T-shirt and dark jeans that highlighted her figure, she looked enchanting.

"Welcome to my humble abode, Du. Come on in," she said brightly and stepped aside.

He paused on the doorstep, gave her a peck on the cheek, and held out a bouquet of wild Australian flowers. "For you."

"Wow, I love banksias. Thank you." She spent a moment looking at the sylvan reds, pink ice proteas, green leucadendrons, privet berry, and banksias arranged within a lotus leaf, and sniffed them. She pointed at a paper wine bag in his left hand. "What's that?"

"A local merlot to complement whatever you're cooking."

"And if it's white meat?" she asked with an arched eyebrow.

He shrugged. "Doesn't make any difference. I don't subscribe to the notion that one should only drink red wine with red meat."

"That must get you talked about when you go out or entertain."

"It does, but I derive sardonic pleasure sabotaging what I consider snobbish notions."

Her laugh a tinkle of bright water. "And if I should happen to have those notions?"

"In that case, I guess it's crash and burn."

Still laughing, she grabbed his arm and dragged him in. "You're safe, this time. However, my dad follows that snobbish notion. So, be warned."

"Duly noted."

"He can be a bit intimidating at times, and tends to be a bit gruff, but he's actually a dear."

"Darling girl. I'm going out with you, not your old man." He held out the wine bag.

"I want you to like him when you see him." She took the bag and led him into a spacious dining/lounge area divided from the kitchen by a breakfast bench. Against the wall, steep stairs led to the upper level. Three modernistic abstract paintings filled empty wall spaces.

"This is nice. Similar to my place," he observed.

"You should have seen it when I first bought it," she said as she placed the bouquet into a fluted blue porcelain vase. "Dark, a narrow corridor opening into a cubbyhole lounge with a separate door to the kitchen. Instant claustrophobia. Fortunately, the wall isn't loadbearing, otherwise my renovation would have been more complicated. I now have an open, airy place I can enjoy. Come, sit down." She waved at two soft seats flanking a low wooden coffee table. A bookcase guarded a large LED TV. "Drink?" she offered as she strode into the kitchen.

"A bourbon if you have it," he said as he sprawled into the seat. "Or a cognac. Either one will do."

"I have both. I don't drink much spirits, but my dad does and I keep stuff just for him. My mom is strictly a wine drinker, like me."

"What do you prefer?"

"Mostly light reds, but I occasionally indulge in something with more body," she said as she poured his whiskey. She took an almost empty bottle from the refrigerator, filled herself a glass, placed his tumbler on the coffee table, then fetched a porcelain bowl of mixed nuts. Glass in hand, she sat down with a sigh.

"So, what do you think of my place?"

"Elegant and modern," he said seriously and touched his tumbler to her glass. "It suits you. Next time, we'll do this at my place."

"And get trapped in a wolf's den?" she demanded with a chuckle, and he grinned. "I don't know."

"I'll put my fangs in the drawer," he promised and took a sip.

She tried her wine and held the glass between her hands. "Sorry about this week, Du. I just couldn't get away."

"Don't worry about it. I've had one of those mad weeks myself."

She tilted her head. "How's the arm?"

He glanced at his brace. "I had to beat off my partners with it. They all wanted to autograph it."

She flashed white teeth. "Any room there for mine?"

"No way. My patients would be horrified if they saw it full of graffiti."

Aviana laughed outright. "Not a professional image at all."

"Better believe it. In a curious way, though, it helped break the ice with some patients. I guess it made me look human and fallible like everyone else."

"Mmm. I can relate to that."

Dural did not want to go there, suspecting he knew what she meant.

"Any headache?"

"On and off for the first few days, but it's gone now."

"Did you file against Uber Eats?" she asked, and the moment passed.

"It's in the works. They're grumbling and making defensive noises, but I'm told they might be prepared to settle rather than face a lot of negative publicity if we went to court." He took another sip of whiskey. "I want to ask you something. Would you mind if I named you as a co-claimant?"

Her eyebrows climbed. "Goodness! Whatever for?"

"Ruined shirt, a scrape on your arm, emotional distress, and psychological trauma. My lawyer suggested it. If I'm going to do this, he said, I might as well make Uber suffer."

"You're cruel, did you know that?"

"Yeah, it's been mentioned," he said slowly, and she grinned.

"Well, I don't mind being a co-claimant, but I still feel it's not necessary."

"I'll talk it over with my lawyer. You said you had a hard week."

"The case against Philip Kresta. I got him a plea bargain. He was fined, got fifty hours of community service, but no criminal conviction. He was also banned from engaging in any activity relating to providing financial services for a period of two years. I'm not breaking client privilege telling you this, as the ruling is in the public domain. Personally, I would not have minded seeing him behind bars, but that ban had to hurt. After the hearing, he wanted me to launch an appeal, claiming the ban would ruin him. Secretly, I hope it will. Instead, I told him he got off easy. He started to abuse me then, threatening to get me fired." She waved a hand. "Hollow bluster."

Dural was immediately concerned. "Do you think he'll try something?"

"I doubt it. He was upset, understandably enough, but once he calms down, I hope he will reflect on his life's choices," she mused and took a long pull of wine. Her dark eyes regarded him over the rim of her glass. "Sorry, I shouldn't be loading my personal baggage on you."

"None better," he told her evenly. "Any time you want to stretch out on my consulting couch…"

"Wolf. Seriously, Du. My conscience goes on a rampage when I see the type of clients Wellard takes on. Not outright underworld criminals, but some corporate cases we handle make my teeth grate. It's the nature of our business, I guess." She placed her glass on the coffee table and slapped her thighs. "Enough of this psycho gloom. Let's eat."

"Now you're talking. Is there anything I can do?"

Aviana pointed at the dining table laid out with dishes, cutlery, and condiments. "Sit and talk about yourself," she said as she walked into the compact kitchen.

He picked up his tumbler and followed her. She donned heavy gloves, opened the oven door, and extracted a baking tray, which she carried to the dining table. He leaned against the breakfast bench.

"I was thinking how things have changed since I was a carefree kid. Have you heard about the Christchurch shooting on Thursday?"

"Oh, Lord. Fifty-one killed and around fifty more injured. Such senseless deaths. I sometimes wonder what's going on in the world."

"It's been a crazy week, all right. Airlines are grounding the Boeing 737-MAX aircraft, and the House of Commons has knocked back Teresa May's Brexit deal again. They certainly made a mess of it for themselves."

Aviana raised both hands. "Stop! I don't want to hear it. Not tonight. You were supposed to talk about yourself."

He grinned. "Sorry. What do you want to know?"

"Anything. Just talk."

"Well, like all kids, I spent my childhood keeping my parents from finding out what I was up to. I collected Superman comics and slowly built up my library of books. When computers became available in the early 1980s, my old man got me one and I created programs using DOS. I had four close friends through my high school years, and we did crazy things like camping, weekend fishing trips, and shooting rabbits with .22s. We liked playing billiards and pool between classes, and during summer, we hung around Williamstown Beach admiring the girls." He took a sip of whiskey and watched Aviana retrieve bowls of salad from the fridge.

"That must have given them a thrill," she quipped with a grin.

"Not as much as they gave us."

She tittered. "Are you still friends with them?"

"One went for Army officer training at Duntroon in Canberra. We exchanged an occasional email, but I haven't seen him in years. One is an electrical engineer, and when he married, they moved to Sydney, and that was that. The other two went to RMIT and I went to Monash Uni for my bachelor's. We met from time to time, but it was inevitable that we would drift apart. At university, I met Gerard and Leonard who also studied clinical psychology. We remained together right through our PhD studies. They're my business partners now."

Aviana bit her lip. "All those years glued to books and exams. I don't know if I could handle it."

"A lot of them fell by the wayside," he admitted. "Getting my bachelor's was the hardest. Master's and PhD degrees were easier and more fun, as they involved research and actual patient handling."

She placed his bottle of wine on the table and swept her hand at the spread. "Dinner is served, sir."

He bowed low. "My lady is too gracious."

As he walked toward the table, he looked at the baking tray.

"Veal strips in gravy with baked pumpkin," she declared. "And there, you have mixed greens and a potato salad."

"I make it myself sometimes," he said and sat down. He reached for the bottle and filled their glasses. "My mother's Polish influence." He raised his glass. "Cheers."

Aviana nodded. "Cheers." She took a sip. "Nice and smooth. What else rubbed off on you?"

"Oh, making strudel, gnocchi, crepes, stuffed peppers, stews. Things like that. Frying steaks is easy."

"Wow, a gourmet chef. You could be handy around the house."

"I also drive a mean vacuum cleaner," he deadpanned.

"Definitely a valuable skill."

He tilted his head. "Are you still weighing me up?"

"Checking the wrapper before I open the package." She pointed at the baking tray. "Help yourself."

He used the large metal spoon to grab two veal medallions, added golden pumpkin wedges, and smothered everything with thick gravy, then heaped the salads into a small bowl beside the plate. The veal melted in his mouth, and he locked eyes with Aviana pretending not to be watching him.

"Absolutely delicious," he said earnestly. "I could get used to this."

She smiled faintly. "Careful what you wish for, Doctor. You know what they say."

"What do they say?"

"When the gods want to punish us, they grant us our wishes."

Dural wagged a finger. "I never believed in that stuff. In many ways, we fulfill our own wishes, and some are beyond reach no matter what one does."

She studied him. "You don't believe a person can achieve anything if he wants it badly enough?"

"Unrealistic expectation, Aviana, and delusional. There are many obstacles around us that stop us realizing our dreams."

"Such as?"

"Take me for instance. I can be a full-time writer, but no matter how many submissions I make to publishers or literary agents is no guarantee one of them will pick me up. I'm sure you have seen some of the trash that gets published, and I cannot help wonder how that author did it, hating his guts, when my stuff is so much better."

She smiled. "Maybe I should read some of your stuff and judge for myself."

"I'll get you something."

"I understand what you're saying, Du, but many first-time authors get published."

"They do, but when you look at their background, most of the time it was a case of knowing someone in the industry."

Aviana shook her head. "I refuse to believe things are hopeless."

"All right. Let's look at something closer to home. When Toyota closed car production in 2017, they provided worker training programs. For younger guys with skills, they probably found another job. For those on assembly lines or in their mid-fifties, chances of getting a job were almost non-existent, regardless of any retraining. Go to TAFE or college, the government tells them, which is not only silly, but condescending and insensitive. Whatever dreams that person might have had would be just that, frustrated dreams." Dural picked up his glass and sipped. "Sorry. You pressed one of my buttons and I got carried away."

"Don't worry. I won't press them all tonight, but I see your point."

"I'm not saying a person cannot achieve his dreams, but the odds are stacked against him."

"Ah, such gloom. Let's talk about something else."

"Your buttons? Which ones shouldn't I push?"

"My big red one is law, of course. These days, judges don't dispense justice, they rule on law, and that stinks."

"Is that why you want to be a magistrate or judge?"

"Society needs laws to operate, but most of all people want justice, and an equal opportunity to get it regardless of their economic status. A bloated millionaire can literally get away with murder, whereas the poor shmuck who steals a loaf of bread gets three years. It makes me pull my hair out."

He grinned. "I'll try not to lean on that button. What else gets you going?"

"Oh, mostly helplessness when I see short-term profiteering at the expense of long-term sustainability; and politicians held to ransom by industrial and religious lobby groups. It's no wonder the millennials are disenchanted." She searched his face with a pondering expression. "You don't agree?"

"I definitely do, and it's the reason why some of my patients end up seeing me." He leaned toward her. "That was your public persona talking, but what do you want for yourself? What are your drivers?"

She shrugged. "What any woman wants these days, I guess. Career, security, perhaps even a family, but that's not likely at my age."

"It's not too late, you know."

"I'm thirty-eight, Du. Let's get real."

There were many things Dural could say to that, but he refrained and concentrated on his food. He took a second helping of veal, to Aviana's evident satisfaction.

He searched her eyes. "Mind if I ask you something personal?"

"You can ask, but I reserve the right not to answer."

"Fair enough, counselor. Why didn't you ever get married?"

"I made choices in life, and early on, having a family wasn't part of the plan. And something else happened." She placed her knife and fork on the plate and her face turned cold. Seeing the barrier, he regretted bringing this up.

"I'm sorry. I shouldn't have pried."

"It's okay. I don't mind talking about it. Toward the end of my stay with the Victorian Corrections Department, my supervisor made it clear he was sweet on me. We dated twice, but I did not feel a connection. He didn't see it that way. When he kept pestering me, I told him he should stop his advances. After almost four years at the same job, I started looking around. I lived in Box Hill at the time. After a particularly long and heavy day, I was somewhat tired and he offered to take me home. Better than chasing trains. Against my better judgment, I said yes. When I got home, I invited him in for coffee. I don't know what made me do that, as I kept our relationship at arm's length. That's when he forced himself on me."

"Shit. I'm sorry, Aviana."

"Afterward, I smashed a plastic container of orange juice over his head. He charged me with assault, and I charged him with rape, although he claimed it was consensual. During the trial, his lawyer tried to make it appear it was all my fault. Three days into the hearing, thinking it would get him a reduced sentence, he pleaded guilty. The magistrate didn't go for it and gave him six years. It restored my faith in the justice system and left me with a totally new perspective on rape victims."

"That wasn't the end of it, was it?"

"No, it wasn't. He left me pregnant and I had an abortion. After that, men did not play a prominent role in my life."

"Yeah. There hasn't been anyone special afterward?"

"It took a while to dispel the demons, but four years ago, I found somebody at Wellard. A junior partner. I even lived with him for two months, and I thought I had met the right one. Some of the girls at the office tried to warn me about him, but I wouldn't listen. I guess he swept me away in a romantic haze with his charm, flowers, great nights out, and witty conversation. Living with him, I got to see what he really was: a domineering, authoritarian, egocentric pig."

Dural chuckled. "Well, you certainly sorted him out, psychologically speaking."

"Prong. I broke it off and he left Wellard soon after. No more men for me, I decided." She exhaled and played with the stem of her glass. "There it is. The story of my life."

"I'm certain there are lots more pages in that book," he said softly.

"And maybe you'll get to read them. What about you? Only one wife?"

"Only one. I met her on a flight. She was going to Sydney to visit her brother."

"And we met on a flight," she observed. "Is that how you pick up your women?"

He grinned. "It appears to be my MO, doesn't it?"

"Do you miss her?"

"Lenora? It ripped me up when we divorced, and deep down, I still love her, but it's only a memory now." He took a sip of wine. "Six weeks after our divorce, she came to see me. She wanted to get back together again."

"Wow. What did you do?"

"Too many burnt bridges."

"I'm sure there must be more to it than that. She married again?"

"No, but her old man told me it's on the cards. I wish her well."

"Nobody since then?"

"I don't go out much, and I haven't been looking. I had my practice and I thought I was satisfied."

"But…"

He looked into her eyes. "Then you came into the picture."

"Hitting on me again, Doctor?" she said with a smile.

"Yes, I am."

She dabbed her lips with a napkin and pointed at his plate. "Done?"

He sat back and patted his stomach. "That was great. Thank you."

She quickly cleared the table and brought out two small plates, followed by a tray of square pastries.

"Coffee, tea?"

"Coffee, please." He took a pastry, the cinnamon scent pervasive, and bit into it. The ground poppy seed filling with a hint of rum exploded in his mouth. "Wow."

"I don't make cakes often," she announced, fussing with the percolator, "but I like eating them. My mom is a great cook. You should try her walnut roll. Heavenly."

"I'm a glutton for cakes," he declared. "I rarely make or buy them, though, but every now and then…"

She laughed. "Me too. It reminds me that life is meant to be relished."

"My philosophy exactly," he agreed. "Give into temptation, I say. You never know if it will come your way again."

Aviana stared at him, then cracked up. After a moment, she wiped her eyes. "That's the most insane thing I ever heard. I hope that's not the kind of sage counseling you give your patients."

He took another bite of pastry. "Strictly a personal philosophy."

She tittered. "I should hope so. Any thoughts I might have had to call on you professionally are firmly dispelled." She brought two large cups to the table, followed by a porcelain container of milk and a wooden bowl of raw crystal sugar.

Dural sighed dejectedly. "I am crushed."

"You'll recover," she told him bluntly.

Glass carafe in hand, she poured him the fragrant brew. He added sugar and milk and stirred, then took a sip. "You're a wonderful cook, Aviana, and a charming host. I don't know if I could top this."

She raised an inquiring eyebrow. "Was that an invitation?"

"Next Saturday. My place?"

"Okay."

Her ready response made him smile. That's what he liked about her. No equivocation or qualification.

She picked up her cup and saucer and cake bowl, and headed for the lounge. He sat down while she poured him a whiskey. Tumbler held between his hands, he peered at her. Her short raven hair glistened under the lighting and he wanted to run his fingers through it. He wanted to trace the delicate line of her jaw, the golden skin of her cheeks, kiss her full lips, and feel every part of her body. Right then, he wanted to take her into his arms and crush her against him, never letting go. He wanted to hold her, protect her, and shield her from the world's hurts. Perhaps she would let him…one day. After Lenora, he never thought he would feel this way again, but Aviana's presence had set his body on fire.

"What?" she asked.

"Oh, just admiring."

"Wolf."

"Anything special on for tomorrow?"

"Lunch with my parents, otherwise a quiet day."

"Your sister Dinah. Part of the lunch deal?"

"And her little demons. Not so little now. The whole Kinsley brood will be in attendance. My mom does this sort of get-to-gether every three months or so. It's a chance to catch up on the latest gossip without getting serious."

"My mom used to do the same thing for the same reason. These days, it's more a random thing. Depends if they're in Melbourne."

"You said that you don't go to Nelson Bay much."

"I was there three weeks ago for the weekend. It's a very attractive place to retire. That's a long way off, though, and I like it here. I cannot imagine myself relocating. Still, who knows? When I get old and rickety, I may change my mind."

She smiled. "I'm trying to picture you old and rickety."

"It happens to all of us." He finished his whiskey and took a sip of coffee.

"What about you? Any plans?"

"Work on my book a little. Take a stroll through the Botanic Gardens. Just enjoy being alive. Nothing too exciting."

She pursed her lips and shook her head. "I see I'll have to add some spice into that boring life, Doctor."

"You already have. More than you know," he said gently.

She blushed and her aura flickered in a shade of confused colors. "Du…"

He raised his palm. "I know."

"You've been sweet, but I need to get comfortable being around you. It's been a while since I did this sort of thing and you'll have to give me time."

He searched her face. "Are you afraid I will hurt you?"

"You might. Not physically, I know you would never do that, but…"

"What then?"

Her eyes shifted away. "It is hard to read you sometimes. You can be pretty intimidating, you know."

Dural gaped at her in shock. "Intimidating?"

"Maybe you don't even realize it, but at times, you project an impression that you're amused with everything around you, including me. You seem to understand and grasp things so quickly it leaves me floundering. One moment you're warm and sensitive, then you look at me with a detached attitude, and I wonder if I'm merely another study subject for you. It's unnerving."

He gave a loud exhale, his mind a jumble of conflicting thoughts. To have his persona penetrated so easily and accurately…He reached for her hand and kissed her palm.

"Aviana—"

"I'm sorry. I shouldn't have said that." She averted her eyes and clutched the wine glass stem. In the ensuing silence, he waded through the cascade of emotions coursing through him.

"You're right about everything," he said at length. "I am cold and clinical sometimes, and you're not the first to tell me that. I've been trying to fight it, but I don't know if I can."

Her hazel eyes turned dark. "What do you mean?"

"The lightning strike? It left me with an eidetic memory, but it did more than that. It changed my personality somewhat. I have always been sensitive to people's reactions, now more than ever.

The price of that sensitivity is that I have also become more ob-jective and detached." He gave a wry smile. "Which you obvi-ously picked up." He looked deep into her eyes. "I seem to un-derstand people better and resolve things more quickly, but I don't feel superior. Wrap it all up, the accident has made me a better psychologist."

"Has it helped you understand yourself better?" she asked softly.

He gave a wry grin. "A question I have been battling to answer for the last four years. In some respects it has, but I don't know what else is lurking deep down inside me, waiting to emerge. Something darker and ugly? If the gods wanted to grant me a wish, I would want to become the person I was. Many things might have been different." He stroked her cheek with a feathery finger. "But then, I would not have met you. Whatever you think of me, Aviana, I want to make what we have last. If I'm rushing things, I'll back off until you're ready. If you see me as just a friend, I will treasure that, happy to share whatever you're pre-pared to give, but you should never feel intimidated by me. Never. You're definitely not a clinical subject of study, even if I do appear detached at times."

Her eyes glistened, and he wondered what went on behind those enchanting orbs. She took a gulp of coffee and sighed.

"Thank you for telling me that, Du. I guess I'll simply have to get used to you, detachment and all."

He did not tell her everything, but he did not want to overload her right now. The atmosphere between them was fragile enough. He had time…

"With that out of the way, could we get together for lunch sometime?"

"Wednesday looks good," she said promptly. "I'll text you."

He reached across the low coffee table and brushed her fore-arm. "Thank you," he said softly. Her aura flared bright silver, bordered by a golden glow. Feeling he should go, he stood. He did not want to, but he sensed she needed to digest what he said.

She nodded and got up.

He held her hands, relishing the tingle that raced up his arms. Seeing she was willing, he gently brushed his lips against her soft mouth. She leaned into him and allowed the kiss to linger for a fleeting, intense moment. He could have kissed her deeply then, and knew she would not have resisted, but he refrained. There were ghosts in her eyes to dispel first before he would go down that path, but he wanted her. Gods, how he wanted her. Not just to make desperate love to her, he wanted her with him for all time. He wanted to hear her silvery voice every day, watch how she moved, absorb the little mannerisms that made her unique, cherish her. The prospect of that happening also unnerved him a little. Four long, lonely years had created a chasm between him and a person he last loved, and if Aviana needed time to get used to him, he realized he also needed time to adjust having someone close again, understanding her wants, likes and dislikes, with all the implications such a relationship entailed, but he wanted that relationship badly.

He pulled back and smiled.

"Sorry to unload all that emotional baggage on you," she whispered.

"My consultancy fee is very reasonable."

"Wolf. Do you want me to call a cab?" she offered with a grin.

"I'll walk to Kings Way and catch one there. They're always around in the evening, especially on a Saturday, and I want to stretch my legs."

"I liked having you here, Du." Suddenly, she was tight against him, head on his shoulder. His arms went around her and he stroked her back. After a moment, she pulled away, eyes large and bright.

"Thank you for not being a wolf."

After the terrible experience she had with a colleague at work, the last thing he wanted was have her think of him as another insensitive male preoccupied with himself and his wants. Sadly, the social context within which they lived still condoned such behavior, as many of his female patients attested.

He smiled and kissed the tip of her nose. "Wait until you know me better."

She giggled and lightly fisted his shoulder. "Prong…Thank you for the flowers."

"And you're my favorite banksia among them."

Hand in hand, they walked toward the front door. The warm look she gave him standing there filled him with contentment. Everything would be all right.

"Good night, Aviana."

"Night."

She unlocked the door and he stepped into dusk.

Chapter Nine

Rosalyn looked around the table, calm and professional in a pale gray business jacket and skirt. "Don't forget to update your billables, or your monthly drawings won't be right. If there are no more points…that's it then. Thank you everybody. The minutes will be available on PAX within the hour."

Gerard glanced at Suyin, stood, pushed up his glasses, and cleared his throat. A tinge of brown uncertainty enveloped his otherwise normal green aura.

"I have a personal announcement. Suyin and I are getting married."

"Way to go!" Dural cheered and banged the table.

Leonard offered a ribald remark, which made Suyin blush, and stuck out his hand. "I'm happy for you, partner."

"Thanks, Len."

Rosalyn took Suyin's hand and cooed over the ring on her finger. "Wow. A yellow diamond. When did he propose?"

"Last night over a candlelight dinner at his place," Suyin said, giving Gerard a sidewise look. "I thought he never would."

"At his place?" Leonard queried with a suggestive smile.

"Nothing like that at all, you dirty old man," Gerard growled, and everybody laughed.

"So, when is the big day?" Leonard demanded.

"We haven't decided on a date," Gerard said, having regained his confidence. "Probably in a couple of months. There are lots of things to take care of before then. We also need to pick a venue. Treasury Gardens perhaps; and then there is the bridal shower and bachelor party. I'm not sure I want all that." He turned and smiled at Suyin, his eyes shining. "But I don't think I'll have much say in it."

"You won't," she told him gleefully, "but we'll talk about it."

Gerard turned to Leonard. "I would like you to be my best man, if you would."

Clearly touched, especially after the misunderstanding with Suyin, Leonard walked around the table and gave Gerard a tight hug.

"I would be honored, Ger."

"We're having an informal engagement party at my parents' place on Saturday the 30th," Suyin announced. "I hope all of you can make it."

"Count on it," Dural told her warmly, radiantly happy that Gerard had overcome his moment of terror. Judging by his bright green aura, he now had everything he wanted in life: love, companionship, and a family. Suyin would take care of him, he reflected.

His cellphone went off and he swiped the green answer icon. "Dr. Sinclair."

"This is Dr. Pollack. My apologies for disturbing you, but under the circumstances, I thought you should know."

Puzzled, Dural frowned. What the hell would the man want with him? "Know what, Doctor?"

"The young lady who visited you after your accident? Ordinarily, I would not violate her privacy rights, but she insisted I tell you. She just underwent surgery for two gunshot wounds."

Something cold wrapped itself around his insides and squeezed, and he felt his face drain. Aviana shot? All sorts of terrible images stampeded through his mind. After several seconds, he took a deep breath and exhaled slowly, trying to calm his racing heart.

"How bad?"

"Nothing serious. She was shot by small caliber rounds, probably a .22. One went through her upper biceps brachii, and the other penetrated the pleural space and grazed the left lung's lower lobe inducing a partial collapse, which we have stabilized. Both were clean penetrations and did not require bullet removal. We basically treated her entry and exit wounds under local anesthetic."

"Do you have any details about the shooter?"

"She asked me to tell you that she thinks it was someone called Kresta."

Kresta! Aviana told him how he threatened her, but Dural found it difficult to believe the young man would actually carry out his threat. It did not seem in character. Still, people did many things that were out of character.

"By the time the police arrived, she was in surgery," Pollack went on.

"Thank you very much for letting me know, Doctor," Dural said gravely. "Can she receive visitors?"

"Ordinarily, I would not allow it, not this soon. However, it has been well over an hour since her surgery, and she should be okay."

"I'll be right over." Dural switched off and pocketed the cell. Everyone around him looked expectant. "That was Dr. Pollack from The Alfred Trauma Center. A client shot my lawyer friend I've been going out with. I'm told it's nothing serious, but I'm going over there. Rosalyn—"

"I'll reschedule your morning patients."

"Thanks."

"I hope she'll be all right," Suyin said, clearly upset.

"Hell of a way to start the week," Leonard growled.

Dural nodded and turned abruptly. He strode out of the meeting room, hurried to his office, grabbed his jacket, and headed toward the elevators. He glanced at his Rado: 10:09.

This was not happening, his mind raged as he ran out of the building toward a taxi rank at the High Street corner. The image of Aviana torn and hurt sent his guts twisting. He could almost feel her pain, wanting to be in that hospital bed instead of her. The shot in the arm, presumably through muscle only, otherwise Pollack would have said, was nothing, but a collapsed lung sounded more serious, and likely very painful. A .22 bullet might be small, but its high velocity made it lethal at close range. Fortunately, it does not savage the surrounding tissue a larger caliber round would.

The cab dropped him off at The Alfred main entrance and he bounded up the stairs toward the large double glass doors. He identified himself at the Admissions desk and asked for Dr. Pollack. He only had to wait some ten minutes before he saw the surgeon's tall, skeletal figure draped in a white lab coat emerge from the elevator. He spotted Dural and strode briskly toward him.

"Come with me, Doctor," he said and led Dural down a crowded corridor.

"How is she?" Dural asked gravely, suppressing the flood of auras around him.

"Minor treatment under a local. We had to insert a tube into her side to release air that seeped into the chest cavity through the entry and exit holes, which induced the partial lung collapse. With the lung fully inflated again and excess blood drained, she's breathing normally and resting comfortably."

"Prognosis on the lung?"

"Only a bullet graze and the MRI did not show any residual garment material in the wound, which would have meant endoscopic surgery to remove it. I'll keep her here for four days to monitor possible infection, but she should recover fully."

"Did you operate?"

"One of the residents did it." Pollack gave a fleeting smile. "Rest easy, Doctor. She was in good hands."

On the fifth floor, Pollack led him through the ward and walked into a four-bed room. An elderly lady lay in a bed on his right wearing a headset watched the wall TV, a drip tube attached to her arm. Dural paused when he saw Aviana in the far left corner propped up by two pillows, a drip in her right arm, the upper left arm bandaged and held in a sling. A large window showed a jungle of buildings and rooftops. She turned her head and beamed, her purple/blue aura flaring with pleasure.

"Du…" she managed softly. "Sorry, I can't talk normally. I'm still sore inside."

Pollack cleared his throat. "Don't strain her too much."

Dural nodded and hurried to her side. Without saying anything, he leaned over her and gently kissed her. Her right arm wrapped itself around his neck and she pressed her face against him.

"It's only a few flesh wounds," she whispered, eyes glowing with feeling.

"That's not what Pollack said." Dural dragged a chair closer and sat down. He took her hand and stroked it. "First me, and now you. This has got to stop."

She smiled, then winced. "Don't say anything funny or I'll rip something."

"Are you in pain?"

"Still a little numb from the operation, but that drip is feeding me painkillers and antibiotics. I watched everything as they sewed me up." She made a face. "It might have been better if I slept through it."

"When Pollack called…" he swallowed hard.

Aviana brushed his cheek. "Everything is all right."

"What happened?"

"I got out of the house around 7:10 and was walking toward the sidewalk. I heard a sharp crack and my left arm felt like it was on fire. Then the second shot came. Something stabbed my side and I sagged against the fence. I heard a screech of tires and looked up in time to see a white Honda or Hyundai race up the street. The badges are similar. I couldn't see the driver, and I have no proof, but I suspect it might be Kresta."

"It could be him, but as you said, there is no proof, and he does not strike me as the revenge type."

"I don't know anybody else I've made mad lately to do this. The two-year ban prohibiting him from engaging in any form of financial service will hurt him badly."

"It could be somebody going after your firm."

She shrugged. "It's possible. We've been involved with some very shady characters. I don't know why someone would want to go after me, though."

"Have you spoken to the police?"

"Not yet, but I gave the details to the paramedics when the ambulance came." Aviana crunched her face. "It's funny, but I didn't feel much pain in my side, except for the arm, which stung like hell. Leaning against the fence, I felt like I had all the time in the world to ring triple zero."

"Lucky for you The Alfred is practically around the corner from where you live."

"I don't know how long I stood there waiting for the ambulance, but it must have been only a few minutes. At one point, I looked at my side and wished I hadn't. Blood everywhere and my arm was covered with it. After a while, I had a bit of difficulty breathing and my chest was killing me. I thought I was going to puke. Then the ambulance came and they put an oxygen mask on my face. One of the medics stuck me with a needle and I don't remember the trip to the hospital."

"What about the neighbors?"

"I didn't see anybody. I could have been the only living person there, which was unusual, as people are always about at that time of morning. A car drove past, but didn't stop. The driver must have been blind not to see me and all the blood."

Dural sighed and squeezed her hand. "My wounded bird. I would gladly swap places with you."

"You had your turn last weekend."

"Still…" He raised her hand and kissed her palm. "I wanted to die after Pollack called."

"I'm glad you didn't," she said softly. "It would have made things awkward for me."

"Get well. That's all I ask."

"That's the general idea," she agreed. "Thankfully, I'm told there weren't any complications, and the surgeon said my arm should recover fully. It'll be sore for a while, and I'll have to do a regimen of exercises, but there will not be any lasting muscle damage."

"You'll need that arm to whack Kresta on the jaw," Dural said grimly, and Aviana grinned. "Better still, I'll do the whacking."

Her face twisted with pain. "Nothing funny, Du!"

He was immediately contrite. "Sorry."

A knock and the door opened. Two uniformed cops walked slowly toward the bed. The chunky bald senior officer carried himself with assurance, expecting deference and instant obedience. Of average height, yellow Asian appearance, thin mouth, his intense black eyes were set to intimidate anyone they happened to be focused on. His young companion, freckles sprinkled liberally across his cheeks, wore a suffering expression of someone resigned to be trodden on.

"Ms. Kinsley?" the senior cop queried in a pleasant enough voice.

"That's right."

"I'm Sergeant Vincety, and this is my partner, Constable Prowler," he said and gave his partner a scowl. Prowler plunged his hand into his jacket and pulled out a small writing pad. "If you're up to it, ma'am, we need a statement of this morning's incident." He gave Dural a close look. "Mind saying who you are, sir?"

Dural studied the man's intense red aura of someone totally in control, possessing high inner strength, determination, and drive. He decided Vincety would be a hard man to work with, but very good at his job.

"Dr. Dural Sinclair. Ms. Kinsley is a close friend, and I am indirectly involved."

"I see." Vincety peered at him as though he were a prime suspect, then turned to Aviana. "Can you tell us what exactly happened this morning?"

She repeated her story, beginning to look tired. The cop saw this and nodded to his partner.

"That's enough for now, thank you. We'll be in touch if we need to see you again for additional details." He dug a business card out of his pocket and placed it on the side cabinet. "Call me immediately if you should remember anything else." He turned to Dural and frowned. "And how are you involved in this…Doctor?"

Dural quickly outlined his visit to Sydney, and Prowler busily scribbled more notes into his pad.

"So you see, breaking his testimony led to the subsequent hearing and Mr. Kresta's conviction, which in turn may have resulted in a revenge attack on Ms. Kinsley."

"If it was Mr. Kresta," Vincety said heavily. "There is no direct evidence to suggest he was the perpetrator, but that's not your concern. We'll be interviewing him to ascertain his whereabouts this morning, and whether he owns a firearm. Until we apprehend him, I suggest you take a cab when you're moving around, Doctor. If he is involved, you may also be a target."

Dural blanched, something he never considered, but it made sense. In a way, he was really the reason why Kresta faced a magistrate. If it was him, he reminded himself, not wanting to be judgmental.

Vincety nodded to Aviana. "Ms. Kinsley…" He gathered his partner with a glare and they walked out.

When the door closed, she sagged against the pillows. "An intense character, our Sergeant."

Intense was exactly the right word, Dural mused, but felt slightly sorry for Prowler. He brushed it away. It wasn't his business how they worked together.

"He can be Jack the Ripper as long as he gets the guy who shot you," Dural growled

Aviana sighed. "Do you mind if I close my eyes for a minute? I haven't realized I was so tired."

"Of course. You have your rest," he said, patted her shoulder, and pushed back his chair.

She reached for his hand. "Don't go."

"I don't mind staying." He swept a wayward lock of hair off her cheek.

She gave a faint smile and her face relaxed. After a while, he wanted to let go, but she held him fast. He slowly stroked her hand with his thumb.

There was no time, no today, no tomorrow. Only the now, the silent room, dark TV, the lady in the other bed sleeping. Sleeping like Aviana, and he wondered if she was dreaming and the dreams she had. He hoped they were happy dreams, bathed in the soft glow of her aura, the glow of her warm soul. He hoped his touch gave her some of his strength in the same way her touch gave him hers. His aura pulsed and merged with her glow until they were one fire, a fire that burned without heat and cast no shadows, but it cast a light. One light. Their light, and Dural basked in its radiance. If only others could see what he saw, the world might not need people like him to heal broken minds and torn spirits.

Her hand in his, her face serene, he sat there and watched her, not believing the depth of attachment he had for this woman. After Lenora, something he never expected to feel again. At least not like this. Was it possible to let himself go so completely that merely having Aviana out of his sight left a bottomless hole only she could fill? What if she walked away leaving the hole behind? If that happened, he fervently believed he would not survive. He would not want to. A world without her in it would be a dark, solitary thing where ghosts of yesterday walked aimlessly; lost, abandoned, unloved. An endless torment of hollow tomorrows. He would rather die.

What if she could not, or did not, want to love him back? Was he building an unrealizable fantasy over a couple of lunches and a dinner? He was a friend, a diversion from an endless grind of cases, endless briefs, crimes, and strife. She liked him, but he could not presume there was anything more. Her hand in his, he did not believe it. She had reached out to him, not wanting to let him go. Even if she did not say the words, perhaps she did not know how, her touch said the words for her, and that was enough.

Do you want to go down this path, Doctor?

He sat there watching her. Yes, he did. Thorns and all.

A light knock and the door opened. The tall man who walked in had a gaunt, thin Michael Rennie look. Pale blue eyes swept the room and rested bleakly on the bed. Pepper hair combed straight back accentuated the man's drawn face and pursed lips. Dural had an instant visceral reaction that had no underlying reason. Perhaps it was the man's stern expression, dominant bearing, or unstated air of superiority. His dirty brown aura, overlaid with streaks of dull gray, indicated a guarded, self-centered personality. He might be a dear to Aviana, but that did not mean Dural had to embrace him.

The slim woman beside him, her radiant orange aura a startling contrast to the man's gloomy demeanor, stood in the doorway with poise and confidence. Her dark golden complexion harbored large black eyes, full mouth, and a face still beautiful. She must have been stunning in her younger years. Her gaze rested on Dural and she smiled.

"Is that your standard bedside manner, Dr. Sinclair?" Her velvety voice conveyed restrained amusement. "Dr. Pollack told us you were here."

Liking her immediately, Dural grinned and disengaged himself from Aviana's hand. "Only with special patients, Mrs. Kinsley," he told the Spanish woman.

Her husband's scowl deepened. "So, you're the one going out with my daughter," the man grated, his aura turning dark.

Mrs. Kinsley slapped him on the shoulder. "Do behave yourself, Taylor, and don't be rude." She turned to Dural. "I apologize, Doctor. My husband was worried about Aviana, and when he saw you holding her hand…"

Dural slowly rose and his eyes bored into the other man. "If you want to be alone with her, I'll leave."

"Don't be so touchy, you two," Mrs. Kinsley admonished.

"Humph!" Taylor cleared his throat and extended his hand. "Sorry," he said gruffly.

Dural shook the hand with his left, but there was no warmth or reconciliation in Taylor's look. Why the instant dislike, he could not say, but he would be forever damned if he would kowtow to him. The clash of wills subsided and Dural looked at the woman, clearly uncomfortable and somewhat embarrassed on her husband's behalf.

"Do stay, Doctor," she said. "Aviana told us how you two met. I think it's priceless." She glanced at her husband. "Don't you think so, Tyler?"

"And now they're dating," he growled in disapproval.

"Don't be a clown, dear. It's about time she decided to go out with someone."

Taylor's scowl deepened, then his face cleared and he smiled. "You're right. I'll behave." He turned to Dural. "How is she?"

"The wound on her arm is superficial and should heal completely, and so will her lung. She just needs rest."

"That's what Dr. Pollack said." Mrs. Kinsley elbowed her husband's side and looked at Dural. "Tyler thinks it's your fault Aviana got hurt," she said with an amused twinkle in her eyes. "He said he would break your arms when he saw you."

"If you want to break someone's arms, Mr. Kinsley, do it to the man who shot her," Dural said darkly.

"Aw, hell. I came on a bit strong, and I'm sorry," Taylor announced. "When the hospital called, my guts turned to stone and I wanted to murder the guy who did it."

"Aviana told me something about you," Dural said guardedly.

"I can imagine what she said." Taylor laughed, transforming him instantly.

Dural was not entirely convinced at this turnaround, harboring a lingering dislike for the man.

"What's going on here?" Aviana mumbled, and everyone looked at her. "Mom…Dad?"

Mrs. Kinsley stepped quickly to the bed and gave her daughter a gentle hug and kiss.

"How are you, my little pie?"

Dural glanced at Taylor, who shrugged. Little pie? He'll remember to use that and see how Aviana reacted.

"Don't call me that, Mom!"

"And why not, my darling dear? You are my precious pie."

Taylor walked to the bed and brushed Aviana's cheek. "How are you feeling?"

"A bit sore, but they have me doped up." She blinked. "I heard arguing. What's going on?"

Mrs. Kinsley stroked Aviana's shoulder. "Nothing, dear. Just your father being a clown."

"Gianna!"

Aviana smiled. "You were always overprotective, Dad." She turned to Dural. "My parents," she said as though that explained everything.

Dural stroked her hand and nodded. "I'll see you later," he said softly and turned. "Mr. Kinsley…Mrs. Kinsley, I hope to meet both of you under better circumstances."

Mrs. Kinsley touched his shoulder. "Gianna, okay?" She glanced at Aviana. "Don't let this one slip through your fingers."

Aviana blushed deep red. "Mom!"

"Until next time, Doctor," Kinsley said gruffly.

Outside the room, Dural paused, trying to make sense of it all.

Aviana was very much like her mother, and he liked her without reservation, but her old man was a cold piece of meat Dural was not sure he would ever be comfortable with. Wary forming a permanent impression from a single meeting, he nevertheless took pains to remember everything. First impressions did not always reveal a person's true nature, but they were a good indicator. With familiarity, a person tailors his behavior to suit the occasion, and Taylor's unguarded attitude when he walked in told Dural a lot about the man. He was prepared to make a fresh start, provided Taylor's moment of contrition was genuine. He would see.

You are dating Aviana, not her parents, Doctor.

True, but he did not want his relationship to damage what she had with her parents. That would be a road paved with emotional thorns for everybody; one he did not want to walk. Taylor was being a jerk as Gianna said.

He grinned and strode down the broad corridor toward the elevators, ignoring the sights, sounds, and hospital smells around him.

When he stepped out of the main entrance, he looked up and scowled. Muddy gray clouds were drifting in from the west, driven by a thin, fresh breeze. He was glad to have his jacket. It was supposed to be 28C today and sunny! The meteorology boys must have blinds over the windows again, he mused sardonically. The planned walk back to Gap Consulting scrapped, he took a cab from a rank at the bottom of the steps. The cabby not impressed driving only three blocks, but Dural had no time for him, his thoughts on Aviana and the shooting…and her parents.

Taylor Kinsley's disapproving frown when they first locked eyes made him smile. Definitely a forceful character. His wife, on the other hand, could not have been more different. Warm, considerate, caring, the two were like poles on a magnet. Dural wondered who dominated the relationship, and decided that Taylor probably did not have it all his way. Gianna had shown steel beneath her engaging smile. He reminded himself to get Aviana's take on the Kinsley clan. Her father was a dear, she had said. At home perhaps, but Dural suspected her old man was a hard taskmaster at work. Well, as long as Taylor did not interfere in his relationship with Aviana, Dural was prepared to cut him some slack.

Heightened empathy was supposed to mean greater understanding and tolerance. Wasn't it?

The cab dropped him off and immediately pulled into traffic when Dural slammed the door. He had not added a tip to the fare, not for three blocks. Besides, he did not believe tipping someone for doing their job. A creeping American disease without a cure. Knowing how little they made, he did not mind tipping a waitress or waiter, but he would be damned if he gave a dollar to a hotel doorman for opening a door. A service he neither wanted nor needed. Soon, he would be required to tip a serviceman for fixing his washing machine! Where would it end?

He took the elevator up and waited stoically. It stopped at the fourth floor and the polished double doors gaped. He strode toward the glass panel with the Gap Psychology Consulting logo carved into the frosted surface, and it slid out of his way. Rosalyn looked up and beamed.

"How is your friend, Du?"

"She'll be fine. The wounds were not serious, but she'll be in hospital for a few days."

"I'm glad to hear it. To think that someone would shoot her…"

"Yeah. Anything I need to know?"

"I squeezed one of your patients into a four-thirty slot this afternoon. The other is at eight o'clock tomorrow morning. Sorry about that. It's the only time she could come in. You're booked pretty much solid for the rest of the week."

Dural brought up the image of his appointments—totally booked out.

"Don't worry about it. You did the right thing."

As he strode toward the kitchenette, he glanced at the Rado on his wrist: 11:50. His next appointment at 12:30, which did not leave much time for lunch. He would ask Rosalyn to order in some sandwiches. It would not be the first time he and his partners had a takeaway. Coffee mug in hand, he headed for his consulting room.

He took two quick, thirsty swallows and powered up the computer. His Outlook In box had the usual sprinkling of emails from professional organizations, colleagues, and several referral requests from GPs. He would look at those more closely later. One Gmail entry without a subject line caught his attention and he clicked on it. It had one sentence, 'Payback time'.

Everybody at the practice received their share of junk mail and occasional scam notifications advising him he had won five million from an unknown beneficiary. To collect, all he had to do was send three thousand dollars for 'handling fees'. The money would then be deposited into his bank account. Provide details, please. A variation of the gag was winning a lottery with a similar demand for a fee payment. The other one he liked was getting an official looking invoice from AT&T, reminding him he was in arrears and should pay promptly or face legal action. There were not many of those, though. Most such demands were made directly to the Gap Consulting address, which Rosalyn deleted without opening any attachment.

Dural stared at the screen digesting the message. It could be a crank email, but it did not have the feel of one. Usually, cranks tended to rant as they pounded their particular pulpit. This one had the flavor of intimidation and warning, and more to come, which meant someone else close to him might be a target. Dural did not like that line of reasoning at all. Then again, the whole thing might be someone's macabre idea of a joke. He did not believe it.

Kresta might be the shooter, but sending that email did not fit the young man's profile. He was arrogant, scheming, and calculating, but Dural could not picture him conducting psychological warfare in a campaign of revenge. A direct in your face attack would be more his style. That is how Aviana got shot, he reminded himself.

Logically, if not Kresta, someone else sent the email. If this was a revenge act, why not simply kill? Make him suffer? He would have suffered all right if Aviana were killed. Perhaps the shooter was a bad shot.

Aviana said she did not know anyone mad enough at her to shoot her. If someone was sore at Wellard, Wellard and Starke, and she happened to be a convenient target, why send the email to him? The cold, inescapable conclusion did nothing to settle his nerves. This was a nemesis from his past.

If somebody was after him, he needed to do some mental sifting. None of his patients came to mind as possible perpetrators. That left only one other possibility—his Victoria Police cases. In the last four years, excluding Kresta, he had handled nine profiles, of which two were exonerated. Out of the remaining seven, three were part of a drug importation ring with Hong Kong and Shanghai connections. If somebody crossed them, these people would not bother sending emails. They would take him out, and that was that. A supposition on his part only.

One suspect was a local underworld hitman and Dural had broken his alibi. He never actually interviewed the suspect, the police considering that too dangerous. He observed the proceedings through a one-way panel and provided telling questions. He could scratch that one off the list. The man was still in prison.

In 2017, the police asked him to look at a real estate scammer who preyed on elderly owners of inner city properties. His scheme was to convince victims their property was sought by a major development firm to build a tenement block. He understated the property value, then sold high. Dural conducted a psychological profile and was never told what happened to him.

Last year, he handled two investment fraudsters offering unrealistic returns if the victims assigned their shares to them. In Australia, anybody can call himself an investment advisor. There were no formal qualification or accreditation requirements. Promising a high rate of return to gullible investors might be unethical, but had no penalty under law. The fraudsters used their client's investments to fund a lavish lifestyle by charging inflated management fees.

In both cases, they claimed the vagaries of the stock market for the losses, which superficially their company's books confirmed, and they made no attempt to hide their operation behind a web of shell companies. The police lacked direct proof of intent to defraud, and the perpetrators could not be convicted for maintaining sloppy bookkeeping and inept share trading. That was something for the Tax Department. The police asked Dural to break down their testimony and establish intent. Difficult, as there was a fine line dividing incompetence and a deliberate scheme to defraud. Over several interviews, Dural managed to extract small inconsistencies in testimony from both, sufficient for indictment. The police never told him whether the fraudsters went to trial or were convicted, and he did not ask.

With drug traffickers and the hitman off the list, that left the real estate scammer and the investment fraudsters. The fraudsters were both polished operators: engaging, sincere, persuasive, projecting confidence and sophistication. Easy to see how they were able to deceive ignorant mom and pop investors. None of them, though, exhibited an underlying violent trait. Dural did not see either of them engaging in revenge, which left the real estate scammer. Raking through his memory, nothing stood out to identify him as the shooter.

People engage in revenge for many reasons. Betrayal being top of the list. It bolstered the perpetrator's ego and reinforced his sense of superiority. Curiously enough, instead of quenching hostility, revenge prolongs the unpleasantness of the original offense. Instead of delivering justice, it often created a cycle of retaliation, which was consistent with the email he received.

Another consideration for dismissing the drug dealers and the hitman was the timespan for the shooting. All of them were likely to be still in prison. That, however, did not preclude the possibility they would engage someone to hit Aviana, but why wait this long? The more he thought about it, the remaining three became the likely suspects.

Dural took a sip of coffee and sighed. He punched a white button on the desk phone and pressed the speaker button.

"Rosalyn?"

"Yes, Doctor?"

"Please get hold of Sergeant Vincety at Victoria Police. If he's not available, leave a message to call me back."

"Will do. Are you going out to lunch?"

"I'm staying in. Can you order a sandwich or something?"

"Leonard and Gerard are also staying in and ordered a tray."

"Great."

Dural took care of several emails when the phone rang.

"Sergeant Vincety is on line two, Du."

"Thank you," he said and pressed a blinking yellow button. "Sergeant Vincety? Dr. Sinclair."

"Good morning, Doctor. What can I do for you?"

"Can you give me your direct email address, please? I found an unusual email in my computer when I returned from the hospital. All it said was, 'Payback time'. Maybe your cyber people can identify who sent it and where it came from."

"Even if we could do something like that, what is the relevance, Doctor? You must get your share of unusual emails."

"We certainly do, but I suspect this is more serious."

"Has this anything to do with Ms. Kinsley?"

"It might."

"Okay, talk to me, Doctor."

Dural outlined his line of reasoning. When he finished, there were several seconds of silence.

"Although your chain of suppositions are logical, what happened to Ms. Kinsley could also be a random act. We have these all too often. A check on Mr. Kresta revealed he does not carry a current firearms license and never had one. That, of course, does not mean he has no firearm. The vehicle Ms. Kinsley mentioned? Mr. Kresta owns a blue Corolla. I'm obtaining a warrant to search his premises. We're still to establish his whereabouts. However, although tenuous, the information you provided is too important to ignore and I shall raise this with my superior. Got a pen?"

"I don't need one, Sergeant."

"Yes, your funny memory. I checked up on you," Vincety said and gave his email address.

"Thank you, Sergeant. I'll send you the email immediately."

"I'll be in touch if anything happens, Doctor," Vincety said and switched off.

Dural replaced the phone in its cradle, sat back, and exhaled loudly.

He possibly had a crazed gunman after him and those around him. This could also be fairy floss suppositions as Vincety said. Until some solid evidence emerged one way or another, he would simply have to figuratively gnaw his fingernails.

During lunch, he bumped into Gerard and Leonard in the kitchenette and told them Aviana was fine when they asked. He thought to tell them about a possible vendetta against him, then decided against it, not wanting to fret them needlessly.

With patients coming and going all afternoon, he had little time to fiddle with his worry beads. Not exactly worried, more like sifting through his case notes and memory for a detail that might help identify the shooter. By late afternoon, he gave up.

The police would handle it, he told himself, not convinced. How much manpower would they assign to what was essentially a drive-by shooting and his suspicions?

When he got home, not in the mood to cook, he made himself a chicken and tuna salad. Done, he switched on the TV to watch the news. Steel bowl in lap—not very dignified at all—a tall glass of pineapple juice to wash down the salad, he began to eat. Afterward, he indulged himself with a snifter of cognac.

Everybody talked about the Mueller report. Although direct collusion with the Russians in the 2016 election not proven, the report stopped short of exonerating President Trump. After three years in office, America appeared to be getting weary of Trump's growing instability and irrationality, while his stalwart Republican Senate and evangelical far-right supporters continued to polarize the country.

In London, people were marching in protest, disgusted with politicians from all sides for not honoring the Brexit referendum. Dural did not want to go there, revolted with Australian politicians of every persuasion.

Trump further eroded a possible Palestinian settlement when he announced that the U.S. recognized the Golan Heights as part of Israel, which prompted an immediate rocket attack by Hamas. Ignoring several UN Security Council resolutions, Israel continued to expand its construction program in East Jerusalem. As far as Dural was concerned, there was no hope that Palestinians would ever have a state of their own as long as ultra-conservative far-right religious parties held the balance of power in the Knesset. It was a doomed land.

Worn down by creeping helplessness at a world slowly sliding into extremist nationalism, political partisanship, and religious polarization, Dural switched off. *It should not be this hard to fix things,* he told himself. It only took a bit of calm discussion and some compromise…and a measure of political will. Regrettably, evidence demonstrated a chronic shortage of these things. Somewhere in the pursuit of happiness, a two-car garage, and a muscular bank account, the Western world had lost compassion, accelerating its decline into authoritarian autocracies. Everything was too complex, and people had become disillusioned and disinterested, not wanting to be bothered, preoccupied with merely surviving while the entrenched politicians continued to play their games.

Let the world destroy itself, O Lord, but not yet, seemed to be the popular sentiment.

Hell of a legacy to leave for the children.

In the kitchen, he washed the glass, placed cling wrap on the salad bowl and shoved it into the fridge. He called a cab and had it drive him to The Alfred.

Aviana watched news on the ABC, remnants of a dinner on the side cabinet. He noted the old lady was gone.

"Hi, Du. Great to see you. I've been all alone this afternoon."

"Poor you."

"Prong."

He kissed her forehead and dragged up a chair. "How is my favorite patient?"

"Well, I'm sort of lying down, Doctor, which means I can start regaling you with my life's problems."

"Okay, the meter is ticking."

She suppressed a chuckle and touched her side. "I'm not supposed to laugh, Du."

"Right, no funnies." He glanced at her arm. "No drip?"

"They figured I can help myself to a glass of water or juice without one, and there are pills for pain and other stuff." She pointed at the TV. "I'm a celebrity!"

Dural did a double take and the pieces clicked. "You were on the news?"

"They just showed it."

"That explains why I missed it. Has Sergeant Vincety called?"

"He rang around four. Kresta accounted for his movements this morning, and he doesn't own a firearm." She noted his frown. "What? You know who did this?"

"I don't, but I spoke to Vincety about a possibility."

"And?"

"This could be a grudge statement against me."

"Your evil past catching up with you?"

"It might be," he said and told her about the email.

"What did Vincety say?"

"He would look into it."

"I hope he looks hard. I don't relish the prospect of getting shot again."

"Although possible, I don't believe the shooter intended to kill. I think he wants to intimidate me."

"Which implies he might go after someone else close to you?"

"I'm afraid so."

She snorted and shook her head. "My instincts told me I shouldn't get involved with you."

Dural blanched, then relaxed when he saw her impish grin.

"Just kidding."

"You have a low sense of humor. Did you know that?" he growled.

"Dad told me. By the way, how do you like my parents?"

"Your dad is a dear, just like you said," he deadpanned, and she chuckled. "I'll get used to him. Your mom, though, is a darling."

"She is. I knew you'd like her. Give Dad a chance. He's a dear once he lowers the barrier."

"For you, anything, my little pie."

She glared. "You call me that again and you'll be on the floor."

He raised a hand. "I couldn't resist."

"Prong." Her face clouded. "What if the shooter goes after you and—"

He lifted his hand. "Stop right there. The police are on top of it."

"You hope."

"Look, if someone wants to take a shot at me, there is damn little I can do about it."

"And if you get killed?" Her eyes filled and she sniffed.

"I don't particularly relish the idea, or someone else getting hurt because of me."

"What if—"

"Aviana…"

She cleared her throat and sighed. After a moment, she gave a small smile.

"Well, I can scratch myself off the list. I've already been shot."

"If I get shot," he added, "I'll get us a private room and we can convalesce together."

"That would be exciting," she drawled.

He patted her hand. "Try not to dwell on it."

"This afternoon, with nothing but time on my hands, I've been asking myself how the shooter knew that you and I…you know…"

"I've been asking myself the same question. This did not look like some off-the-wall impulse act. The only thing that makes sense is that I've been under surveillance. Perhaps the shooter initially had somebody else in mind. When he saw us together, and assuming he wanted to cause me maximum emotional stress, you became the target of choice."

"And you cannot think of anyone who might be behind this?"

"I'm a blank file."

She smiled. "You have yourself a situation, Doctor."

"Thank you for that startling insight."

"You're welcome."

Dural stood and gently brushed her cheek. "You take it easy and I'll see you tomorrow." He bent over her and kissed her full lips. "Night."

Her face a cascade of emotions, she grasped his hand and squeezed. "You take it easy yourself."

He nodded and walked out.

The elevator took him down and he strode quickly through the noisy, crowded foyer awash with shifting auras. After a short sigh, he blinked hard. When he opened his eyes, the auras were gone, much to his relief, thankful for his ability to blot them out. That's what he feared all those years ago, not able to shut out the flood of conflicting colors. Over time, as with most things, he would probably have gotten used to it, if it had not driven him mad first.

Already after eight, the hospital showed no sign of slowing down. It probably never did.

The main entrance panels slid back and he paused at the landing. Visitors and patients were coming up the steps and moved around him to get in, or were going down to catch a cab, tram, or simply merge with other pedestrians and vanish in the gloom, glad to be out of the depressing building. He could not say why hospitals were such depressing places, but they were. Intellectually, he knew, of course, but did not want to think about that right now. Knowing why did not stop them being depressing.

A tram pulled away from the stop and clattered down the road. A major thoroughfare, Commercial Road was lit with car headlights. Laden with the acrid stink of exhausts, the mild air made him look up at a totally black sky devoid of stars, their flickering points drowned by the city's glare. He wondered absently if people living in downtown apartments ever got to see stars. They must sometimes. He saw stars from his place. A few; the largest and brightest. Did a star exist if there was no one to see it? A moot philosophical riddle.

Dural walked down the steps and turned left, deciding to enjoy the evening by stretching his legs. At the corner of St. Kilda Road, he glanced at the glowing spires piercing the pervasive darkness and pondered what all the people there were searching for in the brightly lit streets, surrounded by a sea of seething pedestrians, inviting storefronts, and places of entertainment. A tide of humanity that washed in every morning and ebbed late into the night. There was nothing more dismal than a city empty of life, empty of cars, silent, an occasional piece of paper or plastic bag fluttering along the tram tracks. Lost souls…damned souls condemned to wander endlessly, seeking and never finding.

He turned left and began walking briskly toward High Street, golden elms whispering to him like sirens. Trinion Street an oasis of dark shadows and deep silence, with islands of yellow light painted from tall poles. It would be easy to imagine himself in a thick forest of ancient gnarled trees hissing to themselves as a light breeze stirred the leaves, unknown glowing eyes peering at him. At midnight, strange creatures would be about, wary of daysiders intruding into their domain.

Daniela used to love stories about witches, goblins, and things fluttering through the night, even though they scared her. He made them bleak and creepy to set her imagination on fire, but ensured they were never actually terrifying.

My little grub, I hope only light and joy surround you now. Can you see me? Could I see you and your bright aura just once? Surely not too much to ask.

His footfalls echoed on the empty, dark sidewalk.

* * *

The sight of two police cars, their roof lights cycling from side to side, channel Seven and Ten news vans double-parked in the inner lane before the Gap Consulting building, made Dural pause. In a flash of foreboding, he hurried. Two lady reporters chatting to each other, cameramen trailing behind them, emerged from the entrance. In the foyer, sprinkled with men and women coming into the building to start another working day, he almost ran toward the elevators. Everybody wore expressions of mild curiosity as they tried to discern the presence of TV crews and the police.

He stepped into the elevator, waited for others to squeeze in, and rode it up. When the doors opened on the fourth floor, four uniformed cops were waiting to go down. He recognized Vincety and Prowler and stopped.

"Sergeant, what's going on here?"

"Dr. Sinclair…" Vincent looked momentarily distracted. "One of your partners, Dr. Morton, was shot twice in the right shoulder in front of the building."

Leonard shot? A flood of memories and images stormed through Dural's head. They had been friends since university, hung together, did crazy things together, and trusted each other implicitly to partner in a business. Without Leonard's experience and guidance, the practice would never have gotten off the ground. Now, his close friend had paid a penalty for something Dural did out of hubris and expression of unstated superiority.

Two close friends had now paid.

"How bad?"

"Unknown. Witnesses say a small black sedan sped into the traffic immediately after the shots were fired. It appears the perpetrator waited for him to arrive. Nobody got the registration number. The ambulance took Dr. Morton to The Alfred." Vincety pursed his lips, staring intently at Dural. "Search of the area failed to locate any spent cartridges."

Dural's mind went into overdrive. The wounds pattern suggested an expert shooter. This guy knew exactly what he was doing. To hit someone from a vehicle on a crowded sidewalk without hitting an innocent bystander took skill.

"My police cases…have you checked if any had military training?" A long shot at best, as anybody can become a proficient marksman with enough practice popping cans on a fence.

"We'll look into it. As for you, Doc, check your emails."

"I'll do that. Thank you, Sergeant."

"This is no longer a case of random assault, Doctor, but deliberate terrorism. You might consider lying low for a while until we apprehend your attacker."

Dural stared hard at the cop. "I'll consider it."

Vincety nodded as the elevator doors opened and stepped in.

Suyin and Rosalyn were huddled in conversation when he walked into the reception area. Rosalyn wiped her eyes and sniffed.

"Du, this is awful."

"I have a profile case on June 10. Please call Inspector Frank Farmer and cancel it. Also, tell him that Gap Consulting is no longer available for any police work," Dural told her harshly. He would never again inadvertently place people he knew in jeopardy.

She looked at him for a moment, glanced at Suyin, and nodded. "I'll get it done right away."

Suyin walked up to him, hesitated, and grasped his left arm.

"What's going on, Du?"

"Is Gerard here?"

She shook her head. "Not yet."

"It appears that somebody is after me, Suyin. A case I did for Victoria Police. That person has now targeted two people close to me and might be planning more attacks."

Her black eyes regarded him without flinching, absorbing the information.

"I don't know if any of us is safe anymore," he added.

"The police—"

"Are on it," he said and sighed. "I hope they catch him before someone else gets hurt, perhaps seriously."

The telephone rang, scattering whatever thoughts he had. Rosalyn reached over the counter and picked up. Dural could only hear fragments of the conversation.

"Thank you. I'll tell him," she said and replaced the receiver, her face grave. "That was Dr. Pollack. Leonard is out of surgery.

Two .22 bullets were removed from his right shoulder blade, but there were no complications and he'll be all right."

Dural pulled at his right ear. "Please call Pollack as ask if he can move Leonard and Ms. Kinsley into a private room."

She nodded. "What now, Du?"

He looked at them. "We close up until this is resolved, or we keep working. Your choice, but bear this in mind. Both of you have a child who is dependent on you."

Suyin glanced at Rosalyn, then gave Dural a determined look. "I have patients to look after."

"I'm staying," Rosalyn said and walked briskly to her chair.

Dural glanced at his watch: 07:50. "I have a patient of my own in a few minutes. Rosalyn, try to reschedule my eleven o'clock for five today. If not, then at eight tomorrow. I'll give Leonard a quick visit at eleven."

"Leave it with me, Du."

Suyin touched his arm. "When Gerard gets in—"

"Tell him what's going on, but he is not to rush off to the hospital. A lunchtime visit might be more appropriate. Somebody has to keep this consultancy going," he said with a grin, more for their benefit than anything else, and strode toward his office, his thoughts dark.

He powered up the computer and brought up Outlook. One message without a subject line stood out. He hesitated for a second, then clicked on it.

It said, 'Not done yet'.

Mouth clenched, he forwarded it to Sergeant Vincety.

Chapter Ten

A troubled, drama filled day, Dural reflected as he walked home, relieved it had ended. A late patient, a talk with Gerard and Suyin, Inspector Farmer attempting to change his mind, by 6:20, he had enough. Cooped up in his consulting room all day, he needed to stretch his legs and take in some fresh air. A brisk trek home gave him both, even though the air had a faint whiff of car exhaust stinks from a long queue of vehicles patiently crawling out of the city. For some, it would take a while before they reached home and a measure of peace, having to do it all over again tomorrow.

Sometimes, he wondered at the point of it all. A man spends upwards of forty years toiling every week under the weight of a mortgage, which in some cases his children would have to pay off if they wanted to keep the house, meet grocery and utility bills, maintain a car or two, send kids through school, and if lucky, have a bit of time to go out and take his family for a holiday somewhere. Most people dreamed of having a nice brick veneer house, little backyard and garden, and some money for a secure retirement. Regrettably for many, it remained only a dream. The modern lifestyle offered conveniences and luxuries parents of Dural's generation never envisaged, but it also took a heavy psychological toll in broken marriages, traumatized children, and general social stress. He saw such people every day.

A simple rural existence had a charming attraction, drawing city dwellers into the countryside every weekend. It satisfied a yearning to escape, forget, refresh inner energy before returning to the grind on Monday. It might be charming for a weekend or holiday for a few days, but most people were unwilling to trade their modern lifestyles for an elusive inner peace that did nothing for the bank account. A perfect social dilemma. A subconscious desire to escape somewhere for spiritual fulfillment and the rational realization that an easier materialistic life meant putting up with the daily chore of work. Dural was not surprised that some found it impossible to reconcile the two conflicting wants.

As he turned the corner into Trinion Street, he felt cold drops on his head and face. Somewhat appropriate, he thought. The world was pissing on him. He glanced at the heavy gray clouds and pursed his lips. Let it pour, they needed it, but not until he got home, he pleaded, now only a few houses away.

Gerard had invited him to have dinner at Suyin's place, but Dural politely refused. Another time, he said. He wanted to clear his head, impatient and frustrated that Sergeant Vincety had not called. His probably not the only case the cop handled, but Dural did not care about other cases. He wanted the shooter behind bars for a hundred years, but acknowledged it took time to sift through available information and trace down leads. He'd been around Victoria Police long enough to understand that, but it did nothing to settle his nerves, and he was unsettled, dreading the idea of having someone else hurt. He should have anticipated something this when he agreed to work with Farmer, but it honestly never occurred to him. Some genius he turned out to be.

Dural did not linger long at the hospital that morning. Leonard looked pale and weary propped against the wall, his right arm held in a black shoulder sling. According to Pollack, the clavicle was not fractured and should heal cleanly, although Len would have an uncomfortable four weeks or so walking around with a sling. It could have been worse, Len said after Dural explained why he had been shot, more concerned about the effect on the practice during his absence over the next few days. Len did not hold the shooting against him, something he appreciated, and lifted a load off his mind. Leonard's positive psychological attitude, Dural observed, would also help the recovery process enormously. There were many examples of patients dying from relatively minor wounds because they simply gave up.

At least Pollack managed to get Aviana and Len into one room. Although comfortable, it held only two beds. Not enough space if someone else got hurt, Dural thought wryly. Having company would make the day pass more quickly for both. She was delighted to see him, but he did not linger long, telling them he would be around that evening, wanting to make sure Leonard was okay, with a 'You too' for Aviana.

When Gerard returned from his lunchtime visit, he told everybody how Len harangued the nurses to let him out of there, which raised a few indulgent smiles. Typical of Leonard. During the afternoon coffee break, Dural called Helen, offering an apology for what he considered his fault that Leonard got shot. She listened without interruption to the chain of events that led to the two shootings, then thanked him gravely, assuring him she bore no ill will, which eased Dural's heavy conscience somewhat. He told her he would be at the hospital around eight and they would have a chance to talk more if she came.

A pattern of wet spots marred the sidewalk as he neared his house, and the air had taken on a fresh scent that always preceded a downpour. He reached into his jacket and fondled the keyring.

He sensed a figure behind him and glanced over his shoulder. Of medium height, stocky, wearing a black leather jacket, black jeans, the man gave a sardonic grin. Dural recognized him immediately—the real estate scammer.

"Ponting!"

"Hello, Dr. Sinclair," Ponting said pleasantly. "Someone appears to have gotten to you ahead of me," he added, nodding at Dural's arm. "No matter. I wanted you to see me before I depart somewhere more peaceful. And you know what? I'll need it after fourteen months in the cooler thinking about you," Ponting grated, his voice savage. "You have no idea what I went through during those fourteen months." He reached into his jacket and pulled out a slim handgun. "It's payback time, Doc, for ruining my life."

The crack sounded unnaturally loud in the quiet street. Fire seared Dural's left thigh. He gasped and instinctively clutched his leg, feeling a trickle of warm blood.

"The other one next, but it won't be as pleasant," Ponting smirked.

"Drop it! Now!"

Vincety stood beside the prickly holly bush in Mrs. Parker's front yard. A revolver held in both hands pointed unwaveringly at Ponting.

"Don't even think about it," a calm voice announced close to Dural.

He turned to see Prowler standing behind the fence of his front yard, gun leveled.

Ponting squeezed off a shot and Dural grunted at the light blow to his stomach. Two sharp cracks made his ears tingle, and Ponting crumpled to the sidewalk clutching his chest. Prowler scrambled over the fence and kicked Ponting's gun into the gutter.

Leg throbbing with fire, Dural gingerly opened his jacket expecting to see blood, surprised that he did not feel any pain. He stared at his shirt, but there was nothing. Vincety ran to him and grabbed his left arm.

"Where are you hit?"

"My…my stomach," Dural mumbled, waiting for the agony to start.

Vincety looked up with a grim smile. "This is your lucky day, Doc. The bullet hit your belt buckle."

Dural touched the bright indentation in the plate buckle. Two centimeters up or down…

"How's the leg?" Vincety demanded.

"Burning, but I'm able to stand."

"Sorry we didn't react faster. Ponting didn't waste time taking his shot."

"He could have killed me!" Dural snarled in outrage.

"No, he wouldn't. He wanted to cripple you. That last shot of his was instinctive. He may not even have meant it."

"I don't think much of your tactics, Sergeant, or your sense of humor."

Vincety shrugged. "We got him, that's what counts." He turned to his partner. "How is he?"

"Two chest wounds," Prowler said. "He's still alive."

"Call an ambulance."

Prowler nodded and dug out his cellphone.

Dural looked Vincety in the eye. "You staked out my place," he made it a statement.

"After securing two victims, we figured the attacker would be coming after you. Prolonging his vendetta, regardless how pleasurable to his ego, would have been an exercise of diminishing returns. We have profilers of our own, Doc," Vincety added dryly.

"And the most logical place to get me was in front of my house," Dural said in disgust. "You could have told me!"

"No, we couldn't. I did not want to change your normal behavior pattern. Your Mr. Ponting could not be allowed to suspect a trap."

Dural glared at the cop, then glanced at the wet stain on his leg. He wanted to see how badly he'd been hit, but short of dropping his pants—not something he wanted to do in front of Vincety—he would have to wait for the ambulance and a ride to the hospital.

The situation made him grin.

"What's funny?" Vincety demanded.

"The room with Ponting's two victims? It only holds two beds."

The cop scowled. "Maybe you won't need a bed."

"How did you identify Ponting as the shooter?"

"We didn't. He was released two months ago and my best suspect. The two investment scammers were out since last October. Any of the three could have been the shooter."

Calmed somewhat, Dural extended his left hand. "I want to thank you, Sergeant, but not for the leg."

"You're breathing, Doc, and that's thanks enough," Vincety said bleakly as they shook hands.

Dural heard an ambulance siren and glanced up the street. It turned the corner and slowed, the siren winding down as it stopped. With the shooting over, he looked around, surprised to see a small crowd hovering around them. He nodded to two of his neighbors.

"What the hell happened, Dural?" one of them demanded.

Mrs. Parker pushed through and gaped when she saw Ponting on the sidewalk, blood all over him.

"Goodness!"

Vincety raised his arms. "It's all over. Go back to your homes."

Two paramedics hurried to Ponting, slapped on pressure bandages, lifted him onto a gurney, and wheeled him into the ambulance. One medic glanced at Dural.

"Better get in."

Dural hobbled toward the back and the medic helped him climb in. His thigh protested with sharp lances of pain at this mistreatment. The medic banged the back of the cabin with his fist and the ambulance lurched from the curb, siren wailing. His partner was fixing a drip to Ponting's arm.

"Let's take a look at that leg." The medic reached into a tray, pulled on surgical gloves, and held up scissors. He cut away the trouser around the wounds with impersonal efficiency, ruining a pair of five hundred dollar pants, and exposed two small weeping holes.

Dural glanced down and winced. The round had gone straight through the muscle part of his thigh. The medic dabbed antiseptic on it and Dural gasped at its sting.

"Doesn't look too bad," the medic said briskly as he affixed pressure pads onto the entry and exit holes. "Shallow with minimal muscle trauma."

Dural hated Ponting with scorching intensity. He could have had a shattered femur or a severed sciatic nerve, which would have left him crippled. The medic held out two yellow pills and a large brown one.

"Antibiotics and pain killer. You'll need both."

"Thanks." Dural mumbled and swallowed all three in one go.

At The Alfred's Emergency, they took an MRI to make sure no trouser material was left in the wound and closed the holes with a couple of stitches. A nurse wrapped a large waterproof pad over both wounds and bound the thigh with a thick bandage. They gave him a walking crutch and he was free to go.

"Keep your weight off the leg for two or three days," the attending resident told him cheerfully. "Come back tomorrow and we'll change the dressing."

Dural filled the prescription for antibiotics and painkiller at the downstairs pharmacy and hobbled toward the elevators. His thigh numb from the anesthetic and he didn't feel much discomfort. That, he was sure, would change once the anesthetic wore off. Since he was already here, he would visit Aviana and Leonard, relishing seeing their expressions, torn bloody pants and all. He could also use a bit of gratuitous sympathy right then.

"My God, Du!" Aviana gasped when he walked in. "What the hell happened to you?"

"A gift from my nemesis," he grated and pulled up a chair, his leg grateful for the gesture.

"How bad?" Leonard demanded.

"A shallow wound. The cops got him before he could do more. He's in surgery now with a couple of bullets in him."

"Does that mean it's over?" Aviana asked.

Dural nodded. "No more police consulting for Dr. Sinclair."

"Are you in a lot of pain?" she asked, distress all over her face.

"One arm in a brace, a bum leg, I figure I'm still ahead."

"Prong."

"They're not keeping you here?" Leonard put in.

"The wound is not that bad. How's the shoulder?"

"Sore, but Ms. Kinsley—"

"Aviana."

"—kept me entertained."

Dural pointed a finger at her. "Take care, hear? Len's the real wolf here."

She grinned broadly. "He has been a perfect gentleman."

"With that shoulder sling, he couldn't do much," Dural growled, and Aviana laughed, then clutched her side. "And you?" he asked.

She shrugged. "Fine, all things considered."

"Yeah." Dural heaved himself up. "Sorry to cut this short, but I need to clean myself up." He hobbled to her side and kissed her. "I'll see you tomorrow," he whispered as he gazed into her fathomless hazel eyes.

She stroked his cheek and nodded.

"What about me?" Leonard protested. "Don't I rate a kiss?"

"Get them off Helen," Dural snapped, and everyone chuckled. "See you later, guys."

"Night, Du!" Aviana called after him.

In the corridor, he sighed with satisfaction. It was over, but not without some collateral damage, though. Walking crutch tapping against the hard linoleum floor, he slowly made his way toward the elevator.

Ponting…he would never have figured it.

Some profiler you turned out to be, Doctor.

A drama filled day, all right.

Outside, the clouds had lifted. The cabby hardly gave his torn pants a look when Dural climbed in. He guessed the man must have seen a lot worse things around here.

The cab dropped him off in front of his house and the cabby helped him to the front entrance, much to Dural's pleased surprise. He gave him fifty bucks and did not ask for change.

He locked the door and headed for the bar cabinet. The whiskey seared his insides as it went down. He shouldn't be mixing spirits and medication, but he figured just this once would not kill him. After a nod, he lifted the tumbler in a salute to the gods. He glanced at the deeply indented belt plate and shook his head. The margin between death or a serious wound had only been a couple of centimeters. He shrugged and headed for the stairs to change, considering himself lucky.

Damn, the leg had started to hurt.

* * *

The doorbell chimed and Dural swept his eyes around the set dining table and lounge. Everything in order, he walked to the front door with barely a limp and unlocked it. Aviana's small mouth lifted in a delicate smile.

"You have a nice neighborhood here, Du. Quiet," she said in a ripple of musical notes.

He leaned toward her and brushed his lips against her cheek. "Welcome to my den. Come on in."

Very stylish in olive pants and white T-shirt, she left a lingering fresh scent as she moved past him. Her shoulder grazed his chest and he felt a tingle of energy race through him. Her aura flickered bright yellow, then faded, clearly feeling the connection between them. He glanced at her red Mazda parked in his driveway and closed the door with a backhanded shove.

"Any problems coming in?" He planned to pick her up, but she insisted she would drive over. Not wanting to make a big deal out of it, he respected her choice.

"Traffic was a bit heavy, but not too bad."

Not unusual for a Saturday evening as people headed into the city hunting for a restaurant or entertainment.

"Lucky you have a driveway, otherwise I would have had a tough time finding an empty spot." She looked around with pursed lips. "You're right. Your place does look similar to mine, but it's lots roomier."

Dural tore his eyes off her and waved at the couch. "Make yourself comfortable. Care for a drink? Sherry or wine? Some whiskey or cognac perhaps?"

"A medium sherry would be nice, thank you." She sauntered to the wall shelf and peered at his collection of books and DVDs. "I thought you didn't like fantasy?"

"I don't. Those are Lenora's. She was into Harry Potter and magic," Dural remarked, fixing their drinks. "I should get rid of them, as I'll never read them, but I'm a book hoarder. I've been meaning to take the whole lot to the local op shop, but I keep putting it off. I'll have to do it soon, though, to make room for the stuff I like."

He *had* been putting it off. A lingering psychological block? A reminder of days past? Right now, he did not care to analyze it too much.

She sat on the couch, crossed her legs, and took the offered sherry glass. Dural raised his cognac balloon.

"To the walking wounded."

Her clear laugh made him feel good inside as they touched glasses. She showed no discomfort from her side, while he still favored his left leg a little. At least he no longer used the crutch.

"I'm glad to be home, I tell you," she added. "Leonard practically climbed the walls the last two days."

Pollack released him yesterday to stop his irascible patient haranguing the nurses. Make your wife's life difficult, he told him. Len would be at the office next week, which would relieve the other partners from the extra load of looking after some of his patients.

Aviana glanced at his arm. "No golf for a while."

Dural smiled. "True, but it's going to be harder on Leonard. He loves his game."

She took a sip of sherry. "I still cannot believe someone would actually shoot people around you in revenge for something he did to himself."

"Blame transference is common among those who consider themselves superior," Dural said. "Anyway, he won't be bothering any of us for a long time to come." He took a swallow of cognac. "Back to work on Monday?"

"I'm afraid so. Wellard doesn't believe in idle hands, and I have been putting in some work at the hospital."

"I noticed the laptop on Tuesday."

"I had our secretary bring it over." Aviana chuckled. "It made me laugh watching Leonard struggle with his, left hand pounding the keyboard."

"His supplementary notes helped the rest of us deal with some of his patients we took on."

"Talking to him, he can be very intense," Aviana remarked.

"That's Len. I'll never be able to make it up to him for getting hurt because of me." He looked steadily at her eyes. "Or to you."

Her aura flowed in golden orange hues at his words.

"You couldn't have known this would happen, Du," she said softly.

"I should have considered the possibility. A touch of hubris, I guess. I thought I knew it all."

"Don't beat yourself up over it." She pointed at his leg. "You seem to be walking okay."

"It's still a little sore, but I'm getting there, and the walks are helping rebuild the muscle. And your arm?"

"Sore as well, but the exercise program is slowly giving me my strength back. I'll live," she said with a shrug and took a sip of sherry. "I'm glad you're starting to like my dad," she added with a whimsical smile.

"I must admit, he does have a charming side."

"Once he pockets his horns," she mused, then tilted her head slightly. "I'm interested to compare him with your dad."

"No horns. At least not while I'm around anyway. He and my mom are coming down on Tuesday and we've been invited for lunch next Sunday…if you can make it."

"I'd love to, thanks. Unless something comes up before then." She noted his hesitation. "What?"

"I have one other thing in mind as well. My partner Gerard is getting engaged—"

"I know. Leonard told me."

"And I would like you to come with me to the engagement party. Nothing formal or fancy, just an afternoon get-together at Suyin's parents' place as far as I know. I want to show you off."

"A traditional Chinese party with costumes and all?"

"They're Aussies through and through. Her ancestors came here during the 1850s Ballarat gold rush. You can probably expect party pies and sausage rolls."

She chuckled. "I can clearly picture that combination. When is it?"

"Next Saturday. You don't have to if you don't want to," he added hastily.

"And have you as the only bachelor there? I'll come."

He smiled broadly and nodded. "Thanks. I'm curious to see what Suyin and her parents will come up with." He finished his cognac and stood. "Ready for the main event?"

"I'm dying to sample your culinary experiments."

He raised a finger. "Not experiments, my dear, but high art. And I assure you, you won't be dying."

"That remains to be seen."

Dural led her to the dining table and pulled back a chair for her. She sat down and looked with interest at the black porcelain plates adorned with a gold border, laid out over a light green tablecloth. Gold cutlery gleamed under the overhead light, resting on dark green cloth napkins.

She picked up a knife. "Real gold?"

"Plated, I'm afraid," he said from the kitchen. He filled a black tureen with thick soup from a pot on a hotplate and brought it to the table, followed by a basket of small rolls. He sat down and nodded to her.

"Please…"

Aviana ladled the rich soup into her bowl and sniffed appreciatively. She took a spoonful, blew on it, and had a taste.

"Wow. This is divine, whatever it is."

"Plain old pureed chicken soup. With real chicken and one or two other things," he added, helping himself.

"It didn't come from a can, that's for sure. You'll have to give me the recipe."

"I'll email it to you."

She took a small roll and bit into it. "Nice flavor."

"I get them from a Chinese bakery on High Street. Guaranteed no chemicals or preservatives," he assured her.

They spent the next few minutes concentrating on their soup. When finished, Aviana glanced at him, smiled, and helped herself to more. Dural grinned, pleased to see her relaxed and enjoying herself.

When she finally finished, she patted her mouth with the napkin, sighed, and leaned back.

"That was good. Do you cook like this all the time?"

"It depends on how I feel. If I have a long day and come home late, I keep things simple, which means most of the week. I try to be more creative on weekends."

"Same with me," she said. "Sometimes, by the time I get home, it's a grilled sandwich, or I pop into a local restaurant for something if I don't feel like making anything." She gave him a speculative appraisal. "You have managed to keep the love handles at bay."

He snorted. "If only it came off as quickly as it went on."

Aviana laughed, her purple/blue aura flowing in pleasing pulses.

"And some men don't care to take it off."

"Looking at you, you've nothing to worry about," he told her, wanting her to see the glow of desire in his eyes.

He wanted her to see this was not a passing infatuation, a fleeting satisfaction of flesh, a momentary convenience for both. He wanted to tell her he cared for her, but uncertain this was the right moment. Then again, when was the right moment to tell her everything? Was there ever such a thing?

Should he tell her about his tumor? He decided not. At least not tonight. This evening was for enjoying themselves, not dwelling on something gloomy, and he did not want gratuitous sympathy and commiseration.

Should he tell her about his ability to see auras? Tempted, he refrained. This also wasn't the right moment either. He would recognize it when it came. She would have to know sometime, but not tonight.

Aviana lowered her eyes, then looked up. "You're a curious man, Dural, and I haven't made up my mind about you yet. You have secret drawers you keep closed, and I want to see what's inside them before I do."

"I haven't told you everything about myself, but one day I will."

"Not tonight, though?"

"A mysterious package should be opened slowly," he quipped with a teasing smile.

"Mysterious and witty."

He reached across the table and laid his hand over hers. "One thing is not a mystery, Aviana. You have enchanted me from the first moment I saw you. I don't want the magic to stop, and I hope you're sharing some of it."

The tip of her tongue ran over her lips. "I am. I don't know if I'm ready to let it sweep me into its embrace."

He stroked her hand. "I'm content with what I have now, although I do want more, you need to decide if you're willing to give more."

Her aura merged in a cascade of turquoise, blue, and soft greens. She wanted him, he could tell. It could also be a transitory emotional attraction brought on by a moment of mutual connection, which did not necessarily represent her logical, reasoning self. She might be willing to give herself to him now, but she might resent him afterward if he exploited her vulnerability. Something he was not prepared to do for a fleeting spark of pleasure. He wanted a flame that would burn forever, no matter what.

"Time for the main treat," he declared and broke the spell.

He brushed her cheek with a finger and started to collect the dishes.

"For a moment there, I wondered if those bread rolls were all we were having," she mused with a twinkle in her eye.

She had recognized they had treaded exciting, but dangerous ground. Better to be on firm footing for the time being, he reflected.

"Never fear, my dear. Your patience shall be rewarded, as will your taste buds."

She laughed, stood, picked up the soup tureen and placed it on a cork mat beside the hotplates.

"Anything I can help with?"

He pointed at the fridge. "You can take out the salad. Some wine with the meal?"

"I wouldn't mind a shiraz. I don't usually have a heavy wine, but this seems to be the night for it."

"I have a very smooth one from the Barossa Clare Valley. You'll like it. At least I hope you will."

He took out two large vol-au-vents from the small pantry, placed them on flat plates, and spooned in the veal filling simmering on a hotplate. After serving them, he strode to the liquor cabinet and opened the cooler. He sat down and poured for both of them.

Aviana helped herself to a mixed salad and picked up her glass. The crystal sang when they touched glasses. She sipped and her eyes widened.

"Very smooth like you said. It also has a nice berry aftertaste. What is it?"

"Taylors. Not an expensive wine, but I think it's better than many pricier wines. You can pick it up at most liquor stores."

"I'll have to get some."

"I found most Clare Valley wines are just as good. Must be the soil and the local climate, as other Barossa wines have a different taste."

She cut off a piece of vol-au-vent and filling and popped it into her mouth. After a moment, she shook her head.

"If this is a sample of your cooking, I'll have to come around more often."

"And risk falling into the wolf's claws?"

She smiled. "I might be prepared to take that chance."

She ate with relish, but refused a top up of wine. Driving, she explained, and he understood, always careful himself when behind the wheel.

"Psychology…" she said after a time. "You must meet a lot of weird people. Sorry, I didn't mean weird. People with a lot of different problems."

"Some of them *were* weird," he told her after taking a sip. "Mostly, they're confused and uncertain how to get themselves out of an emotional hole they have fallen into or dug for themselves. More often than not, over a protracted period. Some problems surface quickly, such as postnatal depression."

"You must charge quite a bit for your service."

"It's $290 for a one-hour consultation."

"You and your partners are doing well."

"That's not clear profit, mind you. We have overheads and expenses, but we're doing all right. You probably find yourself in a similar situation."

"I do. My firm charges 40% of any settlement with no upfront client fees, but it depends on the case. If a partner feels the risk is excessive, we work on an hourly fee. Some cases require a lot of research and detective work before they get to court, and that can run into tens of thousands of dollars."

"We sometimes take on pro bono patients when government services fail them, or the waiting time threatens their mental well-being, but we don't do many of those."

"Same with Wellard. It's all a question of profit, unfortunately."

"It is," Dural agreed. "I could have taken a residency position with one of the public hospitals and lived off a government salary. Perhaps a more humanitarian application of my training. I didn't do it because I'm selfish and I wanted a comfortable lifestyle a private practice gave me."

"I didn't judge, Du. I want that same comfortable lifestyle."

He shook his head. "I wonder what a psychologist would say after I bared my capitalistic approach to life?"

She grinned. "Probably sympathize…then hand you a $290 fee."

He laughed. "*Touché!* You have skewered me."

Done with the main course, she helped him clear the table, then waited with lively interest as he served a bowl of bread and custard pudding smeared with dark chocolate. As an extra treat, he poured her a small glass of golden dessert wine.

Studying the pudding, she sighed and looked at him. "I can see you're determined to ruin my waistline."

"A little indulgence now and then is good for the soul," he told her comfortably. "I remember you saying that."

"If not the waistline," she added tartly and picked up her glass. She took a sip of the honey liquid and gaped. "Nectar of the gods. What is this?"

"Ice wine. The best stuff is made in Germany and Austria, although Canada is also a producer."

"Sweet and delicate, but not cloying. I never had it before."

"I'll give you a bottle."

"Must be expensive," she said, eyeing the slim brown bottle.

"The quality ones are."

"Indulgence for the soul?"

"You got it."

"Where can I buy it?"

"You won't find it displayed, but you can order it."

"You've sold me. This is definitely something I want in my bar cabinet."

Finished with her pudding, she glanced at the tray, then raised her hand.

"I'm tempted, but I won't. I've had too much already." She pointed an accusing finger at him. "And it's all your fault."

"Guilty as charged," he agreed promptly. "I was fattening you up for the wolf."

She laughed, eyes sparkling. "I knew you had a hidden agenda."

"What can you expect from a wolf? Coffee or tea?" he offered.

"I wouldn't mind a coffee."

Dural got up and set the percolator going. Aviana followed him to the kitchen.

"Cups and saucers?"

He pointed at them already laid out next to the fridge. "I'll bring the milk and sugar."

A bowl of chocolates in hand, he walked to the table, poured for both of them, and laid the glass carafe on a cork mat. She eyed the chocolates, bit her lip, and reached for one. She popped it into her mouth.

"Liquor centers, yummy. What are they? Lind?"

"I find Lind chocolates too sweet. These are from a candy store in High Street. They make their own."

She sighed and patted her stomach. "You are an evil man, Du, tempting me like this."

"Indulgence, remember?"

She stirred milk and sugar into her coffee and took a sip. She glanced around the lounge and looked at him.

"You're not much into decoration."

"You mean flowers and stuff? Not really. I like things simple and functional."

"I can see that."

"You? I noticed the abstract paintings and the elegant simplicity of everything at your place. You have good taste."

"I like modern things," she said and sipped her coffee.

They spent the next few minutes chatting about nothing in particular, Dural enjoying her company. Coffee finished, she patted her thighs.

"I'll pick you up at five on Saturday," he said.

She pushed back her chair and stood. "I had a great time, Du, and you have been very gracious."

"I liked having you here."

He stepped up to her and gathered her in his arms. She flowed against him without resistance. He brought his mouth against her yielding lips and closed his eyes. Her mouth opened and her tongue touched his, sending a jolt of fire through his body. They stood locked in the embrace, the kiss filled with a promise of tomorrow.

After an eternal time, he pulled back and gazed into the depths of her hazel eyes.

"Thank you for bringing sunshine back into my life," he whispered hoarsely.

"Wolf," she murmured and brushed his cheek. "I better go before your claws come out."

"Don't worry. You're safe…tonight."

"I'm looking forward to seeing what's in that mysterious package of yours," she said softly.

"Next time."

He strode to the cooler and pulled out a bottle of ice wine. He slid it into a paper bottle holder and held it for her. She took it and nodded.

"Good night, Du."

"Take care, Aviana."

He opened the front door and walked her to her car. She started the engine, and with a flutter of fingers, backed out of the driveway. He waved at her as the car whispered up the street.

The night warm and silent, light poles casting yellow pools, Dural glanced at a black sky, patchy clouds having obscured the stars. He did not need to see the stars. One already shone for him in his heart.

* * *

Something was badly wrong, but Dural could not tell what or why. He only knew that Aviana avoided him. He could sense it; sense her withdrawal, the hesitation in her voice, the excuses. He understood work commitments and late hours. Nevertheless, they could still have an odd evening together when lunch was not possible. A dinner somewhere in a relaxing, congenial atmosphere would be a welcome break for her. A break for both of them and an opportunity to knit more firmly what they had begun between them. However, she had rejected all his advances, and he felt growing dismay and trepidation. Was it something he said?

He remembered Lenora's periods of moodiness and introspection, and learned to let her get over it in her own good time without bothering her. Even Daniela behaved herself when Mom wore a scowl for a few days. Lenora would then snap out of it and become her happy, loving self, to everyone's relief. With Aviana, it had to be something else than moodiness. It gnawed at him, and Dural was uncertain what to do.

He finished his coffee and glanced at the computer timestamp. He still had eight minutes before the next scheduled patient. A woman in a supposedly happy marriage who suddenly found herself in a casual affair with a younger man who had time for her and made her feel special in a way she had not felt in a long while. She loved her husband and dreaded the thought of hurting him, or disgracing herself in the eyes of her children. Revolted with herself and ashamed, she was at a loss how to deal with her dilemma. Was it possible to love two men with equal passion, she asked during their last session. Was her lover prepared to commit to something lasting? Questions Dural needed to help her answer in eight minutes.

His phone rang. He read the caller name on the small screen and smiled as his heart lifted. Perhaps this was one answer he sought for himself. He picked up, wearing a grin.

"Aviana, good to hear from you."

The silence on the other end lasted only a fraction of a second, but it felt like an eternity of emptiness.

"I'm sorry for the late call, Du, but I won't be able to make it this weekend," she said in a rush.

Dural felt his mouth go dry and he grasped the receiver harder.

"What is it?" he asked, perhaps a touch more coldly than intended.

"I've been put as point on a big case due to go before the court next Thursday. The partner handling it had a burst appendix and is out of it. I know how much you looked forward to this weekend, and I'm sorry to mess it up for you, but there is a ton of work I need to do and I want to make sure I'm prepared."

A wave of resentment raced through him. Wellard, Wellard and Starke had six partners. No one else could take the case? He had everything organized and told everybody they would at last meet his lady friend outside a hospital bed. His parents were particularly pleased that he found someone after having his heart minced by Lenora, dropping not very subtle hints that getting married again would be good for him. He had not thought of their relationship in those terms yet, but did not reject the idea outright. After all, they had only known each other a few weeks.

A tumble of thoughts tripped over each other as he took in Aviana's words.

"Du? Are you there?"

"Sorry, you caught me by surprise."

"This is a major case, something that will lead to bigger things with Wellard if I do well."

"I understand, and I'm glad you got this break. Still, I am a little disappointed about the weekend. Couldn't you make it for lunch at my parents' place on Sunday? I looked forward to showing you off."

He could picture her biting her lip.

"I would love to, really, but I don't have the time. Mad at me?"

"A little, but you haven't lived until you have tasted my mom's cooking."

She chuckled. "It will have to be a rain check. Sorry, Du, I've got to go," she said and broke contact.

"Good luck with the case, Aviana," he murmured into the dead phone and replaced the receiver, smelling ashes in the air.

Ashes of what might have been. A future fading into a pale dream of lost hopes.

Dural stared at the wall, not actually seeing it. Was she giving him the brushoff, or was he being overly sensitive and insecure? He knew her work kept her busy, and an important case was an opportunity to shine, personal considerations notwithstanding, however inconvenient for him. A professional, she looked after her career. Something far more important than a pleasant, diverting weekend. *There would be other weekends,* he told himself.

Let's not build this into something that might not be there, Doctor.

Sage advice, he agreed, but he could not shake off the feeling that she avoided him. If she was, why? During dinner at his place, she was warm, enjoying his company, and appeared willing to build on what they had beyond mere friendship. Everything she said, her small gestures, radiant aura, told him that. By Monday, something had changed. She could not meet him for lunch and he did not think anything of it. These things happened. How about Tuesday, he offered. She would call him, she said, then begged off, refusing a dinner date.

That planted a dark seed of doubt in his mind and set his heart fluttering. The seed had now sprouted leaves of insecurity in him, but what grew might be a weed he should pluck out. If he had the smarts he supposedly had, he should uproot it and excise the burn on his heart.

He wanted to banish his doubts, but could not bring himself to do it. She had an important case, fine, but she had to eat sometime. A couple of hours at his parents' place would not compromise her preparation work. Was he being selfish? Staring at nothing, he decided he might be a little. She had her own life and priorities. Priorities…and he might be at the bottom of the list.

If this was a major case, did that mean she would not be able to see him for some time? He did not know, and she had not said, how long these things took, but what he knew, a court case could run for weeks if not months. He did not like the thought of that at all. Even if her days were filled, that still left evenings, and all this week, she had refused to meet him.

The phone rang and he picked up. "Yes, Rosalyn?"

"Mrs. Ward is here to see you."

"Thanks. Show her in, please."

The smell of ashes strong in the air.

A sharp buzz invaded his head and a wave of nausea swept through him. His vision blurred and he clutched the edge of his desk for support. For a panicked second, he thought he would pass out. Gradually, the buzzing stopped and the nausea receded. He blinked hard and his vision steadied. His hand shook when he wiped his wet brow.

What the hell?

He took a deep breath and exhaled loudly. Mental exhaustion, that was it.

Before going home, feeling his normal self, he told Suyin that Aviana would not be able to make it on Saturday. She was understanding and wished his friend success with her case. The call to his mom more difficult, sensing her disappointment at not meeting someone who might be a possible daughter-in-law. Was everything all right between them, she asked. Dural told her things were great, not sure he sounded convincing. His mom did not pontificate or offer hollow advice, for which he was grateful.

Around seven, finished for the day, he walked out of the building and immersed himself among pedestrians hurrying to wherever they were going, the sounds of cars and clattering trams, and the pervasive smells of a city alive. He walked toward High Street a thoughtful man, his anchor of stability dragging in the mud of uncertainty.

Hormones, they can screw up even the most rational person.

That's what happens when you allow yourself to love, his dispassionate self declared.

What if Aviana no longer wanted to see him, whatever the reason? Should he wish her well and simply walk away, shelving the experience as a pleasurable interlude in his otherwise stable, comfortable life? He did not need the emotional baggage of commitment, sharing, arguments, disappointments, joys; everything that came with love. His life was complete now, his cold self said.

Yeah, he had everything…except Aviana.

If she *was* walking away from him, he would pursue her and get her back. He would convince her that together, they would have more than the solitary lives they now had. That had to be better for both of them.

He recalled Barbra Streisand's 1981 song *Memory*, something he thought rather apt at this moment. Were memories all he would have left of Aviana? He did not want to believe it. He could not, startled by the depth of his feelings for her. He had not sought her, had not sought anybody, but fates had brought them together, and now a bond existed between them. A bond he would not allow to be broken, but it looked like it might be broken, and he did not know why.

Then again, he might be overreacting and being a fool.

* * *

After five rings, her voice came on.

"This is Aviana Kinsley. I am not available right now. Please leave a message and I'll get back to you." Followed by a beep.

Dural took a deep breath and exhaled slowly.

"Hi, Aviana. It's Du. Please call back."

He hung up and stared at the phone, intensely frustrated. He called her on Monday without receiving a response. He called yesterday. Nothing. The way things were going, he did not expect a reply today either.

What the hell was going on?

This limbo of uncertainty had started to affect his concentration and work. He tried to hide it from the others, but it had not come off. They knew something had gone wrong in his relationship. He could see it in their eyes and worried faces. Gerard tried to sound him out about it, but Dural did not feel like talking and brushed him off. He apologized later, not sure whether to be irritated at this unwanted attention, or pleased that his friends were concerned about his welfare.

Why didn't she answer his calls?

If this was her idea of an April fool's gag, she had pulled it off beautifully.

If she did not want to see him anymore, she should simply say so and be done with it. He would be devastated, but at least, he would know. He could understand her evasiveness last week—somewhat. The silent treatment over the last few days something else. Did she lack the courage to tell him it was all over? It certainly felt like it, something he found strange. She had a strong, determined personality, and did not hesitate to tell it like she saw it. This silence hardly in character. Then again, breaking off a relationship was not something one did every day. If she were that busy, why not just text him? He might not like it, but he would understand and support her. Her silence echoed in his mind and would not let go.

On impulse, he brought up the contact list and tapped an icon on a preset number.

"Wellard, Wellard and Starke. This is Tamara. How can I help you?"

At least they had a real live person to answer calls rather than an irritating menu of options that sometimes did not get him anywhere. The worst ones were when a luscious voice asked him to tell her in a few words his query, when a few words could not explain his query. He would say nothing and she would repeat her request. Finally, the stupid system would switch him to a human operator, which he wanted to begin with.

"This is Dr. Dural Sinclair. I have been trying to get hold of Ms. Kinsley, but she has not been answering my calls, and I thought it might be because of her court appearance tomorrow."

"She has mentioned you, Doctor. She has been spending all her time preparing for the case, but the hearing won't be tomorrow. She was granted a continuance for April 15."

A cold ball materialized in his stomach and something heavy constricted his chest.

Aviana was walking away from him.

"Thank you for letting me know, Tamara. Is she in?"

"She is, but I cannot tell you more."

"Please don't let her know I called."

"I won't tell her. Goodbye, Doctor."

Dural placed the cell on his desk and glanced at his watch: 10:50. He needed to see her and try to sort things out. He had a patient at 1:30, but he figured he would be done by then, one way or another. He pulled on his jacket and strode out. Although still pleasant, the days had lost their summer feel and the nights had become fresh. He might not need a coat, but he could always take it off if it turned out too warm.

He stopped before the reception counter and Rosalyn looked up.

"I'm going out for a while, but I should be back in time for my next appointment. I'll call you if I have to reschedule."

"Is everything all right, Du?"

"No, everything is not all right. It's Aviana."

"It's none of my business, but sometimes a woman needs a little time before deciding she's ready to commit. It's a major step for a girl. It was for me."

"Did you talk it out with Evans?"

"I did, and I was grateful for his understanding."

"That's been my problem, Rosalyn. She's avoiding me and won't talk to me. I need to find out what's going on."

"I hope it works out for you," she said, eyes filled with concern.

"Thanks. You've been a good friend."

She grinned. "Perhaps a whack on the head with that brace will bring her around."

He could not hold back a smile. "Not a bad idea. I'll keep it in mind. Then again, I might be the one getting the whack."

"Then you'll know, won't you."

He would indeed. The not knowing, that was the worst part. Truth, he could handle, whatever it might be.

"I'll give you an update when I get back."

"Too bad your friend missed Suyin's engagement party. It was great, wasn't it?"

Rosalyn could not stop gushing about the party, and it was great, he admitted. There were around fifty people or so at the rooftop venue of The Mission Caters in Chapel Street. He thought it would be at her parents' place. Everybody enjoyed fine food and a grand view of Melbourne as evening descended. Suyin's parents were unpretentious and straightforward, mingling among the quests, most of them not Chinese, Dural was surprised to see. After living in Australia for such a long time, they clearly had a wide range of friends. Sharing a table with Rosalyn and her husband, Leonard, and Helen, he felt a little out of place without a partner, but that soon wore off as he mingled.

"I had a good time."

"Luck with Aviana." She waved at him.

Outside, he hurried across St. Kilda Road and waited at the tram stop. It only took a couple of minutes for one to show up. He stepped on board and tapped his Myki against the sensor pad. Almost empty, the tram surged toward downtown. Dural sat down and gazed absently at office buildings and apartment complexes passing by, not seeing them, his mind on other things—like what he would say to Aviana when he saw her.

He got off at Collins Street and looked around. At a little corner box selling general knickknacks, he bought a bunch of banksias. He waited for the lights to turn green, and was swept across the street in a tide of pedestrians. His left leg protested, only a little painful. As always, the city center seethed with people and a clash of conflicting auras. He switched off the colorful menagerie and strode with determination toward the Louis Vuitton Building. His watch said 11:25. He took the elevator up and walked to the reception desk.

A pretty Asian girl looked up and smiled, her round face framed by long black hair.

"May I help you?"

"I'm Dr. Dural—"

"We spoke earlier! I'm Tamara."

"Is she in?"

"In her office," she said and picked up the phone. "I'll let her know you're here."

"Thank you."

"A lunch date?" she asked seeing the flowers.

He grinned, although his insides did not feel cheerful at all. "I hope so."

Apart from the open entrance area and a formidably long reception counter surrounded by tall potted plants, Wellard, Wellard and Starke written in bold gold lettering on a dark wood paneled wall behind it, the place had a subdued atmosphere of competent, expensive lawyers. He had seen one of them at work during his divorce.

"Ms. Kinsley? Dr. Dural is here to see you...very well." Tamara replaced the receiver and looked at him. "She'll be out in a minute."

Don't screw this up, he told himself and opened the door.

Aviana walked out from the last office at end of a short corridor and stood there.

"Du..."

"Nice to see you, Aviana."

He walked past her and took in the spacious office, the walls on either side taken up with ceiling-high shelves filled with thick volumes. A large window behind her heavy desk opened to Collins Street. Neat piles of paperwork surrounded a laptop connected to a large screen. Two thick red-bound volumes lay open over the papers.

She closed the door and stood there, her face expressionless. Dressed in a cream blouse and black skirt, she looked striking, and his heart constricted as he stared at her.

"For you," he said and held out the flowers. "Since you haven't returned my calls, I thought I'd come and see you," he said, trying to sound casual.

She took the flowers and placed them on her desk. "Thank you." She pointed at a dark gray soft chair. "Please…"

He nodded, pushed back the chair, and eased himself into it. "Comfortable," he added.

Her mouth firmed. "You must understand. I've been running myself ragged preparing for the case."

"I can understand that, but you could have called to let me know how you were. Have I offended you or said something—"

She raised a hand. "It's nothing like that."

"Then what? Do you need time to sort yourself out? Have I been pushing you into something you don't want? I need to understand. What's killing me is your silence. Talk to me. Please?"

Eyes bright, she looked at him and he waited, dreading what she might say, but he had to hear what she thought and felt, no matter how it came out. At least he would know and deal with it.

"If there is somebody else, I'll break his arms."

The pixie light returned to her eyes. "It's not that."

"What then?"

She pulled a chair closer to him, sat down, and clasped her hands in her lap, fingers working in agitation. Her pale yellow aura betrayed her uncertainty, and he suppressed it. He wanted to hear her words, watch her expressions untainted by colors of her inner self.

"I *have* been avoiding you," she whispered, her face full of churning emotions. "I wanted to call you, but every time I picked up the phone, I couldn't go through with it. With each day, it became harder and my resolve crumbled. This must have hurt you, and I'm sorry for that, but I couldn't help myself. I didn't know how to reach out to you."

He took her hands and squeezed. "I love you, Aviana," he told her softly, relieved the words were said, because it was true. If ever there was a moment to say them, he knew with unshakeable certainty, this was it.

"I know," she whispered, her voice choking. "I've known it for a while. You haven't done anything to rush me, Du, and you were not looking for a casual affair. I could tell from the start. It would have been easier if you were. I could have handled it then. We would have a little fun, a few laughs, some dinners, and that would have been it. I could walk away and life would return to its placid, comfortable routine, but you were different. You did not want a casual fling, and that frightened me. For a while, I treated our outings as though it were a casual affair, thinking it would end and I wouldn't have to think about it anymore...or you."

She fell silent and Dural waited, not wanting to disrupt the train of her thoughts.

"Then everything changed. Your accident, me getting shot, the dinner at your place...I couldn't sleep that night, my mind on fire. You see, I realized I had fallen for you, and the realization terrified me."

"You were afraid of me?" he asked in surprise.

"Of what you were—a man. In my mind, all men are wolves, and two of them mauled me. When I called you a wolf, I used it as a joke, but deep down, I waited in fear for you to reveal yourself as one, but you never did. You were not going to maul me like the others. Instead, you seemed to understand me, hoping I would love you as much as I sensed you loved me." She snorted and brushed back a lock of hair. "Love…I never had real love, and being with you, it took a while for me to recognize it…and I was petrified." She sniffed and blinked several times, eyes glistening.

"I didn't know how to handle real love. I had my ordered, predictable life, a promising career unburdened by a family, and thought I had it all. No cares. Then you showed up and I realized how empty and shallow my days really were. Still, I preferred those days to something I never experienced before and did not understand. Driving home on Saturday night, happy, looking forward to spending more time with you, it came to me with crashing realization that this was not a casual relationship, but something frighteningly real. It hit me that I loved you, and I panicked. I couldn't handle it." She looked at him and a glistening tear slid down her cheek. "I didn't know how," she choked.

"That's why you haven't answered my calls?"

She nodded, misery written on her face.

He brought her hands to his lips and kissed them.

"My beautiful, enchanting bird. I was going out of my mind waiting for you to call, gnawing my fingers when you didn't, not knowing why you had turned away, afraid that somehow, I caused you to flee." He stroked the back of her hands.

"I told you once that I would be happy to take what you were able to give and be a friend, but I can no longer be satisfied with that. I want much more. Without wanting to sound like a wolf, I want you, Aviana. Not for a day or a night, but for always, and I will love you and protect you from the little hurts and big hurts life may dish out. I'm not saying there will not be any. Life is like that, but you don't have to fear walking with me because of it.

"After Lenora, I never expected to love again, and I gradually allowed myself to drift, my life comfortable and predictable like yours had become. It was, and I thought I wanted for nothing.

Looking back, I realized it was a trap. A wall I built around myself to ward off the pain I felt when Lenora and I broke up. I did not want to go through that again. Then you came, and you filled my days with light, dispelling the shadows I had gathered around me. I could not believe my luck, afraid you would walk away and the shadows would return. When I thought you *had* walked away, I didn't know if I should let you go or fight for your hand. I had no right to force myself on you if you did not want to see me, but I knew I was more than a friend to you."

"And that's why you came today," she whispered.

"To tell you in my clumsy way that I love you, and I won't let you go. I can't. You have become part of me. A very important part. If you want time to sort out what you want, take as much time as you need. If you decide we don't have a future together, I won't bother you again." He swallowed a lump in his throat. "It will be difficult getting back into my old life, but I'll adjust, knowing you're happy, even if I'm not there to share your happiness." The words came out hard, and left a deep burn across his heart, but he meant them. He was prepared to do anything to see her happy and glowing.

"Prong," she gushed, tears spilling, and wrapped her arms around his neck. Her sweet mouth clamped onto his and he held her tight, relief washing away his doubts and fears. He kissed her with abandon, never wanting to let her go. Gods, he would have been lost without her.

He pulled back, smiled into her eyes, and wiped away the wetness on her cheeks. She melted against him and rested her head on his shoulder.

"I knew you were a wolf when I saw you in my seat on that plane," she purred contentedly.

"Seeing you in the aisle, your captivating face radiant, mouth made to be kissed, I must admit my thoughts were less than honorable."

Her light laugh sent tingling prickles through him. She brushed his cheek with a finger, leaving a trail of fire.

"My wolf," she whispered and kissed him again.

Their tongues danced in a frenzy of desire, and he did not want the moment to end, content to hold her in his embrace forever. She pulled back and searched his face.

"What now?"

"I want you for all time, Aviana. Will you be mine? Will you marry me? This is somewhat sudden, I know, and I don't have a ring or flowers or anything—"

"You did bring the flowers, and the answer is yes," she said simply, and he felt his heart swell with unaccountable joy, not believing it.

"Say that again."

"I'll marry you, my wolf. You can eat me now, and I won't be afraid."

"My soaring bird…"

He held her against him and stroked her hair, her warmth suffusing through him. He wanted to tear off her clothing and make fierce love to her right there on the carpet, but there was no need. It was enough to know she was his, in the same way he was hers for as long as she wanted him. They were one in spirit now, and joining of their bodies would come at a more appropriate moment and place.

"I want to eat you right now, but what if Tamara walked in?"

Aviana laughed and punched him lightly in the ribs.

"Randy old wolf."

"Believe it." He kissed the tip of her nose and gazed deeply into her eyes. "Thank you. You have made me radiantly happy," he whispered, and her eyes shone.

"I love you, Du…totally." She pulled back and sighed. "I never knew saying it would be so liberating…and I'm not frightened anymore. Not when I am with you." She ran a finger across his chin. "You haven't manipulated me with some psychological trick, have you, Dr. Sinclair?"

"The oldest one there is, Ms. Kinsley," Dural said and allowed her golden aura to envelope him.

She sat back in her chair, eyes lively. After a moment, she shivered.

"I feel so many things right now, it's overwhelming, but satisfying. The thought of marriage, living together, doing things…I like it, but I am also daunted a little."

"We'll handle it. All of it. We have all the time in the world now." He stood and helped her up. "How about dinner tonight?"

Her eyes gleamed with a mischievous glint. "I'm in your hands."

"You will be…later," he told her with a straight face, and she laughed with glee.

"What do you have in mind?"

"It'll be a surprise. Dress formally, that's all I can tell you."

"Sounds mysterious, like you."

"All shall be revealed tonight."

Her eyes glinted. "You don't know the half of it," she said softly and rubbed her hip against him. Her purple/blue aura flared bright and Dural pushed back a rush of enticing images.

He pulled her against him. "Maybe we should skip dinner altogether," he murmured into her ear.

"Careful, your claws are showing."

"You're making it difficult not to."

"Patience, my wolf."

He released her and exhaled softly. "Right! I'll pick you up at six-thirty."

"I'll be waiting."

"By the way, don't have anything heavy for lunch. You'll need space for what's coming tonight."

She nodded. "I am warned."

The sun seemed to shine brighter when Dural stepped out, and he did not mind the heavy stream of pedestrians carrying him toward Swanston Street. Waiting for the tram, he could not help grinning, wanting to prance with joy. Finally, everything was right with the world.

Chapter Eleven

The Uber driver pulled up in front of Aviana's house and Dural got out. He opened the small picket fence gate and strode toward the entrance. Soft sunshine spilled shadows along the empty street. Some leaves had already started to change color, the trees preparing for the onset of autumn. The air had a dreamy, lazy quality that set his heart at peace. He pressed the doorbell button and waited.

Aviana opened the door and paused, a small smile lingering in the corner of her mouth. She wore an ankle-length light brown dress with a plunging neckline. Her black high-heeled pumps made her look very tall. A broad dark brown sash draped over her left shoulder fell across her left breast to her hip. A necklace of yellow pearls adorned her slim throat. She wore matching earrings. Light lipstick highlighted her small mouth, her cheeks accentuated by a touch of blush.

Dural stared, unable to take his eyes off her.

"Gods," he whispered. "You look stunning."

"Why, thank you, kind sir. You don't look so bad yourself."

Dressed in a black suit, a cream silk shirt, black cashmere tie, he thought himself presentable. He offered his arm.

"Shall we, my lady?"

She smiled broadly and locked the door. She wrapped her arm around his, and they walked slowly toward the car, her fresh spring fragrance complemented by a pink glow of contentment from her aura. He opened the back door for her and waited until she slid in, then walked quickly around the other side. They buckled in and the car surged down the street. It took a left onto Kings

Way and headed for the city, some of its towers already lit from within as twilight slowly descended.

"Where are we going?" Aviana asked.

Dural grinned at her. "It's a surprise."

"Okay, I'm willing to be surprised."

"You will be…and delighted, I hope."

Traffic built up quickly as they approached downtown. The driver steered past the Crown Casino complex and threaded its way along two narrow streets shrouded in gloom from the surrounding skyscrapers. The car stopped at a small square in front of the Eureka Tower and Dural nodded to Aviana.

"End of the line. We're there," he said and got out. He strode around the car and opened the rear door.

She slid out and looked up at the looming tower before her. It rose and rose until it pierced the sky. Although full of pedestrians, the square not crowded. A fair number of people were going in and coming out of the building. A narrow alleyway opened to the Southbank promenade along the Yarra River, the city looming on the other side.

Dural thanked the driver and escorted Aviana toward the main entrance. Several men passing by gave her appreciative glances, which she appeared to accept as her due. She looked grand, knew it, and appeared not to mind the looks. At the far left entry, a short queue of oldies and kids waited to get in. Their target, the popular 88th floor observation deck, one of Melbourne's major tourist must-see attractions.

He waited for the gleaming steel elevator doors to open and they strode in. He pressed the 89th floor button and the high-speed car surged up. It took some forty-five seconds before it slowed and stopped. The doors slid away and he showed her into the broad reception area of the Southern Point Room. A tall young woman in a white blouse and black trousers, a black choker around her throat, hurried toward them.

"Welcome to Eureka 89. Do you have a reservation?"

"Dural Sinclair."

She checked her tablet, nodded, and extended her arm. "This way, please."

The place smelled of fine food and expensive wines. Ceiling-high surround windows showed Melbourne in its full glory, the city stretching endlessly toward the horizon. They padded softly across a hard carpet made of various shades of gray squares broken by pale yellow streaks. Chattering, laughing patrons enjoying their meal and drinks filled some of the large round tables. The hostess led them to a small corner table and beamed.

"I'll be back in a few minutes. Enjoy the view."

Dural pulled back a chair and waited for Aviana to sit, then sat opposite her. Everything done in black: tables, chairs, napkins tucked into tall glasses, it all blended in under subdued ceiling lighting.

She looked around with lively interest. "This is elegant, Du. I am impressed."

"Wait until it gets dark. That's when you'll be impressed."

Their minder came bearing a silver tray in her left hand with two cocktail glasses of pale yellow liquid. She placed them down and undulated off. Dural picked his up and held it.

"To my light. May you shine for me always."

Aviana lifted hers and their glasses touched. "To my romantic wolf." She took a sip and her eyebrows lifted. "Nice."

He reached for her hand and gazed into her eyes. "No regrets?"

Outlined against the city's backdrop, her aura shone bright; no hesitation, doubts, or uncertainty. She had given herself to him without reservation. He hoped he was worthy of such trust.

"No regrets. However, I am still digesting the changes this will mean for me. After living by myself for such a long time, having you around every day will be a major adjustment." She grinned and her eyes sparkled. "I imagine I'll get used to it."

"I dare say you will."

"And you?"

"A voyage of discovery. One I am anxious to start."

She took a sip, the tip of her tongue worrying the corner of her mouth.

"Are you expecting me to move in with you?"

"My darling girl, I'm not expecting or asking for anything. This is a major change for both of us, and I want you to be comfortable with whatever you decide."

"Thank you," she said softly. "That's what I adore about you, Du. You're prepared to give me time and space without suddenly becoming an overbearing alpha type."

"We have years ahead of us, my gold. Whatever makes you happy will make me happy."

Their minder appeared carrying two square white porcelain plates and set them down. Next to each plate, she placed a glass of pale yellow wine.

"Enjoy."

Aviana glanced at her plate of pickled cobia fish, spiced tomato, and horseradish, and looked up.

"No menu?"

"It's a set course," Dural told her. "Saves wear and tear on the nervous system trying to decide what to have. I hope you don't mind."

"I'm willing to be adventurous," she said and tried the wine. "Nice and crisp. Not bad."

They nibbled their entrée for a few minutes. The restaurant began to fill, although there were still plenty of empty tables, a Wednesday night not being very busy.

A dish of scallops, grilled nori, and spring peas followed the entrée, accompanied by a Pinot Blanc. The small serves did not look filling, but Dural assured Aviana, she would struggle by evening's end.

She finished, patted her mouth with a napkin, and took a sip of wine.

"Do you wine and dine like this often?"

"Special occasions only. I'm a more stay at home type."

"I remember you mentioning that."

"And you said you'll have to work on that. Well, you'll now have time to turn me into a cosmopolitan playboy."

She chuckled. "I wouldn't go that far, but a little cultural infusion will do you good." She lifted a finger. "No opera, though. My parents will be startled when I tell them I'm engaged. Especially my mom. She has been trying to get me married off for years, extoling the virtues of her friends' bachelor sons."

Dural laughed. "My mom was the same. Being Polish, she had set ideas when a man should take a wife. With university studies, getting my PhD, then setting up our practice, didn't leave much time for wife hunting."

"And when your ex left, you gave up altogether," she observed.

"I did. She left a deep hole in me, one I have been filling ever since. You seem to have settled well into life alone."

Her eyebrows lifted. "Was that a diagnosis, Doctor?"

"Just an observation. No fee."

She grinned. "I was doing fine, I guess. There were moments when being alone gnawed a little, and some nights were cold inside an empty house, but I had my work to keep me occupied. I did not feel I needed anything more…until you came along."

The quail in a mushroom-garlic sauce with pickled fennel a dish they could sink their teeth into. Their glasses were collected and fresh wine delivered.

"A different wine with every dish. Something unusual," Aviana noted.

"It's an opportunity to sample some fine vintages," he agreed. "If I like one, I can always buy it somewhere." Feeling content, he searched her face and decided to reveal one of his secrets. He did not want to postpone it any longer.

"There is something I must tell you before you commit yourself fully. It will probably never amount to anything, but you deserve to know."

She waited expectantly, eyes searching.

"I have a benign brain tumor, courtesy of my indirect lightning strike."

Her expression did not change. "How…"

"The voltage surge induced accelerated neurogenesis—growth of new brain cells. Somewhere in that process, a mutation-induced development of tumor cells."

"Can it be removed?"

"Easily. The growth is in a membrane sack, and there is no tendril spread into the cortex."

"You mentioned accelerated brain growth. Does that mean you're now smarter?"

"Somewhat."

"How much smarter?"

"Quite a bit, actually."

"You mean, I've been courted by a genius?"

"A very human and fallible genius."

"This growth, it doesn't bother you?"

"I cannot even tell it's there. A routine MRI scan found it when I cracked my head outside the La Pesce."

She sat back and exhaled. "Wow. Any other secrets?"

"One, but I'll save that for later, and it's in no way dangerous or detrimental to my health."

"When you first told me about your accident, I did some reading. By all accounts, you were very lucky."

"Extremely so." He looked into her eyes. "Now that you know—"

"No big deal," she said and shrugged. "I appreciate you telling me this now, but I know you would not have prolonged our relationship if your condition was in any way threatening. You didn't take advantage of me, Du."

He stroked her hand. "I couldn't let us go on without you knowing."

The Cape Grim beef, charred leek, and bone marrow, filled whatever space they had left. The beef tender and hardly required chewing. Definitely different from the cuts he usually had at home.

"That was grand," Aviana remarked with satisfaction. "You were right about the small serves at the start, but this was worth waiting for." She glanced at the darkness outside, the city lit in glory. "Magical," she whispered.

He brushed her cheek with a finger. "You are magical," he told her and watched golden streaks race over her aura.

"You keep saying that, and I'm liable to jump you here and now."

He looked around. "With everybody watching?"

She laughed. "Well, perhaps not right now, but I like hearing it. It has been a while since somebody said such words to me."

"You'll be hearing lots more."

"I won't mind."

When offered dessert, both refused, but agreed to an expresso with thin dark chocolate fingers as nibbles. Enjoying the atmosphere and Aviana's company, Dural regretted ending it. However, as she reminded him, tomorrow was a working day for both of them.

"My parents are still in town this weekend," he told her. "Are you okay if we have lunch there on Sunday? We don't have to if you have other plans."

"I would love to meet your parents," she said simply.

"They're certainly looking forward to seeing you. My mom was disappointed about last Sunday."

"I'm sorry about that."

"Not to worry. You made up for everything."

He thanked their attendant and left a generous tip. He ordered an Uber pickup from his cell and escorted Aviana toward the elevators.

Completely dark now, the small square outside teemed with people, the air filled with background noises of a lively city.

Arm wound around his, Aviana leaned her head against his shoulder.

"Thank you for a lovely time, Du."

"You made it special, my gold," he told her tenderly, amazed how at peace he felt. There were no tomorrows, only the endless now with her beside him. It had been a long time since he felt so content. He looked forward to many more days like this, determined to make her equally content and fulfilled without any misgivings for choosing to be with him, enormously grateful that she made light of his tumor. She had to know, though. It was unthinkable to keep something like that from her. Especially if things turned grim in times to come.

The Uber car came and they got in, the drive to her place spent in comfortable silence, her warm hand in his. No need for words, her gently pulsing aura entwined with his bright halo. They were one in spirit. He could not ask for more.

The driver pulled up in front of her place and Aviana turned. "Care for a nightcap?"

Dural hesitated. "Well, I would not mind a whiskey to chase down all those wines. You don't mind?"

"Come," she said and got out.

Dural followed her to the entrance. She glanced at him and walked into the lit lounge/kitchen. He closed the door with a backhanded push. She stood there, regal and beautiful, and he longed to run his fingers through her short hair, cup her face in his hands and hold her against him. He wanted to kiss her lips, never letting go.

Something of his desire must have shown, for she smiled faintly and walked into his embrace. Her arms went around his neck and she reached up with her mouth. He met her open lips and abandoned himself in the wonderful sensations coursing through him.

"My nightcap," he mumbled.

"You're holding it." She smiled into his eyes and her mouth sought him.

When time finally resumed, she pulled back, stroked his cheek and took his hand. Without saying anything, she led him toward the stairs, and his heart hammered with anticipation. It had been a while since he did this, and he hoped he would not disappoint her.

Her bedroom opened and she flicked on the light. Tasteful cream walls, a walk-in robe, vanity cabinet tucked into a corner, left room for an elegant queen-size bed. Aviana reached for his jacket and pulled it off, her invitation unmistakable. Dural slipped his hands behind her and tugged down the long zipper with a faint rasp. She shrugged her shoulders and the dress slithered to her feet, revealing a black bra and lace panties. Her fingers pulled at his tie and dragged it over his head, then worked the buttons of his shirt as he undid his trousers and pushed them down. She pressed herself against him, her body burning, and pulled at his boxer shorts, his hand fumbling to unclip her bra. Her firm breasts pressed into his bare chest, hard nipples teasing him with fire. Her mouth clamped itself against his in a deep, prolonged kiss.

"My sweet," she whispered tenderly.

His hands slid down her smooth skin, lingering at the curve of her hips. Her right leg came up and wound itself around him. When he looked up, she pushed him toward the bed. Throwing off the last of their clothing and his arm brace, they merged, her cry of ecstasy echoing his groan of intense pleasure, never wanting the moment to end.

"Love you, Aviana Kinsley, and I don't care who knows it," he told her softly.

They lay entwined, her leg over him, head resting in the crook of his arm, long fingers marching playfully through the sprinkle of fine hairs on his chest, her sharp fingernails pinpricks of arousal. With a look of total contentment, she slid a slender finger along the line of his jaw.

"You are a very tender lover," she purred from deep inside. "I had forgotten how good it felt having a man in my bed."

Dural kissed the tip of her nose. "I'll remind you," he said.

"I'll hold you to that," she murmured and stretched like a cat.

He held her and gently ran his fingers down her back. She caught him smiling and lifted her head.

"What?"

"Did you know that you have the most enchanting golden glow when we loved?"

"Golden glow?"

"It lit the whole room when it blended with mine, and you're glowing right now."

"What are you saying, Du?"

"I can see your aura, Aviana," he said simply.

"My aura?"

"Every living thing has a bioelectromagnetic field. Some people can see it, but the medical community has not accepted it as a real physical phenomena. Those who claim to see someone's aura are labeled cranks and charlatans, but they do exist. That lightning strike? It changed me and I can see auras."

She blanched. "All this time, you were able to see my thoughts and emotions?"

"Not your thoughts."

"I understand now some of your looks. I always wondered what went on behind those gray eyes of yours." She licked her lips. "It must be confusing for you in a crowd."

"I learned to suppress it. At first, the assault of colors almost painful."

"Have you told anybody?"

He shook his head. "You're the only one."

She studied him for a moment. "I can imagine why you would want to keep this a secret."

"Professional ruin if this became known."

"And probably turned into a lab subject."

"Almost certainly. End of life as I know it."

"Why did you tell me this, Du?"

"I don't want anything to stand between us, my lovely bird. If we're going to be together, share everything, I had to share this with you as well."

Her head sank against his chest and her fingers resumed their march.

"This ability must make you a first-rate psychologist," she said after a while.

"It helps, but I don't rely on it exclusively." He stroked her bare arm.

She snuggled closer and her hand drifted down past his stomach. Bottomless eyes locked with his, she climbed on top of him and took him in. He lifted his arms and cupped her breasts as she leaned back, eyes squeezed shut in pleasure.

Her aura flared, merged with his, and the world disappeared.

* * *

Dawn had already broken when he woke, Aviana's warm body curled beside him. He gazed at her saintly face and gently brushed back a lock of wayward hair from her eye. She stirred, but did not wake. He did not want to wake fully either, wanting the dream to go on and on forever, because it had to be a dream. Seeing her beside him, a living reality, glad she was not a dream, a fantasy he conjured in the basement corridors of his desire. He leaned toward her and gently kissed her cheek, a fleeting, gossamer touch. He wanted to embrace her, crush her against him, never letting go, his love for her unbound, basking in the glow of her aura.

Her eyes fluttered and she smiled, a teasing lift of her lips. "Morning."

"Morning, my sunshine. You okay?"

"Radiant. You?"

"Bewitched, but I've got to come crashing down to earth. Patients."

"Stay and call in sick."

"I *am* sick. Sick with dizzy joy, my sweet, and you made me dizzy."

She ran a finger across his rasping stubble. "Guilty as charged," she murmured. "What's the sentence?"

"A lifetime of happiness."

She gave a tinkling laugh. "Well, if there is no escape…"

"And there is no parole."

"That's harsh, and I might appeal. When does the sentence start?"

"Right now," he murmured and sought her mouth with his. The kiss progressed and she rolled on top of him. When they finally broke, his hands roaming over her smooth back, he sighed with resignation.

"I don't want to leave you for one second, but I must."

"I know. Duty before pleasure."

"One word from you, and I could easily forget about duty."

"Me too, but you're right, and I'm also not free to lose myself in your arms." She slid off him and rested her head on his shoulder. "I want to feel you for a while longer."

He stroked her side, abandoning himself in the moment. With a grunt, he swung out his legs.

"I've got to go before we start something."

She grinned. "I wouldn't mind if we started something."

He stared into her eyes. "God, how I want to!"

He dressed quickly and glanced at his watch: 06:32. He would just have enough time to get home, shower, and make it to the practice by eight.

Aviana propped herself against the bedrest, thin blanket against her chin, and watched him.

"Du…"

He looked at her.

"Thank you," she whispered.

He strode to the bed and kissed the top of her head. "Thank *you*! See you tonight? Most of my day is packed and I won't have time for lunch."

"Come over around six-thirty and I'll fix us something. I don't feel like going out." Her eyes glittered mischievously. "It will give us more time for other things."

His skin rippled with desire as he pictured the other things waiting for him.

"Deal." He brushed her chin with a finger and hurried out of the bedroom, impatient for the day to end.

That's how his day started.

Dural ambled in and Rosalyn looked up.

"Well, someone is a happy chappy this morning."

He smiled, wanting to dance among the clouds, run in swirling surf, but not quite in the reception area of Gap Psychology Consulting. Not with three patients waiting, heads buried in glossy magazines. If he started acting silly, they would be justified calling for restraints, doubting his professional credentials.

Nevertheless, he felt grand, his heart and soul soaring the heights of bliss. He was happy, ecstatically so, and he did not mind if it showed. Aviana had made him happy, and he was determined to make her equally happy. He had not felt such contentment and fulfillment since he held Daniela in his arms for the first time, her angelic eyes staring at him without recognition.

"I'm glowing!" he declared, and he *was* glowing, his aura radiating like sunshine. Since Rosalyn could not see it, he would share something of what he felt with her. "Aviana and I had dinner last night at the Eureka 89—"

Her eyebrows rose. "My, aren't we lavish."

"It was worth it. I proposed to her earlier."

"From your satisfied expression, she obviously said yes."

"She did." He shook his head in wonder. "I'm still finding it surreal that I'm getting married."

"It will grow on you. Congratulations, Du."

"Thanks, Rosalyn. These last few days were pure torture. I thought I did something to push her away."

"I'm glad it all worked out."

Dural cleared his throat and glanced at the patients.

"Give me a couple of minutes, then send in Mrs. Fleming."

The phone rang and she picked up. He nodded to her and walked briskly to his consulting room.

Aviana would be his wife. Incredible.

He mumbled another thanks to the gods looking after their creation. Which, of course, an utterly ridiculous thing to do for a rational scientist. He did not care if the whole world knew. Nothing was going to spoil this moment for him.

A knock and Rosalyn peered in. "Mrs. Fleming, Doctor."

Reality came down with a thump.

During the brief lunchbreak with everybody gathered in the kitchenette, Dural told them the wonderful news. Gerard and Leonard pounded his back in congratulation, and Suyin kissed him on the cheek, wishing him joy. Her radiance told him she was also joyous, adoring Gerard's admiring looks.

When was the engagement, the wedding? They were yet to decide, Dural told them. A civil ceremony probably, unless Aviana had other ideas. Whatever she wanted was fine with him. His mom would not mind a church wedding, but she had resigned herself a long time ago to having an atheist son.

Crap me dead! He must call her about Sunday. Should he tell her about Aviana or make it a surprise? Why hold back? He still had a few minutes before his 12:30 patient and took out his cell.

"Hi, Mom."

"Du! Is everything all right, dear?"

"Everything is fine. The lunch on Sunday? I'm bringing Aviana."

"That's wonderful. You patched things up with her?"

"I proposed yesterday, and she said yes. I still have to get an engagement ring, though. Everything was kind of rushed."

His mother squealed with delight. "I can't believe it! My son getting married again. After Lenora…" She sniffed, and Dural could picture her crying happy tears.

"For a while there, I did not think it would happen. Sorry, Mom, I need to cut this short. Love you."

"Love you too, Du. Wait till your father hears this."

"I'll call you later. Bye." He hung up, smiled and sat back.

Around four-thirty, done for the day, he began to get himself mentally ready for the evening. The telephone rang and he picked up.

"Yes, Rosalyn?"

"Dr. Pollack is on line two."

"Thanks." Puzzled, he pressed a glowing yellow button. "Dr. Sinclair."

"Good afternoon, Doctor. Apologies for disturbing you, but could you come to the hospital?"

"What's the problem?"

"I would like to run another MRI on you. It's probably nothing, but I want to eliminate the possibility that your meningioma is not mutating."

A cold shiver ran down Dural's back. "I thought you said it was benign."

"That's what the consulting neurologist confirmed at the time. However, I had an opportunity to discuss your case with a visiting specialist from the Johns Hopkins Meningioma Center, and he suggested taking another look."

"When do you want me to come in?"

"Right now, if convenient. I want the specialist to examine the scan and get his opinion. He's flying back tomorrow morning. I would not be too concerned, Doctor," Pollack added, "but it is best to eliminate every possibility."

Dural bit his lip. Don't be concerned? And why the urgency? The Alfred had world-class neurologists. It would not hurt to have himself checked out by a specialist in the field, but he could not help gnawing at possible negative scenarios.

"I'll be there as soon as I can, Doctor, and thanks for the call."

"Get Admissions to call me when you get in," Pollack said and hung up.

Unnerved by the call, Dural punched numbers into the phone.

"Aviana Kinsley."

"Hi there, gorgeous. About tonight—"

"Is everything all right?"

"I just had a call from the hospital. They want to do another MRI on me. It's probably nothing, but I might be a few minutes late coming over."

"What's going on, Du?"

"A routine checkup, hon. I'll fill you in later."

He took a cab to The Alfred and took two steps at a time to the entrance landing. He identified himself at the Admissions desk and they paged Pollack. The crowded reception area made him uncomfortable. The press of people, glum patients, screaming children running up and down corridors, bright convenience store lights, the food smells, all contributed to make him depressed. Hospitals were not his favorite places.

Pollack emerged from the elevator, walked quickly toward him, and held out his hand.

"Thanks for coming, Doctor, and I regret any anxiety you may feel, but it's better that we do this."

Dural shook hands. "I appreciate your concern."

"This way," Pollack said and led Dural toward a bank of elevators near the end of the corridor.

"How long before you know the result?" Dural asked.

"Within ten minutes or so of getting the scan."

Two levels down in Radiology, a nurse injected him with a slightly radioactive glucose molecule, which helped highlight active brain areas, and took him to the MRI room. He emptied his pockets of everything metallic and lay on a bench protruding from the machine. The nurse positioned a plastic cradle to hold his head in place and walked out. Dural waited, his thoughts disordered. The bench suddenly slid into the scanner. A few seconds later, the machine spun up and the bench slowly moved deeper into the machine, paused, and slowly moved back.

"The test is finished, Doctor," the nurse announced over the speaker. "You can come out now."

His aura grim gray, he got up, pocketed his belongings, slipped on his jacket, and strode out. The nurse smiled at him and waved at tree chairs.

"Please wait here. Dr. Pollack will be with you shortly."

He nodded and sat down, feeling the sands of life dribbling away one slow grain at a time. An eternity of fifteen minutes passed before Pollack emerged from the control room. He smiled at a short, bald individual beside him and offered his hand.

"Thank you for your time, Professor."

"You're welcome, Doctor. A most interesting case," the man answered, clearly American. He glanced at Dural, pursed his lips, and walked out.

Dural stood and waited.

Pollack held a large white envelope in his hand, gave Dural a penetrating look, and extended his arm at the door.

"Let's go to my office, Doctor."

On the fourth floor of another wing, Pollack strode into his office, pulled back a chair behind his desk and sat down. Dural eased himself into a guest chair and waited, studying the surgeon. Pollack looked like a man tasked with an unpleasant chore, but was nonetheless determined to carry it out.

"What is it, Doctor?" Dural asked softly, the suspense stifling him.

Pollack cleared his throat. "Have you experienced any unusual symptoms lately?"

"Well, a couple of days ago, I had a sudden intense buzzing in my head, violent nausea akin to vertigo, and my vision became blurred."

"How long did the episode last?"

"I would say around fifteen seconds."

"Dr. Sinclair, the MRI revealed that your meningioma sack has burst, and new nodules have spread through your brain mass. You have glioblastoma, Doctor."

Crap me dead.

Dural felt blood drain from his face and his mouth became dry. He pulled at his earlobe.

"Is it treatable?"

"The spread is extremely virulent and is now at Grade 4 stage. The last time we spoke, I told you I was somewhat surprised how quickly your meningioma has grown. In your case, the DREAD complex that acts as a brake for cell division has failed. Subsequently, your cells were not able to properly regulate division, which led to their malignant transformation."

"What's the prognosis?" Dural asked in a disembodied voice. *This is not happening,* he kept telling himself.

"Due to the extremely rapid migration into other parts of the brain, invasive surgery to remove the nodes is impossible. It also denies us the use of radiation, chemotherapy, and some of the more exotic treatment options. Not in the time available."

Dural stared, then swallowed hard. "Are you telling me the condition is terminal?"

"Within a few weeks, the cancerous nodes will begin to interfere with your brain's capacity to regulate body functions. You'll begin to experience increased levels of nausea, muscular weakness, potential memory loss, and double vision. This may also affect your cognitive processes. I'm sorry, Doctor."

Sorry, Dural mused, his world crumbling around him, his hopes and dreams shattered. Something gripped his chest and squeezed, forcing him to exhale loudly. He clenched his fists until the fingernails bit into his palms.

He had his life ahead of him, for Chrissake! A great life and things to be done. This wasn't *fair*!

He had counseled a number of terminal patients, providing solace and techniques to cope with the condition and reconcile themselves with the prospect of death. Those techniques were suddenly shallow and banal when faced with the same situation.

Pollack saw his distress and made to stand, but Dural waved him back.

"I'm okay. Give me a moment."

"Of course."

After a few deep breaths, Dural settled down. "How much time do I have?"

"Five weeks. Perhaps less. Depends on the rate of spread."

"Will there be much pain?"

"It varies greatly from patient to patient. You should be comfortable over the next four weeks, but once your symptoms become advanced, there will be a degree of pain. The final phase will progress quickly, leading to termination."

"In the meantime..."

"Do whatever you want. You'll be able to judge the degree of your deterioration. However, if you start to develop cognitive impairment, you must report yourself to the hospital immediately, or have someone bring you."

Dural looked at him, eyes pleading. "There is nothing you can do?"

"The growth has been abnormally rapid. If I had operated when I saw your scan—"

"Not your fault," Dural told him heavily and slowly rose. He shook his head and snorted. "You have a hell of a way of ruining a good day."

"Dr. Sinclair—"

"I'll make my own way out," Dural said.

On the steps landing outside, he took a deep breath and looked up at the fluffy white clouds building in the west. A light breeze stirred his hair. Cars flowed along Commercial Road, most of them heading for the suburbs. Enough pedestrians filled the sidewalks to keep the place from looking lonely. Sights, sounds, smells, a city pulsing with life, uncaring and impersonal. What was one more life among millions? A computer bit in a database. No relevance, no meaning, just cold numbers.

His life had *meaning,* he told himself. It may have been cut short, but looking back over his forty-two years, he'd had a rich, fulfilling life. The fates had thrown him a few curveballs along the way, but those potholes and speedbumps also enriched him and gave him a measure of wisdom. He helped and healed many people, enabling them to resume productive lives. That had to account for something, didn't it?

He could not pass the curveball he'd been handed now, though.

You could have been run over by a bus, you know, his inner self said.

Yeah, except he had not.

Ever since the lightning strike, he held a dread of developing some debilitating psychological or physiological impairment. *As the years went on and nothing happened,* he told himself he had beaten the game, when all this time, the fates had it in for him. He should be enraged, screaming at the unfairness of it all, smashing everything in sight. If he looked at things objectively, he realized, he *had* been given a fair deal. He had four wonderful, memorable years of satisfying, healthy life enjoying the benefits of his eidetic memory, increased intelligence, and ability to perceive auras. Time to pay the bill.

What now, Doctor?

Some deep thinking was in order—while he could still think.

Numb, in denial somewhat, he took a cab home. He immediately strode to the liquor cabinet and pulled out a bottle of 21-year-old Chivas Regal. He wanted to get stoned until he passed out. Ready to pour, he paused. Getting pissed would not solve anything, and he would be mighty sorry tomorrow. He corked the bottle and put it away, then went up to shower and change. He glanced at the bedside electronic clock. Almost six.

Aviana…

He could take everything, but having to face her, watch her horror, watch her broken spirit, he would rather avoid drinking that cup. She had to know, of course. In a way, he was thankful to find this out now rather than in the months ahead when they had a new life together. It would not be so painful to break up now. She was strong. She would move on. At least he hoped so. It would take a while before the pain faded, but it would fade. It would fade.

He called Uber and arranged a pickup for 6:15.

He lost Daniela, lost Lenora, and now, he would lose Aviana. What else can go shitty?

Life sucks, he decided.

He did not pay attention to what went around him as the driver threaded through the traffic, his mind far away in a world of what might have been.

The car stopped and Dural got out. He watched it run down the street, then strolled slowly toward the small gate. No need to hurry with anything anymore. At the entrance, he hesitated, wanting to walk away. Wanting to spare her the pain and misery. He reached up and pressed the doorbell button. Footsteps came from inside and she opened the door, beaming broadly. She flowed into his arms and melted against him, her soft lips seeking his. He kissed her deeply, holding her with desperation. When she pulled back, he cupped her head between his hands.

"My precious bird…"

Something in his eyes gave him away and her color drained.

"What is it, Du?"

"Let's go in."

In the lounge, he took her hands and squeezed.

"Du?"

"Aviana…" He gulped and felt his eyes sting. "I cannot marry you."

She gaped. "What are you talking about? What happened?"

"I'm dying," he managed to choke out, the weight of the world on his shoulders.

"What do you mean, you're dying?"

"That brain tumor I told you? This afternoon, I had an MRI. The meningioma has developed into a Grade 4 glioblastoma. I have five weeks at most."

She swayed and he helped her to the couch, then sat beside her.

"No, no," she moaned. "This is not possible. You told me it was benign."

"That's what they said."

Tears leaked down her cheeks and she brushed them away with an impatient swipe.

"My God, Du. This is horrible, a nightmare."

"I know, my sweet."

She clung to him and sobbed. He stroked her back and waited for the catharsis to run its course. With a final sniff, she drew back and reached for the tissue box on the coffee table. She blew her nose and tossed the tissue into a small bin beside the couch.

Eyes red, she searched his face. "What now?"

He shrugged. "Take each day as it comes."

"Will you be in a lot of pain?"

"Toward the end. I should be all right until then. Depends on the symptoms." He told her what he might expect.

Her tears flowed again unchecked. He smiled wanly and brushed them away.

"I'll miss the years I hoped we would have together, but I am thankful for what we had. You have enriched my life in so many ways, my precious bird. You gave me light when I walked in darkness. You saved me, Aviana. I'm sorry we won't have those years. In a way, I feel I've betrayed you."

"Prong." It came out as a sob. She sniffed and her face became determined. "I want to marry you, Dural Sinclair. If it is to be for five weeks or a day, I want to do this."

Startled, he shook his head. "My sweet, think what you're saying. I cannot ask you to do this."

"You're not asking. I am telling. If there is anything in this world that I want, it's you, and I don't care if we don't have those years. Whatever time is given to us will be a lifetime. I'll never leave you."

Her hands wound around his neck and she kissed him. At war with his cold, calculating self, Dural was at a loss what to do.

He pulled back and sighed. "You're in shock, Aviana, and reacting emotionally. Once you start thinking objectively, you'll realize how impractical this is."

Her eyes blazed. "I may be in shock, but I'm not in any way reacting emotionally. I fully appreciate all the arguments against doing this. Nevertheless, this is my choice, not yours. If you deny me this, I'll…I'll break your other arm."

Dural smiled. "I believe you would."

"I would," she choked, fighting for control. "I love you, Dural, and I want to have you for all the days that are given to us. Do you understand that, you thick lug?"

He reached for her and crushed her against him. This was insane, madness, but his soul lifted with joy.

"For all the days that are given to us," he murmured into her hair.

She stood and looked down at him. "Come."

He slowly rose, a faint smile playing at the corner of his mouth.

"A dying man's last wish?"

"Hopefully, not the last," she purred, her face serene, her aura flaring with pure radiance.

* * *

Not fully awake, Dural luxuriated in the comforting warmth of Aviana's body against him, not wanting to open his eyes just yet. One arm across his chest, her head against his shoulder, she hardly let him go all night, as though afraid is she lost that touch, he would disappear forever. She clung to him as they made love, her arms and legs entwined around him, wanting to merge with him until they were one body.

He clung to her with equal desperation, afraid she was nothing but a fantasy conjured by his deranged mind. Every time he touched her, hands exploring her curves, gave him reassurance of her tangible reality. Somewhere in the night, she cleansed him of whatever self-pity he had, replacing it with bliss and contentment. There was no tomorrow, no darkness, only light and love in her aura.

They loved repeatedly until both were exhausted and finally satiated. Then, among the deep shadows, they talked. Her head on his chest, she listened as he told her everything, revealing secrets he'd buried in the bottomless recesses of his mind, unloading a lifetime of experiences and feelings. She listened as her aura shifted in response to his words and her emotions. Uninhibited, free, they talked.

In the small hours, they raided the kitchen, had an overdue dinner, and drank wine. As he ate, his eyes consumed her, not wanting to miss one second of her presence. Perhaps for the first time in his life, he realized that right then, in that timeless moment, he really lived, unburdened by his yesterdays and the nebulous phantoms of tomorrows that might never come for either of them.

Later, entwined, liberated as he never felt before, he basked in her glow, deliriously happy.

"I wish I could see your aura," she murmured and kissed his chest.

"White, with a touch of lavender and gold."

"And you know what each color means?"

"I studied and learned by observing. They're very reliable indicators of what a person feels and actually is. A lie may sound like truth, but an aura reveals the real truth."

"What is my aura?"

He smiled and brushed her cheek. "Indigo of deep intuition and sensitivity, overlaid with blue of peace, clarity, generosity, and contentment. Surrounding it all is a band of pulsing yellow. It's a color of optimism, kindness, and fulfillment. Even as I look at you, our auras are merging and the room shines like a torch. I want that light to shine for all time."

"It will shine, my magical prince," she whispered.

"It's enough that it shines for me right now."

"In the morning, I'm going to see Mr. Wellard and ask for six weeks' leave," she said suddenly, "and I'm moving in with you. Enough of lunch meetings and one-night dinners. I don't want to lose one precious moment away from you."

"I like the sound of that," he said easily, his hands stroking her back. "What about your court case?"

"I don't care. One of the other partners can take it." She looked at him. "What about you? What are you going to do?"

"Quit the practice. But first, I need to get some rings." He searched her eyes. "Come with me?"

"I would love to. Thank you."

Time drifted and so did Dural. He sighed and she pulled him against her.

"Do your parents know?"

"I'll tell them on Sunday. Mom will probably go all out preparing lunch, and I'll wait until we're done. I don't want to spoil it for her. It might be the last lunch we'll ever have together, but you'll be there, and that will make her very happy."

"I'm looking forward to meeting them."

"They'll adore you, in the same way, I adore you. Less, because no one can adore or love you more than me, my soaring bird."

Her mouth sought his and she rolled on top of him. He cried out when they merged and time stopped.

A stray ray of light danced between the drapes and splashed against the bed. He watched dust motes floating in the beam, his mind free associating. He did not want to get up or do anything. He only wanted this moment to continue with a wondrous woman at his side. Aviana was wondrous. Once the shock wore off, she behaved as though nothing had happened, and loved him unreservedly. Not denial on her part, merely acceptance. That was the gift she gave him; the ability to accept his condition and move on. A gift beyond price, freeing him from guilt, regrets, and destructive self-pity.

Her eyes fluttered and she smiled. "Sleep well, my randy wolf?"

"Wonderfully well, my sweet."

"I've been thinking, Du. Let's get married. Today!"

"What's the rush?"

She laughed and fisted him in the ribs. "Prong."

"How about next Saturday," he suggested. "Nothing big. Family and close friends only. My mom would never ever forgive me if we didn't have some sort of reception. I'm sure your parents would like that as well."

"I suppose. Okay, next Saturday it is. I'll let my dad know and he'll arrange everything."

"Your parents shouldn't carry this alone. My mom will want to get involved."

She exhaled loudly. "I never appreciated how complicated getting married can be."

"You'll want to pick out a dress for yourself, arrange brides-maids—"

She raised a finger. "I don't want an elaborate wedding. A simple civil celebrant ceremony with no fuss and a small reception. We'll run ourselves ragged otherwise."

"Suits me."

"Let's get away after the wedding, okay? Somewhere quiet and peaceful. Somewhere with a beach, palms, tall cocktails, and no phones."

"I wouldn't mind. Any particular place?"

"One of the Whitsunday islands perhaps?"

"I'll book it today. Four, five days okay?"

"Whatever. I want to spend quality time with you away from fawning sympathy if we stayed here."

He looked deeply into her eyes. "Did I tell you I love you with every fiber of my being?"

"Not this morning."

"Well, I do, and I will never stop loving you."

Her face clouded. "Oh, Du. Why did this have to happen? We were supposed to have a life together. Just when I thought all my dreams had come true, I have woken to a nightmare." Tears welled in her bright eyes and ran. "It's not fair."

Dural leaned over her and kissed them away. "I know, my sweet. I know."

She sniffed and gave a brave smile. "Sorry. I told myself I would not get emotional."

"I'm crying also, Aviana, but men aren't supposed to show tears."

She buried her face in his chest and sobbed quietly.

All he could do was hold her while dry tears burned his soul. He swallowed hard and looked at the ceiling.

If you are there, God, look after her for me.

It was well after eight when they reluctantly left the comfort of her bed. As Aviana made breakfast, he pulled out his cell.

"Morning, Rosalyn."

"Du! I was worried when you didn't come in. Is everything all right?"

"I'll explain on Monday. In the meantime, please cancel all my appointments for the day. I'm not coming in."

"Du—"

"Don't worry, Rosalyn. Everything is fine. Give my regards to others," he said and hung up.

Eggs done over easy, coffee beside him, he ate with relish. Aviana smiled over the rim of her mug.

"Who's the hungry boy?"

"I need to replenish my energy," he deadpanned, and she threw a piece of toast at him.

"You're going to work on Monday?"

"No more work. We have a partners' meeting every Monday where we go over the books, our billables, and general business. I'll pop in long enough to tell them what's going on and announce our wedding. I'll want them there."

He needed to clean out his desk, update his case notes on PAX, give Rosalyn his login details, and do the goodbyes. That one was going to be tough.

Thinking about administration, he would have to see Paul Becker about revising his will and settlement of his assets. He also had to assign copyright for his two textbooks. Gerard would get that, including the royalties. Then there was Aviana...

"You're pretty close to Gerard and Leonard. This will hit them hard."

"It will hit Rosalyn just as hard. My dad loaned her to us while we were setting up the practice, and she's been with us ever since. We couldn't have made it without her."

"Sounds like a wonderful person."

"She is. I'll miss her. I'll miss all of them."

"Do you need to go home before we go to the city?"

"I have everything I need with me."

"In that case, mind doing the dishes while I get ready?"

He grinned at her. "I have done this once or twice before, you know."

"Prong."

* * *

They greeted dawn early in their luxury Whitsunday Apartments suite.

"Good morning, Mrs. Sinclair," he whispered and her sparkling eyes danced.

"Good morning, Mr. Sinclair."

"Sleep well?"

"Deliriously well. If I knew marriage would be like this, I should have tried it a long time ago."

"It's not all that's been cracked up to be, you know."

"Evil man." Her finger traced the outline of his lips. "Happy, Du?"

"Crazy. Sometimes, a moment comes and I cannot believe this is happening, or that you're my wife, but I'm so glad you are."

The week before the wedding kept them busy, even though Aviana's parents arranged most everything. As expected, his mom took the news of his cancer badly, but she braced up and did not turn into an emotional wreck—at least not while he was around. His dad looked grim, in shock, and he could not do enough for Aviana. His mom loved her at first sight and kept hugging her every few minutes. They must have gotten along with her parents, as all the preparations were done smoothly and without fuss. Her dad had some reservations about her marrying what he termed a dead man, but he never complained to Dural, which was just as well. He would have pasted him one. Aviana had inherited strength and determination from her father, and he witnessed that determination in action.

A simple civil ceremony in Treasury Gardens, a small reception in the Docklands Sheraton Hotel Sky Room, completed a memorable day, Aviana a walking angel in her stunning white shoulders-bare dress. They chose not to have a band or music, preferring to mingle with guests and dredge up fond memories without noisy distractions.

He laughed with Gerard and Leonard, ignoring the cloud of death lingering over him, but he could see its reflection in their eyes. They all wished him well, and that was all he could ask for. Nevertheless, his eyes stung when he said his goodbyes, and Rosalyn did not hide her tears. Hard letting go of the past and tomorrows that would never come, but he had indelible memories of what they had together: friendship, respect, and trust. It was enough.

On Sunday morning, Aviana bubbling with excitement and anticipation—and he shared that excitement—they took a cab to the Melbourne Airport and five days of paradise.

Now, four of those days were already gone.

Below their balcony, tall palms lined Catseye Beach. Dark water glittered as the ocean stretched into nothingness. Dressed in a light bathrobe courtesy of the management, not really a courtesy, as everything was calculated into the price, teacup in hand, Aviana gazed at the ocean and sighed dreamily.

She had given him four days of rare happiness, and he hoped he repaid her with interest. Regrettably, they would have to leave tomorrow and return to the real world. A world where death waited to claim him, but he pushed those thoughts away. Each day with Aviana, he had lived a lifetime. The resort gave them space to enjoy each other's company without the clamor and bustle of pressing guests. They wanted natural scenery, seclusion, places where they could be alone, but within reach of modern conveniences and a measure of luxury. Hamilton Island gave them that and more.

They climbed Passage Peak—not a real climb, as the outcrop was only 900 meters, although the last section was rather steep. Once at the top, they had a stunning view of the surrounding islands. Islands of paradise. They visited the lively marina, a short walk across the island along Resort Drive, sampled various seafoods, and ice creams, and browsed through local souvenir shops. People were everywhere, the constant crush out of place with the serene, placid setting of the Lagoon Pool and Catseye Beach they preferred. One day of that bustle had been enough for both of them. Thereafter, they lounged in the pool, enjoyed being pampered by quick waiters, swam in the ocean, or simply forgot the world as they strolled along the beaches hand in hand. They took long walks through the enveloping rainforest, hardly meeting anyone, taking in the smells, sights, and sounds of twittering, squawking birdlife. Mixing it with other hotel guests did not interest them, or participating in the many day and evening activities. They had each other, much more fulfilling and satisfying.

Aviana sipped her tea and turned toward him.

"Can't we stay a couple more days?"

"You really want to?"

"I do. I have everything I want here, Du, and I want to make this last." She suddenly looked concerned. "Unless you're not feeling well."

She never asked about the progression of his cancer, but from some of the looks she gave him, he knew she watched him.

A mild headache developed yesterday, but it went. He had another episode where his head threatened to explode, filled with an intense buzz, nausea making the lounge sway, but it passed. Fortunately, Aviana was in the bathroom and did not see it. Otherwise, he felt strong, alert, and full of energy—except for his right arm. He sometimes felt pins and needles shoot up and down, and had trouble lifting it. That too came and went, as did periods of double vision, something he found most unsettling.

"I'm fine, my sweet. I'll talk to Reception and extend our stay."

She beamed at him and grasped his hand. "Thank you."

"What do you want to do today?" he asked.

"Let's walk somewhere quiet, shall we? We'll find an empty beach, soak in the rays, and do silly things in the water. Perhaps we could go snorkeling tomorrow."

"Done!"

Her hand firmly held in his, warm surf whispered around their feet as it rushed to swallow the pristine sugary sand, they walked along the deserted Hideaway Bay, the sun hot, but did not burn. Sapphire water cleaved the azure sky free of clouds. The ocean stretched endlessly into an endless sky, and time had no meaning. There was only the now, and it lasted forever because he had no plans, commitments, or schedules to keep. He felt free of the shackles that bound him to a life he thought complete. Perhaps it had been, and it gave him a lot, but at this transcending moment, with Aviana at his side, he lived at another altogether soul-fulfilling level. A fleeting, fluttering thought made him wonder why he had not done this before. It did not matter. Nothing mattered except having the woman he loved share this timeless wedge of existence with him.

Aviana paused and bent to dig out a common cockle shell buried in the wet sand. She hit him with her carefree smile and swirled the shell in frothy water to clean it. She brought it to her ear and listened. Still beaming, she offered it to him. He placed it against his ear and the sea sang to him. Beside them, low surf rippled along the lonely beach.

Her previously olive skin now the color of burnished bronze glowing with health. The skimpy black bikini she wore left little to the imagination, but he did not have to imagine anything, having explored every part of her body in endless days and nights of passion, content to be merely close. Her mere presence beside him gave him comfort and peace. She would sometimes wake in the middle of the night and take him to peaks of inexplicable pleasure. By morning, she denied doing any such thing. He did not press her. If this was an unconscious desire to possess him completely, he did not resist, giving himself to her totally.

Aviana was sunshine. She was moonlight, glittering water, surging surf. A creature of the sea as she gulped raw oysters and crunched crab legs, fingers and mouth smeared with butter sauce, her laughing eyes fixed on his face. When she laughed, his soul laughed with her and he was content.

They walked the mostly empty beaches in the shadow of Passage Peak towering protectively over them, exploring the little inlets and shallow pools. Aviana would slowly wade into such a pool, glance at him with a secret smile, and lower herself into the warm water. She would rise, her skin glistening in a rainbow of clear droplets, pause and untie her bikini top. Her breasts lighter than the surrounding skin, jutted out firm, her nipples hard. Then she undid the string that held her bottom part and stood regal and tall. The first time she did that, Dural could only gape, drinking in her unbelievable beauty. Her body fully mature did not have the coltish slimness of a younger woman, but those women could not compare with Aviana's density and richness of form. Her intense gaze burning into him, he did not wait to be asked twice. Lying on the soft, hot sand beside the pool with a woman more extraordinary than any in his erotic dreams, he returned the love she gave him.

In the evening, they watched a crimson sunset from the Lagoon Pool gradually turn the sky into red and orange streaks, the sight broken by surrounding palms towering protectively over them, tall cocktail glasses and exotic seafood nibbles on a tray beside them. Dural lay back on his cushioned beach chair smoking an exquisitely mild cigar, totally content and at peace, Aviana beside him not saying anything, taking in the enchanting atmosphere. He could hear surf break on the beach, hissing as it rushed over cool sands, and smelled salt in the air.

He turned, smiled, and reached for her hand, devastated by the warmth in her glittering eyes. She squeezed his hand and mouthed 'I love you'. His heart melted, not believing this was real, not believing she was his. He kissed her hand and held it fast, never wanting to let go, wishing this moment to continue forever. In his mind, it would last forever. Nothing would tear it from him.

The waiter brought a platter of various seafood and replaced their drinks. Dural nodded to him, sighed, and watched the sun touch the sea, turning it into ripples of silver and copper. He nibbled the fresh oysters, golden calamari rings, crunched on crab legs, and was satisfied. Aviana ate with appetite, glancing at him from time to time, hitting him with her radiant gaze. Sensation faded in his right leg and he could not move it. After a while, feeling returned. He pretended that nothing had happened, not wanting to spoil this moment for her.

Beneath a purple sky, they slowly made their way inside. In bed, Aviana cradled him against her and lay quietly, her eyes never leaving him. He brushed her face with a finger, and after a long time, slowly closed his eyes.

He woke extraordinarily refreshed and hungry. After a hurried breakfast, they went downstairs and ran toward the beach, ignoring other beachgoers and children frolicking in the cold sand. After a refreshing swim, they picked up their snorkeling gear and raced toward an aluminum boat moored a couple of meters from the shore. They scrambled in and Dural started the motor. The ocean a sheet of silver glass with hardly any swell. Farther out, small waves placidly drifted inward. They dropped anchor in a deserted inlet at the island's eastern tip, and put on their masks and flippers. Aviana sat on the boat's edge, hit him with a beaming smile, and flipped backward into the water. It creamed white, hiding her slender form. With somewhat more leisurely dignity, Dural dangled his legs over the side and slipped in. Coming up, he cleared his snorkel and followed her into the crystal clear water. With the sun high overhead, the brightly colored corals showed their magical hues with fish darting between them clothed in rainbows.

A spasm hit his right side. He surfaced and flipped onto his back, waiting for it to pass. His vision blurred and a wave of nausea churned his stomach. Suddenly, Aviana was beside him.

"Du! Are you all right?"

He gasped for air unable to say anything. Feeling slowly returned and his vision cleared. After a moment, he looked at her and nodded.

"I'm fine."

"Let's get back into the boat," she said firmly and grasped his arm.

She got in and helped him clamber over the side. He lay sprawled on the bottom for a few seconds, sat up and gave a loud exhale.

"I'm fine, Aviana. Truly."

"Are you sure? You didn't look all that fine in the water."

"I'm all right now," he said, and he was. He took a deep breath of scented air and reached for the cooler stashed in the stern. He cracked a can of Sprite and drank deeply, relishing the cold drink as it filled his insides.

Concern twisted her face as she bit her lip and stared at him. "Do you want to go back?"

"No, it's all right. Just let me rest for a minute." He hooked his thumb at the cooler. "Want a drink?"

She shook her head. "You sure you're all right?"

He nodded and sat against the gunwale. The boat rocked gently beneath him.

Aviana sat beside him, cupped his face between her hands and kissed him. He wrapped his arms around her and held her. At peace, he drank his soda, her warm body against him giving him comfort. Afterward, they swam to a little strip of beach and lay there without words having to be said, the sun hot on his skin.

That evening, they treated themselves to a sumptuous seafood smorgasbord and drank a little too much in celebration of their last day in paradise.

In the morning, the hotel shuttle took them to the airport.

* * *

They were all there waiting. Waiting for him to die.

Dural could feel it coming for him. Bit by bit, his body slowly shut down. Lying there, the pain gone, he felt disembodied without need or expectation. He wanted so many things, now beyond his reach—Aviana above all else. He did not want to lose her, his precious bird.

He gripped her hand and smiled into her eyes. She smiled back radiating love. He could sense her aura as though seeing it, but he no longer could. His cancer had taken that from him. He did not have to see it, though, his memory conjuring it for him. Thankfully, his mind had not been savaged. He had difficulty remembering some things, and the people around him were strangers, but Aviana shone bright for him, indelible. Something stirred in the depths of his mind and the faces focused into recognition.

"Gerard…Len?"

"How you doing, Du?" Gerard asked, his voice thick with emotion.

"So, so."

"Hang in there, partner," Leonard said and patted his shoulder.

Dural turned his head. "Rosalyn?"

The image faded and he did not know her. The woman buried her face against Len's chest and cried.

Who was she, and why did she cry?

Why couldn't he remember?

Dural recalled being on a tropical island with Aviana. Those memories burned bright. He remembered the flight to Melbourne...and the sudden pain that gripped his body. By the time the cab brought them home, he felt fine. The next few days were a blur. There were walks they had in the Botanic Gardens, along St. Kilda Beach, and strolling around streets near his place. One evening, they had dinner with an older couple who seem to know him, but the faces eluded him now. He did remember cheerful conversation, some laughter, drinking, and good food, although he did not have much of an appetite. He wished he could remember who those people were. The woman kissed him when they were leaving, but he did not know why. His right side became numb one night and he had difficulty moving. He did not recall how he came to be in this room, or why these strangers were hovering around him.

What shone for him was seeing Aviana's face, always with him.

His eyes strayed to an elderly woman, eyes tragic, face torn with emotion. A flicker of vague recognition came to him.

"Mom?"

She gasped and made to step toward him, but the man beside her held her back. Recognition faded.

All feeling ebbed away and warmth stole through his body. Warmth and peace. It felt wonderful and he reveled in the sensation.

Dural focused on a face hovering above him.

"I...love you...Aviana, my magical bird," he managed to say, laboring over every word.

"And I shall always love you, Du," she whispered, smiling, eyes bright.

"I am...sorry that I cannot...soar...with you."

"You did. You did," she said, but he did not hear her.

Autumn leaves fell when he closed his eyes.

About the Author

Stefan Vučak has written twenty-one novels, which include eight SF books in the Shadow Gods Saga. His *Cry of Eagles* won the coveted Readers' Favorite silver medal award, and his *All the Evils* was the prestigious Eric Hoffer contest finalist and Readers' Favorite silver medal winner. *Strike for Honor* won the gold medal.

Stefan leveraged a successful career in the Information Technology industry, which took him to the Middle East working on cellphone systems. Writing has been a road of discovery, helping him broaden his horizons. He also spends time as an editor and book reviewer. Stefan lives in Melbourne, Australia.

To learn more about Stefan, visit his:
Website: www.stefanvucak.com
Facebook: www.facebook.com/StefanVucakAuthor
Twitter: @stefanvucak

More Books by Stefan Vučak

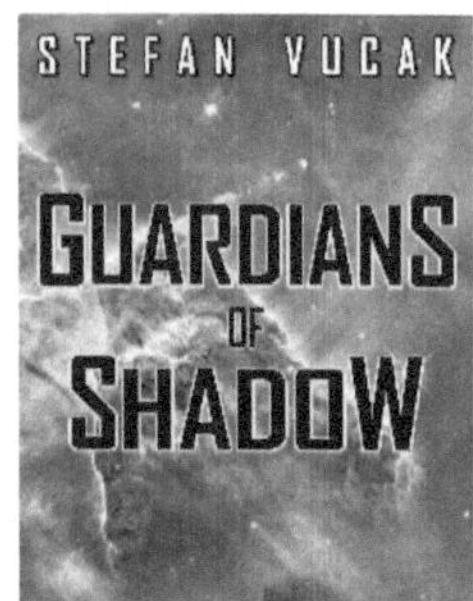